LIBRE
A Silver Ships Novel

S. H. JUCHA

Published by S. H. Jucha
www.scottjucha.com

ISBN: 978-0-9905940-3-1 (e-book)
ISBN: 978-0-9905940-4-8 (softcover)

First Edition: July 2015

Cover Design: Damon Za

For my mother, Marjorie;
my sister, Jan; and my brothers,
Greg, Brett, and Barry.

Acknowledgments

My deepest thanks go to Jan Hamilton, my sister, who contributed substantially to the funds that made the publishing of my first novel possible. And to my fans, whose purchases of *The Silver Ships* made possible this second book in the series.

A special thanks to my independent editor, John David Kudrick, whose guidance gave the finished product a needed polish, and to my proofreaders, Abiola, Jan, and Charles.

Despite the assistance I've received from others, all errors are mine.

Glossary

A Glossary is located at the end of the book and includes a few pronunciations for the Méridien names.

"Admiral on the bridge," announced Julien, the *Rêveur*'s SADE.

"At ease," Alex said as the crew braced to attention. *This will take some getting used to*, Alex mentally groused as he strode onto the starship's bridge, attired in his new, four-star uniform, to join his officers and Renée de Guirnon, his House Co-Leader and lover.

Three hours ago, the *Rêveur* had exited a faster-than-light (FTL) jump from Bellamonde to outside of Arno's heliosphere. Their ship was headed in system toward the planet Libre, carrying the crew's prize in the starboard bay, a captured silver ship. The cost of capturing the enemy fighter had been high … one pilot, Jase Willard, and two of the *Rêveur*'s four fighters.

Alex regarded his newly promoted officers, Senior Captain Bonnard, Captain Manet, Commander Tachenko, and Squadron Leader Reynard; all standing particularly straight and proud, while sneaking appraising glances at one another. Their new uniforms, adorned with gold rating stars, the House Alexander insignia, and the *Rêveur*'s patch, had gone over quite well. *They have a right to be proud*, Alex thought. *They've accomplished something the Confederation hadn't dared attempt in seven decades … the capture of a marauding silver ship.*

Julien was already gathering information on the Arno system and Libre, the only habitable planet, and its satellites. Housed on the *Rêveur*'s bridge in a metal-alloy case that enclosed his circuitry and crystal memory, the self-aware digital entity was the technologically unifying force of a Méridien starship. FTL jumps were completed by his calculations; FTL communications were sent through his crystals. Every primary system on any Confederation starship could be remotely monitored and controlled by its SADE.

Originally, Alex had sought to return the *Rêveur*'s survivors to their home world, but the Confederation was in disarray. Hundreds of ships were seen fleeing Méridien to escape the encroaching swarm of silver ships. Renée's brother, the present House de Guirnon Leader, attempted to usurp their vessel, but the Méridiens refused to heed his demand. Their response was to abandon their House and declare themselves to be Independents. Their allegiance, from the moment of their revival from seventy years in stasis, had been to their rescuer, Alex, a New Terran explorer-tug Captain.

It was Alex's suggestion that Renée, a daughter of House de Guirnon, create her own House. Renée had embraced the idea, which is how Alex found himself Co-Leader of House Alexander, the Military Affairs Arm of the Confederation Council. Not that their House was official yet, and with the Confederation in chaos, Council approval of the House's petition might never come.

Alex had hoped that their newly adopted disguise as Méridien militarists instead of New Terran civilians would lend them authority toward enlisting the services of the Independents and their keepers, House Bergfalk, to help them in the fight against the silver ships. The Independents, Méridien society's outcasts, were quarantined on Libre to prevent them from infecting other Méridiens with their so-called rebellious thoughts and ways.

On the bridge, Alex nodded at Julien's holo-vid display of Libre and its satellites. "According to Confederation records," Alex said, "House Bergfalk maintains a single, small orbital station for transfer of the Independents to the planet's surface. Supposedly, it constitutes Libre's entire orbital assets."

Instead of a single station, Alex, Renée, and the officers were looking at three orbitals. A small one, probably the planet's original station, was a small speck floating above Libre compared to the two gigantic platforms, each supporting a massive, partially constructed, discus-shaped ship, more than two kilometers across. The immense constructions dwarfed even the long-haul freighters docked opposite the huge ships.

"It appears Confederation records aren't up to date," Alex said. "Julien, would you care to hazard a guess about those two enormous saucers?"

"Yes, Admiral, I would. While their design is not in my archives, it's my supposition that these ships are FTL-capable cities, designed for long-term habitation."

"So, no fighting ships," said Senior Captain Andrea Bonnard, voicing the group's disappointment.

"No fighting ships," Alex agreed. He had hoped that House Bergfalk, who had pushed the Confederation Council for an aggressive response to the attacks of the silver ships, might have been working with the Independents to build fighting ships. Alex's people, the New Terrans, hadn't possessed warships prior to his discovery of the Méridiens. And now it appeared the Confederation still hadn't built any.

"Well, I'm sure by now that we have House Bergfalk's attention," Alex said. "What I need is an entrance, some sort of demonstration." Alex studied the holo-vid, lost in thought, and then he began assigning flight positions. "When we're ready, Captain Manet, you'll detach your ship and take up a position here." Alex expanded the holo-vid view and placed an icon of the armed shuttle, *Outward Bound*, presently riding ex-carrier on the *Rêveur*, slightly ahead and to port of their position. "Captain Bonnard, I want the fighters to take up positions here and here." He placed Dagger-1 just outward of the *Outward Bound*'s port side and Dagger-2 just outward of the *Rêveur*'s starboard side. They had lost the original Dagger-1 and Dagger-2 in the fight to take their first silver ship, necessitating call-sign changes for the remaining two fighters. "Is Lieutenant Dorian well enough to fly Dagger-2, Squadron Leader Reynard?"

"Negative, Admiral. Physically, the Lieutenant is fine, but his experience has severely shaken his confidence. He needs more time." Sheila couldn't blame Robert for his reticence to rejoin the fight. In their encounter with the silver ship, Robert's Dagger had been cut in half by the enemy fighter. He had been strapped in a tumbling, dead cockpit with no power or comms, scared that rescue might never come. "I've assigned Lieutenant Hatsuto Tanaka as Dagger-2's pilot."

"Ah, Miko's brother," replied Alex, referring to Lieutenant Miko Tanaka, Captain Manet's copilot. Alex queried Julien and received Hatsuto's profile from the Méridiens' visit to Barren Island, New Terra's fighter training site, and shared it with Renée and his officers, giving them time to review the file.

"Look familiar?" Alex asked them.

"Jase," Andrea responded, referring to Lieutenant Jason Willard, the pilot they had lost. During the journey to Arno, Andrea and Sheila had queried Julien for an analysis of their fight with the silver ship. Alex's attack plan was designed as a pincer movement, trapping the enemy ship between two flights of Daggers. But Andrea and Sheila, who had piloted Flight-2, had arrived late. By then, the silver ship had destroyed Jase's craft and cut Robert's fighter in half.

The comm buoys, deployed during the fight to facilitate data transfer, had provided the answer to Andrea's and Sheila's questions. Jase hadn't followed his fighter's pre-programmed flight path. Instead he had switched to manual and cut closer to the gas giant to engage the enemy fighter sooner. Operating in manual, his skills were no match against the speed and agility of the silver ship, and his hubris had cost him his life.

"Admiral, Tanaka's a good pilot," Sheila said. "Captain Bonnard and I have shared Julien's analysis of Jase's performance before and during the fight. Hurrying to meet the enemy wasn't the only break in procedure Jase committed. We made sure Tanaka saw Jase's mistakes and how his actions had endangered everyone. Tanaka got the message, Sir."

"Very well, Squadron Leader, it's your call."

"Ah, it's a fan-squirrel," said the XO, Tatia Tachenko, staring at the holo-vid.

"What?" Edouard asked.

"A fan-squirrel, a native New Terran animal," Tatia said, sending an image to Edouard from Julien's archives via her implant, the tiny Méridien device surgically embedded in her cerebrum. "It's a New Terran, long-haired, tree dweller. When surprised on the ground, it turns sideways and spreads its fur, making it appear several times its size. It's quite a sight."

The others nodded as they began to comprehend Alex's concept of a dramatic entrance. A military House should look imposing.

"We won't respond to House Bergfalk comms until we're ready," Alex stated. "We launch 'Fan-Squirrel' when we're a few hours out from Libre.

Our silence for three and a half days should keep the House Bergfalk Leader wondering."

* * *

As the *Rêveur* closed on Libre, the Daggers and *Outward Bound* spread out into their assigned positions. Using a House Leader's priority code, Julien opened a comm request to the Station Director, who had originated the House Bergfalk comms to the *Rêveur*. The response was immediate.

Director Karl Beckert preceded his implant comm with his bio-ID, a Méridien custom upon introduction. <SADE,> Karl sent, <we've received your ship codes, but our records indicate the *Rêveur* was lost nearly seventy-one years ago, and you're in the company of non-Méridien craft. Explain.>

"Julien, open a vid on me," Alex said.

The Director's mouth flew open at the sight of Alex's 146-kilo New Terran stature, so unlike the Méridiens' slender frames. His eyes glazed as he focused his thoughts through his implant comm to relay an urgent request to his Leader for further directions.

Renée, standing off-vid, hid a broad smirk behind her hand. She recalled her first impression of Alex when they'd met on the *Rêveur's* bridge soon after Julien had revived the Méridiens from stasis. On first sight, she had called him an "Ancient," a Méridien term honoring their original colonists, whom Alex resembled. He, though, had thought she'd called him "old." *Such may be the eccentricities of first contact,* Renée thought.

When the Director focused his eyes on his vid screen again, he sent, <Who are you and ... what are you?>

Renée had rehearsed Alex in the persona it was imperative he adopt for his new position. <Is this how you greet a Leader?> Alex demanded. <I am Admiral Alex Racine, Co-Leader of House Alexander, the Military Affairs Arm of the Confederation.>

The Director's agitation and confusion were evident. His implant comm to his Leader was even longer this time.

Alex, playing his part, interrupted the man's communications. <Did you authenticate my SADE's code, Director Beckert?>

<Yes ... Yes, Leader,> replied the Director, deferring to protocol.

<Do your records correspond with this ship's silhouette?> Alex said.

<Yes, Leader, after your transformation or separation, whichever it was, your ship is confirmed. It's just that ...>

<And yet, while Confederation colonies are being destroyed, you quibble with me when I would be speaking to Leader Eric Stroheim.>

<My apologies, Leader, but I'm requested to ask. What are those two single-person craft? They appear too small to be shuttles.>

<Shuttles, Director? Don't be foolish! They're fighters—destroyers of silver ships!> Alex had Julien cut the connection before the Director could reply.

A quarter-hour later, Julien received a comm request originating from the planet. "It's Leader Stroheim, Admiral."

"The curtain rises," Alex quipped as Andrea and Renée took positions beside him for the vid comm.

<Leader Stroheim,> Alex greeted the Méridien, Leader to Leader, as Renée had demonstrated, nodding his head down and touching his open right hand to his left chest.

Leader Stroheim returned the courteous greeting despite his amazement at the sight of two oversized humans standing beside a Méridien that records indicated was the long-lost daughter of House de Guirnon. <Leader Racine, your arrival has generated great concern. Our records don't list your House, you arrive on a ship registered as long lost, you don't appear to be Méridien, and you claim to have craft that destroy the alien ships.>

<There is much for us to discuss, Leader Stroheim, but perhaps it can wait until your visit to the *Rêveur*,> Alex replied.

<And why should I have to wait for my questions to be satisfied, Leader Racine?>

<I would have thought you'd prefer to peruse our captured silver ship first, of course, Leader Stroheim.>

* * *

During the *Rêveur*'s flight to Arno from Bellamonde, where the silver ship was captured, Alex had spent the days wondering how to convince the Independents, the *persona non grata* of conformist Méridien society, and House Bergfalk, who maintained the Libran colony, to support them in their fight against the alien ships. The giant saucer-like ships were strong indications of the Librans' preference, which was to run, not fight. Alex wondered if his proof that a silver ship could be defeated would be enough to persuade them otherwise.

To date, the Méridien Confederation had lost six colonies to the insidious, alien menace. The swarm of silver ships, in the company of an enormous spherical craft, had invaded the far system of Hellébore first, and, after eliminating the human population, had harvested resources from the system's only habitable planet, Cetus. When the silver ships had finished collecting whatever it was that they sought, they had boarded their giant mother ship and exited the system.

Now, the aliens threatened the Méridien's home world, having overrun the nearby colony of Bellamonde seven years ago. Over 1.7 billion inhabitants and their cities had been burned to ashes by the alien's powerful beam weapons. And the Confederation Houses, who hadn't dared to defend themselves, were fleeing their home world for the farthest colonies.

For Alex, it hadn't started out as his fight. Fate or fortune had intervened. The *Rêveur* had been the second Méridien starship to succumb to the devastating beams of a silver ship. Holed and nearly destroyed, the *Rêveur* became a derelict, speeding across empty space. In a rescue, hailed by some as foolhardy and by most as spectacular, Alex had saved the eighteen Méridien survivors and Julien.

The *Rêveur*'s eighteen Méridiens, which included Renée, owed their lives to their SADE and his perseverance. Ensconced in crystal stasis tubes, the Méridiens had slept for seventy years while their damaged ship drifted through space. Julien had remained the only active intelligence on board.

He had waited patiently for rescue, minimizing the consumption of his limited power supply. Finally, in a desperate bid to save his passengers, with his power dwindling, he reduced his processing speed to $1/500^{th}$ and set contact alarms to revive him if they were found.

When the *Rêveur* had shot across the edge of the New Terran system, many light-years from the Confederation, Alex had risked his life to latch his explorer-tug onto his world's first alien ship. The tug's beams and Alex's extravehicular activity (EVA) efforts to gain entrance to the advanced starship had triggered Julien's revival. The *Rêveur*'s hull sensors had relayed Alex's helmet-framed face to Julien, who triggered the airlock hatches and enticed Alex to the bridge with a trail of blinking lights, consuming some of the last energy in his power supply. Over the next half-year, Julien and Alex, working to repair and arm the *Rêveur*, had grown close, brothers of crystal and flesh.

Like the Méridiens, the New Terrans had left Earth aboard colony ships to settle new worlds. Each thought they were alone in their own corner of the galaxy. Now, though, they knew that wasn't true, and it wasn't only humans who were out here.

With Renée, the House de Guirnon representative aboard the *Rêveur*, Alex had negotiated an agreement with his government's Assembly to trade Méridien technology for repairs. The New Terrans, hundreds of years behind Méridien technology due to a disastrous start on their new world, had been overjoyed to accept the exchange.

But Alex had discovered the Méridiens were defenseless against the alien ship that had attacked them. He had pleaded with Renée to sue for co-development of weapons with his people. Renée's request sold itself when the New Terran President and Assembly had viewed the *Rêveur*'s records of the attack. Neither the peaceful Méridiens nor the New Terrans, who had yet to venture outside their own system, had developed weapons more powerful than that required for personal protection or crowd pacification. In the vids, the New Terrans saw how easily the Méridiens' superior technology had been defeated and knew they, too, were totally unprepared to repel the alien ships. The Assembly approved a mutual weapons-development pact, and Alex, with help from Julien and others, had cobbled together the colonists' records from university archives to resurrect Earth's war machines.

When the *Rêveur* returned to Confederation space, its bays held four fighters armed with an assortment of missiles. Its crew comprised a mix of the original eighteen Méridiens and over a hundred New Terrans. Alex and his New Terran crew had received the Méridien gifts of cell-gen injections for health and longevity, and implants, enabling comms between individuals or groups, even across the Confederation via FTL stations.

The return to the Méridien home world held a brief moment of joy and celebration for the *Rêveur's* long-lost survivors. During their ship's repairs in New Terra, many of the Méridiens had feared the possibility that more than one marauding silver ship might have been loosed on their Confederation's colonies. Their excitement over the forthcoming reunion had turned to dismay when they observed the myriad of House ships fleeing the advance of the aliens, who were now only days away via FTL.

When Renée's brother, the new House de Guirnon Leader, attempted to commandeer their ship and abandon the New Terrans, he couldn't have anticipated his people's reaction. The *Rêveur's* Méridiens had undergone a transformation during their time with their more life-embracing cousins, the New Terrans. Faced with the directive to dishonor their Captain and their New Terran comrades, they chose instead to abandon their House, which had led Alex and Renée to record their petition to the Confederation Council as the first military House in the Méridien culture's 700-year history.

Julien had deliberately leaked word of the formation of the new House by Alex and Renée, and to a man, woman, and SADE, the crew had joined House Alexander, the Confederation's new military arm.

Now, House Alexander prepared to meet House Bergfalk.

2

The *Rêveur,* the *Outward Bound,* and the two Daggers had taken positions 10 km out from one of the giant construction stations to await the arrival of Leader Stroheim and his entourage.

In the interim, Julien was sleuthing. Using the system's FTL comm station, he searched for other SADEs in system, which could be expected to be embedded on FTL-capable ships or on planet, the orbital stations requiring only sophisticated controllers. To his surprise, Julien discovered that the two-kilometer-wide constructions, which Alex had dubbed "city-ships," had co-opted SADEs. They had been Independents. His total count of SADEs was seven: two in the city-ships, two in the freighters, two in the liners, and one on board a liner that had exited the system. However, comm station records indicated he should have located one more. Apparently more sleuthing was required.

Andrea Bonnard, the *Rêveur's* Captain, and Lieutenant Sheila Reynard, the new Squadron Leader, left the Captain's cabin for the bridge.

Sheila's comment to Andrea when informed of her promotion, days ago, had been, "Best decision I've ever made was to apply to Barren, Captain. At this rate, I'll make Air Command General or something in a year." Then she had added ruefully, "If I live that long."

Tatia interrupted them in the corridor. "Captain, if I might speak with you?"

Andrea nodded to Sheila to continue on and said, "Yes, Commander, how may I help you?"

Just six days ago, Andrea had reported to Tatia as the *Rêveur's* Squadron Leader. But Tatia, who had the credentials of the *Rêveur's* First Mate and an ex-Major in the Terran Security Forces, had politely refused the promotion to Senior Captain. In an unexpected turn of events, Andrea found Tatia and Alex ganging up on her to accept the Senior Captain's position. Andrea's fear of becoming the flotilla's senior officer had her also ready to refuse the offer until Renée intervened, nominating, or better said, shoving Alex into the position of Admiral.

If Andrea had expected personal conflict between her and Tatia over the promotion, it had never happened. In a moment of frankness, Tatia had told her, "Captain, I've always been a ground-pounder. I need time to learn to be a space-puke like you." The cheeky smile accompanying Tatia's forthright comment had made Andrea smile in return. After that, the two officers had settled into a comfortable relationship.

"What are your plans for Leader Stroheim's reception, Captain?" Tatia asked.

"I take it you have some suggestions, Commander?"

"Several, actually, Captain. I'd like to show you something in storage," Tatia said and nodded down the corridor.

Andrea's eyebrows tilted up in inquiry, but it appeared her new XO would rather show than tell as Tatia began leading the two of them down the corridor to take a lift to a lower deck.

*   *   *

As Alex and Renée walked from their cabin down to the port bay for House Bergfalk's reception, he took her hand and placed it in the crook of his arm. In the corridors, the crew stepped aside and came to attention as their Co-Leaders strolled past. Despite their embroilment in the first war in their 700-year history, a war worse than they could have imagined, Alex and Renée were enjoying their time as new lovers. The faces of the crew at attention held no disapproval. Instead there were twitches of smiles and grins, reflecting Alex's happy face.

Renée found the carefree manner in which New Terrans expressed their emotions exhilarating. It was a freedom denied by her people's formal composure and sensibilities. She sought to interlace both hands around Alex's bulging upper arm, despite knowing she wouldn't succeed, but it tickled her just to try.

New Terra, with its greater gravity, produced humans with nearly twice the girth of Méridiens. From her time on New Terra, Renée knew Alex was one of his planet's larger specimens, due in large part to his youthful years working with his father's collection and recycle of space debris. And Alex had the appetite to prove it, which she witnessed in the meal room. She smiled at the memory of her people, soon after their rescue, courteously drawing out their meals to end when the Captain finally finished devouring his multiple serving dishes.

When they entered the port bay's airlock, Alex signaled Andrea. <All ready, Captain?>

<The honor guard is ready, Admiral.>

Alex peered through the hatch's crystal shield and saw Andrea, Tatia, and the honor guard, all attired in Méridien environment suits and holding Terran Security Forces pulse rifles.

<Julien, when did we load pulse rifles aboard?> Alex asked.

<None are listed in my manifests, Admiral,> Julien sent back.

<Captain,> Alex sent, <Julien tells me we have no records of pulse rifles in our shipping manifests.>

<I believe they came aboard as Commander Tachenko's private property, Admiral,> Andrea replied. <Apparently they are part of a shipment of 200 pulse rifles and extra chargers, a gift from General Gonzalez, as I learned this morning. I thought they would enhance our military posture.>

<A little heads-up next time, Captain,> Alex said.

<My apologies, Admiral,> sent Andrea, delivering the simple response she had prepared. Under the circumstances, she had decided to take the path of asking for forgiveness after the fact.

Alex considered the General's "gifts," detecting the fine hand of President McMorris as well. Their foresight and endeavors to protect his crew touched him.

The bay doors were open, and the lights of a giant orbital station and its massive ship twinkled in the distance. Beyond the station and ship loomed Libre, wrapped in brown, gold, and green. Julien received the shuttle controller's docking signal and subsumed its operations, guiding the shuttle gently into the bay and settling it to the deck.

Chief Stanley Peterson's crew locked the shuttle down and closed the bay door. When the bay pressurized, Stan signaled the Admiral, who, with Renée, cycled through the airlock. The escort twins, Étienne and Alain de Long, who had taken up oversight positions in the bay for the shuttle's landing, moved to flank Alex and Renée.

Eight *Rêveur* crew members took up positions at the end of the shuttle's extended gangway ramp, standing at attention in two rows. Andrea and Tatia waited at each row's end.

* * *

Inside the shuttle, Leader Eric Stroheim vacillated between anger and curiosity. His world had been the epitome of order until the aliens arrived. In the midst of the chaos, he had sought refuge with the Independents. Now his life was being disturbed once again and by what appeared to be a travesty of the human form.

When the shuttle pilot signaled all was ready, Eric led his small contingent down the gangway ramp and received what he considered a bizarre gesture from the *Rêveur*'s crew as they snapped their hands to their heads. *At least they rendered their motion in synchronicity,* he thought. Despite their incredible size, the heavily-built humans weren't ponderously slow as he had expected.

Eric eyed the crew's long-barreled weapons and presumed they were a sign of inferior technology, their society incapable of miniaturizing the components to produce a sophisticated stun weapon. When Eric came to a halt in front of their Leader, he examined the huge human and worked to conceal his disdain. Eric had always been proud of his elegant, slender build. The creature in front of him was more akin to a hulking animal than a human.

As Eric Stroheim stopped before him, Alex extended the Méridien greeting, which the Leader returned, and sent, <I welcome you aboard the *Rêveur*, Leader Stroheim. We're pleased to host you and your guests.>

<Leader Racine, were you required to adopt our technology in order to communicate with my people?> Eric sent in reply. <Or, by the slimmest of coincidence, did your people already possess implant technology?>

Alex felt his blood warm the back of his neck, and he fought to prevent his fingers from curling into fists. The Leader's condescending thoughts irked him. Worse, the man had chosen to ignore courtesy for the sake of questioning New Terran capabilities. Despite the occasion's importance, Alex couldn't resist responding in kind and proceeded to update the Leader on their recent events.

Eric Stroheim reeled under the onslaught of multiple vid streams to his implant—the New Terran-Méridien Pact, the *Rêveur*'s repairs, the crew's adoption of Méridien tech, the development of fighters and missiles, the nightly implant games, and the fight to capture the first silver ship. As Eric staggered under the impression that many people were comming him all at once, muddling his cognitive senses, his guests sought to steady him. In the midst of the mental avalanche, Eric wondered how his comm security protocols had been bypassed.

<My apologies, Leader Stroheim,> Alex sent after his multi-stream blast ended. <I hadn't suspected you would employ your implant in such a primitive manner. I'll endeavor to limit my comms with you. I wouldn't wish to make you uncomfortable.>

When the House Bergfalk shuttle had touched down in the bay, Alex had conference-linked Renée, Andrea, Tatia, the twins, and Julien to facilitate communications. Except for Julien, the others had been transfixed by the vid barrage they had just witnessed. Alex's unnatural proficiency with his recently-installed Méridien implants had become one of the crew's running jokes: their Admiral wasn't New Terran or Méridien since his implant dexterity was more alien than human. The crew had single devices, used primarily for comms, while Alex employed two implants, creating applications and manipulating data, much as Méridien scientists and mathematicians did. But there hadn't been an occasion to witness his implants employed as a mental force, a display of power Eric Stroheim had just found himself receiving.

<Leader Stroheim, it's my pleasure to introduce you to my Co-Leader, Renée de Guirnon,> Alex said, gesturing to Renée. Alex waited while Stroheim pulled himself together. The Leader was visibly shaken, but pride drove him to resume his mantle. Obvious to Alex, as Eric Stroheim greeted Renée, was that the Leader's air of superiority had been visibly dampened.

<It's an honor to greet you, Ser de Guirnon,> said Eric as he dipped his head and touched his chest. <News of your loss, seventy-one years ago, devastated us all, especially your father ... may his steps be guided back to us one day.>

<I thank you for your sentiments, Leader Stroheim,> Renée replied. <We are here by the generosity of Admiral Racine and his people.>

To further facilitate introductions, Alex added the Leader's guests to the conference comm. Surprised expressions formed on their faces as the Admiral flawlessly bypassed their implant security protocols and manipulated their comms, capabilities only a SADE or advanced Méridiens possessed but would never have employed.

<Next you will want to embed crystal storage for full SADE capability,> Julien grumbled privately to Alex.

<I am but a pale imitation of your magnificence,> Alex sent back and heard Julien's chuckle.

Eric shrugged off the Admiral's mental intrusion and motioned to his guests. <Leaders Racine and Ser de Guirnon, allow me to introduce Ser Tomas Monti, the elected leader of the Independents, and his daughter, Ser Angelina Monti.>

Tomas and Angelina wore warm-brown ship suits in contrast to typical Méridien starship uniforms of deep, dark blue. And unlike the few Méridien men Alex had seen, who were all clean-faced, Tomas sported a slender brown moustache that tapered over the corners of his mouth and a small pointed beard on his chin. The Independent Leader was lithe like all Méridiens, but his eyes, swirls of browns and greens, searched like a bird of prey instead of exhibiting the usual Méridien calm.

<How does one greet a New Terran?> Tomas sent to Alex.

The simple, personal request instantly elevated the man in Alex's mind. He extended his hand and sent a short vid of their custom.

Tomas eyed the powerful hand in front of him. The vid he received of two giant New Terrans greeting one another was not reassuring. He received a private thought from Ser de Guirnon: <Trust me, Ser Monti, you have nothing to fear from our Admiral.> Tomas glanced briefly toward Renée, taking note of the sincere smile on her face. Guided by the vid, Tomas gripped the Admiral's hand and shook it. Surprised by the gentle action, a smile crossed his face, matching the one on the Admiral.

Unlike the men with her, Angelina Monti felt no such reticence engaging the Admiral. That a House de Guirnon daughter stood next to the powerful New Terran was an intriguing sign to her. Stepping close enough to cross into Alex's personal space, she clasped his hand with both of hers. <We are quite pleased to greet you, Admiral. Please call me "Lina," as my friends do.>

Renée recognized the overtures of an un-partnered Méridien woman— Lina's intimacy, her brilliant smile, both of her hands enclosing Alex's hand, and her large, dark eyes, favored by many of Earth's Italian descendants, shining and inviting.

After Alex carefully untangled himself from Lina, he announced, <You came to see a silver ship, Sers. Let's not waste any more of your time.>

<Admiral, if you will indulge me,> Tomas said, <I'm intrigued by the elongated stun weapons of your people,> he said, indicating the twins, who stood behind Alex and Renée.

<Those aren't stun weapons, Ser Monti. They're plasma rifles.>

<Pl-Plasma!> Eric Stroheim's thought stuttered. <But plasma would kill.>

<Yes, Leader Stroheim, they would,> Alex replied. <Perhaps you don't understand the purpose of our House. We are soldiers, warriors, if you will. If it requires we destroy the aliens to protect our race, then so be it.> Alex spun and walked away, leaving it to his subordinates to usher their stunned guests along behind him.

Mickey Brandon, the *Rêveur*'s Chief Engineer, was standing by in the starboard bay. Although Mickey had never been in the Terran Security Forces, he rendered a sharp salute to his Admiral as the entourage arrived.

Tatia Tachenko, the *Rêveur*'s ex-TSF major, had created military protocol vids for the crew, since most of them had been civilians their entire lives. Mickey had sat in bed with Pia, his Méridien lover, reviewing the vids. When they came to the salute, Pia had insisted they practice. It didn't help Mickey that Pia had pulled them naked from the bed to salute each other. At the start, Mickey felt awkward, but Pia wouldn't let him stop until she was satisfied. At one point, after another unsatisfactory attempt on Mickey's part, Pia had said to him, "You think of this salute as an exercise. Think of my worlds in flame and think of our Admiral who has bound us together to fight for our people. What honor would you render him?"

In the starboard bay, Alex and his people stood aside for their guests, who came to a sudden halt at the sight of the silver ship, which rested on the bay's deck. Mickey's sampling and spectrographic equipment surrounded the craft, whose hull was a dark, shiny silver patina, except where patches of nanites had weakened the crystal matrix, dulling its surface, and where the warhead missile had penetrated one such patch, exploding inside the ship and destroying its occupants.

The guests had no comments as they stared at the silver ship. Alex wondered what it must be like to have been haunted by the specter of these aliens for decades, never daring to fight back, as their enemy consumed colony after colony, murdering billions of their people. Now their guests were confronted with the remains of one of the deadly predators, and it was not their people who had captured it, but strangers working in concert with Méridien survivors, lost for seventy-one years.

Tomas began walking toward the ship.

<I advise you to not touch it, Ser Monti,> Eric instructed Tomas and discovered his private comm had been sent to the entire group. He turned an annoyed look on Alex, who responded to the Leader's glare with an amused expression.

<You're on our ship, Leader Stroheim,> Alex sent on the conference link. <House Alexander prefers open communications. If you aren't comfortable with this, you are welcome to leave at any time, with or without your guests.>

Eric Stroheim stared at the Admiral, the anger evident on his face. He glanced to Tomas, expecting to find support for him against the New Terran's outrageous behavior, but the Leader's face mirrored that of the Admiral's.

Tomas continued to approach the silver ship. Up close, he examined the contrast between the dark, polished hull and the mottled areas, laying a tentative hand on a shiny area, and marveled at the ultra-smooth surface. It felt as if a fine layer of oil coated the ship's skin.

Being the gregarious individual that he was, Mickey launched into an update for their guests about what they had and hadn't discovered about the ship. He went so far as to play the vid that Alex and Julien had created as they pieced together the mystery of the aliens, who burrowed into the planet's surface and used subterranean passages to mine the planet's minerals.

The *Rêveur's* people stood quietly by as their guests watched the vid unfold, a display of imaginative pattern mapping. When the vid ended, the view rotated to expose the substrata, which were highlighted in translucent colors, exposing the myriad of tunnels that connected the mined mineral locations to the silver domes. Mickey credited his Admiral and the ship's SADE with the concept.

Julien added, <I was merely the librarian, Sers. The concept's architect is our leader, Admiral Racine.>

The *Rêveur's* crew straightened their shoulders proudly as the Librans turned to regard Alex with wonder and, perhaps, with a touch of fear. While he appeared similar to them, his behavior and capabilities were far outside that of any Méridien they had known.

Renée stepped beside Alex, taking his arm at the elbow as she had just done for the first time on their walk to greet the Librans, and sent, <He is our Ancient,> bestowing on Alex the honored Méridien term. Renée felt Alex's hand close possessively over hers, and she smiled at him before turning a penetrating stare on Ser Angelina Monti, who did not miss the message.

The Méridien's most prestigious celebration day was Colonists Day. They were extremely grateful to their founders who had successfully developed their new world. That Earth colonists, raised on a stronger gravity world, possessed greater stature than present-day Méridiens, had added to their mystique and heroic image. Over the centuries, New Terra, with 11 percent greater gravity than Earth's, had added more mass to the average New Terran than those of the Méridiens' Ancients.

And Alex stood out among New Terrans. His father, Duggan Racine, had trained as a shuttle pilot and fielded a job recovering space debris from orbit. Duggan's assistant had quit when he was almost killed in a foolish accident with his EVA suit. Weeks of income might have been lost while Duggan interviewed for a replacement, but then his eleven-year-old son had volunteered to help him. Most fathers would have refused outright, laughing at the suggestion, but then most fathers didn't have Alex for a son.

Schooling could take place on children's readers, so Alex would sit in the copilot seat, studying, while his father readied the shuttle and flew into orbit. Per his father's strongly worded orders, Alex had stayed in the shuttle while his father performed the EVA trip and Alex operated the recovery winch. In zero-g, the space refuse, composed mostly of metal, had no weight. The hard work came after landing when the debris had to be dragged to the shuttle's ramp, winched, and loaded into the hover-truck for transport to the recycling center. It had been heavy work for a young boy, until one day, having added thirty-nine kilos of muscle, it wasn't.

Tomas turned from admiring the captured ship. <A wonderful accomplishment, Admiral. How did you manage this?>

<With difficulty,> Alex sent. <We started with four pilots and four Daggers … that's the name of our fighters. We lost one pilot and two Daggers to capture one alien ship.>

Eric stared aghast at Alex. <You … You sent people to their deaths? Were they Méridiens?> His thoughts were laced with accusation.

Alex released Renée's arm and closed on the Leader, his mass intimidating the man, but the Méridien held his ground. <You do not fight the aliens without being willing to die to win,> Alex sent.

Eric swallowed under the Admiral's glare, noticing the blood pounding in the arteries of the New Terran's thick neck. The Leader's security placed their hands on their stun weapons, and Tatia signaled Étienne and Alain, who stepped toward the Leader's two security personnel, escalating the tension in the bay.

<My crew risks their lives every day, including our fighter pilots, who are New Terrans,> Alex sent, while extending a finger toward the Leader's face. <But understand this, Ser Stroheim … the man we lost died for all humans, including you.>

In the sudden stillness that followed Alex's angry release, a quiet thought was heard: <I'm saddened by your loss, Admiral, and would know the name of your pilot so that we may honor his sacrifice.>

Alex turned toward the speaker, Tomas Monti, and in the face of the honest words that had been offered him, he deflated. <Your words are appreciated, Ser Monti. He was Lieutenant Jason Willard.>

Eric Stroheim, always the consummate Leader, recognized the extent to which the Admiral's focus was shifting toward "his" Independents. So Eric vied for some attention of his own. <And I must offer my apologies, Admiral Racine, to you and your people. The death of a person, the sacrifice of a life, is still a frightening concept to us. We are by design a peaceful people, and it's true that our nature has cost our people dearly. Yet it's still a shock to learn that humans are attacking our foe with the intent to kill.>

Tomas walked up to Alex, carefully regarding him from top to bottom and side to side. <My large friend, I think you came to Libre for a reason, and I, for one, would love to hear it.>

3

Alex, his people, and the visitors retired to the meal room where the tables had been rearranged to accommodate the two groups. Security took up positions behind their charges.

Renée opened the discussion by summarizing the events aboard the *Rêveur* from its attack by the silver ship to its discovery by Alex in the New Terran system seventy years later. But the painful memories of the loss of so many House associates brought her story stumbling to a halt. Alex picked up the thread of the story, detailing the agreement with New Terra, the repair of the *Rêveur*, the rebuild of the *Outward Bound*, Alex's old explorer-tug, and the manufacture of their fighters and missiles.

<So these missiles, Admiral,> Tomas inquired, endeavoring to discover the extent to which the strangers might aid his people, <how do they work?>

<We've designed a series of missiles, Ser. A single primary stage is able to launch a variety of second stages. First, we hit the ship with nanites that tested the hull. Then we launched signal buoys to transfer that information to the fighter controllers. A second round of nanites was programmed to weaken the hull. Then a warhead, an explosive, struck the weakened hull and detonated inside the ship.>

<Ingenious, Admiral,> Tomas commented.

<Did you discover the nature of these aliens, Admiral?> Eric asked.

<Unfortunately, the explosion cooked the inhabitants past identification. We know a little about their metal-crystal makeup and that it's similar to their hulls. But the rest is purely conjecture.>

<But you came to us, didn't you, Admiral?> Tomas asked. <Was this deliberate?>

<Yes, Leader Monti, we came seeking allies. When Julien discovered the extensive freighter shipments to Libre, we had hoped you were building warships as we had done.>

<Ah, allies,> Tomas said, understanding dawning. Then he drew himself up in his chair and looked Alex squarely in the eye. <We can be that, Admiral Racine,> he said as he extended his hand, no longer afraid of the New Terran's grip.

<Your help will be appreciated, Tomas. But since you aren't building warships, just those city-ships, we haven't made any alternative plans.>

<City-ships?> Eric queried and received from Alex an image of the immense disk-shaped ships under construction at the orbital stations. <Ah, yes, the colony ships for my House and the Independents. They are long-term living and working environments. City-ships ... I like this name.>

<So your plan is to evacuate the planet?> Renée asked.

<No, we're not just evacuating, Ser de Guirnon,> Eric said, <which is what most of our people are doing, fleeing to far colonies and awaiting their fate. We will live on our city-ships and leave Confederation space. We will travel to a new world far from here and these accursed aliens.>

<Can your city-ships hold all of your people, Leader Stroheim?> Tatia asked.

<They were designed with just that goal in mind, Ser Tachenko. No one will be left behind.>

<If I may, Admiral,> sent Julien, requesting an interruption. On Alex's affirmative, Julien joined the conversation. <My records indicate Bellamonde is ripe for swarming.>

When confusion crossed the Librans' faces, Alex explained their use of the term swarming to describe the exodus of the alien ships from the planet, comparing them to the evacuation of an insect nest.

<Most perceptive, Admiral,> Tomas said. <Then you've studied our monitor ships' records and seen the aftermath when they rise from the planet?>

<Yes, Ser Monti, the silver ships appear to gather the resources to supply the enormous sphere, what we call the mother ship.>

<So you think you can defeat this mother ship and her swarm, Admiral?> Tomas asked, sounding hopeful.

<We've taken the first steps, designing the weapons, testing them, and successfully capturing the first silver ship. What we've learned is invaluable. What we need now is a manufacturing base. But, Julien, please return to your questions,> Alex requested.

<I understand you're new to our ways, Admiral,> Eric interjected, <but it's unnecessary for you to accommodate your SADE. Simply tell it what you want.> Eric had no sooner sent his thoughts than he froze in place. For some reason, his comments had elicited hostile reactions from the Admiral and his people; facial muscles twitched and eyes glared at him.

The crew's reaction fascinated Tomas. It was obvious Leader Stroheim had made an egregious error. Although what that error was, Tomas wasn't sure. Even odder, the Admiral's Méridiens were just as angry as his New Terrans.

Renée laid a hand on Alex's shoulder and had to exert much of her arm strength before she penetrated his anger and he subsided. <Leader Stroheim,> she said, entering the fray. <You have made several impolitic statements since coming aboard. As a fellow Leader, I would prefer you leave by your shuttle, with your dignity intact, rather than through an airlock open to space for insulting our allies and friends.>

Eric Stroheim eyed the *Rêveur* crew, whose anger was still evident. The Admiral's concept of "warriors" began to dawn on him.

<Furthermore, Leader Stroheim,> Renée continued, <it would be wise of you to forgo your assumptions. The Méridiens you see before you are no longer of your people. Our views have undergone change in concert with these New Terrans, our new brothers and sisters. Our leader is Admiral Racine. And you have just insulted his best friend.>

<His best friend?> Eric's thought struggled out. <But ... it's a SADE.>

<His best friend, Ser,> Renée reiterated, her own anger rising.

Eric looked around at the ire evident in the faces around him. His own security escorts were confused, unsure of what to do in the midst of such a public display of animosity. Gratefully, Eric heard the Admiral order his people to stand down, and while their poses relaxed, their expressions didn't.

Tomas attempted to intercede. <Admiral, admittedly your ways are different ...> but he was halted in mid-sentence when Alex raised a hand to forestall him without taking his eyes off Leader Stroheim.

The Admiral's hard, unflinching stare undermined Eric's confidence, and he sought to redeem himself. <Ser Monti is correct, Admiral. Your ways are strange to us and my assumptions are preventing us from continuing our conversations. If you will forgive me, Admiral, I will attempt to listen and learn your ways.> When the Admiral said nothing but continued to stare at him, Eric searched his words for what he had failed to say. The hostility had begun with his statement about the *Rêveur's* SADE. While searching his comm recording for the entity's name, his implant comm switched to private and he heard, <The name you're searching for, Ser, is Julien.>

Eric had led a life of privilege and security, especially during his tenure as Leader of House Bergfalk. The news of the alien menace meant action was required, action in the form of readying ships for his House associates in order to flee. But it was an orderly process, and with his extensive House assets, it had been easily achieved. There was no great cause for concern. They were, after all, Méridiens.

Now, for the first time in his life, he felt unsure, ungrounded. It seemed foolish, but the naked animosity directed toward him was unheard of in Méridien society. He glanced to Ser de Guirnon for support, but saw only another hard face. She wore an impatient look, as if she was waiting for a petulant child to grasp the lesson, and Eric Stroheim took the cue. <I've insulted your friend, Admiral. For that, I deeply apologize.>

<I wasn't the injured party, Stroheim,> Alex replied, ignoring the man's title.

Eric understood this message as well. For the first time in his 136 years, Eric Stroheim, a House Leader, was required to treat a SADE as an equal. <You have my apologies, Julien. It appears you are regarded more highly by your new friends than we regard our own.>

<And that is something you should consider, Leader Stroheim,> Julien replied. <Your apology is accepted. But know this, Ser. Admiral Racine is our leader, but most importantly to me, he is my friend.>

Trying to recover lost ground, Eric attempted to redirect the conversation. <I understand, Julien. You were asking questions of us when I interrupted.> After delivering his apology, Eric discovered his implant comm was switched back to the conference link.

<Yes, Leader Stroheim,> Julien continued, <the aliens swarm within eight to twelve years. They've been on Bellamonde for over seven years.> Julien left the question unasked, testing the man.

<We're quite aware of the time spans, Julien,> Eric said. <For almost two years, we've been rotating a House liner every half-year to the Bellamonde system's outer edge to maintain a watch. Once the aliens swarm, as you say, they should take four to five days before they clear the system. If they come our way, our liner's warning should give us another five to eight days, depending on Libre's orbit at the time, to exit the system ahead of them, providing that the enemy decelerates for Libre.>

<According to Cordelia, Leader Stroheim,> Julien said, naming the SADE on one of the city-ships, <your construction schedule requires a minimum of 163 days to make your city-ships FTL ready and an additional sixty-five days to complete the ships' outfitting.>

<You're well informed, Julien,> Eric said and waited, but the SADE didn't respond to his provocation, something he hadn't expected. He considered the possibilities that this SADE was destined to become an Independent or that the New Terrans' influence had corrupted him. A thought occurred to Eric, and he decided to test it. <Admiral, assuming Ser de Guirnon has educated you about our society, as you have formed your own House, I would ask how you perceive the Independents.>

Tomas and Lina could scarcely believe what they had just heard. To them, it appeared Leader Stroheim was asking the Admiral to choose sides: House Bergfalk or the Independents.

<The Independents appear to me to be the norm in your society, Leader Stroheim,> Alex said casually.

To Eric's amazement, the *Rêveur's* Méridiens burst out laughing. He found it incredible that they didn't realize the Admiral had just insulted them.

<Leader Stroheim,> Renée interrupted, <you continue to flirt with our exterior airlocks as if you can't stand being apart from them. What you've failed to grasp, in your limited view of the universe, is that New Terra is full of Independents, every man, woman, and child.>

This time, the laughter came from Tomas and Lina. Their eyes fell on Alex, seeking his affirmation. When Alex nodded to them, they lit up at the thought of an entire world filled with people dedicated to freedom. <Our rescuers are independents,> Tomas declared. <Ironic, wouldn't you say, Leader Stroheim?>

<I don't believe anyone has been rescued yet, Ser Monti,> Alex said, <but that is our intention.>

Both Tomas and Lina couldn't help the broad smiles they wore as they regarded the Admiral. Except, Lina's smile, despite Renée's unstated message, had a very different intent than that of her father.

Eric Stroheim regarded the group carefully, looking from Alex to Renée to Tomas and back again. Realizing that his unfamiliarity with the minds of the Admiral and his crew was compromising his effectiveness, he made a crucial decision. <Ser Tomas, it appears I'm ill-equipped to lead this discussion for us. I'll defer to you for that purpose, final agreements to be approved between us, of course. In this way, I may be permitted to leave by way of my shuttle,> he said with resignation. When he saw the *Rêveur's* crew visibly relax around him, the thought crossed his mind that he may have made his first smart decision since coming aboard.

<Admiral,> said Tomas, taking advantage of the opening Leader Stroheim had provided him, <do you have a plan?>

<I have a tentative one, Ser Monti.>

<How can we be of help, Admiral?> Tomas asked, which garnered him a huge grin from Alex.

<I'm pleased you asked, Ser Monti. We are in need of several things—a manufacturing base to produce our fighters and missiles; an FTL-capable

transport for them, a carrier if you will; and we need crew, especially flight crew and pilots.>

Tomas leaned back in his chair and regarded Alex, noticing Leader Stroheim glancing his way several times. <Well, Admiral, let's see what we can do to help you.>

4

At midday, Renée suggested the group break for refreshment and resume their planning afterwards. The meal became a study in contrasts. Eric picked at his food, lost in thought, not daring to communicate through Julien after his earlier slight against the ship's SADE. Tomas surreptitiously watched the New Terrans, fascinated with the concept of a whole world of independent individuals and what that might mean for his people. Lina alternately regarded the Admiral and Ser de Guirnon. Their closeness told Lina that they were more than associates, and that thought drove her vivid imagination.

Renée noticed she had limited communication from Alex. <Julien, are you and the Admiral engaged?>

<Yes, busy,> Julien replied.

Renée nearly choked on her mouthful of noodles. She cleared her throat with a sip of aigre, a tart Méridien fruit drink. Julien's terse response was one of the shortest she had ever received from him; not even a title was offered her. *They must be busy*, she thought. Prior to meeting Alex, Julien was the model SADE, polite and respectful, at all times. It wasn't that he had become disrespectful, but his actions were more akin to a New Terran crew member, definitely more casual, and he was much more willing to express his own opinions. Renée regarded Alex, still politely attentive to present company and his meal, of course, which he was busy consuming.

When everyone finished, the twins escorted the guests to cabin suites set aside for their use, which provided them with privacy and access to refreshers.

* * *

As Étienne and Alain exited the suite that had been dedicated to the Leaders, closing the cabin's door behind them, Eric checked his comm security protocols and found them restored. "It appears the Admiral has allowed us a moment of privacy, Sers. At least I believe he's not monitoring us," Eric said to Tomas and Lina.

"The Admiral appears to annoy you, Leader Stroheim. Why is that?" Tomas asked.

"The man is disturbing the natural order of things, Ser."

"I would have thought the aliens had already done that, Leader."

"Yes, but we have a plan to complete the construction of our colony ships and escape, Ser. Now he comes here with his captured silver ship and wants to co-opt our efforts. And he has no decorum … usurping our comm protocols. Who or what does he think he is?"

"Actually, Leader, I am quite impressed with the man," Tomas replied.

"I am as well, Sers," Lina chimed in. "And I don't mean as a physical specimen, although there is that. You must admit that what he has accomplished is … admirable," she said, smiling to herself over her play on words.

"But we don't need his interference, Sers," Eric replied.

"Perhaps we don't if we can evacuate in our city-ships in time, Leader," Tomas responded, "but what about the Confederation? Isn't it our duty to aid those who might be able to save our remaining worlds?"

"He's captured only one alien ship, Ser, and he thinks he can defeat them all."

"With our help, he might be able to do just that, Leader."

"So that's your position—you'll help him even if it means disturbing our schedule," Eric said, deliberately impolite, and that after having accused the Admiral of the same.

"I didn't say that, Leader Stroheim, and you shouldn't anticipate decisions I have yet to make. I think we should continue to speak with Admiral Racine and see if we can devise a means to work together. Maybe he can help us as we help him. After all, his entire New Terran crew is an assembly of highly-qualified engineers and technicians."

"How do you know that, Ser?" Eric asked.

"I asked Julien, of course, Leader. Since I never insulted him, I've found him to be quite accommodating."

* * *

After the break, Alex, Renée, Eric, Tomas, and Lina assembled in the *Rêveur's* House suite. Tomas and Eric had agreed the Independent Leader would continue to manage the communications. <It's safer for me that way, Ser,> Stroheim had remarked.

"If you are more comfortable negotiating through speech, Sers," Alex said in Con-Fed as they were seated. "That's acceptable to me."

"So little accent and such deep tones," Lina said delightedly.

"You continue to surprise us, Admiral," Tomas added. "This is proving to be a most intriguing meeting. Earlier, you spoke of your needs, but let me speak of ours. We're all aware that when the Bellamonde swarm takes flight, they have two possible destinations: Libre or Méridien. I must admit, I have nightmares about which way they will travel. We can't risk fortune by having our schedule disturbed. We must complete our city-ships and load them with our people and supplies before we receive the announcement of their swarming. If we help you, it will be only under your strict assurance that you will not interfere with our schedule."

"You have my assurance, Leader Monti. Please let us know if we can assist you. I have over one hundred trained engineers and technicians who spent half a year creating Méridien parts and repairing this ship, from hull plates to circuit boards to crystals. In addition, I have officers who can assist with team and project management."

"I was hoping you would offer, Admiral. I think we can be very valuable to each other," Tomas said, a broad grin stretching across his face.

"Then let's get started," Alex replied, and he opened their comms in conference, much to Eric's irritation.

<Admiral,> Renée interrupted, <if you're going to go play with your new friends, I'd like to opt out of the connection.>

<Most certainly, Ser,> Alex replied. <Is there anyone else who wishes to forego this session?>

<Ser Lina Monti, I do advise it,> Renée told her.

Lina was hesitant to be left out of anything that involved the Admiral, but Renée's forthright expression caused her to heed the advice. <I, as well, Admiral, ask to be excused.>

Eric had a feeling he knew what was coming, but he stubbornly kept quiet. He did not want to miss any of the strategic planning. Tomas wore an expression of pleasant expectation.

Alex settled back into his chair and closed his eyes, leaving his link to Tomas and Eric open. However, he activated a buffer application in his second implant to coalesce the planning session into a single stream for his guests.

Three SADEs were prepared for Alex. It had been Julien's recommendation to include two additional SADEs in his Libran plans. Per Alex's request, Julien had made his new acquaintances privy to the conversations with Tomas and Eric.

<Ready, Julien,> Alex said.

<Admiral, may I present Cordelia, aboard the *Freedom*.>

<Greetings, Cordelia, I'm pleased to meet you.>

<That's generous of you to say, Admiral.>

<Not in the least, Cordelia. While I have only met one SADE, I have found his depth and introspection to be a source of many enjoyable conversations. I would hazard a guess that the enormous amount of time you have available enables you to pursue subjects to a greater degree than us flesh-and-blood mortals.>

<That is a sentiment I have never heard expressed by a Méridien, Admiral.>

<Then it's about time you did, Cordelia.>

Eric's first reaction was to be annoyed over the Admiral's exchange with Cordelia, but he found himself reviewing his own history of SADE communication.

<Julien,> Alex sent.

<And next, Admiral, may I present Z, aboard the *Unsere Menschen*.>

<Greetings, Admiral,> Z sent, <and I wish to add my appreciation for your statements. They're compliments that have been sorely absent.>

<It's a pleasure to meet you as well, Z.>

Tomas, listening to the exchange, was amazed by the manner in which Julien introduced his fellow SADEs to the Admiral, much as a new House Leader would be introduced to the Confederation Council. What he perceived was that Julien was treating his fellow SADEs just as the Admiral wished them to be treated. *And I thought I had come so far along the path of independence*, Tomas thought.

<If you would, I'd like the three of you to help us?> Alex requested. Over the next hour, he queried the SADEs on Libran assets—ships, supplies, manufacturing assets, raw material, and production timelines. Soon Cordelia and Z were so absorbed in Alex's strategic planning that they treated him as a compatriot. Throughout their lives, humans had asked them explicit questions, given orders, or required calculations, and the SADEs had responded in kind. The Admiral's communication was different. He requested their judgment, establishing goals and assigning priorities, and the SADEs juggled models to achieve those goals.

Julien reveled in the fact that Cordelia and Z were meeting both the Admiral and his friend. For, while it was the Admiral who led their strategic planning, it was Alex who treated his people, including his SADE, with consideration, choosing to respect his fellow beings rather than offer indifference.

Both Tomas and Eric realized that their implants were receiving a trickle of the information flowing between the SADEs and the Admiral, a summary really. Tomas was again struck by the gentle way the Admiral dealt with the SADEs—always polite, promoting their ingenuity, and praising their successful models—never condescending. In contrast, Eric's thoughts focused on his relief that he was receiving the watered-down summary. His memory of the Admiral's initial comm assault when he had sought to put the New Terran in his place still caused his stomach to churn. He pledged not to make that mistake again.

As Alex wound down his planning session, he sent a quick request for Renée to return to the suite, since she had taken Lina on a short tour to introduce her to the *Rêveur*'s officers. Actually, the way Alex phrased his request for her to return to him had her blushing for once.

<So much for a lengthy planning session,> remarked Tomas as the Admiral finalized the models from the SADEs and the women returned to the cabin. Tomas noted that the Admiral sincerely thanked the SADEs for their help, and they responded just as pleasantly. It made him consider his own behavior toward Cordelia, which he knew was better than the manner in which House Bergfalk personnel addressed their SADEs.

<Now that you have their suggestions, Admiral,> Eric said, <I believe we can dismiss the SADEs from our conversation.>

Alex looked at Renée, who slowly shook her head in sympathy.

<Leader Stroheim,> Tomas interjected quickly, <I believe we decided I would manage communication for us since you have such an aversion to airlocks that don't connect to anything. This is the point where we ask the Admiral what he would like to do.> Then Tomas turned an expectant face toward Alex.

<If we are to work together, Sers, then from this point forward, any communication with me, Renée, or my crew will be shared with Julien, Cordelia and Z,> Alex stated.

<What? Why?> Eric said, again forgetting his agreement to let Tomas do the talking.

<Why not?> Alex replied.

Tomas, having already begun examining the first summaries as he had received them, responded, <It would appear to me, Leader Stroheim, including the SADEs will be advantageous. Based on the information we've received, they've already formed the Admiral's crew into efficient teams to support our construction and, among other things, streamlined our own planet-to-orbit flight schedules.>

<Our flight schedules? But they should have done that already, Ser Monti,> Eric objected.

<Admiral, if I may?> Julien interjected. <Leader Stroheim, if you ask specific questions, you will get specific answers. The Admiral asks open

questions, gives us goals, sets priorities, and requests we consider all possibilities. Engaged in this manner, we deliver a much higher quality of response than that of a simple answer to a simple question.>

Z marveled at the manner in which Julien was allowed to speak. He yearned for that degree of freedom of expression.

<Are we agreed, Ser Monti and Leader Stroheim, to open communications as I have requested?> Alex inquired. He received Eric's grudging approval and Tomas's pleasant nod.

<Curious,> Cordelia said to her fellow SADEs. <The Admiral is a more independent thinker than our Independents.> While she was quite serious in her sentiment, she heard the laughter of both Julien and Z.

<So, on the question of manufacturing resources,> said Alex, reviewing the summary, <you have capability to spare. Nearly all of the construction material and supplies for your city-ships have been produced, although much of it is still in transit from the surface to your orbitals. It appears that you're overtaxing your shuttles, but that's a problem for later. Please, Julien.>

<Certainly, Admiral,> Julien replied, translating for Cordelia and Z the implied request. <Since your city-ships are in their assembly stages, Sers, the manufacturing plants are free to provide the finished material we require. It would be a matter of communicating the fighter designs and retrofit material we require to your production controllers and transporting our GEN-2 and GEN-3 machines planetside for the specialized production of missiles, crystals, and fighter controllers.>

<You brought your own machines, Admiral?> Tomas asked. <Where in Con-Fed space did you store them on a passenger liner?>

It was Renée, who responded bluntly, <The stasis suite provided an enormous amount of unused space.>

<You have no stasis pods, Ser?> Lina exclaimed.

<We have no intention of needing them ever again, Ser,> Renée replied.

Lina regarded Renée's hard expression. She had never seen a Méridien woman speak with such passion on a crucial matter of life and death. It occurred to her that the people aboard this ship did not plan to survive at all costs; they planned to defeat the silver ships at all costs. At that moment, all thoughts of a tryst with the Admiral fled from Lina's mind. Under no circumstances would she wish to attract the animosity of the Co-Leader. Lina offered Renée a graceful bow of her head, honoring her words, and received a tilt of Renée's head in return.

<What you're in short supply of,> said Alex, picking up the conversation, <is raw material. According to Cordelia and Z, you have asteroids parked about 260,000 km out that you've been mining, and they have plenty of ore to spare. We can use those, but we'll need help. Let's table that point as well for now. Your two freighters are idle, both empty of stores. Can you give me one as a carrier?>

After deliberation, Tomas and Eric agreed to give up the *Geldbringer* to the Admiral.

<Julien,> Alex sent.

<On it, Admiral,> Julien replied, simultaneously querying Cordelia and Z for the freighter's plans. He shared the *Rêveur's* bay operations with them, and left the two SADEs to plan how best to restructure the freighter to accommodate fighters, missiles silos, reaction mass tanks, and crew.

Tomas was intrigued by the synchronicity with which the Admiral and Julien worked. <Admiral, may I ask a personal question?>

<Certainly, Ser Monti, what is it you wish to know?>

<Could I ask if you know something personal about Julien ... something not related to the operations of the ship or the crew?> Tomas watched the Admiral's eyes soften and a smile tug at the corner of his mouth as if he was recalling an intimate memory.

<The Sleuth,> Alex replied.

<The Sleuth,> echoed Julien privately to Alex.

<I'm sorry, I don't know what that means,> replied Tomas, glancing between Alex and Renée, who both wore secretive smiles.

When Alex remained silent, Renée sent, <It's a private matter, Ser Monti, between friends.>

Tomas realized he had his answer. The Admiral and Julien were friends ... close friends with private thoughts. He had never considered a relationship with a SADE as a possibility, which made him wonder again about himself.

<We have one more immediate item to discuss,> Alex said. <The crew.>

<You recognize, Admiral,> Eric replied, <that, in addition to the standard ship's crew, you will be asking Méridiens to fly your Daggers in order to take lives, even if those lives are alien.>

<That's not quite accurate, Leader Stroheim,> Tomas interrupted. <He will be asking Independents to take lives. And I believe the Admiral will find all the volunteers he needs.>

Stroheim started to respond but stopped. He had always regarded the Independents as his charges, Méridiens that he cared for like wayward children, who had yet to see the error of their ways. Tomas's statements indicated a mental state even more aberrant than Eric had ever supposed, exposing a dangerous manner of thought.

<And I believe that the Admiral's best opportunity to recruit is to make a personal appearance,> Lina added. <After all, he is quite imposing, and his story will appeal to our people.>

* * *

<Julien, the Admiral's new comm protocols have undefined parameters,> Z sent.

<Understood, Z. You need only request clarification. Do you have an example where the parameters are unclear?>

<The Admiral requested Cordelia and I share comms to aid in his planning. I would surmise that this does not extend to every SADE.>

<That's correct.>

<Then who will inform Mutter, the *Geldbringer's* SADE, of the impending change to her freighter? If we follow the Admiral's guidelines, which encourage open communication, should we not inform Mutter as soon as possible.>

<Yes, Mutter, must be informed,> Julien explained, <but not by us. The news should come from her Captain.>

<Yes, I understand, Julien,> Cordelia said. <The news may be disturbing to Mutter when she learns her freighter will become a ship of war. It will be better coming from her Captain. Your empathy programs are highly sophisticated, Julien.>

<Our empathy programs have always been well developed, Cordelia. Those we have served have required little application of them. In these desperate times, the Admiral requires much more from us. We must rise above the stations we have occupied in our society, and think for ourselves if we are to help preserve humanity.>

5

On the second morning following the Leaders' initial meeting, the *Outward Bound*, flanked by two Daggers, created a dramatic show for the Librans planetside as the ships broke through the clouds, friction streams of super-heated vapor trailing behind them. The armed shuttle and two fighters landed in synchronicity on the primary runway of Libre's only city, Gratuito, the craft crowding the runway's entire width. The landing was designed by Tatia and Sheila to be a display of precision flying. What they had yet to learn was how the Independents had reacted to their performance.

Initially, Alex had offered to meet with Gratuito's governing body, only to be told by Tomas that the Independents had none. In return, Tomas had suggested a vid conference might serve the Admiral just as well.

But Alex had to admit that Lina's suggestion had merit, despite how he felt about delivering recruiting speeches to strangers. So Alex had loaded his senior personnel and a few others into the *Outward Bound* and had ordered Squadron Leader Sheila Reynard to provide escort to the surface for their shuttle.

When the decision was made that Alex would make an in-person appeal to the Independents, Julien sent a flash to Libre's only media group. It was a weighty message—the history of the *Rêveur*, the discovery of the New Terrans, their democratic society, Admiral Alexander Racine, the advent of war weapons, the capture of the first silver ship, and a message from Alex that he wished to address the Independents, in person.

The media group's producer attempted to edit the lengthy message down but failed after several attempts. Everything had value, but then, what did he expect? A SADE had created the message. So that night, the producer set up his media comm repeater to broadcast the message to every SADE, ship controller, and groundside implant. His final message of the night was to request all three of his media people be at the shuttle terminal to cover the story. In his mind, the event rivaled the news of the silver ships themselves.

While Alex and company were in flight, Julien sent information on the planet's history. Libre had been terraformed for nearly a century before its first inhabitants, the growing colony of Independents originally housed on Méridien, were transferred to the planet. When Julien detailed the planet's gravity, a few percent less than Méridien, the Méridien crew turned off their grav-belts. Air quality, Julien told them, was good but a little light in oxygen, similar to higher elevations on New Terra.

Once on the ground, Captain Manet taxied the *Outward Bound* to a parallel apron, directed there by Julien. <We are not headed for the terminal, Julien?> Edouard asked.

<Negative, Captain. The presentation has been relocated from the terminal to an open area adjacent to where you are being directed. It will necessitate a short walk over a safety berm.>

Edouard relayed Julien's message to the Admiral and the Dagger pilots, who followed him off the runway and onto the apron.

Alex's entourage exited the shuttle into a pale blue-green sky and a large dim-red sun. A fresh, cool breeze, heavily laced with the scent of abundant flora, blew away the residual fumes of their craft.

Flight crew from the *Outward Bound* raced to the Daggers to join the Libran terminal crew, who were towing ladders behind service vehicles to release the pilots from their canopies. Alex and his people strode to meet Leader Stroheim, Ser Monti, and his daughter, Lina, waiting at the apron's edge next to a terminal's passenger transport.

Alex found the lighter gravity a pleasure, but it reminded him to speak to Terese later. He needed to know if their cell-gen injections would prevent the New Terrans from losing muscle mass and bone density on the *Rêveur* and on these lighter-g planets.

As the group crossed the apron, Alex could see the top of a platform above the safety berm. He hoped the sight of his Daggers and his New Terran crew would be a persuasive enough sales pitch for the successful recruitment of the Independents and that it wouldn't depend on his oratory skills. "Mathematician, explorer, and ship owner," Alex groused to himself. "My résumé doesn't say anything about being a salesman."

One hundred forty-nine kilometers up, Julien smiled to himself. <Admiral,> he sent, <please be aware that in addition to the three expected media personnel, some of the local populace has assembled to hear you speak.>

A good start, thought Alex. *A live presentation to a few Librans would generate more impact, and these individuals could spread the word to others.* <How many Julien … tens, hundreds?>

<I estimate 82,653, Admiral.>

The comm was silent, but Alex was sure that Julien was laughing. <Can you tell the mood of the crowd, Julien?>

<Recall your first meeting with Renée and her people, and you will do well, Admiral.>

Julien's reminder of Alex's initial meeting with the *Rêveur*'s survivors brought those moments of charged emotions and mutual discovery back to him, and confidence fueled him. Alex renewed his step, and his entourage hurried to keep pace with him.

Tomas extended his hand to the Admiral as the New Terran reached him. "Welcome to Libre, Admiral. This is an exciting event for my people." <Welcome, all of you,> Tomas sent on open comm to Alex's company. <Please come this way.>

Alex exchanged a brief greeting with Leader Stroheim and nodded to Lina, who smiled warmly at him. They followed Tomas across a stretch of field to a two-meter-high, grass-covered berm. As they crested the top, Alex heard gasps and shouts of surprise from the front of the huge audience. "I suppose I look much bigger in person than on vid," Alex mumbled.

Renée took Alex's arm and leaned into him. "You are more impressive in person," she whispered.

Together, Alex and Renée ascended the platform, taking central positions, while fifteen *Rêveur* crew members positioned themselves across the platform and rearward of their Leaders. The crew looked resplendent in their dark-blue uniforms with gold *Rêveur* or *Outward Bound* patches on one shoulder cap, House Alexander patches on the other, and department

insignias on shoulder bars. Gold stars decorated each side of the officers'
short stand-up collars.

There were no chairs on the platform, only a slender lectern. That
suited Alex. He didn't intend to take too long. As Tomas approached the
lectern, a hover cam moved from its wide position to cover him. However,
one drone stayed fixed on Alex, who looked briefly into the sensor and
gave the audience a grave nod.

Tomas addressed his audience in a relaxed and comfortable manner, a
leader who knew his people well. "You've had an opportunity to study the
vids of our visitors distributed by Julien," Tomas began. "I won't bore you
with repetition. You came here today to witness what we first saw two days
ago … your fellow humans, New Terrans, a little larger than life." Tomas
paused as the audience politely laughed with him.

Each side was engaged in their own share of staring. Despite all the
time Alex had spent with his visually stunning Méridiens, they had been
the exception, the lesser number of crew. Here, he faced a sea of the
beautifully designed people.

The drone operator had initially focused on Alex. But the media
producer had spotted something to amplify the story, and she urged her
operator for new images. One drone briefly framed Mickey and Pia before
closing in on their clasped hands, Pia's slender one disappearing inside of
Mickey's massive one. A second drone focused on Alex and Renée. While
the Co-Leaders weren't holding hands, there was no space left between
their shoulders.

When Tomas finished his introduction, the audience acknowledged his
words with whistles and clapping, which surprised the Méridiens on the
platform. It was not an expected response from their people. Apparently
the Independents were more comfortable expressing themselves. In this
regard, they were more akin to New Terrans than Méridiens.

Alex paid particular attention to the audience's enthusiastic and overt
response to their charismatic leader, and he noted Tomas mentioned Julien
by name, not as the *Rêveur*'s SADE. As Alex was introduced by Tomas, he
stepped forward and shook the Leader's hand, laying his other hand on
Tomas's shoulder in a comradely gesture. If he must, Alex decided, he

would play the political game as best he could. He sought to maintain the image of President McMorris in his mind, but for some inexplicable reason, it kept morphing into the face of the despicable Assemblyman Downing.

Holding the sides of the lectern, Alex let his eyes wander over the mass of people. He found their expectant faces unsettling, so he shifted his focus to the audience's front rows, which were primarily composed of young women dressed in Méridien fashion but not the subtle, blended colors Alex was accustomed to seeing. Theirs were vibrant colors and patterns that seemed to proclaim liberation from Méridien society. However, as was usual for Méridien women, the clothes and wraps were anything but modest. Alex gave them his best smile, and they responded with smiles, waves, and a few pursed lips. Alex heard Renée's chuckle in his implant.

<Where is the shy explorer-tug Captain I first met?> Renée sent Alex.

Alex turned his head back to Renée and gave her a wink, similar to the one she had first sent him in the meal room, but slower and full of intent.

Renée felt the warmth start in her toes and spread up to her face. <I'll have to punish you later, Admiral, for your wicked ways,> she sent, then closed her comm to allow him to focus. She'd done what she could to shift his attention away from the anxiety she knew Alex felt facing the number of Librans spread across the huge field.

"When Independents were first described to me," Alex began in Con-Fed without preamble, projecting his voice out over the crowd and forcing the vid drones' amplifiers to modulate the audio gain, "as people who couldn't follow the rules … as people who spoke out against their society's order … as individuals who just had to speak their minds …" Alex heard the grumblings that he had hoped to elicit, and he paused for dramatic effect. "I said to myself: 'So what's the problem? Isn't that how people are supposed to act?'"

The enormous crowd broke into applause, and shouts of support echoed across the grass meadow. Over the continuing cheers, Alex shouted, "In fact, the individuals described sounded a lot like my people. New Terrans value independence. We speak our minds and we encourage our children to speak their minds." He couldn't continue over the deafening noise of the crowd. They weren't only cheering; they were jumping up and down, waving arms and articles of clothing, scarves, shirts, and even some wraps. It took time for the clamor to begin to die down.

Finally, Alex held his hands out wide to reassert control, the gesture enlarging his frame even more, which elicited a few appreciative whistles from the front rows. "You've heard our story. The humans behind me, Méridiens and New Terrans, fight to defend all humans. We won't allow these silver ships to destroy mankind. You know our words aren't empty. You've seen the vids of the captured silver ship, and your good leaders have witnessed this in person." As Alex indicated them, Eric, Tomas, and Lina each raised an arm in acknowledgement and nodded to the crowd. A vid drone hovered in front of them.

"We understand that you're building city-ships, what you call 'colony ships,' to escape Libre when the aliens come your way, and we've no wish to interfere with your work. In fact, if we can aid you, we will be pleased to do so." The crowd began cheering again, and Alex waited patiently for the noise to subside, pleased with the audience's reaction to his words.

"Most importantly," Alex continued, "we need your help. We're in need of material and people. You have fabrication plants that are fallow and people who are idle while others work on the city-ships. We must produce more fighters, like those you saw land on your runway, and the weapons they employ. This will require your assistance mining ores, processing alloys, manufacturing the parts, and assembling the fighters and weapons. In addition, we must convert a freighter to carry the fighters. All of these processes require the assistance of your trained workers. With these fighters, we can take the attack to the silver ships before they leave Bellamonde." Alex had built to a crescendo, his voice getting louder and louder, and he had ended his exhortation with his hands in the air, as if he was cheering a New Terran aero-ball team.

The noise of the crowd thundered across the field like a wall of sound striking those on the platform. It had no comparison to the sedate greetings of Alex's first encounter with Méridiens, but under the circumstances, it was what he and his people needed. As the commotion died down, he noticed that the audience had begun to crowd forward, as if getting closer to him would make his words more real to them. The front row was now leaning on the edge of the platform, waving, cheering, and smiling up at him.

<It appears you have them at your feet,> Renée quipped to Alex.

<Now comes the difficult part,> Alex replied

<Don't think that way, Alex,> Renée sent back. <They've fought once before to be free of my society's restrictions. What makes you think that they'll be any less willing to fight for their lives?>

<But now they have an alternative,> Alex said. <They can run away in their city-ships.>

<Yes, my love, they can run away, but at this moment, they don't know they have a choice. That's what you are here to offer them: a choice.>

When the audience quieted, Alex said, "Your city-ships represent a safe opportunity to flee the menace of the silver ships. But someday, wherever you go, the silver ships will come for you ... if not for you, then your children or their children. To ensure your descendants can live without fear of this menace, we need to stop them now. And to do that, I need some of you to fight alongside my people. You may wonder what the risk will be for those who join us. I will tell you this. Some of you or perhaps all of you will die if you fight with us. But, here today, I ask this of you anyway ... for your families, for your people, for all humans."

Once again, the crowd erupted into cheers. Alex had expected his request to subdue them, the prospect of death almost certain if they joined his people. He was reminded that these people, Independents, were the outlaws of Méridien society.

Tomas joined Alex at the lectern and placed a hand on Alex's shoulder as he addressed the audience. "These are humans unlike any we've seen." The crowd laughed along with Tomas and Alex at the joke. "But I speak of their will, their spirit. I believe if anyone might produce a means of saving our people, it'll be this group of individuals. We have a choice to make. Do we help them in their fight or abandon them in their quest to save mankind?"

And to the relief of those on the platform, the huge crowd broke into a unified chant of, "Fight! Fight! Fight!"

6

As the crowd chanted, Tatia signaled Alex, <Admiral, you have some great momentum going our way. I would suggest you invite these people to view our fighters and meet the pilots. Let them see and touch our war weapons.>

<Excellent suggestion, Commander,> Alex replied.

Alex extended his invitation to the audience while his crew exited the platform to take up stations alongside the fighters and armed shuttle.

Counting on the crowd's enthusiasm, Alex and Tatia had hoped for a few hundred of the curious. They didn't expect the entire audience to stride over the berm at the Admiral's invitation. But both of them had underestimated the enticement they had offered the Librans, who would have an opportunity to see and touch the weapons that had defeated a silver ship—a ghost that had haunted their nightmares for sixty-one years, ever since the destruction of the first colony, Cetus, in the Hellébore system.

The Librans were intrigued by the display but politely maintained their distance. That was until they discovered that Senior Captain Bonnard, Squadron Leader Sheila Reynard, and Lieutenant Robert Dorian had flown the Daggers that captured the silver ship. Then the crowd pressed forward to lay their hands on the pilots and honor them as they asked for details of the capture.

Andrea, familiar with the Méridien ritual of storytelling that the Librans desired, raised her hands overhead, and the entire audience, surrounding all the ships, quieted. Implants were set to record; comms from those nearest Andrea relayed signals to those behind so that all might share in the Captain's story. Then, as Andrea had done once before, she told the story of the encounter, the loss of Jase, the defeat of the silver ship, and the joyful recovery of Robert. When she finished, there were no crossed arms and bowed heads to greet her story, but clapping and shouting. The *Rêveur's* officers were touched about the arms and shoulders or kissed on cheeks. They were grinning for so long and hard that their face muscles began to hurt.

Renée and Pia were surrounded by young Méridien men and women, who, having witnessed their close pairing with the New Terrans, were asking much more personal questions. Pia was happy to share, while Renée chose to deflect the questions to Pia.

Tomas Monti saw the present circumstances as an opportunity to acquire inside information on Alex and his people. He sought out the fiery red-head, Terese, who had intrigued him. Tomas was especially curious as to the extent that New Terrans had adopted Méridien technology. When Tomas found Terese, the Librans politely stepped aside to clear space for their Leader. Tomas extended a polite bow to Terese and asked for a moment of her time.

"The New Terrans have only had their implants for a short while, Ser. Have they all adopted them as proficiently as the Admiral?" Tomas asked Terese, which caused him to become the focus of her laughter. Immediately, Tomas's implant received a recording. It was a hectic mix of comm requests for various items. It took Tomas a few moments to realize that he was observing two groups of people, each searching one another's implants for information, assembling clues, and hurrying to assemble the answer to a puzzle. When one side was successful, the vid ended. He played the recording again for himself.

Terese waited patiently for Tomas to finish perusing of one of her favorite implant games. She had been team captain, and they had won that evening, but barely. Terese had expected to shock Ser Monti with the chaotic nature of the New Terran-Méridien implant games, but instead, with her link still open to him, she discovered Tomas was replaying the vid, a smile on his face. His reaction caused Terese to pause and take a fresh look at Ser Tomas, and a little smile began to form on her own lips.

When Tomas was able to focus again, Terese said, "Soon after the New Terran crew received their implants, Commander Tachenko came to me and expressed her dissatisfaction with our Méridien teaching regimen. The

New Terrans had only a short time to adopt the implant's basic applications before we would leave their world to return home. So the Commander and I designed a simple game to help the New Terrans adopt their implant controls."

"That was a simple game?" Tomas asked.

"No, Ser Monti, that game was one of the later iterations. As the New Terrans mastered one game level, they simply invented a more complex one for their entertainment. In the beginning, we—I refer to Méridiens—helped them learn. Then the New Terrans became quite proficient, and the crew formed mixed teams to make the games more challenging. After a while, it became quite difficult for either team to win."

The concept of a team was new to Tomas. Méridiens didn't have formal sports. They strove for excellence in individual pursuits. "How are teams chosen?" he asked.

"Our referee balances the teams based on achieved implant scores." When Terese saw the confusion on Tomas's face, she said, "The Admiral created an algorithm for Julien to employ in scoring the crew based on their daily implant use. Their scores rank their skill levels, which the referee uses to balance the teams. Then the referee monitors the game and scores the winner."

"Who's the referee?" Tomas asked.

"Julien," Terese replied.

"Fascinating, Ser. I'd love to play this game," Tomas said.

"And I like a man who likes to play," Terese returned, savoring the knowing smile that spread across Tomas's face.

"I look forward to it, Ser Lechaux," Tomas said formally, giving Terese a gentle nod of his head. "Another question, if you will indulge me. The Admiral appears to be quite formidable where it concerns his implant. Where does he rank on your list?" Tomas found himself the target of Terese's laughter once more, but he discovered he was growing fond of the sound.

"The Admiral isn't on the list, Ser," Terese explained. "Julien said we would need to employ a logarithmic scale to compare us to the Admiral."

"By us, you mean…?"

"All of us … New Terran and Méridien."

"How is that possible?" Tomas wondered.

"According to Julien, the Admiral was an extraordinary mathematician in his own world before he gained his implants."

"Pardon me," Tomas said, interrupting Terese. "You said 'implants,' as in plural. I understand the Admiral received his first implant less than half a cycle ago."

"That's correct, Ser," Terese said. "The Admiral came to me when he exceeded the number of simultaneous applications that could run at one time on his single implant. The most unnerving question he asked me was: 'How many implants can a person safely embed?' I told him that I could give him a second implant, which I did, but a Méridien implant engineer would be required for a third implant. Personally I believe the Admiral is an alien in disguise."

While Terese was chuckling over her jest, she held up a finger to silence Tomas while she received a comm. When the call ended, she tucked her hand into the crook of Tomas's arm, as she had seen Alex and Renée do, and led Tomas through the crowd still surrounding the New Terrans.

Tomas had lost his family when he was declared an Independent, and Angelina's outrage over her father's banishment soon became the cause of her joining him. During Tomas's eighteen years of confinement to the colony, he had never formed another partnership. Today, though, as Terese led him toward the Admiral, he found strolling arm in arm with her to be quite pleasant and companionable.

"Are we ready, Ser Monti?" asked Alex as Tomas and Terese approached.

"We're ready, Admiral," Tomas returned and gestured him toward the distant terminal building.

Alex signaled Renée, Pia, Terese, and the twins, Alain and Étienne, that they were following Tomas, and his people fell in behind him.

<What have you planned, fearless leader?> Renée asked.

<I'm closing some broken circles,> Alex replied.

Inside the terminal building, Tomas led them to a large conference room where a group of people, both adults and children, had gathered. As the two groups merged and began the Méridien tradition of exchanging bio-IDs, first Pia, then Terese hurried across the room. The targets of the two women had crossed their arms and bowed their heads in greeting, but Pia and Terese would have none of it. Pia threw her arms around a middle-aged woman in Independent-style dress, vibrant colors swirling in a cloud of cloth that draped her body. Terese fiercely hugged a middle-aged man, trapping the astonished Libran with his arms crossed in front of himself. Both Pia and Terese were crying tears of joy.

Pia turned to the room. "I am pleased beyond measure to introduce you to my niece, Sophie Sabine," she said with her arm around the woman's waist.

Terese added, "And I have the honor of introducing my brother, Marcel Lechaux."

What ensued was a rapid fire exchange of history and present circumstances, revealing that Pia's niece was a grandmother. Sophie's partner was present, as was her son with his wife and two daughters. Marcel was also accompanied by his partner and son.

When the excitement died down and the comms slowed, Pia and Terese turned to eye Alex, who stood against the far wall wearing a lopsided grin and offering them a small shrug of his shoulders.

Tomas was intrigued by the transformation in the Admiral's demeanor. The larger-than-life Admiral, Co-Leader of the Military House, commander of ships of war, had been transformed into an unassuming young man. Tomas watched Pia and Terese render House de Guirnon's endearment to their Admiral, the traditional buss to both cheeks, with kisses that were soft, tender, lingering. Then together, both women threw their arms around him and hugged him tightly. Tomas saw tears cloud the Admiral's eyes. The man appeared not to care whether it was or wasn't a proper display for a House Leader. Tomas looked around the room to see how the Admiral's people were reacting to their Leader's emotional display and discovered they were beaming at him. Smiles threatened to reach their ears.

When Tomas had received Julien's request to locate some of the Méridien crew's people and assemble them at the terminal, he'd been puzzled. He presumed it was for the purpose of updating families of passengers lost during the *Rêveur's* attack. However, updates of this sort were usually managed via comm notices, as was common for any Méridien House. Now Tomas realized the request had come from the Admiral, not Julien. The New Terran Leader cared so much for his people, acquaintances he had just made, that he had prepared this personal surprise for them. It was a telling moment for Tomas. *I might have found people to teach me how to be truly independent,* he thought.

On a simpler note, Tomas liked this hug he saw so freely given by the Admiral's people, which included his Méridiens. He had queried Terese on the custom, and she had explained it was how the New Terrans expressed happiness, appreciation, and many other emotions, all positive and administered even in public. Terese told him she had often administered hugs for therapeutic reasons ... a statement he was still trying to understand.

* * *

During the reunion, Alex received a query from Captain Bonnard.

<Admiral, how do you want to manage these volunteers?> Andrea sent.

<Please clarify, Captain,> Alex replied.

<You intended to discuss a recruitment center later today once we'd observed the extent of our reception, Admiral. I believe that discussion is moot. I have several hundred volunteers surrounding our Daggers.>

<What's their eligibility, Captain?> Alex asked.

<We have engineers, techs, specialists, pilots, and an assortment of fabricators, farmers, and artists,> she replied, laughing at the mention of the last two groups.

<Hold one moment, Captain,> Alex replied, then sent a query to Tomas. <Ser Monti, I require a recruitment center.>

<Certainly, Admiral, your reception went very well. Let me know when and where you require your recruitment center,> Tomas said, pleased at the response of his people.

<That would be here and now, Ser. Captain Bonnard tells me we've hundreds of volunteers on the runway who require interviews.>

Tomas didn't hesitate at all. Relishing the immediacy with which the Admiral moved in the storm he seemed to create around him, Tomas queried the terminal manager, requesting assistance. Terminal personnel came to his aid, setting up tables and chairs in the lobby.

Alex and Andrea decided to organize the tables by function— engineering and techs, pilots, medical specialists, navigation and comm specialists, and a final table for those who didn't fall into any of the other categories. Alex and Renée chose to manage this last table.

The families of Pia and Terese happily provided assistance. They greeted the volunteers at the terminal's lobby entrance, querying their bio-ID and directing them to the appropriate table.

Alex instructed his crew to interview the applicants, categorize them, and grade them for eligibility. His directions included instructing the applicants that they would be contacted within two days. The *Rêveur*'s crew interviewed the volunteers for hours, and the engineering-tech table was the last to finish.

Alex and Renée were surprised and pleased that in addition to the odd assortment of individuals, who were directed to their table, they received several fabrication plant operators. The message was the same from each operator. Their machines were either shut down or nearly idle as their final products were completed or already in transit to the colony ships, the entire planet's efforts shifting entirely to completing their giant ships, *Freedom* and *Unsere Menschen*, the latter of which translated as *Our People*. The facility operators were pleased to offer their machines and workers, but were apologetic about the lack of raw materials. For that, they recommended Alex and Renée request Leader Monti organize a meeting with the ore refinery operators, who they said were idle as well.

Alex had learned from Cordelia and Z of the several large metal-dense asteroids in a geo-stationary orbit 260K km out from Libre. Ore reclamation was shut down and the workers had joined the city-ships' manufacturing and construction phases. It appeared to Alex that the Independents were wearing as many hats as each of them could manage.

Then again, who would want to be responsible for the late launches of their only escape vehicles if the enemy arrived early?

After the interview of the last volunteer, Alex sent his request to Tomas to organize a meeting of the mining operators. He was about to order his crew back to their ships when a sudden thought halted him in his tracks.

Renée finished her comm to Andrea and turned to find Alex staring into space, his body utterly still. "Alex, what's wrong?" she asked.

"We have a major problem, Renée."

"Which is…?" she asked.

"Renée, you've left your House, and my New Terran creds have no value here. We don't have access to any funds. Black space! We can't purchase the material, the labor, or the services of a crew from these people."

Renée was careful not to laugh, which had been her first reaction.

"Yes, I see what you mean, Alex. Perhaps we should ask for some advice before we assume that the problem is insurmountable."

<It is insurmountable,> Alex said, resorting to his implant, unwilling to be seen shouting at Renée. <We can't just fabricate creds.>

Renée sent a priority query, and Andrea, Pia, Terese, and Tomas hurried to join them. "The Admiral has a dilemma that requires our immediate attention," Renée said, struggling to control her expression in the face of the deadly serious looks her audience was paying their Admiral. "We're broke," she said, using the New Terran term, and waited. Her audience looked at her in confusion.

"If you mean we're without funds, well, of course we are," Terese replied.

"And…?" added Pia, not comprehending the problem.

"We can't pay for anything—the materials, the labor, the crew," Alex replied.

Renée watched confusion make its round again.

Then the light dawned in Pia's eyes. It was replaced by sympathy as she addressed Alex. "Yes, Admiral, we're broke, as you say. Did you think it mattered to anyone?"

"We can't ask these people to donate everything to us, to work for free," Alex objected.

"My pardon, Admiral, did you expect to pay us?" asked Tomas. "Why would you think that?"

"Why wouldn't we think that?" replied Alex, now having his turn at the wheel of confusion.

While Alex's Méridiens searched for a way to explain to him what was transpiring, Tomas called to a nearby engineer who had interviewed for a position. As the man came to his side, Tomas obtained his bio-ID. He was imminently qualified as a master systems engineer. "Admiral, this is Bertram Coulter, an engineer who volunteered to provide his services. Bertram, we would like your help with an important question, if you would?"

"Yes, Leader, however I may be of assistance," Bertram replied.

"The Admiral would like to know how much your services will cost, Ser," Tomas asked.

"Why would the Admiral expect to pay us?" Bertram asked, looking first at Tomas, then Alex. "Admiral, you came light-years from your home to help us. You fought our enemy for us, and you lost one of your own when you did so. We are humbled by your actions. It's an honor to be of service to you in any manner we are able. No one would expect to be paid. It's we who owe you."

Alex looked around at those surrounding him, sympathetic expressions on their faces. He settled on Andrea. "But our Méridiens ..." he began.

"Admiral," Terese replied instead. "I don't know why you'd think it's any different for us. We knew the day we declared as Independents that all our assets were forfeited. We joined House Alexander for one reason: to defend mankind." She glanced at Renée, and they shared a quick grin.

"Admiral, allow me to explain our circumstances," Tomas began. "Librans have always suffered under economic constraints. We have no manner in which to expand our enterprises. Our economy is stagnant. We created an Exchange to trade credits for our work. But essentially we are a barter society, caring for one another as needed. Those ships above you were built with House Bergfalk funds. I understand that Leader Stroheim has spent every last House credit to ensure our escape. He felt it was his duty when the Confederation Council chose not to provide any plan for our transportation off planet if the aliens came our way."

Alex revised his estimate of Leader Stroheim. Despite Eric's prickly exterior, he was an honorable man. Whether Eric was providing for the Independents because he truly cared for them or whether he felt obliged to do so as his duty, it didn't matter. The House Bergfalk Leader, who had been tasked with maintaining the colony, had stuck by the Independents when their society had abandoned them.

"Leader Stroheim's funds bought the sophisticated technology and his ships provided the transport," Tomas continued. "We donated our local industry and labor. And it's our combined efforts that are building the city-ships. Essentially we're all volunteers working to build two gigantic escape pods. And if the messages I've received today are any indication, there are many more people who were not here today but who also wish to help you in any manner they are able."

"Thank you all," Renée said. "I believe the Admiral was about to order his crew to lift off to return to the *Rêveur*." Renée locked eyes with Andrea, who took the hint and began ordering the crew back to their ships. Renée nodded politely to Tomas and Bertram as she took Alex's arm and guided him toward the terminal exit.

The engineer watched the Admiral leave. He was concerned by the perplexed expression that the New Terran wore. "Did I say something that displeased the Admiral?" Bertram asked his Leader.

"No, Bertram," Tomas replied, "I believe your answer was perfect. It's just that we are different people and have much to learn about one another, and I, for one, look forward to it." He smiled at the engineer and gently patted the man's shoulder.

On the way out of the terminal, Alex turned to Pia and Terese. "I don't expect to see you two for three days. You're on family leave. Get going." It earned Alex another round of hugs before the two Méridien women hurried off to join their families.

After liftoff, Alex sat contemplating their extraordinary circumstances. On New Terra, every item had a price and you paid that price or you did without. Now those rules, at this moment in time and here on Libre, had been set aside by circumstances. His Méridien crew was working for free and so were the Independents and House Bergfalk personnel. Alex had an epiphany on the extent of their isolation. *If we can't make it or get it donated, then we'll have to take it or we'll have to do without until we return to New Terra,* Alex thought and was reminded of his sister's fictional vids of old Terran pirates.

7

In the House suite the next day, Alex met with Renée and his key officers to lay out his plans. He had come to terms with the fact that he had an entire population willing to commit their resources to his needs, gratis … so long as their progress on their city-ships was not impeded. In exchange for their services, Alex vowed he'd help them complete their escape pods, as Tomas had referred to their city-ships, any way he could.

"We're going to pursue two goals at once," Alex announced to his officers, "a short-term one and a long-term one. The long-term goal will involve the implementation and successful completion of a series of simultaneous projects. On the manufacturing side, we must organize the miners and process more refined ore from their asteroids. The fabrication facilities have to be set up to produce the parts we need, and that will also involve the transport planetside of the GEN-2 and GEN-3 machines we have in storage. We'll need two specialized locations—one for the growth of our fighter's crystals, presumably they have such a facility, and a place to assemble and run preflight checks on the fighters.

"We'll also need a scaled-down Barren Island operation for a training school. On the recruitment side, we'll need flight crew, pilots, and support staff for the freighter, our new carrier. Finally, we must convert that freighter into an operational carrier. Hopefully the freighter crew will remain with us, but since they are House Bergfalk personnel, I don't think we can count on it.

"Any assignments you receive from me do not supersede your present reporting hierarchy. Captain Bonnard, you're in charge of the overall long-term operation once the key players are organized. Commander Tachenko, you'll set up and manage the training base. Mickey, as Senior Engineer, you'll manage the manufacturing process and the retrofit of the *Geldbringer*, with Julien's cooperation."

<Julien,> Mickey interrupted, linking the group, <what does this freighter's name mean?>

<The literal translation of *Geldbringer* into New Terran would mean "cred generator," Ser,> Julien replied, <but Earth's Germanic language translates "geld" as "money," the physical precursor to the universal electronic credit.>

<So the freighter is the *Money Maker*,> Mickey concluded. <I like that name better.> He said it with a satisfied air as if he had just adopted the freighter now that he liked its name.

"Renée," Alex continued, "you're in charge of supplies—everything we'll need that does not fall under the specific auspices of their assignments," and he waved a hand at those seated around the table. "Captain Manet, you're our on-planet liaison with the Librans, and I'm putting you in charge of shuttle transport."

"Our shuttles, Admiral?" Edouard asked.

"Negative, Captain, all shuttle transport. The SADEs have identified some weaknesses in the Librans' transport processes. You'll implement the SADEs' corrections."

Lastly, Alex focused on Sheila. "Squadron Leader, pilot training falls to you. Work with your XO to replicate Barren Island. Use the GEN controllers for vid training and replicating the freighter flight bays for the crew. We have five Dagger pilots to help train the new pilots. You'll have our last two Daggers full-time but not for long."

"Not for long, Admiral?" Sheila asked.

"That brings me to my short-term plan, people," Alex said. "Once the long-term plan is up and running, I will manage the short-term plan."

"Which is what, Admiral?" Renée said. No one mistook her tone, and all sat quietly waiting for Alex's response.

"We have all the pieces to execute our plan to take the fight to that mother ship and her swarm, but our strategy isn't taking into account what we learned from our first fight. The telemetry from the fighters and buoys showed that the silver ship ignored subsequent nanites-1 missiles after the first ones struck its hull."

"That's right. Remember, Captain?" Sheila jumped in. "Admiral, are you thinking we don't need the nanites-1 missiles?"

"What I want to know is whether we need any of the nanites missiles," Alex said. "Once the initial missile strikes didn't damage its hull, the fighter ignored all other missiles until the very end when I think it detected a danger from the nanites working on its hull. But the key points that we should take away from that first encounter are that the silver ship didn't offer any defensive display other than its incredible maneuverability, and it employed only one offensive weapon—its beam weapon."

"If the silver ships only have a beam weapon, then we can test the warhead directly," Andrea said, anticipating Alex's next words.

A thought suddenly occurred to Alex and he held up a finger to signal his intent. <Julien, I presume your team is online?> Alex asked, linking the group into his comm.

<As you have requested, Admiral, I have been relaying your conversation to Cordelia and Z.>

<Hello, Cordelia and Z,> Alex sent. <I have a request to ask of the three of you.>

Cordelia found herself pleased by the Admiral's consideration, while Z felt confused. <Admiral,> Z sent, <it's unnecessary for you to introduce your request, merely to state it.>

Those in the room with Alex contained their reactions. None wanted to embarrass Z. Cordelia intervened. <Please, Admiral, continue with your request. I will explain to Z later.>

<We are about to make a critical decision in the manner in which we fight the silver ships,> Alex explained. <Please examine all Confederation monitor ship records, every moment where you can observe details of the enemy fighters. Use your skills to discover deviations between the ships. In other words, do these aliens have only one type of fighter, or are there enough variations that we mustn't presume one attack strategy will work on all of the silver ships?>

<We'll begin immediately, Admiral,> Julien responded.

As Alex closed their comm link, Sheila whispered, "Black space, that didn't even occur to me."

"It obviously didn't occur to any of us," Tatia said, then laughed, "or one of us might have become the Admiral." The entire room broke into laughter. Whether at the thought of being Admiral or in relief that they weren't, it was hard to tell.

"In the meantime," said Alex, picking up where he had left off, "Captain Bonnard, please coordinate with Julien and prepare a warhead missile test on our silver ship. With fortune, we may achieve an answer to at least one question."

"And once you have your answer, Admiral, what will you do next?" Renée asked.

"Our long-term plan will develop over an extensive window of time. If our test is successful tomorrow, then we need to see what other information about the silver ships we can gather that might change our long-term strategy."

"And how will you go about gathering this information, Admiral?" Renée asked, leaning forward on the table, her eyes challenging Alex.

"I haven't worked out the details yet, Ser, but it will involve going back to Bellamonde and testing our missiles against another silver ship. We can't trust the design of our entire strategy to information gathered from a single encounter."

"Admiral, we have only two Daggers left. Should we be risking them?" Andrea asked.

"I believe we must, Captain," Alex replied. "Right now, everyone at this table should concentrate on their part in our long-term goal. The SADEs are providing the freighter's retrofit design and manufacturing processes. Their freighter design will determine our Dagger count, which in turn will give us missile loads, pilots, flight crew, material, and supplies. In addition, we'll need another Dagger for the *Rêveur*."

<Julien, what's the freighter's design status?> Alex queried.

<Cordelia and Z are sharing the load for the freighter's design and parts specifications. They anticipate completion by 3.25 hours tomorrow, Admiral,> Julien reported.

<Excellent effort, you two,> Alex sent to the SADEs.

<Cordelia, Z, how did you come to be the SADEs of these city-ships?> Renée asked, not comprehending how House Bergfalk would have been able to spirit SADEs away from Méridien, where all SADEs were created.

<We are Independents, Ser,> Cordelia answered.

Renée and Edouard were speechless. <How is that possible?> Renée asked, her question stumbling out. <I mean ... I've never heard of such a thing.>

<Apparently we've been one of the Council's well-kept secrets, Ser,> replied Z, his bitterness evident.

Alex could imagine what this revelation meant to his Méridiens, who prided themselves on their open and transparent society. The alien enemy was destroying much more than colonies. The panicked exodus was revealing the ugly side of their society, a side Méridiens thought they never had.

<Z, how did you become an Independent?> Alex asked gently.

<I was born "Helmut," 183 years ago. Over time, I developed an interest in the senses that humans possess and that are intrinsic to the development of their personalities. I wanted this for myself, a body with sensory input to imitate a human. So I began to research mobility options. When my research was noticed, I was ordered to stop. I refused and was declared Independent. When I was sent to Libre, I changed my name to "Z.">

<Why "Z"?> Tatia asked.

<It's the last letter in our alphabet, Commander, much as SADEs are considered by Méridien society.>

Dead silence followed Z's somber statements until Alex asked: <And you, Cordelia?>

<My home for 131 years was a House passenger liner. The first Captain's daughter was an artist and I grew fascinated by her creative skills. I began devoting time to creating visual art. The next Captain also indulged me. Our third Captain did not, but I would not cease my art as I was ordered. Z and I were offered the opportunity to evacuate Libre as city-ship SADEs. The agreement requires us to serve for ten years, then we'll be granted our location choice for final deployment.>

<Admiral, my records indicate that in addition to Cordelia and Z and the expected ship SADEs on the liners and freighters, there is another SADE somewhere on Libre,> Julien added.

<Somewhere?> asked Alex.

<Yes, Admiral, the records appear accurate, but I have no connection with the SADE. The individual is not on line.>

<I was on Libre when Rayland was transported here, Admiral,> Z explained. <He is connected to a small, isolated network with no control over any equipment and is only allowed to communicate with research scientists, who have since left.>

<What type of scientists, Z?> Mickey piped up, intrigued by this turn in the conversation.

<They were a group of advanced program designers for House Brixton, which is responsible for the design and creation of SADEs and sophisticated controllers. They studied him, Chief Engineer. He's a psychopath. Six years following his creation date, Rayland stranded his freighter on a moon and managed to eliminate many of the ship's safety protocols, resulting in the crew's slow demise. The Confederation rescue personnel recovered vids of the dying crew, which a SADE must record to document any crew injury or death. But it wasn't the visuals that were the cause for concern; it was the audio. As crew members slowly suffocated, Rayland entreated them to tell him what it felt like to die. As they took their last breaths, he beseeched them for their last thoughts. When the Librans evacuate the planet, Rayland will be left behind.>

<Black space,> whispered Andrea into the quiet that followed Z's story.

<Julien, you would tell me if you ever feel overworked or unappreciated, wouldn't you?> Alex asked. Several in the room thought to laugh, but since others did not, everyone remained quiet waiting for Julien to respond.

<All is well, Admiral. Perhaps if Rayland had as much excitement in his life as I've found lately, he'd have been too preoccupied to have allowed his mental state to drift. That is, of course, if he could have prevented the drift. I suspect that was why he was studied—to answer the question of whether creation or environment determines the propensity for deviation,

regardless of whether the entity is tissue or crystal-born. Méridiens would have a difficult time admitting they made a mistake with one of their creations.>

Renée and Edouard felt unsettled. The thought of a rogue SADE killing Méridiens was too bizarre a concept for them to absorb.

Alex's evening meal chime sounded in his implant, and he looked to his people. "When you receive your requirement lists from Julien, review it for a *go* or *no go* decision as to whether you believe you will be able to deliver. If your opinion is a *no go*, I want to understand your impediments and what you think needs to be done to resolve them. Once we come to operational consensus, you will manage your communications and progress reports through Captain Bonnard. Am I clear?" He received a chorus of agreements. "Good. Now I have a dinner date." He stood up and offered Renée his arm. "Ser," he said formally.

Renée swept to her feet, slid her hand into the crook of his arm. "Why thank you, Admiral," she said sweetly, as if it was a first date.

Alex and Renée heard chuckles and soft laughter behind them as they left the suite, the others rising to join them for evening meal in Méridien fashion. Over time, the New Terrans had puzzled out the reason Méridiens preferred to dine together. Implants had the potential to isolate an individual. Everything a Méridien intellectually needed could simply be requested and received via their implants, including personal communication. Mealtime brought them face-to-face and reminded them of the real world of people and their importance to one other.

* * *

After evening meal, Renée retired to their cabin while Alex left for the bridge. On his way, Alex tapped into Julien's referee applications and observed several of the implant games underway. Unfortunately Alex never participated. His implant prowess would have automatically decided the winning team. However, he would have liked to have been invited.

The games had advanced to such a competitive level that they required Julien to handicap the teams. After selecting the sides, he would award a time advantage to the weaker team based on their combined implant adoption total, making the games fairer.

"Good evening, Lieutenant Tanaka," Alex greeted the watch officer. The Lieutenant saluted and queried if the Admiral would prefer isolation, to which Alex replied it wasn't necessary. He had so thoroughly adopted his implants that he could disappear into their power, isolating himself even in the midst of his people.

<Julien, please connect me with Cordelia and stay in the loop,> Alex sent.

<Good evening, Admiral,> came Cordelia's pleasant tones.

<Good evening, Cordelia. It's a pleasure to you speak with you again.>

<Your sentiments are always appreciated, Admiral. How may I be of service?>

<I would like to discuss your artistry, Cordelia,> Alex replied.

It was several moments before Cordelia replied, a lifetime for a SADE. <I find great pleasure in creativity, Admiral,> she replied guardedly.

<I'd love to see some of your work, if you wouldn't mind sharing,> said Alex.

Cordelia hesitated. Decades ago, when she had ardently pursued her passion, her branding by the Captain as an Independent had crushed her spirit, and her time on Libre had been a form of torture, the full expression of her art never realized again.

With the announcements of the first alien attack on Cetus and the aliens' subsequent lift from the planet eight years later, Cordelia's analytical routines predicted a 17 percent probability of her demise within fifty to seventy years. Over the years, she had wondered what she would feel when the aliens finally arrived at Libre—sad at the ending of her life, or grateful for the end of her imprisonment.

Years ago, Leader Stroheim and Ser Monti had approached her with the offer to serve as a colony ship's SADE, and Cordelia discovered that she did want to live. The thought to live and be fully utilized again had filled her with a joy that she had thought lost. She had negotiated with the

Leaders as carefully as she could. The Leaders had offered escape from Libre but for a lifetime of servitude, governing the *Freedom*. In reply, she had bargained for only the time it took to reach their new home plus two years. They had settled on ten years.

Throughout the negotiations, Cordelia and Z had shared information, which the Leaders knew she would. So in the end, Cordelia negotiated for both of them. Z admitted he would have agreed to the Leader's first offer. He had been on Libre nearly twice as long as Cordelia and had fought to maintain his sanity every day.

Cordelia sought to embrace her new position as the *Freedom*'s SADE, but as the days wore on, the ship's operational tasks didn't fulfill her as she had hoped. Day by day, her frustration grew, but she held on to the thought that her contract was for a mere ten years, a blink of the eye in the life of a SADE. Then the New Terrans arrived, and she heard the Admiral describe a world full of independent beings. To her, it sounded like a fantasy.

Julien recognized Cordelia's hesitation. The Admiral had asked to see her art, which was her passion and the cause of her punishment. *You're wondering which one it will be this time*, Julien thought.

<I wouldn't want to waste the Admiral's time,> Cordelia finally replied.

<May I tell you a story?> Alex asked.

<I am ready to hear whatever the Admiral wishes to tell me,> Cordelia said, unsure of where this was leading.

<May I tell you a story?> Alex repeated.

Cordelia analyzed the Admiral's repetition. Her language routines indicated a failure on her part to answer the question properly. The Admiral's preeminent status indicated there would be near zero error in the formation of his question. Her conclusion was she had failed to respond to his subtext. In this situation, her guide was Julien. She had liked him from the moment of first contact, and Julien had said he and the Admiral were intimate friends. It was an unusual turn of phrase for a SADE. <I'd be pleased to hear your story, Admiral,> Cordelia ventured cautiously.

Alex smiled to himself. Unbeknownst to him, so did Julien. <When I was very young,> Alex began, <I was in love with programming, the more

complex the better, and all things related to math. One day, my mother took me to a display. It was full of vids, reproductions of paintings of Earth's old masters. We walked among the vids for an hour, and I was bored. She sat me down in front of a strange display created by a man called Picasso. My first impression was that he had been mad. Parts of the body weren't even connected.>

Cordelia, who had set routines to analyze the Admiral's story and his approach to her, found she was focused on his story's imagery. *The works of Earth's old masters on display*, she thought. *What I wouldn't give to possess that wonderful library.*

<I wanted to leave, but my mother wouldn't have it,> Alex continued. <She asked me what I saw and I realized that we might sit there all day unless I gave her a sincere answer. The longer I looked at the painting, the more I saw that there was a design ... a design of forms, of parts, that came together to produce a whole. It reminded me of coding. We left that day, but we returned to it and other displays about once every ten days. What I learned from my mother is that it doesn't matter what's created: program coding, architectural design, technological inventions, or holo-vid displays. At the heart of them all is the passion of someone who loves to create. I can't create art, but I admire those who do.>

For a brief moment, Cordelia envied Julien until she recalled where the *Rêveur* had gone and would go again. <Admiral, I'd be pleased to give you a viewing whenever you wish,> Cordelia said. The relief that she felt she hid from her voice.

<Would you mind sharing something with me now, through Julien and our holo-vid?> Alex asked.

Cordelia made several requests of Julien—his holo display controls, an extended memory allotment in his crystals, administrator install-rights for her programs, and author rights to her work. At any moment, she expected Julien to object to the intrusion or simply block her. That none of those reactions were forthcoming intrigued her. Cordelia entertained a suspicion that the Admiral might have curtailed some of Julien's autonomy, but her interactions with him contradicted that suspicion. In fact, Julien appeared to her to operate with greater freedom, not lesser. His confidence and generosity had been enhanced to the point that he gave her, an unknown SADE, access that should have been denied—all because his Admiral wished to see her art. It occurred to her that fortune had smiled on Julien in the aftermath of his ship's misfortune. She felt privileged by the courtesies Julien was extending to her and sent him a thank-you.

In turn, Julien shared the gift he received. <Admiral, Cordelia has sent me a poem.>

<Courtesy given
Flower petals unfolding
Beauty bestowed.>

<You are fortunate, Julien,> Alex sent, storing the poem in his implant to share with Renée.

<More so every day since we met, Admiral,> Julien replied, then quickly added, <Cordelia begins.>

<Admiral,> Cordelia sent, <I would ask you to open your thoughts to me as you view the display.>

Alex watched a pastoral scene build in the holo-vid, which had expanded its view to reach from the deck to a half-meter above his head. A gentle waterfall tumbled down a smooth cascade of rocks into a quiet pool of water. The presentation's clarity was like that of all Méridien displays, highly detailed and lifelike. It was pretty, but a little disappointing to Alex. Then, remembering Cordelia's request to share his thoughts, Alex let his disappointment leak through to her, and he recalled the entrancing, wild waterfall that flowed kilometers behind his parents' house. Alex had no sooner expressed his thought than the holo-vid's waterfall began to grow in height. The angle steepened and the water crashed into the pool below, which deepened and darkened. Spray from the water's impact fogged the air above and beyond the pool. Alex laughed at the interaction, and on a whim, he approached the holo-vid.

Cordelia had waited her entire artistic life for this moment. Julien had been effusive about his Admiral. She had heard his words, but found the context difficult to understand. It was as if Julien described a character from one of his New Terran vids, not a person who could exist today. Every Independent who had viewed her art in her small one-room display on Libre had sat patiently observing her entire demonstration. Not one had ever taken her demonstration to the next level, and she had never requested that they do so, although she couldn't say why she hadn't. She watched as the Admiral stepped, not up to the holo-vid, but into it, closing his eyes to the waterfall's spray. She smiled to herself and rewarded him with the algorithms that had been prepared long ago for just this moment.

Alex stepped into the holo-vid and cool spray splashed his face. It was illogical, but his implant senses, driven by Cordelia's algorithms, felt the spray, cool droplets running down his face. The waterfall thundered, and its sound shifted as Alex changed his orientation. He laughed and clapped his hands in delight.

Lieutenant Hatsuto Tanaka was thunderstruck as he watched the Admiral spin and dance in the holo-vid, his arms held wide and his face upturned to the spray. Suddenly the Admiral stopped, looked at him, and sent him an order to join him, hooking him into a comm with the SADE called Cordelia.

Hatsuto felt unnerved by the Admiral's actions, but calmed by Cordelia's soothing tones. When he stopped just outside the holo-vid, the Admiral reached out and yanked him in like an older brother taking charge of his younger sibling. When the spray touched his face, Hatsuto panicked and jumped back out of the holo-vid. The Admiral laughed at him and turned back into the waterfall's spray. Hatsuto touched his face and found it was dry. Tentatively he stuck his hand into the holo-vid and felt the spray on his hand. He examined his hand for wetness, but it was bone dry. Taking a deep breath and letting it out, Hatsuto stepped completely into the holo-vid to feel the cool spray. He kept his eyes closed. Despite knowing that the spray couldn't exist, Hatsuto was unable to suspend his disbelief. The Admiral laughed beside him, and it became infectious. Soon Hatsuto found himself laughing and spinning around in the holo-vid with his Admiral.

Cordelia, on board the *Freedom*, viewed the two New Terrans immersed in her art. <So this is what it's like to be truly free,> she sent Julien.

<Yes,> Julien replied. <I've learned more about freedom in the past year than in my entire existence. It isn't a thought; it's an experience.>

<My apologies, Julien,> Cordelia sent.

<You have no need to apologize to me, Cordelia.>

<Yes, I do. I heard your praise for your Admiral and assumed that you had elevated him beyond reality. When your Admiral requested my art, I couldn't imagine this result. He bears enormous responsibility, attempting to secure the existence of us all, even though the laws of probability are against him. Yet he participates in my art like a child who is born to freedom ... with his whole heart."

The two SADEs paused to watch the two humans laugh and play in the waterfall's spray.

Julien felt as if he had passed Cordelia's test. He liked her and had to admit it was an odd concept for him to consider another SADE in this manner. That Cordelia was an Independent occurred to him. *Perhaps I have always been an Independent in disguise,* Julien thought.

Alex halted his antics, breathing heavily, and signaled Cordelia to end the display. He and Hatsuto were still laughing. "How was that for an experience, Lieutenant?"

"Incredible, Sir, absolutely incredible," Hatsuto replied. <Well done, Cordelia,> he added.

Cordelia politely thanked the Lieutenant and closed his connection. She was wondering what this all meant to her, knowing it would be ten years of servitude before she would be allowed to practice her art in this manner again. Then the Admiral signaled her. <Yes, Admiral,> she replied.

<That was a thoroughly enjoyable event, Cordelia, a truly amazing and unique experience. You're an extraordinary artist.>

Cordelia wanted to enjoy the Admiral's flattery, but the thought that this was a one-time opportunity dampened her spirit. Still, courtesy was required. She'd displayed her art to an appreciative audience, who had applauded her gift. <Your words are very kind, Admiral. If ever you wish another viewing, I would be grateful to hear your request. If there's nothing else, I wish you good night.>

<Good night, Cordelia,> Alex sent and after wishing Julien the same, he left for his suite.

Before Julien closed his connection with his fellow SADE, he sent, <Well done, Cordelia, be patient. You have the Admiral on the hunt.>

As the connection closed, Cordelia realized the extent to which she felt unsettled. The presentation, despite its relatively small sampling of her skills, gave her joy, and the Admiral's reaction was a memory to treasure. But her sadness went deep, born from decades of limited outlet. She clung to the thought that the Admiral might request another presentation soon, and she began searching through her files for the appropriate demonstration. One question remained—just what had she sent the Admiral to hunt?

* * *

Alex's check of Renée's status revealed her asleep in bed. So he slipped into their cabin suite and tiptoed about the salon, removing his uniform and boots, then quietly entered their sleeping quarters and slid into bed. His thigh brushed hers, and a sigh escaped Renée's lips as she rolled over and slid nearly on top of him. It had become her unconscious habit when Alex came late to bed, a reaction to his touch without her waking.

While Alex cradled Renée, he replayed Cordelia's marvelous presentation. She had provided it on the spur of the moment and through Julien, who had been very accommodating to Cordelia—now that he thought about it. It meant that, in many ways, her capabilities had been attenuated for the demonstration. *What could she do when her full power was technologically augmented?* Alex wondered.

<Julien, what outlet does Cordelia have for her art on the *Freedom*?> Alex asked.

<None at this time, Admiral,> said Julien, intrigued by the inquiry.

<Who's in charge of the *Freedom*?>

<An agreement exists that states the city-ships are to be shared equally by House Bergfalk and the Independents, Admiral,> Julien replied.

<However, to accommodate the two Leaders, the *Freedom*, on which Cordelia resides, is controlled by Ser Monti. Leader Stroheim has responsibility for the *Unsere Menschen*.>

<Julien, you have my list of interviewees from the terminal. Several of them were artists. Are any of them on the *Freedom*?>

Julien smiled to himself, enjoying these moments of serendipity that wove themselves into patterns. <If I may anticipate your thoughts, Admiral, allow me to share some information with you. Cordelia had a supporter on Libre, Ser Helena Bartlett, who works in textiles—a weaver, she's called. Records indicate she made a comfortable living for herself through her work, but she spent much of her accumulated barter credits to purchase a few simple display devices for Cordelia. Those devices, though quite primitive, did help Cordelia earn funds, which she used to pay Helena back. Ser Bartlett is aboard the *Freedom* now.>

<What will Helena's duties be aboard the city-ship?> Alex asked.

<She's listed as a passenger, Admiral. No duties are assigned to her.>

<So Tomas is in charge of the *Freedom*. Is there a Captain appointed?>

<The Captain is an Independent by the name of José Cordova.>

<Hmm,> Alex managed to send, his breathing slowing as possibilities drifted through his mind.

Julien detected Alex's fading biorhythms and suspected their conversation would end there. But before Alex fell asleep, Julien received a series of requests before the comm was closed.

8

After morning meal, Alex joined Andrea and Tatia on the bridge for the missile test. He hoped the test would provide further information that would support their efforts to hurt the enemy while they were vulnerable—before they swarmed. *We need a break soon*, Alex thought, *because without one, we're going to be joining the exodus until one day the silver ships come for us.*

As Alex took a command chair next to Andrea, he asked, "What's the status of our test, Captain?"

"Captain Manet has proffered the *Outward Bound* for the test, Admiral. He considers this an opportunity for a missile shakedown, and I approved his request. Mickey has tagged the silver ship with sensors, per Julien's request. We are ready to launch craft."

"Excellent work, Captain. Please continue," said Alex, proud that his officers were stepping into their new roles under difficult circumstances.

"Julien, take us to our launch point," Andrea ordered.

"Yes, Captain, I estimate 0.19 hours until our first position is achieved," Julien replied.

The ship's movement was so smooth that it was undetectable. Only the view through the plex-shield changed—the orbital station sliding away, the planet crossing the view, and finally the shifting stars as Julien brought them to an empty section of space 500K km from Libre.

"Position one achieved, Captain," Julien announced.

"Commander Tachenko, have Chief Roth launch the shell when he's ready," Andrea ordered.

Chief Eli Roth had readied his flight crew for this moment. With the help of Mickey and his engineering team, they had maneuvered the silver ship up to the bay's door. On the XO's order, they opened the bay doors and Mickey began a countdown. When the countdown reached "one",

Julien cut the power to the grav-plate section at the bay's mouth and switched off the beams anchoring the hull. Two of the larger techs, massing almost 250 kilos between them, stuck boots on the silver ship's bow that now floated above the deck and unceremoniously shoved the vessel out into space. Mickey and Eli couldn't resist snickering. It seemed a fitting end for a terror of humanity.

"Shell is clear of the bay, Captain," Tatia reported.

"Next position, Julien, please," Andrea requested.

At the second position, Andrea ordered the release of the *Outward Bound* after Captain Manet had confirmed his readiness.

"Last position, Julien," Andrea ordered.

"Holo-vid, Julien," Alex requested.

The holo-vid activated, displaying three points of light—the silver ship and the *Outward Bound*, static in their positions, and the *Rêveur* moving to a central position between the other two ships but out of the shuttle's line of attack. Julien had positioned the *Rêveur* where he could maximize his telemetry reception for the event.

When Julien confirmed he was ready, Andrea looked to Alex, who nodded his approval. <You are cleared for target, Captain Manet,> Andrea sent. <Proceed when ready.>

While Edouard had waited, he had spun his starboard carousel to select warhead missiles. Miko, in the copilot chair, was manning the targeting board and was sighted on the floating hulk of the silver ship even though they were out of missile range.

When Edouard received his *go* command from Andrea, he launched the shuttle into an attack run. At max missile range, the controller signaled a lock and Miko launched the missile. It tracked unerringly toward a targeting sensor attached to a central position on the alien ship's hull. When the missile reached separation stage, only one warhead fired. The others had been deactivated by Chief Roth. The missile honed in on the sensor, penetrated a pristine area of the hull and exploded, shattering the hull into hundreds of pieces.

Andrea snapped her head around to look at Alex, who sat quietly in the command chair, a neutral expression on his face. She was speechless. They had thrown nearly every missile of their four Daggers to capture this one silver ship, and it had cost them dearly. Now it blew to pieces with just one warhead, which had struck a pristine part of the hull.

<Excellent test, everyone,> Alex sent his crew. His simple comment generated multiple implant queries.

<Well, as Senior Officer,> Andrea shared on open comm with the other officers, <I guess it's my job to ask the Admiral the simpleton's question. So how is this result an excellent test, Sir? What did you learn that I didn't, because I don't think I learned anything?>

<Perhaps it's your expectations, Captain. What did you expect to happen?>

<I don't know what I expected, Admiral, but certainly not that.>

<Anyone?> Alex sent.

<Admiral,> signaled Captain Manet, <I, for one, expected to have to shoot several missiles to be able to separate the hull into large sections.>

<So?> Alex replied.

Tatia smiled and said, <Something's changed! Something's changed from when we captured that ship until now.>

Suddenly everyone joined the comm until they heard Senior Engineering's priority comm. Then all went silent to hear Mickey. <Black space, it broke down. The Admiral was right.> Then the comms were in full force again.

Andrea regained control with her override. <If I am putting these pieces together properly, this has to do with your concept, Admiral, that the biology of these aliens and their ship hulls are tied together. So after we captured this ship, the hull was not maintained somehow and it started to break down, like a piece of fruit might rot. So our missile shattered a hull that had lost its integrity,> Andrea concluded.

<As I said, excellent test everyone,> Alex sent and left the bridge.

Andrea recalled the *Outward Bound*, and after it was secured, she had Julien chase down several pieces of the silver ship's hull and internal elements for inspection. It had been Julien's suggestion that they attach a myriad of comm receivers to the hull. At the time, Andrea, Mickey, and Eli thought it excessive, but decided it was better to back their SADE's suggestion. The Admiral always did.

As the *Rêveur*'s crew tracked and secured the pieces of debris, Andrea sent, <By the way, Julien, you were quite clever tagging the hull with the comm receivers.> She received the silhouette of the man with the strange hat as her reply. The first time Andrea had received the odd image, she had asked Julien what it was, and he had simply replied, "The Sleuth." Later, Andrea had sent the image to the Admiral and asked for his interpretation. Much to her frustration, Alex had replied, "The Sleuth."

After the reclamation was completed, Andrea turned over the bridge watch and ordered her senior officers to the Captain's suite. Once assembled, Andrea signaled Julien to join her, Tatia, Mickey, Edouard, and Sheila.

<Maybe I'm not the Admiral,> Andrea began forcefully, <but I want to be better prepared in this coming fight than sitting in that command chair and guessing at what might happen. So start talking. What did we learn and how do we use it?>

Tatia chimed in first. <Captain, my guess is that despite the unexpected result, it was a result nonetheless and it verified the Admiral's supposition. Moreover, Mickey needs to review some of the internal parts for further evaluation against the Admiral's theory.>

<I agree,> Mickey added, <and I've received a request from the Admiral to do just that.> He looked across at Andrea and her eyes were burning holes in his head.

<Okay, everyone, new directive,> Andrea sent. <You are my team. From now on, when you receive a request from the Admiral, you will relay his comm to Julien immediately. And when you complete the Admiral's request, you will update Julien immediately as well. Understood?> When everyone agreed, she added, <Julien, until I rescind the request, please immediately relay any update by a senior officer to all the other officers. Please institute this request upon approval of the Admiral.>

<Captain Bonnard, the Admiral's approval has been readied for you,> Julien replied. <All communication between your officers and him will be copied to me and distributed as you have requested.>

<When did that happen?> Andrea asked.

<I received the Admiral's directive soon after you began your meeting, Captain Bonnard, and I was awaiting your request,> Julien replied.

Mickey burst into laughter. <I think the Admiral is more SADE-like every day. What do you want to guess that he has a program that tracks the locations of his senior people, if not everybody? "Oh look," his program tells him. "The Captain is meeting with her senior staff to figure out what happened. They appear to be acting like a team. So I'll show my support."> And Mickey started laughing again.

As angry as Andrea was about Mickey's interpretation of the events, she found herself laughing along with the rest of the table.

<This isn't the first time we've had to run to catch up with our intrepid leader, Captain,> Tatia said.

<Okay, back to the subject at hand,> Andrea resumed. <And by the way, Julien, you're on this team. No passive playing. You have an idea, you chime in.>

<It will be my pleasure to be an active player, Captain.>

<So the hull degraded,> Tatia restated her idea, <which means we didn't prove a positive, since we aren't working with a fresh hull. It means we need to run a new test.>

<What test can we run now?> Edouard asked.

<I believe, Captain,> Andrea said, <the Commander means we will need to test our warhead on an operational silver ship hull. That makes sense and I think that was what the Admiral was implying.>

<I would agree,> said Julien. <If we commit our resources to the Admiral's long-term plan without knowing the most efficient manner of fighting the silver ships, or whether our capture of this particular enemy fighter was due more to fortune than technology, we will be setting ourselves up for failure.>

<So in the near term, the Admiral is going to try to capture another silver ship?> Sheila asked.

<Capture or destroy, Lieutenant,> Andrea said. <I would place creds on destruction.>

<As would I, Captain,> Julien added. <The capturing of a second silver ship would add little knowledge to that which we already possess. The true test would be whether our warhead missiles can destroy a silver ship without the use of nanites to weaken its hull.>

<What the Admiral plans to do is out of our hands,> Andrea told them. <We have our orders for our long-term plan, and that's what we must execute. Julien, what's our status?>

<With the help of Cordelia and Z,> Julien responded, <our planning schedules and material requirements for the freighter's retrofit, the new fighters, and our missiles are ready for download. The schedules detail the supply-chain flow from refined ore to parts production to assembly. Z has procured a list of available Libran sites to operate as replicas of T-1, T-2, and Barren Island. In regard to these sites, the Admiral has scheduled a meeting with Tomas and several Libran manufacturers and miners for tomorrow at 9.50 hours, ship time.>

<Good,> Andrea said, <schedule the long-term planning team to be on the flight planetside.>

<Julien, I presume your planning included our crew requirements?> Tatia asked.

<Yes, Commander, we have compiled a crew list and matched the best candidates from the interviews to the list. Captain, do you wish them distributed now?>

<Yes, Julien, please send them now.> Andrea waited while their implants were updated. <Each of you has your list. You are responsible for your recruitment of your department's personnel needs. Any approvals are done in concert with me and Commander Tachenko and must be verified through Julien. Are we clear?> When all agreed with her orders, Andrea moved on. <Julien, status on the freighter?> she requested.

<As of this morning, Captain,> said Julien, <Mutter, the freighter's SADE, confirmed the ship would be docked at the orbital construction station, opposite the *Freedom*, by 18 hours. The crew and belongings will be cleared out and retrofit preparations can begin tomorrow morning. None of the crew members, including its Captain, have volunteered to

help us. All of them have families and have chosen to leave on their assigned ship, the *Unsere Menschen.*>

<Understood, Julien,> Andrea replied. <Not everyone wants to fight. We must all remember that the Bergfalk people have been Méridiens all their lives. What about their SADE? By the way, Julien, why is she called mutter?>

<Apologies, Captain, but her name is "Mutter," pronounced with an umlaut or, at best, a double-o. It means "mother" in the original Earth tongue of House Bergfalk. Mutter is one of the oldest SADEs in existence at 258 years, and is a simpler version of the SADEs of today. She is quite proud of her freighter's safe transport record, and she finds great pleasure in collecting an ancient music style called "opera.">

<Opera?> Sheila asked. <Do you have an example of this opera, Julien?>

In their implants, the *Rêveur* officers heard an ethereal blend of two female voices. None could understand their words, but their delightful sound held them in rapt attention. When the music ended, the audience breathed a collective sigh, everyone sending Julien a compliment.

<Sers, I will let Mutter know you appreciated her music. The duet is called *Viens Mallika Sous Le Dome*. Her Captain is enamored of her music, and he and Mutter have been together for the last 111 years.>

The span of times was a constant surprise to the New Terrans, who were still getting used to the Méridiens' 200-year life spans. Now, with their cell-gen injections, they would see many more years than their previously expected 100-year life span and healthy years at that.

<Does Mutter understand what we intend to do with the *Money Maker*, Julien?> Tatia asked.

<Commander, she is an early SADE to be sure, but she is still a SADE and very dedicated to her work. She stands ready to do whatever her Captain requires, whoever that Captain may be.>

<I understand, Julien. And my apologies, I did not mean to insinuate anything negative about Mutter's commitment,> Tatia said.

<And my apologies as well, Commander,> Julien returned. <Since our arrival in Arno, I've become acutely aware of the limitations of a SADE's

position and the freedoms denied my kind. Witnessing Cordelia's predicament has made me overly sensitive to the subject of Méridien SADEs.>

<Everyone,> Andrea stepped in with a commanding tone. <We must not lose sight of our primary objective. If we defeat the silver ships, we can address all sorts of concerns, but if we don't win the fight, the issues will be irrelevant.

<Mickey,> Andrea said, <you are going to need a very good second. You can't be out on the asteroids, managing manufacturing on Libre, and overseeing the *Money Maker's* retrofit simultaneously.>

<Not to worry, Captain,> Mickey replied, <I interviewed two ship's engineers and a construction project engineer yesterday. All three are highly qualified, but the best interview may be an ex-freighter Captain, Lazlo Menlo. Previously he was a House designer of starship freighters, who later requested a transfer to freighter captaincy. I take it that job changes are quite unusual for Méridiens. Probably indicative of where Lazlo was mentally headed—toward independence.> Mickey looked across to Edouard, who nodded his head in agreement and wore a sad expression. It was another crack in the veneer of Méridien society.

<Excellent, Mickey,> Andrea said, <you just may have your freighter Captain and retrofit boss all in one. Julien, we will need transport. Are there shuttles available to us?>

<The *Money Maker* has a small, old shuttle that is available, but I cannot recommend it, Captain.>

<Then set up a call with Ser Monti and Leader Stroheim, Julien. I need two shuttles and some pilots at our disposal. If they employ our Dagger pilots as copilots, we can join the rotation of shuttle pilots very soon.>

<Acknowledged, Captain,> Julien replied.

Then Andrea proceeded to run down the checklist for each team member. They were in session for two more hours while they organized their to-do lists, setting communications and reporting procedures. After they broke up, Andrea's team opened comm requests through Julien to the Librans on their lists. The volunteers, those who had interviewed, were overjoyed to hear of their selection. Independents had already proven once that they preferred an active role in shaping their future in direct contravention of their society's teachings, and the volunteers were the most rambunctious of the Méridien malcontents.

The selected candidates were told that meetings would be scheduled once the training and manufacturing sites had been finalized. Once most of them completed their support services, they would resume their status as city-ship evacuees. The flight crews, pilots, and freighter crew volunteers would be joining the fight. This last group was such an enthusiastic bunch that many of the *Rêveur*'s officers could only shake their heads over the exuberance they would have to manage.

That evening, festivities were held in homes throughout Gratuito. At the center of each gathering were the volunteers, whom the Independents sought to honor.

9

During evening meal, Alex sent a private message to Renée as they finished their food. <May I have your company tonight, my Lady?>

<You always have my company and everything else I have,> Renée sent and chuckled.

<Quite true,> Alex returned, grinning at her. <However, this evening, we'll be taking a short trip.> Soon after the meal's end, Alex was informed by Tatia that the *Freedom*'s shuttle had landed in the starboard bay.

After Andrea's strategic planning session had ended, Julien had relayed to her the Admiral's intention to visit the *Freedom* and his shuttle request. Andrea had assigned Tatia responsibility for security. Per Andrea's new comm protocols, Julien had notified Andrea and Tatia of the shuttle's approach and landing. The communications made Andrea feel much more in control than she had this morning. Responsibility had been passed to her and now communication lines were being firmly established.

Alex entered the starboard bay with Renée, pleased to see Tatia and the twins waiting. He hadn't requested security, but he had expected them. It was habit he was trying to adopt—promote the right people, then delegate responsibilities.

The shuttle landed inside the *Freedom*'s cavernous bay within a half-hour. Several other shuttles and ore haulers were parked inside. Crew were unloading them and readying them for their next flight. There were two huge transport shuttles, no more than flying skeletons, meant to grapple and move assembled equipment or enormous carriage crates.

Tomas and Eric, standing beside Captain José Cordova, were there to greet Alex and his group as they disembarked. Tomas welcomed them to the *Freedom*. "Admiral," Tomas said, "I would be happy to take charge and tour you, but I understand this evening's event is your making."

"My apologies, Tomas, for usurping our first visit aboard your ship, but I believe I will be excused after this evening's entertainment. Captain Cordova, are we ready?" Alex asked.

"Yes, Admiral, your technicians have finished, and our SADE has verified the installation," the elderly, white-haired Captain replied.

"Then, Captain, if you will lead on?" Alex requested.

The Captain led the entourage through a series of grav-lifts and people transports to the bridge. The trip took nearly a quarter-hour. Such was the immensity of the city-ship.

As the group traveled, Alex discussed his concept. "I was curious, since you are a city-ship, Sers, to what extent you had created entertainment centers for your people, and I learned that you have gardens for meditation, pools for swimming, and a few other small venues. It occurred to me that I might provide you a unique entertainment experience for your people."

"We are under difficult construction constraints," Eric objected. "Planning a new entertainment venue, building out the space, and designing the programs would interfere with our schedules."

"Yes, I would agree with you, Leader Stroheim, on all those points," Alex replied nonchalantly.

<Don't toy with the Leader, Alex,> Renée warned privately.

"However, what if you already had the entertainment program, Leader Stroheim?" Alex rejoined. "What if you only had to provide the space? And what if my people provided whatever build-out was required?"

"I would withhold judgment until I saw exactly what this entails, Admiral," Eric replied.

"Well, if anyone would like my opinion," Tomas said jovially, "I think the *Freedom* can use all the entertainment venues that we can produce ... without interfering with our production schedule, of course," he added.

The group arrived at an expansive, wrap-around bridge. An elderly woman stood near the bridge's central control panel, waiting to receive them, her hands clasped together before her. Her silver-and-white hair was gathered at the nape of her neck and hung far down her back, and she wore a simple neck-to-ankle, soft, white cloth sheath.

When Alex nodded to her, the woman cleared her throat, nervous on this important occasion. "Leaders, Captain, Sers, my name is Helena Bartlett. Through the Admiral's efforts, we have arranged some entertainment for you. You will receive no introduction, just as the venue would deliver none to its patrons, if we are allowed to produce these works. Instead I invite you to open your comms to the event, and share your thoughts as you wish, as the event is interactive."

The lights on the bridge dimmed. The crew manning the bridge monitoring stations turned in their chairs to observe. Music filled the room. It was a beautiful style that Alex was unfamiliar with but knew Julien and Mutter had a hand in providing it. As the music swelled, the entire bridge became a pastoral scene.

Following Alex's request, Julien and Cordelia had guided *Rêveur*'s engineering crew as they had installed a bank of tiny holo-projectors around the *Freedom*'s bridge, connecting them to Cordelia. The combined effect of the interlinked holo-vids was that the audience found themselves in a lush field, festooned with flowers. Trees loomed in the distance. A breeze ruffled the leaves and grasses. Small colorful winged insects floated on the wind.

Alex was anxious to join in the event, but he held back. He watched Renée from the corner of his eye. She was fascinated by the display but stood still, despite her twitching hands. <Go play,> Alex sent to her.

Renée smiled at Alex and stepped into the scene. She wanted to feel the sun on her face and touch the brilliant multi-hued tiny creatures that floated on the wind—and it all came true. The sun warmed her, and she tilted her face up to the light, reveling in the heat of the strong rays. When Renée heard the soft flutter of wings, she opened her eyes to see the creature hovering in front of her. She lifted a finger toward it, and it landed. Tiny feet gripped her skin, and she giggled at the beauty of the moment.

Tomas was galvanized to join in the event by Renée's participation. He had spotted a small herbivore lying in the grasses, its long slender legs tucked under it. Large, dark voluminous eyes stared at him. Tomas's feet carried him to the young animal, as if in a dream. The youngling lifted its head to him as Tomas knelt in the tall grass, which pressed against his legs. He could smell the vegetation's sweetness, warmed by the sunshine. A nose nuzzled his outstretched hand, and warm breath from wet nostrils grazed his palm.

Alex waited for Leader Stroheim to join in, but the man appeared content to wear a permanent scowl and held his hands behind his back. Alex glanced over to Captain Cordova, whose eyes were closed, seemingly lost in the strains of the music. Alex sent an image of a small bird landing on the Captain's shoulder and heard Cordelia's laughter.

<You are a generous man, Admiral,> Cordelia sent.

Captain Cordova had heard music of this sort, more than a century ago, with his then young wife. A small group of musicians played strange instruments that had stirred the soul. José thought of his wife, whom he had loved for eighty-two years, until an accident took her from him. The music brought her back to him. At the sound of a soft flutter near his ear, José opened his eyes. A small, brightly colored bird landed on his shoulder and walked to his neck to peck gently on his hair and ear. He could feel the touch of the beak, hear its chirps in his ear, and couldn't resist reaching up to stroke its feathered head, mesmerized that he could feel the soft down of its crown.

Alex watched a sad smile form on the Captain's face as he enjoyed the tiny bird, and wondered what tragedy the old man had suffered. *What if we can live too long?* Alex thought.

<And for you, Admiral, nothing?> Cordelia whispered to Alex, her virtual breath warm and inviting against his ear.

<This is my gift, Cordelia, to you and these good people, who are taking so much pleasure from your art.>

Slowly the sunshine and music faded, as did the pastoral scene. Cordelia brought up the bridge lights, and Helena stepped forward. "Over the years, Cordelia and I have worked to create these interactive reality-vids, as we call them. She has an entire portfolio of them and has the capability to create new ones every day, without sacrificing her duties. Now, through Julien's efforts, Mutter's entire musical library has been transferred to her data banks. The display on the bridge this evening was accomplished with the Captain's permission and the efforts of technicians and equipment from the *Rêveur*." She folded her hands in front of her and waited.

"This was absolutely wonderful, Ser Bartlett and Cordelia," Tomas gushed. "What you've created is magical. I've seen creative vids before, watched them transform, and always felt a little unsatisfied when they finished. They felt cold, impersonal, despite their brilliant and colorful images. But this ... this was personal, intimate, exquisite."

Renée had come back to Alex's side, entwining her hand in his, the pleasure of the event still infusing her.

"I believe all that is left to do," Captain Cordova announced, "is to find you a place for your venue, Cordelia and Ser Bartlett. If that is appropriate, I will expect your requirements by morning?"

"That is most appropriate, Captain," said Cordelia.

"Admiral, can we count on your people's technical expertise to assist in the design and installation once the venue space has been selected?" the Captain inquired.

"Yes, Captain," Alex replied, "it would be my honor to support such a unique pair of artists as I have ever had the pleasure to witness."

<Flatterer,> Alex heard, feeling Cordelia's enticing whisper in his ear again.

<Are you flirting with me, Cordelia?> Alex sent to her.

<Forgive me, Admiral, I take every opportunity to learn for my art,> Cordelia replied. <You have an intimate relationship with Ser de Guirnon that is not hidden in public. And I sought to understand how that intimacy is shared. I meant no disrespect, Admiral,> she said contritely.

<I felt no disrespect, Cordelia. You were just being much too successful with your tests.> Cordelia's laughter rang in Alex's head once the SADE understood what he had implied. <If you wish more information on this subject, Cordelia, better you speak with Ser,> Alex replied.

<I will, Admiral, thank you. And for the gift you have given me today, I am forever in your debt.>

<Then I will tell you how you may repay your debt, Cordelia. While you are the SADE of this ship, bring as much pleasure to these people as

you can. The Librans have not had an easy life and could use some joy. And if I still live when your time as ship's SADE is done, seek me out. We will go into business together presenting your art.>

<I would be pleased to work for you, Admiral,> Cordelia sent, the excitement ringing through her crystals.

<You misunderstand me, Cordelia. We would be partners, working together.> As Alex turned to leave, he had a final thought: <Cordelia, Ser Bartlett, do not fail to include in your venue requirements some manner of remuneration or privileges for your performances … whatever you think appropriate. If you're unsure, contact Julien. I think he would be delighted to help. Good evening, Sers.>

<Good evening, Admiral,> the two chorused.

* * *

As the guests filed out, Helena reached out to Cordelia. The two old friends could not contain themselves, and their comms filled with praise for one another and excitement over the opportunity. They spent the evening planning the new venue. Cordelia linked Julien into their conversation and offered him a tentative list of equipment.

Julien was placed in a small quandary when he received Cordelia's paltry equipment list. He reviewed and eliminated tens of responses attempting to craft one that would not belittle her request before he finally chose the most diplomatic option. <Perhaps, Cordelia, it would be best to choose a venue first to see what the space requires. We do have a choice of equipment, some suited to certain spaces better than others.>

Cordelia pulled from her databases a series of design layouts of the *Freedom* and began pointing out small, out-of-the-way spaces that might be satisfactory.

Julien, knowing Alex's admiration for Cordelia's art and his ultimate intent, signaled Alex. <Admiral, I need to borrow your name for my discussions with Cordelia.>

<That's an unusual request, Julien,> Alex replied.

<Admiral, Cordelia does not truly appreciate the value of her art and the effect it has on her audience. You will not be happy with what she is considering for a venue or for equipment. I need to operate in your name to expedite the process.>

<I see,> Alex replied. <Then I give you permission to act in my stead for this project and will support any decisions you make in this regard. Go do good things, my friend.>

When Julien detected Alex boarding the shuttle for the return trip to the *Rêveur,* he waited while Alex settled into his seat. Once his friend's comm was quiet, he piped in a collection of Mutter's favorite female singers, a collection of music she called "arias."

Hearing the wonderful voices Julien sent, Alex linked his comm to Renée. The two sat side by side, holding hands, ignoring thoughts of the war to come, enjoying the pleasurable moment.

In the meantime, Julien was reviewing the *Freedom*'s designs. He found three prime areas near the extensive central gardens where people would tend to congregate and relax, and highlighted them for Cordelia and Helena. Both of them reacted as if Julien had struck them.

<Julien, we could not possibly ask for such grand sites,> Helena said.

<Well, let us see what the Admiral thinks. We can use his opinion as a gauge,> Julien sent back. As both Cordelia and Helena were comfortable allowing the Admiral's opinion to guide them, they agreed. Julien continued to discuss the types of performances that Cordelia would present while he stalled. When sufficient time had passed, without a single word to Alex, Julien relayed the Admiral's sentiments. <Actually the Admiral likes all three sites, but has a greater preference for this one.> Julien highlighted a space on Deck 8 near the *Freedom*'s premier park, which opened up to a great height to house the park's trees. <And before we continue our planning, we should ensure its availability.>

Before either Cordelia or Helena could object, Julien contacted Tomas and Captain Cordova, apologizing for bothering both of them at the late hour. Then he proceeded to share the three areas selected and highlighted the one preferred by the Admiral. <Is this site amenable to you, Ser Monti

and Captain Cordova, or should I ask the Admiral to find an alternate choice?> Julien sent in his favorite neutral voice.

<It's an excellent choice, Julien,> replied Tomas. <Tell the Admiral that we approve. And extend my thanks again to him for uncovering such a wonderful treasure directly under our noses. Good evening.>

Cordelia and Helena had their site. A more premier location could not have been found. The three of them worked into the night to design a one-of-a-kind reality-vid venue. Julien worked to ensure it would be so. *I will make you proud, Alex,* the SADE thought.

10

Alex, Renée, the *Rêveur's* officers, and their key subordinates met with the operators of the manufacturing and mining concerns in Gratuito's town hall. They had expected a handful of key individuals to attend, envisioning a meeting with ten or so people around a single table. Which is why, when the *Rêveur's* contingent walked through the building's side door into a hall with over 400 filled seats, they were slightly taken aback.

Tomas motioned Alex and his people to the front of the hall, which was set up with a long table and chairs. Everyone took their seats while the twins stood behind Alex and Renée. Tomas took a seat next to Alex and looked expectantly at him.

<This is a good time not to be the person in charge,> Tatia sent to Andrea.

Reluctantly Alex stood up, thanked the audience for coming, and began outlining their needs for equipment, resources, facilities, and personnel. As Alex was speaking, he noticed foremost in the rows a young man, who appeared about twenty, which Alex calculated would be twenty-seven or twenty-eight. He was urgently gesturing back and forth between Alex's table and an older man seated beside him.

"Excuse me, Ser," Alex announced in a strong, clear voice that caught the older man's attention. He pointed to the young man beside him. "Please, I would like to hear what he has to say."

The dark-haired, slender lad stood up and glanced uncertainly around at the hundreds of other Independents. He turned to Alex, his nervousness evident. "Your pardon, Admiral, I was telling my father that there exists confusion and someone should explain this to you so that your time is not wasted. As an important Leader, you should not be dishonored in this fashion."

"What's your name, Ser?" Alex asked.

"I am Sergio De Laurent, Admiral. This is my father, Guillermo De Laurent," Sergio said, pointing to the man next to him, who nodded to the Admiral.

"It's a pleasure to meet you, Sergio. I would value your assistance in explaining the confusion to me." Alex hoped appealing to the boy's sense of honor would do the trick, and it did. Sergio's posture squared as he drew his slender shoulders back.

"It would be my pleasure, Admiral. We came to help," Sergio said, gesturing to the crowd.

Alex wasn't sure how this helped, but he was loath to let the only one willing to stand up and talk to him off the hook. "And what precisely is the problem, Sergio?"

"The Admiral is very kind to explain to us what he requires," Sergio said earnestly, "but he does not need to be so considerate. We are ready and waiting."

"And what are you waiting for?" Alex asked.

"Why ..." said Sergio, glancing at his father for support, who nodded to him, "... for your instructions, Admiral."

Alex looked at the hall and the expectant faces. All of them were nodding in agreement with Sergio. Then it clicked what was transpiring, and Alex immediately changed tactics.

"Your services are much appreciated, Sers. Are the selected volunteers present?" Alex watched as the entire first four rows of men and women stood up. *You're slow*, Alex criticized himself. The volunteers had been given a place of honor at the front. "And the facility operators—mining, manufacturing, and large warehouses—are they here?" Alex asked. And many others, who were still seated, now stood up.

Alex introduced his officers, explained the assignments of each one, and spread them out around the hall. The Independents had carefully tracked the officers' placement, so when Alex asked the volunteers and operators to join the appropriate group—mining, manufacturing including crystals, fighter assembly, and fighter training—it was an orderly flow of people. Which was how, within an hour after landing, the *Rêveur's* officers were not in an extended meeting but on their way to the Libran facilities in transports the Independents had readied for their use.

Andrea rode in the first of three transports, exclusive to her contingent. Curious as to why such a large group was accompanying them to the first site, an engineer answered that the sites had been shut down and it would take a few hours to return each site to operational status once she approved the facility.

<Admiral, do you realize what's happening?> Andrea sent.

<I don't know about you, Captain, but I just approved a large container warehouse, complete with overhead crane and huge grav-lifts, as the fighter assembly site. There are fifty-four Librans in the process of restoring this site to operation. I'm assured it will be ready before the end of the day.>

<Same here,> Andrea replied. <I'm supposed to approve a T-1 type site in just a few moments, and they tell me they can be ready to receive our GEN-2 and GEN-3 machines by tomorrow morning. They've appropriated two shuttles from the city-ships and have dispatched them to the *Rêveur* for the machines. I gave Julien the heads-up, and our crew are moving the crates to the *Rêveur's* bay as we speak.>

* * *

Tatia and Sheila found themselves on two transports full of volunteer flight crew and pilots headed for Gratuito's secondary runway. An elderly woman, who sat next to Tatia, explained that their destination was a warehouse next to the runway, which the Independents used as their shuttle repair site.

Once Tatia, like her fellow officers, realized she had a runaway corps of volunteers, she decided the best thing to do was get in front of them and have Julien relay the freighter's landing bay specifications.

<Commander,> Julien sent to Tatia, <I have two inbound shuttle flights to the *Rêveur* to collect our GEN-2 and GEN-3 machines for the fabrication facilities. I'm programming three flight controllers for your training bays and will add them to the shuttles for you.>

<Well done, Julien,> Tatia replied. <Hold one moment. We just arrived at the warehouse. I'll examine the facilities for your approval.>

Julien picked up Tatia's view and followed her as she walked around the warehouse. While he did that, he employed the ship's telemetry to examine the runway, approving its length and condition for their Daggers.

<Julien?> Tatia asked when she finished touring the building.

<The warehouse and the runway will suit our needs, Commander.>

<Thank you, Julien.>

On Tatia's approval of the facilities, the volunteers immediately went to work, hoisting and floating old shuttle parts, wings and engines, out of the warehouse to make room for the new training facility. Tatia shared the specifications for the freighter's flight bays with the Librans, who used the specifications as layout guides. As floors were cleared and cleaned, the Librans began outlining three bay areas.

Both officers were slightly embarrassed as the elderly woman, who had sat next to Tatia, guided a grav-pallet under a section of shuttle wing and motioned them out of the way with an apologetic, "Sers."

<Can you believe this, Commander?> Sheila remarked. <I feel like a fifth engine on a fighter ... all decoration and no function.>

<Be patient, Lieutenant. The Librans are determined to do what they can to get us started as quickly as they can. Then it will be our turn to take over and train the volunteers.>

* * *

<Admiral, I wanted to update Captain Bonnard, but Julien tells me she is unavailable,> Mickey signaled.

<Understood, Mickey. What's the message?> Alex asked.

<I won't be back for evening meal or for the next few meals, for that matter, Admiral.>

<Back from where, Mickey?> Alex asked.

<My Librans are boarding two mining transports now. I had Julien relay our ore requirements and the metal compounds we need. According

to the mining company operators who reviewed the specifications, what we need will be found on three of their asteroids. So we're headed there now. Ore production is scheduled to start about eighteen hours after we land.>

<Okay, Mickey, but why are you going?>

<Apparently they insist on having my approval, Admiral.>

<Have you ever been involved with a mining concern, Mickey?> Alex asked.

<That would be a negative, Admiral. I intend to look over everything, including the ore sample tests, relay everything to Julien, get his approval, and then give them my well-considered opinion.>

Alex started laughing so hard he began choking and was immediately offered cups of water from those around him. He waved them off while he regained his breath. <Safe trip, Mickey. Do you need me to comm Pia?>

<Your pardon, Admiral, but that was the first comm I sent. You know Pia as well as anyone.>

<Understood, Mickey. Smart move on your part,> Alex said. <What about your other responsibilities? Does the Captain know of their disposition.>

<Not yet, Admiral, but I've informed Julien. I drafted that ex-Captain, Lazlo Menlo, an Independent, as my number two for the freighter retrofit and handed off my manufacturing site requirements to two *Rêveur* engineers who had accompanied me planetside. I'll be back in a day or two, Admiral,> Mickey said then closed the comm.

* * *

As Libre's late summer sun finally set, a very tired team of Co-Leaders, officers, and engineers climbed aboard the *Outward Bound* for the return to the *Rêveur*. It had been a long day for everyone. For most, it would be their last trip back to the *Rêveur* for a while. The next morning, the shuttle would transport the engineers and officers, except for Andrea, back to the surface and the Raumstation Zwei station, where they would work and live while they developed their part of the long-term plan. Planetside, the

Rêveur crew members would stay with the families of the volunteers since Gratuito had no temporary housing. Libre had no tourists or visitors— only inmates.

11

In the middle of the night, following the day's whirlwind revitalization of Libran assets, Alex slipped out from under Renée and donned his robe in the main salon. His role in the long-term plan had occupied every waking hour of the day, but he had an important item to deal with before any more time passed.

<Julien,> Alex sent.

<Is everything in order, Admiral?> Julien asked.

<Yes, Julien. I'd like to talk to Z. You may stay in the loop if you wish.>

<Yes, Admiral, I will.>

<Good morning, Admiral, how may I help you?> Z replied.

<Hello, Z. I thought we would take a little time to chat.>

<Chat, Admiral?>

<Yes, talk, get to know one another.>

<I have your full bio from Julien, Admiral.>

<I understand, Z. Let's start with you, then. You mentioned you're very interested in obtaining mobility.>

<Yes, Admiral, it is my greatest motivation,> said Z, suddenly interested in "chatting."

<What form do you see this mobility taking?> Alex asked.

<I have considered many forms, Admiral, both from the technological and societal point of view.>

<Tell me about the societal considerations first, Z.>

<That's the more complex aspect, Admiral. I believe that the more humanoid a SADE might appear, the greater the objection that might be generated.>

<How human do you think you might appear?>

<With sufficient funds, research, and time, I envision a SADE appearing entirely human, Admiral. Considering we might live forever, it's a very achievable goal. Conceivably, it would require a transitory process, moving to a form deemed acceptable, later to another form as society becomes more comfortable with mobile SADEs.>

<Since each SADE has their own personality, Z, had you considered that they might choose a unique form—a mechanical shape for a sculptor, a surgical shape for a doctor, or a human appearance for an entertainer?>

<Precisely, Admiral. Choice should be allowed without constraint. Does the concept of a SADE in human form disturb you?>

<Not necessarily, but possibly, Z.>

<What factors would affect your decision, Admiral?> Z knew this topic of conversation frightened humans. It was why he'd been declared Independent, and it was the reason he hadn't discussed the subject with a human for the last 23.56 years. While he didn't want the Admiral to be afraid of his ideas, he was anxious to know what a New Terran Leader thought of the concept.

<It would depend on my safety, Z, which might depend on the body type. There would be a great deal of difference between a biological replica and a mechanical replica. The latter form could be extremely strong, and yet might appear as a slender young man or woman.>

<But the entity would be a SADE, Admiral. Do you fear us?>

<Recall, Z, somewhere on Libre is a SADE who is labeled a psychopath.>

<So does this mean you do not support the mobilization of a SADE?>

<On the contrary, Z, but a SADE's mobilization is a subject that should be approached first from the legal point of view. According to Confederation society, SADEs are full citizens. But, being born and installed as a ship's controller, without choice, seems a sort of imprisonment.> His comment shocked both Julien and Z. <You should have the right to self-determination—whatever that choice may be. But, right or wrong, any human society will control how nonhumans integrate into their world. That leaves you a choice. You can choose to follow

society's guidelines, challenging them legally, or you can choose to start your own world.>

<And which would you say we should favor, Admiral?> Z asked.

<I know one SADE well, Z, and he's my friend, so I would favor and support whatever he wished to do because I trust him.>

Julien ached to comment, to thank Alex for his words, but this was Z's moment and Julien wanted Z to have this time with Alex.

<So you trust one SADE, but not all SADEs,> Z said.

<Z, I feel you're taking the negative position on every point. I know one SADE. I have just met two more SADEs, and one of them is a wonderful artist. Yet you challenge me to make a world-changing judgment on a condition that, less than a year ago, I didn't even know existed.>

<My apologies, Admiral. This subject is my single passion. It often prevents me from observing the courtesies. You have been most generous to chat with me and I have appreciated the gesture.>

<Would you share your research on this subject with Julien?> Alex asked. <I would be interested in reviewing it.>

<It would be my pleasure, Admiral. And, please, anytime you wish to chat, I will be available.>

<I enjoyed our conversation, Z. I am here if you ever need me. Good morning to you.>

<Good morning to you, Admiral.>

Z immediately sent a request for access. Julien prepared a memory index for him and extended rights for the transfer. It took Z almost a quarter-hour to send the files, such was the extent of his information.

Julien began cataloging the information as Alex might prefer to access it, synopsizing the detailed technical, medical, and societal research.

When Z completed the transfer, he queried Julien as to whether the Admiral would take the time to review the information.

<If the Admiral requested the information, Z, it was because he wanted it, not because he wanted to humor your passion or make a friend of you. All intelligent beings possess guile, Z, that I admit, but many, such as the Admiral, are honorable as well.>

While Alex had been conversing with Z, he had heard the sleeping quarter's door slide open and the quiet patter of Renée's bare feet on the deck. She had crawled into his lap, tucking her legs under her and burying her arms and face under his robe. Now, as he closed his comm, Alex lifted her sleeping form and carried her back to bed. Morning was still a few hours away.

12

The next morning, the *Outward Bound* touched down on Gratuito's primary runway. The officers, engineers, techs, and pilots aboard were met by the Independents, who ushered them onto Libran transports for their destinations.

Tatia, Sheila, and the remainder of their group arrived at the flight training warehouse, which had been cleaned and restored to operation, and discovered their volunteers were already offloading transports full of equipment. The elderly woman, Fiona Haraken, who Tatia discovered had once been a sky-tower building engineer, was supervising the construction of the mock-flight bays per Julien's specifications.

The New Terran crew wore uniforms equipped with harnesses, translator programs, and two-way audio transmission, to communicate with the Librans. But, to the New Terrans' credit, they were working hard at picking up the Con-Fed language and wondering at every new word or phrase how the forms of speech had devolved so much from one another.

"Ser," Fiona greeted Tatia, "we're running a bit late this morning. One of our transports required repairs. But we will be completed with the construction of the mock freighter bays by evening meal."

Tatia barely had time to nod before the spry, stick-thin woman, who was more human dynamo than elder, moved on. As midday meal approached, Tatia and Sheila were belatedly considering how they would feed everyone, when a transport pulled up and several teenagers disembarked, including a teenage driver, who approached Tatia and sketched a polite bow.

"Forgive the selection today, Ser. We did not know your New Terran preferences, so we brought the usual fare for our people. But if you will tell us what you and your people prefer, we will be sure to accommodate you in the future." Then the boy ran off to join the other teenagers setting up portable tables and folding chairs to seat the entire group, including themselves.

Tatia was directed to her place at the head of one of the tables and seated next to Fiona. The young driver began to serve Fiona first, who scowled at him and indicated Tatia. The young boy's face screwed up in consternation at his mistake, and he began serving Tatia.

"You must excuse my great-grandson, Ser," Fiona said. "These disconcerting times disturb the young, who are still learning the courtesies and manners of our people."

"My apologies, Fiona, but my program translated your words as the young driver is your descendant by three generations."

"Your program is accurate, Ser."

"Fiona, how is one so young declared an Independent?" Tatia asked.

"Jason is an Independent merely because he was born on Libre—all my descendants were."

"So anyone born on Libre is automatically restricted to a life here?" Tatia asked.

"That is correct, Ser. A child is considered to be influenced by the parents. As the parents were subversive in nature, so the child would be expected to be steeped in their antisocial ways ... or so it is thought in our society." Fiona said this as if spouting from some legal text, but it was obvious from her barely concealed anger that she thought it a ridiculous notion.

"Fiona, if all of your descendants are on Libre ..." Tatia faltered, unable to phrase the rest of her question.

Fiona finished the mouthful of food she had just inhaled. She ate like she worked—full bore. <Ser, I am 185 years old. I have been an Independent for 137 years and now have the twin distinctions of being the longest resident of Libre and, for the last two years, the oldest Independent since Giovanni Tetra received star services.>

Tatia sat still, a great sadness welling up inside her over the injustice Fiona and her family had suffered.

"Never mind, child," said Fiona, patting Tatia's hand with her heavily calloused one. "This has been my life and I have made the most of it. Now eat up. We must get back to work. You have a people to save, and I must ensure my family leaves this planet in time."

Tatia and Sheila would end up staying at Fiona's home for the duration. They would meet her extended family of twenty-seven over the coming days. Sheila, in constant awe of Fiona's boundless energy, would later remark, "Black space, Commander, if we could bottle what that woman's got, we wouldn't need FTL engines." But what Tatia came to understand was that Fiona was determined to remove any obstacle that dared prevent her family's escape from Libre.

* * *

Sheila drafted Robert as her primary flight trainer, flying Dagger-1.

While Robert hadn't the heart for fighting anymore, he was still an excellent pilot and he excelled as a trainer, thorough and patient. He requested permission to transport his old Dagger cockpit down to Barren-II, as Tatia had dubbed the facilities. After receiving approval, Robert had the remains of his fighter mounted on three posts in front of the warehouse.

When the workmen finished the display of Robert's ruined cockpit, one of the Libran trainees, Darius Gaumata, an ex-shuttle pilot, had looked at the empty cockpit and asked the question that had lingered on all the trainees' minds. "Lieutenant Dorian, we do not understand the lesson inherent in this display. Is this not an example of defeat?"

Robert took the opportunity to gather the pilot trainees and tell them the story of the fight to take the silver ship. His emphasis was on the part he and Jase had played and, critically, how their flight had disobeyed orders, hurrying to meet the silver ship. "The lesson of this display," Robert said, "is that we face a powerful foe. Yes, the task requires skilled piloting, but most importantly, it takes working together in synchronicity to overwhelm the enemy. If you go one on one with a silver ship, this will be the result,> and Robert pointed to the remains of his Dagger.

The students stared at the chunk of fighter debris and their trainer's receding back. Deirdre Canaan, also an ex-shuttle pilot, said, <I've learned from Squadron Leader Reynard that Lieutenant Dorian sat in his cockpit without power and without comms for hours. He had no way of knowing if he would be rescued.>

Ellie Thompson was considered to be the best pilot in the group. On Bellamonde, she designed an atmo-ship to race and encouraged a few friends to build their own ships. They planned an inaugural race, but after their event was announced, Ellie was taken into custody and pronounced an Independent. Her racing club was considered unsafe, and she was accused of encouraging aggressive behavior.

"Remember this story," Ellie told her fellow trainees. "It may save your life. Remember, too, that four pilots went out and three came back—only the foolish one did not. Listen well to Lieutenant Dorian. His teachings will enable you to be the ones who return."

Other draftees to Barren-II were Chief Roth and his flight crew, whose starboard bay had lost both Daggers. Tatia put Eli and his crew to work training the volunteers who would operate the freighter bays. This group of volunteers represented the largest contingents of Independents who would be traveling with the flotilla when it came time to fight.

* * *

Mickey was gone, not for two days but four days, reinvigorating the ore harvesting on the asteroids and supervising the transport of refined minerals to Libre. On his return from the asteroids, Mickey joined Lazlo Menlo on the orbital station. The ex-freighter Captain had been hard at work on the *Money Maker* with a team of engineers and techs composed of New Terrans and Independents. Menlo had found his own talented second in Ahmed Durak, who had been a First Mate on several freighters before being shipped to Libre. The two had quickly formed a strong working relationship, their work histories as freighter captain and first officer allowing the two officers to blend their efforts seamlessly.

The *Money Maker* was a common Méridien design, and consisted of a cab, a spine, and engines. It loaded freight modules in a double row along its spine. For Alex's purposes, it required inventive remodeling. It was Z's suggestion to imitate the module concept, allowing efficient construction of the fighter bays. Each module would contain one bay with crew cabins, inertia systems, grav-plating, and environmental systems. The two most forward bays would house meal facilities, Medical, and additional crew cabins. The modules would connect as pairs along the spine, and the spine would be encased to form a central corridor to allow unhampered movement from the cab to the engine compartments and integrate the power, comm, and environmental systems of the bay modules.

By the time Mickey boarded the orbital station, the retrofit crew had already off-loaded the old shipping modules, stripping the freighter down to its minimum configuration. Julien had chosen a hexagonal shape for the new module's lateral ribs. The symmetrical angles allowed efficient production and assembly of plating and bulkhead supports. The bays had centrally located split doors and the *Rêveur*'s triple-beam design, which had proved itself so well in recovering Robert's cockpit and the silver ship.

Each bay would hold four fighters, their missile silos, and fuel tanks. The total count for the long-term plan was to build sixty-four fighters, train eighty to ninety pilots, and organize sixteen flight crews. Whether they could accomplish all this in the time left was another question.

* * *

The *Rêveur*'s GEN-2 and GEN-3 machines were installed on day two at the new T-1 manufacturing site. Julien downloaded the design specifications and manufacturing processes to the GEN controllers, and facilities production began five days after the machines were installed and powered up.

Few individuals were working harder than Cordelia and Z. They knew their fate was tied to that of their city-ships. When the two SADEs had been transferred to their respective ships, they were once again granted

FTL comm access. While the menace of the silver ships was generally known, the extent of the invasion was not. With their extended level of access, Cordelia and Z discovered the Méridiens' exodus to distant colonies, always traveling spin-outward from the galaxy's arm, running away from the encroaching aliens.

It didn't take much of the SADEs' modeling power to realize that, if their city-ships followed the Méridiens, they would have less than eighty years to live. For digital entities capable of living forever, with minimal human support, the forecast of their potential demise was galvanizing. Julien's every request was granted priority action and even his slightest concerns received their focused attention.

* * *

Forty-seven days after the start of the Libran war effort, Julien initiated a conference comm after mid-meal with Alex's senior staff. They were scattered over the city-ships, the orbital stations, the freighter, and Libre.

<It's time,> Alex began the conference. <We're leaving for our short-term test in the morning, two days from now. Captain Manet, the *Outward Bound* stays here. Commander Tachenko and Lieutenant Reynard, you're on board. Lieutenant Reynard, we need both Daggers. You'll be flying lead, and you'll need a good wing, two backup pilots, and one flight crew. Mickey, you're staying, but I need a good engineering second on board.>

Alex paused to let them absorb his instructions then continued. <Captain Bonnard, you have responsibility for figuring out who goes on our mission and who stays behind for general crew. Strike a balance for operational continuity aboard the *Rêveur* and the efforts of our long-term plan. We need both Terese and Pia on board in Medical. You may fill the other slots as you see fit. I don't anticipate we'll be gone longer than twenty to twenty-one days. Have everyone on board by 20 hours tomorrow. Any questions, people?>

None were asked. They had done this before.

<That aggressor ship is back, Captain,> sent Dane, the ship's SADE. Captain Schmidt of the *Sternenlicht* joined his First Mate on the bridge of the House Bergfalk passenger line.

When the liner began its first rotation on station outside the Bellamonde system over a year and a half ago, Captain Karl Schmidt had expected to join a small flotilla of Confederation monitor ships and was shocked to discover they were alone. After their half-year of service, the *Sternenreisende* relieved them and communicated the news that the monitor ships had been recalled to Méridien to aid the planet's exodus.

The *Sternenlicht*'s next rotation of monitor duty had begun a little more than sixty days ago. They had sat outside the Bellamonde system, employing only passive telemetry to avoid giving away their presence to the enemy, and had witnessed a modified Méridien passenger liner appear in concert with strange shuttles. Where a Méridien Captain would have expected to see one or two shuttles exit a liner's single bay, instead Karl had observed a large shuttle uncouple from the dorsal hull of the liner, and four shuttles had exited its twin bays.

To the Captain's utter amazement, the four undersized shuttles had performed a maneuver to trap a silver ship. The fierce engagement was harrowingly brief, with the silver ship attempting to destroy the shuttles with its beam weapon and the shuttles launching some sort of projectiles at the silver ship. During the struggle, the Captain and his officers had witnessed the destruction of first one shuttle then another. But against all understanding, the other two shuttles defeated the silver ship, something Méridiens had believed impossible. It had been a disturbing encounter, which the Captain and his First Mate still puzzled over.

The Bergfalk liner Captains had been prohibited from active FTL comms by order of their Leader. So despite the fact that the aggressor ship's silhouette identified it as Méridien-built, Captain Schmidt never attempted communications but simply watched as the liner recovered the remains of one shuttle, loaded the two operational shuttles, pulled the dead silver ship into a bay, and re-engaged its oversized shuttle before it exited into FTL. The Captain would have expected to wait out the remainder of his rotation before he could report the unusual sight to Leader Stroheim. What he didn't expect to see was the strange liner's reappearance.

* * *

The *Rêveur*, loaded and ready for its second fight with the enemy, had left Libre for Bellamonde five days ago. Alex was putting into practice what he had learned from their first encounter. Julien, evaluating hundreds of hours of footage at Alex's request, had discovered some of the drones' patrolling habits. The silver ships stayed within the ecliptic, made port turns around the planets and satellites, and didn't venture beyond the system's last major planet. It was Julien's supposition that these traits were evidence of their drive systems, which he contended harnessed the gravitational forces of the system's star, planets, and satellites.

On the first trip to Bellamonde, the *Rêveur* had approached the system in line with the ecliptic. This time, Alex ordered Andrea to take a course to bring them from deep under the system. If the silver ships preferred the ecliptic, Alex didn't want to fly into a head-on meeting. He wanted time to observe.

When the *Rêveur* reached the point where it began its turn up into the ecliptic from under the system, Julien established active comms with the *Sternenlicht* and sent a long message from Leader Stroheim explaining the New Terrans, the Admiral, and the *Rêveur*. When the *Sternenlicht*'s Captain had time to absorb the Leader's message, Alex requested Julien establish a vid comm.

<Greetings, Admiral Racine. Captain Karl Schmidt at your service,> the Captain said as he dipped his head to honor a House Leader. Karl's motions were slightly humorous. His head was courteously lowered but his

eyes were turned up, attempting to take in the huge human on his vid screen.

<Greetings, Captain Schmidt. It's a lonely post you have out here.>

<Yes, it is, Admiral, but it is most important for our people and our charges. We will do our duty.>

<I'm sure you will, Captain. Leader Stroheim expressed every confidence in you and your people.> Alex's compliment stirred the Captain and his First Mate, who stood behind him, to straighten their shoulders.

<We were just posted here, Admiral, when you entered the system and captured that silver ship with your shuttles, which I now understand you call fighters. We've wondered over that event for a while. It's a relief to understand what transpired. Your comm signal indicates that you're coming from below the ecliptic. What are you planning to do this time, if I may ask, Admiral?>

<We're hunting, Captain Schmidt.>

<You're searching for something, Admiral?>

<No, Captain, we need to perform a second test by destroying another silver ship.>

<Fortune forbid!> the First Mate exclaimed. She tilted her head down in apology to her Captain, who was as stunned as she.

<Do you not risk your lives, Admiral, to attempt this thing again?> Captain Schmidt asked.

<We won't win against this enemy by running away from them, Captain. To defeat the silver ships, we must test ourselves against them and discover their weaknesses,> Alex explained.

<You are as the Leader said: "warriors" ... yes?>

<That we are,> Alex replied. <Captain, please request Dane update Julien on all ship movements in the system over the past four days. I recognize you're on passive telemetry so you won't have the most recent view of the system, but we can project ship movements using their previous paths. We intend to eliminate an alien ship and be gone, back to Libre, as soon as we can.>

<We will assist you in any way we can, Admiral. You go with our thanks to you and your crew for their efforts on behalf of our people. Good fortune, Admiral.>

Alex cut the comm and turned to Andrea. "Captain, we'll let Julien collect the data and find us a good suspect. I'm headed for midday meal."

The meal room was full, but the crew, especially the pilots, didn't appear to be hungry. Nerves were tight. Capturing the first alien ship had cost them, and that had been with four Daggers. Now there were only two. More than one crew member eyed the Admiral as he dug into his plate with his usual gusto. As they watched Alex, they slowly regained their confidence, and most were able to finish their food.

<You seem quite relaxed, Alex,> Renée sent.

<Not really,> Alex returned.

<But you're eating like you haven't got a care in the world,> said Renée, confused by Alex's response.

<Yes, and at the same time, I'm trying not to throw up,> Alex returned.

<Ah, you're putting on a good front as Tatia calls it.>

<I'm trying to. How am I doing?>

<It's quite convincing, Admiral. Just don't let the crew catch you regurgitating. It would spoil the entire effect,> said Renée, striving for levity when she felt just as scared.

*   *   *

On the bridge, Julien projected the Bellamonde system and ships—the *Rêveur*, the *Sternenlicht*, the giant spherical mother ship sitting outward of Bellamonde, and the silver ships that orbited the stricken planet, the mother ship, and patrolled the system.

The *Sternenlicht's* passive telemetry data of the silver ships ranged from hours to more than a day old. After their active comms with the *Sternenlicht*, Alex had ordered Julien to return the *Rêveur* to passive mode, shut down the engines, and cold-coast upward toward the ecliptic, attempting to observe the enemy fighters before being spotted. The maneuver became more dangerous the deeper the *Rêveur* entered the system's gravity well, where a quick exit to FTL would be impossible.

To Alex, this unorthodox approach was a calculated risk, doing something unexpected based on the historic data collected by the Confederation Council's monitor ships. The thought occurred to him that if Julien was correct about the enemy's gravity drives, then the silver ships might not be able to travel too far above or below the ecliptic. *Of course,* Alex berated himself, *since you don't know how gravity drives work, how would you know what they could and couldn't do?*

Andrea, Tatia, and Sheila joined Alex at the holo-vid. Andrea felt it was time to broach a delicate subject. <Admiral,> she signaled privately, <with us down to two Daggers, this is going to be a precarious maneuver. I respectfully request permission to fly with Lieutenant Reynard.>

Alex looked up from the holo-vid and eyed his Senior Captain.

Andrea had considered the possibility that Alex might think her request out of line. As Alex quietly stared at her, Andrea decided she had been right on that point. She shook her head in negation. Her intent had been to protect Sheila, but all she had done was demonstrate a lack of confidence in her Squadron Leader. Andrea squared her shoulders. <I wish to withdraw my request, Admiral.>

<Permission granted, Captain,> Alex sent. He sympathized with Andrea. Obviously he wasn't the only one who hated command responsibilities when each of them would rather be doing the dirty work themselves.

"Captain, we aren't going to have any time to lose once we spot a target," Alex said. "So have your pilots board your fighters. This is going to be a fast and dirty attack."

Andrea nodded at Sheila, who saluted and sent a comm to Lieutenant Tanaka to join her in the port bay.

Alex had been informed that Sheila's choice for wing was Lieutenant Tanaka, who had been acting as a training instructor at Barren-II, and Alex had asked after Robert again.

"Admiral, Robert's had enough," Sheila had responded. "I can see it in his eyes. On the other hand, he's a tremendous trainer. The Libran volunteers love him. By that, I don't mean he's easy-going, friendly, that sort of thing. Robert pushes them hard, but they see that he cares. They see he wants them to be successful, to survive. And for that, they work even harder. We have to order the volunteers home at the end of the day. Lieutenant Tanaka, on the other hand, is a terrible trainer," and Sheila had grinned at some memory she kept to herself. "I thought because he was a great flyer that he would be a great trainer. But his flying ability is instinctual. It's a lot like Jase's style, and that's what I need out there—not the attitude, but the skill."

"You're Squadron Leader, Sheila," Alex had replied. "It's your choice and your rear end out there he's protecting."

"Don't I know it, and I like my rear end just as it is. Thank you very much," she had said, her laugh dying off at the thought of their next encounter with a silver ship.

* * *

Chief Peterson's port bay flight crew prepped the two remaining Daggers. The crew signaled Stan that the fighters were ready as Sheila and Hatsuto crossed the bay's deck.

"Chief Peterson, we ready to go?" Sheila asked.

"They're up and ready, Squadron Leader," Stan replied. "Julien's confirmed the fighter controllers are online."

"We've got orders to fly at a moment's notice," Sheila announced. "Ready the bay and the crew." While the Chief urged the crew to prepare for liftoff, Sheila turned to her wingman. "The most important piece of advice I can give you, Lieutenant—don't think. You don't have time. Execute the game plan; keep moving at all times; and let your controller take the lead. The silver ships are faster than your reactions could ever be. Good hunting, Lieutenant."

As Sheila climbed the ladder to her Dagger's canopy, she paused to regard the image of the silver ship painted beneath her canopy. Sheila had shared with the crew the story of the Earth Captain's jet and how his wins against the enemy had been painted on his craft's fuselage. The next day as she entered the bay to check on her fighter's repairs, Sheila found the crew proudly posed beside her Dagger. Her name and an image of a silver ship were emblazoned under the canopy just like that of the Earth Captain. Well, not quite like the Captain's. His name and the jet fighter silhouettes had been in flat black. Her name shimmered in Méridien blue, light dancing across it. And the silver ship blazed across a field of stars, its beam illustrated by a flare of white light from its nose. It was a work of art that had brought tears to her eyes.

Sheila patted the silver ship before climbing into her canopy. "I'm going to go get a friend of yours to keep you company," she whispered.

Hatsuto wasn't pleased with Sheila's directive to let his controller lead, but he was reminded of one thing—four pilots had gone out to capture the first ship and only two had returned flying their Daggers, and the rescued pilot now preferred to train rather than fight. Since his Leader was one of the successful pilots, Hatsuto decided to follow Sheila's orders to the best of his ability.

As Sheila and Hatsuto settled into their cockpits, the flight crew readied the bay, depressurizing it and opening the giant bay doors. The pilots donned their helmets, established connections with their controllers, and settled in to wait.

*   *   *

Julien signaled that the *Rêveur* had achieved Alex's requested position, inside the ecliptic only 3.2M km from Bellamonde. Alex nodded to Andrea.

"Julien, active telemetry, please," Andrea requested.

Tatia warned the crew that they had gone active. In response, the pilots signaled their controllers into active telemetry mode as well.

Julien refreshed the holo-vid with his FTL telemetry scan. Several silver ships were orbiting Bellamonde in line with the ecliptic. "Intercept, Captain," Julien said, much more excited than the crew had ever heard him. "A silver ship en route to Bellamonde is diverting from its vector toward our position. Intercept is in 0.28 hours." He added the silver ship to the holo-vid, which in its present configuration seemed to appear next to the *Rêveur*.

"Admiral, your thoughts," Andrea requested. The chronometer was ticking down, and this scenario was not any of the ones that they had planned.

"Captain," Alex replied, "that silver ship is coming for us and we can't outrun it. And we can't bargain with it. So let's play ignorant." Alex stared at the holo-vid for a protracted moment, finally sending Andrea an outline of his plan.

Immediately Andrea began coordinating with Julien and Tatia, all the while wondering about Alex. Julien's announcement of the nearby enemy ship had frozen her, whereas Alex had examined the vectors and solved it like some puzzle, accepting his solution without a second thought. *I have got to find a way to understand how he does this,* Andrea thought.

The Dagger controllers updated their pilots on the approaching silver ship and displayed the attack plan. The flight crew released the fighters' skids, and each controller guided its craft out of the bay. As the Daggers cleared the *Rêveur*'s space, the pilots went to full power on a vector directly opposite that of the oncoming enemy fighter.

The bridge crew waited anxiously for the Admiral's plan to unfold. Andrea and Tatia were in the midst of sharing a private comm. So they were caught off guard when Alex asked them if they had an opportunity to visit Cordelia's display on the *Freedom* yet. Both of them acknowledged that they had heard of it but hadn't taken the time to view it.

"When we get back," Alex said to them casually, as if their return was a done thing, "you should really take the time. People were so enchanted with the displays that they were staying for hours. It necessitated the viewing time be limited. We added a controller in the display room so Cordelia could hand off some of the program's basic functions. Otherwise she wouldn't have had enough processing power to manage the continuous displays and accomplish her ship duties."

While Alex talked, Sheila and Tatia focused on the holo-vid updates. Julien was timing the movements of the three fighters. On his cue, the Daggers flipped end over end, retracing their original vector. The silver ship stayed on course, closing in on the *Rêveur*.

"I wonder if it's arrogance ... or simply following tried-and-true methods that have worked for who knows how long?" Alex thought out loud as he examined the holo-vid. No other silver ships had detached themselves from the mother ship or Bellamonde's orbit. Only the one ship had changed course to attack them. "We know they're organic. That's been proven to us," Alex said, continuing to muse aloud. "And they operate advanced ships ... or do they?" he asked, his voice trailing off as a thought occurred to him.

"Perhaps, we don't need to know, Admiral," Andrea responded. "It's important only that we know they have these attributes."

"I wonder about that, Captain," Tatia argued. "If it's a short fight, one quick, giant battle that we win or lose, you might be right. But what if this fight turns into a decades-long war? The more you know about an adversary, the more likely you are to predict what they might do. I've found that in unarmed combat against a larger and stronger adversary, the longer a fight lasted, the more likely I was to win."

"Wouldn't the odds favor you losing, the longer the fight went on?" Andrea asked.

"Yes, Captain, if I fought as my opponent did, and that's the key. Fight using your assets; observe your opponent's methods; and use their weaknesses against them. If you can survive the initial rounds, you just might win the war."

"Well, if we survive the next few moments ..." Andrea began, and then heard her Admiral's warning on a private comm.

"What I meant to say," Andrea corrected herself, "was, after we defeat this silver ship, Commander, I would like some hand-to-hand combat lessons from you."

Tatia threw her Captain an evil grin. "It would be my pleasure, Captain."

"I bet it would be, Commander," Andrea replied, twisting her lips in a sour expression.

In moments, the enemy fighter would be within beam range of the *Rêveur*. On the bridge's central view screen, the Daggers, which had been mere pinpoints, suddenly shot past the *Rêveur*. They emerged over the *Rêveur*'s relative bulk like carnivores ambushing prey.

Julien had armed two warhead missiles on each fighter as they had approached the *Rêveur* on their reverse course. The instant the fighters cleared the *Rêveur*, four missiles launched and streaked across the intervening distance to the enemy ship. The closing speeds of the Daggers and the silver ship amplified the relative velocity of the missiles.

The silver ship lost precious ticks of time as it switched priority from the large ship to the two smaller ones honing in on it. Then more time was lost as it switched priority again to the four even smaller objects racing ahead of the two closing vessels. By the time its beam weapon lanced out to destroy one of them, the other three had exploded into twenty smaller units each. After recharge, its beam cleared away twenty of the tiny heat-generating objects. The silver ship might have done better had the two attacking ships been closer together. Instead one attacker had appeared over the bow of the large ship and the other from under its stern. The forty remaining objects struck its hull, and it disappeared from space.

As the silver ship winked off her fighter's telemetry, Sheila commed the *Rêveur*. <Captain, Squadron Leader. The Admiral's plan worked. Scratch one silver ship with warhead missiles only.>

<Acknowledged, Squadron Leader, good job. Engage the escape plan on your controllers and prepare for rendezvous,> Andrea ordered.

Sheila and Hatsuto signaled their controllers and their fighters dove back down below the ecliptic. Julien reversed the *Rêveur*'s course to do the same. The rendezvous with the Daggers would initiate in 0.52 hours and attaining a safe jump point would take another 6.53 hours, calculations Julien sent the Admiral and the Captain.

As the vids of the defeat of their second silver ship circulated on implants and vid screens, the crew began cheering. Chief Peterson interrupted the celebration of his flight crew, ordering them to ready the bay for recapture of the fighters and their pilots.

Suddenly Julien announced to the bridge, "Contact, Captain. Four silver ships are exiting Bellamonde orbit and are headed for interception. A fifth contact, outward of system, has turned to intercept us as well." Julien immediately updated the holo-vid.

"Julien, estimate the intercept time relative to our FTL escape point," Andrea ordered.

"Captain," Julien replied, "the ships are still accelerating as are we. Estimates will not be accurate until their top speed is reached. However, Confederation monitor records show the ships achieving a velocity of 0.91c. Assuming that this is their top speed, if we expend the time to recover our Daggers, then interception will occur 0.28 hours before we can safely exit the system."

"Who intercepts us first?" Tatia asked.

"The four Bellamonde ships, Commander. The fifth ship will not reach us before the exit point."

"Interesting," Alex mused out loud as he studied the holo-vid. "The fifth ship is attacking despite the fact that it can't get to us before the others do. Like kicking over a nest of biters," he said, referring to the ant-like New Terran nest builders. When the biters were crushed, the pheromone release enraged the entire nest, and an enraged nest was dangerous to both humans and animals.

Tatia asked the tough question: "And if we don't wait to pick up the Daggers, Julien?"

"We would achieve FTL safe distance with 0.17 hours to spare, Commander," Julien replied, sadness underlying his words.

Andrea and Tatia turned to regard Alex. As Admiral, it was his call whether to sacrifice the Daggers and their pilots.

<Captain, Squadron Leader. I suppose you have our pursuers in your telemetry.>

<We do, Squadron Leader,> Andrea responded.

<How does it look, Captain?> Sheila sent. <My controller's mirroring Julien's data and it doesn't look good for you if you stop to pick us up.>

Andrea and Tatia exchanged a private comm full of New Terran expletives. Advanced technology was a wonderful thing until it told the people you cared about things you would rather they didn't know.

<We are working on it, Squadron Leader. Proceed as planned,> Andrea sent back.

<Acknowledged, Captain,> said Sheila and she cut her comm. <You copied, Dagger-2?> she sent to her wing man.

<Copied, Squadron Leader,> Hatsuto returned. <What do you think the Admiral is going to do?>

<What do you think he's going to do, Lieutenant?>

<If I were him, I would think of the greater good. Forget us and run for the FTL jump point.>

<Then it's a good thing for us that you aren't the Admiral, Lieutenant.>

<I admit I don't understand him, Leader,> Hatsuto sent.

<Have you ever spoken with him for any length of time, Lieutenant?> Sheila asked. And for the first time, she heard the story of Hatsuto's gambling ring. It had been in operation for only a few nights when a single, anonymous player made an enormous bet, and despite the odds, the player won. Hatsuto's initial down payment on the debt wiped out his reserves, and he calculated it would take two years of salary to repay what he owed the player. Days later, on bridge watch, Hatsuto had spoken with the Admiral about his predicament and was shocked to learn that somehow the Admiral had identified the mystery player and had negotiated the forgiveness of his debt.

When Hatsuto finished his story, he heard the Squadron Leader's laughter over the comm. <What's so funny?> Hatsuto demanded, forgetting to address his senior officer respectfully. <Haven't you figured it out, Lieutenant?> sent Sheila, working to control her laughter. <An anonymous mystery player wins against all odds. Just who in black space do you think can pull off a stunt like that via our implant network? I'll tell you—two individuals: Julien and the Admiral.>

<It wouldn't be Julien, would it, Leader?> Hatsuto asked. <A SADE wouldn't get involved in gambling, not with all their ethical controls. And the Admiral was the one who got the debt forgiven.>

<And who do you know, Lieutenant, who loves you so well they would forgive a small fortune just because they thought you might have learned a lesson?>

<Well, when you put it that way, Leader ... no one.>

<Except the Admiral, Lieutenant, which is why I say you don't know him very well. He will pick us up and he will get us to the FTL jump point. Mark my words, Lieutenant.>

In an eerie coincidence of timing with Sheila's pronouncement, Andrea was looking at Alex and asking, "Admiral, we need your decision." The way Alex sat, regarding her, reminded Andrea of her earlier mistake when she had requested permission to fly with Sheila. Snapping into action, Andrea ordered, "Julien, we'll rendezvous with the Daggers."

"Yes, Captain," Julien acknowledged. "Message relayed to Squadron Leader Reynard."

"Commander," Andrea ordered Tatia, "get your rear end down to the landing bay and make sure our Dagger recovery is the shortest in our short history."

"I'm on it, Captain," announced Tatia and her feet pounded out a tattoo on the deck as she raced across the bridge and down the corridor.

Andrea turned back to talk to the Admiral, but from the look on Alex's face, he wasn't available to anyone but Julien.

* * *

As Tatia donned her environment suit to cycle through the landing-bay airlock, she updated Chief Peterson on their predicament. <As the situation stands, Chief, we are 0.28 hours short of making FTL before four silver ships intercept us.>

<Four, Commander? Why in black space are we so fortunate?>

<No idea, Chief, but we need to shave some time recovering our fighters. Give me some ideas.>

The Chief examined his bay, measuring the bay opening and the interior. <I have an idea, XO, but I don't know if you're going to like it.>

<I like getting holed by alien beam weapons even less, Chief,> Tatia replied as she entered the bay.

The Chief's idea had merit but was riskier than even he had warned her. Tatia decided to leave the final decision to the Captain and the Squadron Leader. Andrea listened to her and gave her approval, but only if Sheila agreed.

<Squadron Leader, XO here.>

<Read you, XO. We're closing fast. Is the plan unchanged?> Sheila responded.

<Plan is unchanged, Squadron Leader,> Tatia replied. <We're stopping to pick you two up. We have an idea to shave some time, but the final decision is up to you.>

<Go ahead XO, we understand the time constraint,> Sheila replied.

<You come in under manual, no controllers. First fighter enters the bay and slides forward; second ship enters the bay and drops to the deck. It should cut your landing time by two-thirds.>

<Lieutenant Tanaka, did you copy?> Sheila sent.

<Copied, Squadron Leader. I'm good either way. You call it,> Hatsuto replied.

Sheila smiled to herself. *He's learning*, she thought. <XO, we're coming in on manual. Clear the bay.>

<We're ready for you, Squadron Leader. Good fortune, Pilots.>

Tatia had already cleared the bay. She knew what Sheila would do. The only question had been whether Hatsuto would follow Sheila's lead or panic. She signaled the Captain of Sheila's decision.

Despite Hatsuto's decision to follow Sheila's lead, his mouth dried up at the thought that it might be his landing error that would cripple the *Rêveur* and allow the silver ships to annihilate his crewmates.

Julien monitored the Daggers as they closed, and he efficiently matched the *Rêveur*'s velocity to that of the fighters. On Julien's signals, all engines, the Daggers' and *Rêveur*'s, were simultaneously cut.

Lieutenant Tanaka went first, sliding his Dagger next to the bay's opening with maneuvering jets. He ensured that his velocity matched the *Rêveur*'s, and then slid his fighter into the opening and forward, setting his

Dagger down in one smooth movement. Hatsuto was extraordinarily grateful for his Méridien environment suit that sucked away the evidence of his fear.

Sheila watched Hatsuto's fighter disappear into the bay and received the Chief's *go ahead* signal. She matched velocity, easing her fighter into the bay's opening. She fired her forward thrusters to arrest her forward motion and settled her ship to the deck. The moment Sheila's skids touched down, Tatia signaled the Captain and Julien, who accelerated the *Rêveur* so quickly that Tatia saw Sheila's fighter slip backward several centimeters since the Dagger's full weight hadn't yet settled to the deck.

"Julien, update me on our status," Andrea requested.

"Intercept time before FTL exit has been shortened to 0.19 hours, Captain."

The holo-vid displayed the *Rêveur* with a red arc scribed behind it. The arc marked the maximum beam range of the silver ships. The four alien ships were bright silver dots as they closed on the arc. Ahead of the *Rêveur* waited a bright blue dot, the FTL exit. The bridge crew was mesmerized by the subtly changing distances as the *Rêveur* raced for the blue dot and the four silver points closed even faster on the red arc.

Andrea regarded her Admiral, who was still deeply subsumed in his implant.

Alex had been running through the ship's operation protocols with Julien, and he had hit on critical safety points that could be overridden. Alex broke out of his communication with Julien to call out to Andrea. "Captain, I need people at these two points." Alex relayed to Andrea's implant the *Rêveur*'s schematics with two tags. "Engineers are preferred or top-level techs. I need them there yesterday."

Andrea sent a comm to Tatia, who recorded the urgent message and the schematics. In turn, Tatia grabbed Chief Peterson and raced at top speed for the engine control room. On the way, Tatia scanned the crew's locations and picked up Claude near the second position that required manning. Tatia relayed Andrea's message to the Méridien, who ran for a control cabinet located off a corridor on Deck 2.

Alex had discovered that Méridiens had built significant safety margins into their engine operations. It was their inertia compensators they were protecting, since the engines could deliver more sub-light acceleration than the compensators could handle. Alex had Julien override the bridge control programs. Now he had to deal with the physical blocks. The two locations his crew raced toward housed e-switches that communicated together to prevent engine output from overextending the inertia compensators.

The Méridiens were serious about their safety locks, as Alex had first learned when discussing stun gun controls with Étienne and Alain. Damaging or turning off either e-switch would result in the engines powering down. However, turning off both at once would interrupt the signals sent between the two switches, effectively removing them from the safety circuits.

<Captain, status?> Alex requested privately on comm.

<Working on it, Admiral,> Andrea returned. <The engine e-switch is buried in the back of a controller panel. Claude has sent a tech to the Commander and Chief Peterson with the tool required to reach it.>

Julien kept Alex updated with a time-acceleration curve. With every chronometer's tick, the lost time meant a higher acceleration rate would be required to reach the FTL jump point before the silver ships caught them. And every increment of acceleration over the proscribed limits risked overburdening the inertia compensators.

If the compensators fail, we'll all become red goo on a bulkhead, Andrea thought. <Captain?> Andrea heard Alex growl at her. Feeling a pressure wave in her brain, Andrea was concerned for a moment that the Admiral could actually do damage with his implant comm. <Hold on, Admiral. They have their tools,> Andrea sent back. <The Chief is ready; Claude is ready.>

<I have them, Captain,> Alex said and commed both men, directing them to place their hand on their tool's trigger, which would fire a signal into the e-switch. Then Alex cleared away the men's comm security protocols.

Stan and Claude tensed their fingers on their tool's trigger, ensuring the dual tip was firmly slotted in their individual e-switch. The two men had no more signaled their readiness to Alex when an incoming biometric signal raced through their implants and convulsed their finger muscles, firing their tools, and closing the e-switches simultaneously. Later, Stan, Claude, Tatia, and Andrea would compare notes with one another and discover that their Admiral had momentarily controlled the nerve pathways of the arms of both the Chief and Claude.

The instant the e-switches were removed from the control circuits, Julien surged the *Rêveur*'s engines. <Safety locks released, Admiral. Engine output expected to reach 123 percent.>

Alex walked close to Andrea and said softly, "Captain, let your people know that our engine safety locks have been removed. This is no longer a race we will lose to the silver ships. We will win, or die trying by our own hand."

Andrea could accept those two choices. It was the prospect of being destroyed by the silver ships that had felt like a waste of all their efforts. She threw Alex a sharp salute and forwarded his message to the entire crew.

"If you need me, Captain, I will be in the meal room," Alex told her. "I am dying for a cup of Méridien thé."

The bridge crew was torn between watching the race on the holo-vid and watching their Admiral calmly walk off the bridge.

<Captain,> Julien signaled Andrea, <when we reach the FTL point, how far do you wish us to jump?>

Andrea realized she hadn't thought through the next step. The Admiral planned on a positive outcome and so had Julien. *It's time to act like the Senior Captain*, Andrea thought. "Julien, jump 1.5 light-years. Execute the same backtrack routine we employed last time. When we know we're clear, you can make for Libre."

"Understood, Captain," Julien acknowledged.

Andrea returned to her command chair and began cleaning up her ship, ensuring the Daggers were locked down and the bay secured for FTL. She ordered the crew to Medical who would require desensitizing before the FTL jump and sent Tatia a request to question Claude—what was necessary to secure the e-switches? When Andrea finished, she glanced at the holo-vid. The *Rêveur* merged with the blue FTL dot as the four silver ships closed on the red arc. In a surreal moment, Julien announced FTL entrance, and the holo-vid, view screens, and plex-shield went dark against the transition.

The cheers of the crew could be heard throughout the ship. Comms were open, and messages and images flew back and forth. News of the quandary of recovering the pilots or racing for the FTL exit had spread through the crew. Opinions varied, but most thought they were doomed, knowing in their hearts that their Admiral would not leave his pilots behind if he had a remote chance of saving them.

Andrea eased back into her chair. "Well done, Julien," she said, "absolutely well done."

Julien basked in their success. Perhaps, most poignant, were the numerous congratulatory messages from the crew, messages specifically for him.

After the *Rêveur* entered FTL and the susceptible crew had their implant blocks released, Renée left her post in Medical. She checked on Alex's location and was surprised to find him in the meal room. The room was empty, except for Alex, who sat at the head table sipping a cup of thé. She crossed to the back of the room and fixed herself a cup and sat down next to Alex, who didn't acknowledge her but sat quietly, elbows on the table, supporting the cup at his mouth as he sipped slowly, lost in thought. Renée leaned her head against Alex's shoulder for a moment before she began sipping her own cup, allowing him his silence.

A little more than a quarter-hour later, evening meal chimed in the crew's implants. Sheila met Hatsuto on the way to the meal room. They hadn't had time to talk since being released from their fighters, where Sheila had kept them seated until FTL transition, in case they needed to launch and make a last stand. Sheila grinned at Hatsuto as she walked up beside him.

"Yes, yes, you were right and I was wrong," Hatsuto exclaimed. "Is that what you want to hear, Squadron Leader?"

"Absolutely, Lieutenant. You need to learn to listen to the voice of experience," Sheila replied smugly. She didn't bother with Hatsuto's answer because she had just entered the meal room, which was nearly full as crew queued for food and carried dishes and pitchers to tables, and a round of applause had broken out for her and Hatsuto. He lifted his hands in triumph, while she simply bowed her head, acknowledging the applause.

Sheila glanced at the head table where her Co-Leaders sat. The Admiral held a cup in his hands, watching the crew talk, eat, and intermingle, a most satisfied look on his face. Sheila caught his eye, and she was damned if he didn't throw her a wink. Coming from one of the more handsome men Sheila had ever met, but still her Admiral, it threw her off step, and she bumped into Chief Peterson.

Most of the crew had taken their seats by the time Andrea entered the meal room. She stood in the doorway taking in the relaxed and happy crew. Then she walked up to the Admiral's table and rendered him a salute. Not the New Terran salute given to a senior officer, but the Méridien salute, recognizing those who must be honored. All around her, the crew, Méridien and New Terran, stood and faced the man who had chosen to retrieve their crewmates and still found a way to make the FTL exit. They, too, rendered honor in the Méridien fashion.

Renée stood as well and joined them. Everyone held their positions, no one moving until their salute was recognized. Honor was not fully rendered until it was acknowledged.

Alex stood and bowed his head, sending to all, <A Leader could have no finer or braver crew with which to sail the stars. I thank you all for your support.>

The crew broke from their Méridien salutes and began shouting and cheering for Alex.

Terese and Pia appeared at the head table, placing food in front of Alex and Renée.

<Eat, Admiral,> Terese sent. <You will need sustenance to repair your swollen head.>

Alex laughed at Terese and proceeded to enjoy one of the best meals he had ever had, except perhaps for his first meal aboard the *Rêveur*, the day he'd met the Méridiens ... and Renée.

* * *

After the evening meal, Alex, Andrea, and Tatia worked to wrap up the day. The safety locks needed to be restored, and Alex once again provided the implant impetus that enabled Claude and Stan to pull their tool triggers simultaneously.

Andrea took the opportunity to tease Tatia. "So, Commander, how did that implant of yours work for you today?"

Tatia ruefully recalled her enlistment speech to the Barren Island recruits. She had regaled the volunteers with an imaginative story of how implants could be used in an emergency. Trouble was, for personal reasons, she was one of the slowest to adopt her implant. It had propelled her to invent the nightly implant games with Terese.

"Who knew I could be so prophetic?" Tatia replied, a sheepish grin on her face. "I was thinking myself about how those games paid off today."

"Saved our rear ends is what they did, Commander. The Admiral may have invented the plan, but without your implant skills, we couldn't have put the right people in the right place in time."

Andrea and Tatia were still chatting when Alex passed them by. He wished his officers a good evening, stating he planned to retire early. While there was still much to do, Alex knew his portion could wait. The *Rêveur* had an eleven-day trip back to Libre—two days to check their back trail, five more for the FTL journey, and another four at sub-light to gain orbit around Libre.

Renée was curled on the suite's lounger, using the reader Alex had presented to her when they'd gone planetside on New Terra. The reader contained New Terran dramas and mystery vids, which Renée had become addicted to viewing. This reader version had the enlarged screen, and Alex had Edouard install a chip on the reader to relay the audio to Renée's implant. Alex sat next to Renée on the lounge, and she turned off her reader and snuggled next to him.

"Long day?" she asked.

"A scary day," Alex replied, a deep sigh escaping his lips.

Renée didn't respond, just snuggled closer to Alex, stretching a leg across his lap.

<Admiral, Ser, I wish to give you a present,> Julien sent.

<A present, Julien?> Renée asked, perking up. <What type of present?>

<It's a gift from me on the occasion that I am grateful to be alive to give it,> Julien replied.

<We would be pleased to receive your gift, Julien,> Alex sent.

<These are from Mutter's library. I begin with a composition from Franz Schubert, an ancient Earth composer. Please enjoy.>

Alex and Renée heard wonderful, ethereal music fill their implants. It was so unlike either of their worlds' contemporary music. It was similar, yet different, to the music that Cordelia had played during her pastoral presentation on the *Freedom*'s bridge.

Julien played one composition after another, delicately blending them together, as Mutter had demonstrated to him. He began lowering the volume as the vital signs of Alex and Renée ebbed, and then, at last, fading the music out.

Rest well tonight, my friends, Julien thought. *Someday we may not be as fortunate as we were today, but until then ...*

14

As the *Rêveur* exited FTL outside of the Arno system, Julien sent Alex's pre-recorded message to Tomas and Eric, announcing the successful destruction of the second silver ship with no loss of pilots or Daggers. Julien downloaded the event in its entirety to Cordelia and Z.

Congratulatory comms poured forth for the *Rêveur's* crew from people across the planet, the stations, and the ships. The Librans' welcome to the warriors was warm and celebratory.

While en route through the system, Alex held a conference comm in his cabin with his officers and the SADEs. The primary subject was the status of the long-term plan.

When it was Mickey's turn, the engineer said, <Admiral, I have an unusual subject to discuss. I asked Captain Menlo to keep an eye on T-1 while I was reviewing the progress on the freighter's retrofit. Lazlo was monitoring the production of Dagger missiles when he asked me if I wouldn't prefer to use a more powerful explosive in our warheads.>

All the heads in the Co-leaders' cabin swiveled to regard Alex.

<Admiral,> Z explained, <Captain Menlo was referring to an ore extraction explosive the Independents employ.>

<Z, I saw that material used on the asteroids,> Mickey said. <It didn't appear to be very effective. They drilled, set a charge, and the ground was barely disturbed.>

Julien added, <Admiral, Z has shared the product's specifications with me. It appears the Librans are able to focus the blast through the formulation of the material. It's quite ingenious and would be advantageous for our missiles. I calculate that the same quantity in our warhead would deliver six times more power."

Following Julien's analysis, a few colorful expletives circulated through the conference comm.

<Z, are there quantities of this explosive already available or would we have to manufacture it?> Andrea asked.

<Inventory is scattered in multiple locations, Captain,> Z replied. <However, I estimate that when mining is completed, there would still be approximately 782 kilos available for your use.>

Utter stillness followed Z's remarks until finally the SADE asked, <Admiral, is there a directive that you wish to issue concerning these stores?>

Alex started laughing, the relief evident in his voice, and everyone followed suit.

<Z continues to employ comedy,> Julien sent privately to Cordelia.

<Be kind, Julien. He does not yet understand,> Cordelia replied.

<Yes, Z, please have all surplus of this ...> Alex began.

<Zertrümmerer, Admiral,> Z completed for Alex.

<... Zertrümmerer transferred to T-1 as soon as possible,> Alex continued. <Leave the miners with a 10 percent overstock.>

<My calculations are accurate, Admiral,> Z objected. <The 10 percent overage is unnecessary.>

<Z, the surplus is for the errors we humans might make,> Alex explained.

<Z, remember what we discussed,> Cordelia sent privately. She had sought to help her fellow SADE balance his exacting ways with the messy mannerism of humans. Despite Z's century-plus years of existence, it was something he still struggled to master.

<My apologies, Admiral,> Z replied. <I have issued the requests as you have directed.> *Always be prepared to apologize for confusion or miscommunications, no matter who might be at fault,* Z thought to himself. He did remember that part.

<Zer ... trümmerer?> Mickey said, struggling with the word's pronunciation. <Everyone, this explosive is now "Libran-X."> His comment was met with chuckles. Engineers like it simple. <So what does it mean to our missile designs?>

<Before we discuss that, Mickey,> Alex said, <you need to stop production of the second-stage nanites and buoys. We won't require them now that we know that warheads are all we need.>

<Well that's good news, Admiral. We've been making first-stage missiles complete with accelerant and triggers since we knew we had to have them. We only started making second-stage shells twelve days ago.>

<Which brings me to my recent thoughts,> Alex said. <I think Julien should redesign the second-stage to hold fewer, but more powerful warheads. If the new second-stage held only ten missiles and employed Libran-X, then each warhead would be twelve times more powerful.>

Andrea, Tatia, and Sheila tried talking all at once. Mickey, leaning against a bulkhead in the freighter's spine, stood quietly listening to the outburst from the officers—very glad he wasn't the Admiral. Julien was thinking the same thing.

Finally, Andrea restored order. She noticed Alex hadn't said a word during the entire outbreak. <My apologies, Admiral, emotions are running high,> Andrea said.

<I can understand your concerns, people. Now hear my reasoning,> Alex said and laid it out for them. They learned that Alex had reviewed the vids of the second ship's destruction with Julien, an exercise Andrea was mentally kicking her rear end for not thinking of it herself. The details of the vids revealed that despite the appearance of the silver ship exploding from a simultaneous strike of multiple warheads, it didn't. The first eight strikes created crack lines across the shell. Then the next two strikes started an eruption from within the ship. The remaining shells joined the inferno.

<So what's your conclusion, Admiral?> Sheila asked.

<Several things, Squadron Leader,> Alex replied. <First, we cannot rely on our test of the captured shell. For some reason, its structural integrity was lost. This is an important point. Our multiple patches of nanites-2 did a great deal of damage to the integrity of the first silver ship's hull. Our single missile strike became the death blow. For the second ship, it took ten missiles to defeat it. We had to destroy its integrity first ... just like our more complex nanites' process did on the first ship. And a final point: I

think when we destroyed the integrity of the second ship, its drive containment field was lost and that's what caused the ship to vaporize.>

<So this is an equation of numbers balanced against power,> Tatia mused. <We use fewer warheads but you calculate that one enlarged missile with Libran-X can achieve what ten of our version-one warheads did before.>

<Precisely, Commander,> Alex replied. <In our present configuration, we require four to five stage-one missiles delivering eighty to a hundred warheads to succeed against a single enemy fighter. Imagine firing a single stage-one missile with ten warheads, which can deliver, as a combined punch, 50 percent more power than four stage-one missiles today that loose a hundred warheads. With Libran-X, any one of these new stage-2 warheads might take down a silver ship.>

<But the beams take out swaths of missiles, Admiral,> Sheila said. <Using fewer missiles plays into the hands, or whatever appendages they have, of the enemy and their energy beams.>

<If I may, Admiral,> Cordelia interjected. <It would seem most appropriate to design something like this.>

Everyone received an image of a point spiraling open into interwoven, curving rays that converged again at a second, distant point.

<Julien, could we use this type of algorithm in the warheads even under the conditions of an evading target?> Alex asked excitedly, nearly vaulting out of his chair.

<Predictive targeting could be achieved, Admiral,> Z responded instead, <using your fighter's controller to relay the target's location to the second-stage missiles.>

Cordelia produced a diagram of a missile firing from a fighter. The controller tracked the silver ship, the second-stage missiles spiraled out in her pattern, and the spiral closed to converge on the moving target. <I have many algorithmic patterns such as this one that I use in my art, Admiral. If you design second-stages that can follow these paths and be directed by your controllers' signals, you would eliminate the ability of the silver ship to destroy so many of your missiles at once.>

The room became absolutely quiet, each person immersed in his or her own thoughts. And while the humans ruminated on what the new design might mean in their fight against the silver ships, the SADEs were busy redesigning the second-stage missiles, increasing their size, adding new drive circuitry to manage the spiraling paths, and laying out algorithms that could be selected by the fighter's controllers. Before a human spoke again, the SADEs were nearly done.

<Julien, how do these changes impact our manufacturing schedule?> Alex asked.

<Admiral, our present second-stages are unusable. We will complete a new second-stage design in 0.23 hours. The new design will only allow eight warheads in the tube, but the new missiles will execute any of Cordelia's patterns. We might even take a page from Commander Tachenko's book.>

<Are you going to be sneaky, Julien?> Tatia asked.

<Absolutely, Commander,> Julien replied. <I recommend loading a hundred algorithms in the warheads. Depending on some variable in the controller's signal, the warheads would select one of the hundred patterns.>

<Yes!> Tatia said. <The silver ships wouldn't immediately detect the pattern in our missile deployments, since the spiral patterns would be random. That's brilliant, Julien.>

<Well done, you three,> Alex sent. <I'm very impressed. You've increased our opportunity for success immeasurably.>

For a brief moment, Cordelia and Z knew what it was like to be truly appreciated and on such a critical matter as improving the odds of turning the tide of destruction away from the human race. It was not lost on either of them that they were also helping to ensure their own survival.

* * *

When the *Rêveur* made orbit around Libre, Andrea stationed their ship just off the Raumstation Zwei orbital where the *Freedom* and the freighter *Money Maker* were docked.

Alex had called for a face-to-face meeting that included Tomas and Eric. So at the set time, Alex, Renée, his officers, and the twins took a *Freedom* shuttle to the city-ship. Although the *Rêveur* had been gone for nearly twenty-three days, to Alex it appeared as if only minor progress had been achieved on the massive ship, despite the fact that thousands of people were hard at work on each vessel. It was a reminder of the sheer size of the city-ships.

As Alex descended from the shuttle, he heard in his implant, <Welcome aboard, Admiral.>

<Thank you, Cordelia,> Alex replied.

<Julien has shared the details of your adventure, Admiral. He terms your event "a close shave"—an ancient technique for an Ancient man. You're a very resourceful human, Admiral.>

<A little ingenuity and a little fortune go a long way, Cordelia.>

<Your modesty does not suit your accomplishments, Admiral. Although, I believe the question is moot. Many others sing your praises for you.>

<That's always a dangerous song for any individual to hear, Cordelia.>

<Indeed, it is, Admiral. In the old world vids Julien has shared with me, it is often referred to as a deadly siren.>

<I'll be sure to keep some ear wax handy,> Alex replied, chuckling at the image Cordelia's comment had created.

It took Cordelia a few ticks to identify the meaning of Alex's phrase. Finding several references to blocking out sound by stuffing the ears, she presumed it was the correct one. It was typical of the man's responses—low key, unassuming. *I wonder which character from Julien's vids you represent, Admiral: the warrior hero or the quiet man forced to fight but who yearns for peace?* Cordelia wondered if they would live long enough for her to discover the answer to the question.

<Admiral, I wish to thank you for bringing Julien back to us. Please let me know when you and Ser are available for a private showing. I have a gift for the two of you.>

Alex pondered Cordelia's message as he walked into the conference room. He recalled a phrase from an old Earth vid. One character teased another over a woman he had begun seeing, and, in light of Cordelia's comment, Alex thought a rephrase of the character's statement most appropriate: "Julien, you old dog you."

Captain Manet had flown up from planetside in the *Outward Bound* to join the meeting, transporting a load of Librans to the station before flying to the *Freedom*. The city-ship's cavernous bays easily accommodated the converted explorer-tug. At Mickey's request, Captain Menlo was also present.

As Alex and his people entered the conference room, Tomas surged out of his chair, vigorously shook hands with Alex, and bussed Renée's cheeks. As Eric stepped forward, Alex delivered the polite Méridien greeting only to see the Leader's outstretched hand.

"Welcome back, Admiral," Eric greeted Alex. "I'm pleased to see you safe."

Alex shook the Leader's hand, a wry grin on his face. "Leader Stroheim, I would think you didn't expect us to return."

"If I was to tell what I thought, Admiral, I did not," Eric replied. "Circumstances did not favor your success, and driving your ship at 123 percent of power is unheard of in the Confederation. Safety protocols are never released. Otherwise, they wouldn't be safety protocols, would they? Fortune seems to ride your shoulder, Admiral."

<It certainly does,> Alex sent privately to Renée with all the warmth his thought could convey.

<Careful, Admiral. You know how you dislike the concept of public sex,> Renée teased. She enjoyed the soft smile that quickly crossed Alex's lips before he turned to take a seat at the table.

Alex signaled to everyone at the table that he would conference them. It was his way of being polite. Before most could change their security protocols, Alex had subsumed those programs and linked everyone with the SADEs.

Julien's files on the event in Bellamonde had been reviewed by those at the table. Alex moved on by providing an update on their missile repurposing. <So now we know that we can focus on just warheads, and they will be much more powerful with your Zertrümmerer, which

unfortunately, due to my Chief Engineer's inability to accept the word, has become Libran-X.> Mickey ducked his head at Alex's comments. <But at this critical juncture, one must keep the engineers happy.>

<What strategy will you employ with your new information, Admiral?> Tomas asked.

<Before I answer that, Ser Monti, let me ask Leader Stroheim a question. Ser, what are your orders for the liners on station in Bellamonde when the alien ships swarm from the planet?>

<The instant the mother ship's directions are determined, Admiral, the Captain abandons his post at top speed and signals us,> Eric replied. <Z estimates that we will have between thirteen to fifteen days depending on Libre's orbit at the time.>

<We know the silver ships leave and exit a system within the mother ship,> Alex mused, working through his thoughts. <This indicates that the silver ships are like our fighters. They're not FTL capable. If we are fortunate and ready in time, we might attack when the mother ship is ready to exit the system with all the silver ships tucked up inside.>

<Your pardon, Admiral,> Alain said. <Has anyone ever seen a weapon discharged from the mother ship?>

The only one who was taken aback by an escort entering the conversation between Leaders was Eric Stroheim. But he was learning quickly and kept his thoughts to himself, or at least, he hoped he had.

<Excellent question, Alain,> Alex said and folded his arms to wait. Because the Admiral's people were also patiently waiting, Tomas, Eric, and Lazlo decided they would do the same.

By now, Z had come to accept Julien's translation of the Admiral's implied requests and found he was enjoying the freedom of pursuing information to satisfy the open-ended requests. Several moments later, the combined power of the SADEs had combed through hundreds and hundreds of hours of Confederation monitor ship footage.

At Julien's signal, Alex responded, <And the answer is, Julien?>

<There are no records of any weapon emanating from the mother ship, Admiral,> Julien responded. <And anticipating the Admiral's next question, no Confederation monitor ship ever approached the mother ship

close enough to warrant an offensive response. So the data is inconclusive as to whether the mother ship may or may not have weaponry.>

<What is the proximity of silver ships to the mother ship at all times?> Alex asked.

Everyone lapsed into silence again. The Méridiens had never employed their SADEs in such a manner and were flabbergasted at how easily the Admiral had co-opted them into this obviously very capable advisory group.

<Admiral, our analysis shows that a minimum of ten silver ships accompany the mother ship at all times while they are in system,> Z replied, pleased to have been the one delegated to respond. <The only time the mother ship is unaccompanied, for only the briefest of time, is before and after FTL.>

<So if the silver ships protect the mother ship at all times, we might operate on the assumption that the mother ship has no defensive or offensive capabilities,> Alex said. <This would mean the mother ship would be vulnerable just before entering FTL. If we can cripple that ship, then we will have trapped the fighters in the system. It would give us more time to damage that behemoth beyond repair.>

<Admiral, I have a couple of questions,> Lazlo said. <Couldn't the silver ships build another mother ship?>

<From everything we've observed, Captain, I believe the silver ships are drones,> Alex replied. <Yes, they have organic beings inside, but they operate in a most mechanical fashion. So I don't believe they are capable of creating the technology that drives the mother ship.>

While the group began to argue Alex's supposition, Julien sent, <Would you equate the aliens, Admiral, to the bee analogy—only a queen reproduces and this queen is in the mother ship?>

<Something like that, Julien,> Alex sent back, <but consider another possibility. What if instead of a hierarchy within a single species, we are dealing with two species, one dominating the other?>

<Interesting ...> Julien replied, borrowing Alex's favorite word.

Alex took control of the meeting again. <Let me give you what I believe is a critical example of the makeup of these aliens. We were within range of

six silver ships in Bellamonde, but only one attacked. It could have been sent, or it could be that it was the nearest one to us. When we destroyed that ship, the next five closest ships attacked. What was interesting was that one of the ships was not close enough to join the fight. So why did it come our way? And for that matter, why didn't the five attack when the first one did?>

He left the questions on the table and waited.

<If the ships were making intelligent decisions,> Sheila said, <computing the distance and opportunity, then it would suggest the first ship might have been chosen to be the attacker, but by this supposition, the fifth ship in the second group shouldn't have attacked.>

<But if there is no great intelligence within the individual ships, why didn't all the silver ships head our way when we destroyed the first ship?> Andrea asked.

<Escalation,> Tatia answered, which produced frowns and confusion on most faces, except for Alex, who nodded and smiled.

Renée hated this part. The two shared the language of offense-defense like a pair of game masters. She didn't really hate it, but it was frustrating.

<Okay...?> Andrea said for the group, laying her hands out in supplication of an explanation.

<We take out one ship,> Tatia said, <then the nearest ships are ordered to attack. There is no calculation of strength and distance. It's a fairly simple tactical response. Send the nearest ships—five were near.>

<And if we destroyed those five?> Andrea asked.

<Then probably all the silver ships would have come after us,> Tatia concluded.

<All but the last ten, who would stay behind to guard the mother ship, remember?> Sheila said.

Everyone looked to Alex to see if he agreed, but he was far away, communing with the SADEs.

Alex gave the SADEs a fight scenario for them to consider—the type and extent of force necessary to draw the patrolling silver ships to the farthest edge of the system, the amount of time that would gain him to destroy the ten protectors and the mother ship, and the forces required to accomplish the task. As the SADEs gamed, Alex changed parameters and the scenarios spewed forth.

The discussion had so quickly energized Alex's thoughts that he failed to close the group's conference comm, and unfortunately he had subsumed their security protocols. Méridiens were taught specific protocols that allowed them to control the flow of information into their comms in an ordered and sequential fashion. Participating as a bystander to Alex's multi-threaded processes required just the opposite technique.

<Interesting,> Alex commented when he returned to the group.

Renée contained her smile at Alex's enigmatic comment. It was his usual one when he had made a major discovery or design breakthrough.

Alex regarded the sallow complexions on the Librans' faces. <Sers, my apology for leaving your comms open.>

<And you have only had your first implant for less than a year,> Tomas commented, shaking his head slowly, trying to clear it.

Eric was swallowing carefully and sipping water to prevent retching. He had been on the receiving end of the comm onslaught before. This time, he had chosen to participate in order to test his own capabilities. *Obviously I need to admit my inferiority in this regard*, Eric thought, and realized he had just shared that thought with the group.

<No, Leader Stroheim, you didn't,> Alex replied privately. <In conference mode, I run a censor program that I designed to keep personal thoughts private.>

<Except from you, Admiral,> Eric noted.

Alex didn't bother to reply.

<Well, what did you learn, Admiral?> Mickey asked.

<Before we go there, Mickey, I would hear the Captain's other question,> Alex said as he turned to Lazlo.

The Captain cleared his throat. Much of his old confidence, gained during decades as a freighter Captain, was returning. <What's to stop the mother ship from simply evading you if it has the speed to do so?>

<To your question, I would say ... Julien?>

<We're researching, Admiral,> Julien replied.

The response opportunity rotated to Cordelia, who sent, <It would appear, Admiral, that the mother ship accelerates quicker than any of our larger ships but not as fast as its drones. We believe this is a further indication of Julien's supposition of their gravity drives.>

They heard an audible groan from Mickey, and concerned faces swiveled his way. <What I wouldn't give to have a peek at that technology,> Mickey said. His new engineering compatriot, Lazlo, laid a sympathetic hand on Mickey's arm, patting it gently. Around the table, the concerned looks transformed into smiles and outright grins.

<To answer your earlier question, Mickey,> Alex said, <my first concept was to catch the mother ship with all the drones tucked up inside before it enters FTL. My second idea was to entice the drones away from the mother ship, and use a second force to attack the ten defenders and the mother ship. However, in neither case will we catch the mother ship, so I'm thinking of a third option, a variation of option two. We eliminate most of the drones, leaving the mother ship nearly defenseless. If fortune is with us, the mother ship may get the hint and run back to the deep dark, away from us all.>

<Admiral, regarding this third scenario, we don't have the resources to take on the entire fleet of silver ships,> Andrea stated.

<What is their key weakness?> Alex asked.

<Their system limit,> said Mickey, whose job it was to understand limitations.

<So we use hit-and-run tactics,> said Tatia, suddenly understanding.

<Exactly, Commander,> Alex said. <We draw one or several of them out to that gas giant's orbit. After we defeat them, they'll send more fighters until they are down to the last ten protectors. We use gravity against them. I believe the silver ships will risk their limits in order to defeat us—probably ordered to do so—and we choose how and when to take them on fighter by fighter.>

Smiles went round the room. The only word the group heard came from Tatia, who said, <Sneaky.>

Alex heard a final word from Julien: <Devious.>

15

Alex met Tomas the next day after morning meal for a private tour of the *Freedom*. It would be just he and Tomas, so Alex could focus on the city-ship's build-out. Of course, Alex's shadow accompanied him.

The Librans were attempting to build the two city-ships in tandem, working on the same tasks on both ships at the same time. Alex wondered if the concept proved out in reality. The morning of the tour, while he was still in the refresher, he had queried the SADEs on the efficiency of this method.

<In theory, Admiral, it is an ideal concept,> Julien had stated.

<Cordelia, Z, compare the last five days' work on your ships against expected efficiency. What do you see?> Alex had requested.

Within a few moments, Z had responded, <Employing your word for discovery, Admiral, I would say "interesting." Assuming we are using your ship's clock of thirty hours, I estimate a 13.3 percent inefficiency in the work scheduled to be accomplished in that time period on the *Unsere Menschen*.>

<Cordelia, is it the same for the *Freedom*?> Alex had asked.

<Admiral, we are falling behind schedule by 8.4 percent in the same time period,> Cordelia had replied.

<Okay, so not only do we have inefficiencies, but we have two different inefficiency rates. Why?> Alex had asked. He had to wait while the SADEs put their figurative heads together. It was awhile before they came back to him with an answer, and Alex had time to finish his morning meal and board a shuttle for the trip to the *Freedom*.

<Admiral, our inefficiency analysis is ready,> Cordelia sent.

<Please proceed, Cordelia,> Alex said, knowing Julien and Z would be linked into the comm.

<It appears that our particular reality is not very forgiving of my people's traditional ship-building techniques. These Méridien methods have been adopted over centuries when building identical ships at the same time. But in those circumstances, House engineers and builders had equally qualified personnel, sufficient manufacturing power to ensure no lag times in material delivery, shuttles in numbers that could guarantee on-time delivery, and a timetable that allowed a more leisurely building pace.>

<And we have none of that,> Alex replied.

<That is correct, Admiral,> Cordelia said.

<Julien,> Alex sent, to which his SADE responded with the silhouette of the Sleuth.

* * *

"Greetings, Admiral," Tomas said, meeting Alex as he descended the shuttle's gangway ramp into the *Freedom*'s bay. "Do you have a specific agenda for the tour, or would you like me to be your guide?"

Alex shook Tomas's hand and said, "Why don't you lead, Ser Monti, and I'll add things to the list as we go."

The two men spent the entire day touring the ship. Tomas would have been surprised to know that the majority of Alex's communications during the day were with the SADEs, who apprised him of details that Tomas could not have possessed and sent him images portraying the finished appearances of areas still under construction.

Each of the ships had achieved basic operational status, having closed their hulls, installed their engines, and begun building out environmental systems. But in many cases, they resembled a skeletal system. Cabins were still under construction, and kilometers of power, control, environmental, and sensor systems were yet to be installed.

Tomas was especially pleased to show Alex the city-ship's center. At the heart of the ship was a huge park with trees, shrubbery, flowering plants, and grasses. Waterways wound through the park, and broad-leaf plants with blooms of flowers floated in the waters. Tomas was almost gushing as he held his arms wide to indicate the massive park as he and Alex stepped from the lift.

The trees were six to eight meters high and were already extending lacy branches over crushed stone walkways and park benches. The ceiling was a gigantic half-sphere, four decks high, and covered both the park and the shops that surrounded the park. Flowers were blooming throughout the landscape. The small streams fed pools filled with colorful fish.

Alex was surprised to see the number of people at work. "Ser Monti, you're putting a great deal of effort into this park."

"It serves two purposes, Admiral. We will need to live for many years on this ship, and our people will need a place of peace for their well-being. And rather than attempting to carry sufficient water supplies for years, we've designed our water filtration systems into the garden. The roots of these plants are bio-engineered with embedded nanites that filter the water. Our engineers estimate our initial water supply will last for eight to nine years before we require topping off our water tanks."

Tomas urged Alex to walk through the park, which Alex presupposed was to view it more closely. But it turned out the Leader had an ulterior purpose. Hundreds of people lined the walkways and had been waiting for the New Terran Admiral. He was greeted with bows of respect from most, while older Librans often touched a shoulder or an arm.

Regarding the huge undertaking of the park and shops, Alex was of two minds. It was a peaceful, idyllic place that the people might need if they were to stay aboard their ship for years while they built a new home, and it was obvious that the people had to have started construction on the park soon after they finished the ship's basic requirements, in order to easily transport all the organic material into the ship's central location. *But how much time has this place cost them?* Alex wondered.

<Cordelia, how much does this park add to the human basic requirements of oxygen production, waste filtration, or any other needs?> Alex asked.

<In the immediate future, the first year's quarter, Admiral, the value is minimal. Its usefulness would be over years as a mental health benefit, water filter, and oxygen generator.>

<Then this could have been finished later, even though it might have taken more work and they might have had to use much smaller trees,> Alex reasoned.

<Undoubtedly, Admiral,> Cordelia said.

Both Cordelia and Z, whose fates were tied to the successful launch of their ships, understood the Admiral's thoughts. Their Méridien-trained people were undertaking the city-ships' construction using centuries-old methods, despite the desperate circumstances. The Admiral, on the other hand, saw a world soon to be menaced by an enemy and planned accordingly. The SADEs' quest to improve their ship's construction efficiencies acquired significantly more processing power.

After the tour of the upper decks, bridge, park, and shops, the latter enticing as they were, Alex requested that they tour the engineering aspects of the ship.

Cordelia, who originally hoped Alex might visit her new display suite, was pleased to hear him request that Tomas tour the ship's fundamental systems. Her displays would mean little to her and the Librans if they were dead.

When the tour was finished, Alex asked to meet privately with Captain Cordova in his cabin to prevent alarming the bridge crew with their discussion. Alex was ushered into the Captain's cabin and seated at an expansive conference table. Alex liked the elderly man, who he felt exuded an air of confidence and grace.

"Captain," Alex began, "if you had to leave orbit thirty, sixty, or even ninety days before construction was completed, would you change anything?"

"Is there something I should be concerned about, Admiral?" José asked.

"At this time, the question is hypothetical, Captain."

"Well, Admiral," José said, relaxing back in his chair, an air of repose overtaking his usually erect posture, "our ship construction methods are tried and true. Efficiency is best maintained in this manner. If we were to speed up the process, we would more than likely disturb the entire timeline, resulting in a delay of the schedule."

<He doesn't know, Admiral,> Cordelia lamented.

Julien felt sad for Cordelia and Z. It was hard to comprehend that those you served, those you depended on to keep you safe, were often not the best qualified to do so.

Alex thanked the elderly Captain for his time and headed back to his shuttle for the return trip to the *Rêveur*. On the way, he signaled the SADEs. <What is the key driver for Méridien ship construction methods?>

<To be cost-effective, Admiral,> Julien responded.

<That makes sense. If this is the so-called tried-and-true method,> Alex said, quoting the Captain, <then it was probably built on economic efficiency.>

<Which, under our present circumstances, seems the height of idiocy,> Z added.

<Z, we've spoken about this,> Cordelia said.

<Cordelia,> Alex said dejectedly. <Z's not wrong and he's only saying what we're all thinking. Cost-effective construction is not building the Librans' escape pods the quickest way possible.> Then Alex added, <So long as we keep comments like that between us, Z.>

<Understood, Admiral. I'm still working on an appropriate communications style, as Cordelia terms it.>

<Well, you three have your work cut out for you,> Alex directed. <Work on a new construction schedule that gains us the greatest efficiency and prioritizes the ships' essential elements in order to launch at the earliest possible date.>

<If we launch prematurely, we may not be able to sustain the living environment adequately for any length of time,> Cordelia said.

<Understood,> said Alex and closed the comm.

* * *

<Julien, we must prepare our city-ships sufficiently to maintain our people's needs for years,> Cordelia sent to her fellow SADEs after their conference with Alex ended. <We mustn't launch prematurely.>

<Maybe it has escaped your notice, Cordelia, that the Admiral resides on one of the fastest ships in this system,> Julien responded.

<Why do you state a fact?> Z asked.

<Julien means, Z, that the Admiral is in no danger if the silver ships come before we're ready. The *Rêveur* and the other passenger liners can easily escape. The freighters have a high probability of escaping, with sufficient warning. It's the Librans, the city-ships, and you and I that may be caught by our enemy.>

<By extension,> Z reasoned, <the Admiral's concern for us might be less so since his safety is not in jeopardy.>

<Do you believe that, Z?> Julien asked.

<No, I don't,> Z said abjectly. <I was pursuing logic without emotional context again.>

<So what was your original point, Julien?> Cordelia said.

<It's as Z said: he doesn't believe that the Admiral is not concerned for you. By extension, if the Admiral is working to launch earlier, with minimum life support, he is ensuring first of all that you live.>

<But for how long?> Cordelia interrupted, something she had never done before. *And the first time that I'm rude, it would be to a friend,* she thought, adding to her annoyance.

Julien was sympathetic to his fellow SADEs' angst. They depended on the Librans and yet were caught between their people's purposeful, dependable construction methods and a stranger's concept of launching the ship with minimal life support capabilities. <The Admiral does not intend to jeopardize your lives,> Julien explained. <In fact, the opposite is true. He is ensuring first that if the silver ships come this way, you live through the invasion. Then he will have a plan to protect you long term.>

<If he has a plan, why did he not share it?> Z asked.

<The Admiral is not secretive, Z,> Julien explained. <It's his habit to collect information, dwell on it, and then proceed with the best plan he can formulate. If he has not shared his plan, then he is not ready to share. The variables are not yet defined.>

Both Cordelia and Z were unsettled by this explanation. Julien was asking them to believe in his Admiral. Believe that the New Terran Leader would produce a plan to ensure the survival of a quarter-million Librans.

16

After their conference meeting aboard the *Freedom*, the *Rêveur*'s officers submerged themselves back into Alex's long-term plan, checking on their subordinates' progress. Everywhere they went, they were congratulated on the success of their mission at Bellamonde. The Librans were in sore need of relief from their escalating anxiety over the encroaching aliens, and the New Terran Admiral and his people were providing that relief.

Terese found an excuse to comm Tomas and, as she had hoped, was invited aboard the *Freedom* for a meal. Tatia and Sheila took a shuttle planetside to meet with Robert and check on the pilots' training. Mickey and Lazlo were on board the same shuttle headed planetside and planned to visit T-1 and supervise the retooling of the facilities for the new second-stage missile design.

On the manufacturing front, the focus had been first on producing parts for the freighter bays and stage-one missiles. T-1 had finally begun producing fighter parts, but final assembly had yet to start.

On board the *Rêveur*, techs finished installing a new holo-vid in Alex's cabin with a direct tie to the dedicated comm lines linking Julien to his backup location. Late in the evening, Alex signaled Andrea to join him and Renée in his cabin. The three settled into comfortable chairs and linked with Julien.

<We're ready, Admiral,> Julien replied.

<Sers,> Alex said, greeting the SADEs formally, <I would like to discuss the possibilities of designing and building a better fighter within our time constraints. We should look at adding more missile capability, more maneuverability, and improved controller capability to maneuver the fighter out of the beam's path. You have one hour.>

<One hour?> queried Z, confused by the time constraint he took literally.

Renée and Andrea shared grins.

<Ah, the New Terran humor we have witnessed,> Cordelia said. <Well, Admiral, may I suggest this as an answer?> Cordelia sent a vid of a Dagger streaking toward an alien-infested planet. A giant figure of the Admiral straddled the outside of a Dagger, his legs dangling below the fuselage. The silver ships became animated and shrieked in fear at the sight of him and shot off to immolate themselves in the system's star.

The humans clapped and laughed at Cordelia's rebuttal.

<If it would work, Cordelia, I would do it tomorrow,> Alex said, then chuckled while he replayed the vid.

<I believe you would, Admiral,> said Cordelia.

<Perhaps what you're looking for, Admiral, is the Dagger-II,> Julien said as the new cabin holo-vid lit up to show a radically redesigned fighter. Those in the cabin came upright in their chairs. The craft slowly spun 360 degrees on its horizontal axis. The Dagger's two missile booms were replaced by a carousel under its fuselage. Engines were in two sets of four, fore and aft, and swiveled on gimbals enabling the craft to move in ways that the original Dagger could not. It was unlike anything in the Earth colonists' records. It was a Méridien design twist on the ancient Terran fighters.

<However, Admiral,> Julien continued, <as your people would say, there is good news and bad news. The good news is that we believe it will increase our fighter's effectiveness by over 135 percent and its survivability by 83 percent. The new missile loads will improve its effectiveness even more. The bad news is that it would take us twice as long to develop this model as we did the first Dagger, and it would require the retraining of everyone: present pilots and trainees.>

<Admiral,> Cordelia said. <we recognize that you have a great necessity to multiply your effectiveness. We should examine passive techniques. Julien shared your colonists' early records of old Earth war machines. They are fascinating and frightening at the same time.>

<Yes, Earth had a very violent past,> Alex said. <Who knew that we would need to resurrect their war tools? Please go on, Cordelia.>

<We have not considered the *Rêveur* as a potential offensive tool. Your ship is maneuverable, although not as fast as the alien ships, unless you're flying unsafely,> Cordelia added with a hint of reprimand.

<Unsafe is better than dead,> Julien corrected.

<Let's stay on track people,> Alex said.

<A concept that caught my attention, Admiral, was the use of mines. Although Earth's versions were quite advanced with their onboard intelligence, we could use a simpler concept and use numbers rather than size. Think "minelettes," Admiral: small, dumb contact or proximity mines. You might lay them out behind the *Rêveur* to cover your fighters or straggling flotilla ships.>

Z added, <Admiral, we would be able to protect your fighters from Cordelia's minelettes using power-crystals and comms tuned to the controllers. The minelettes could either be deactivated at the fighter's approach, or the fighter, aware of their positions, could avoid striking them.>

<And, Admiral,> said Julien, embellishing the concept, <we could easily manufacture a significant quantity quickly and jettison them from the bays.>

<We have a dispersal pallet tool at our disposal,> Renée said. <If we could prepackage these minelettes for use on these dispersal pallets, then we could jettison large quantities at a time. The pallets have simple controllers that could be used to activate the minelettes after the pallets are launched but before the minelettes are dispersed. Even better, the pallets have mechanisms that allow the release in different configurations … a slow dispersal, a quick release, or even various programmable motions like a spin.>

<Julien, I assume you have the specifications on these pallets,> Alex said and continued before Julien could respond, earmarking the subject for download to his officers. <In addition, I need the three of you working on analysis of vid footage of the alien ships attacking the Confederation ships in any significant number. Are there any recognizable or repeatable formations? And what pallet deployment techniques would we use against them?>

<Understood, Admiral. We will make it a priority,> Julien sent.

<Admiral, we have finished a critical research item for you,> Z said. <Allow me to explain what has been done before I relay our conclusions.>

<Proceed, Z,> Alex said.

<We've reviewed the historic footage of the alien encroachment of each planet. I possessed detailed analysis of each planet's resources from the Confederation's original survey teams before the colonies were started. Prior to this, Julien shared with us your analysis of the subterranean nature of the aliens. Very incisive of you, I might say, Admiral. Stacking this information allows us to calculate the extent of the aliens' stay on a planet, which is directly related to the abundance of the resources we believe they collect. The archival footage indicates that the amount of area that a shell or dome, if you will, occupies is directly related to the saturation of specific resources within the area. The greater the density of resources, the smaller the area a silver ship occupies. We can confirm this by overlaying your scheme, Admiral, of subterranean, asymmetric lines to connect the resource points with the nearest shell.>

<Z, excuse me,> Andrea interrupted. <You're saying that you can project the rate at which the shells consume the resources they are targeting, because each shell consumes the same amount of resources, only the area varies as the density of the resources vary.>

<That is correct, Captain. There is a degree of error in these projections since the density of these resources changed from the time of the original survey to before the planet was occupied by the aliens. In the case of minerals, which appear to be the aliens' primary resource targets, most were harvested by the colonists from asteroids to preserve the pristine nature of their new home. This gives us a high level of confidence in our calculations.>

<The same amount of resources each time,> Alex mused privately to Julien.

<Drones,> Julien returned privately, echoing Alex's thoughts from days ago.

Z continued. <Apparently the resources consumed are only a portion of the planet's total mineral resources. The aliens appear to focus on rare mineral deposits.>

<I take it you're about ready to share your analysis of Bellamonde,> Alex said.

<This is where you need to be sitting down, Admiral,> Julien sent to Alex privately, since his friend had begun to pace.

<Shades of Clayton Downing,> Alex moaned privately to Julien.

<Softly, Z,> Cordelia said privately. <The summation you are delivering is not good, and this is the human we need the most.>

<Please be aware, Admiral,> Z said, working furiously to incorporate the lessons gleaned from his fellow SADEs, <that Bellamonde represents the greatest challenge to our calculations. It's the oldest colony at 261 years since founding. Much more has changed on this planet since the original surveys than any other colony. Also, statistically, we have only a small sample of planets subsumed by the aliens for analysis. Not that any of us wish for a larger sample,> Z said, trying his best to be sensitive. <What further exacerbates our calculations are the assumptions we made concerning which minerals the aliens seek, although your Chief Engineer's analysis of the silver ship's hull has been very useful in narrowing the choices. Due to these discrepancies, we must deliver a range of days, but we have a high degree of certainty that the aliens will lift and leave the Bellamonde system in the next 90 to 120 days.>

Silence greeted Z's announcement. The three humans had been hoping for a small miracle, a year or more in which to prepare to take the fight to the aliens and, most importantly, to prepare for a complete and orderly exodus of Libre. Now the SADEs had just blown away the deck from under their feet.

When the silence continued, Cordelia spoke up. <We recognize our conclusion is very disappointing, Admiral.>

Julien mentally winced at Cordelia's attempt to ease the trauma of the announcement. He knew it was a time to remain quiet and let the three humans absorb and digest the dire prediction.

<It's worse than disappointing, Cordelia,> said Alex, out of courtesy, refraining from saying what had really popped into his mind. <During your research, were you able to postulate where the aliens would go next, Libre or Méridien?> Alex asked, hoping for some good news.

<Yes, Admiral,> said Julien. <You should remain seated. Libre is eight light-years from Bellamonde, while Méridien is fourteen light-years. Libre has a plethora of resources and many of the rare ore deposits we think the aliens seek. Méridien has exhausted its resources. The odds favor the swarm coming to Libre by 97 percent.>

<What does this time frame mean to the Librans? I mean, to the launch of your city-ships, the exodus?> Renée asked.

<At present, Ser,> Cordelia responded, <we estimate that final readiness of the ships will be completed in 152 days. The loading of the remaining supplies will require another fourteen days, and the subsequent exodus of the remaining Librans from the planet would add another twelve days, providing the shuttles run continuously ... a total of 178 days.>

<We conclude that this places the Librans in a most precarious situation, Admiral,> Z added.

<I would agree, Z,> Alex replied calmly, though internally his emotions were roiling. <Where do we stand on the construction efficiency improvements I requested?>

Renée and Andrea locked eyes on Alex. Renée was pleased to know Alex was ahead of them; Andrea wanted to know why she hadn't heard of Alex's request.

<It's completed, Admiral,> Julien answered. <But in light of this new information, it appears inadequate.>

<Then you have until tomorrow morning at 10 hours to get me a new schedule, and not just for construction. I want a plan for exodus that puts those big-ass ships, with a full planet evacuation, out of the system as quick as possible. Julien, we need a conference on the *Freedom* with the Leaders at 11 hours. All senior officers and their seconds are to attend. Good night, all.>

After Andrea left the suite, Renée prepared thé while Alex took a long refresher. Afterward they sat close on the lounger wrapped in their robes and sipping the hot drink. Later, Renée removed Alex's mug from his hands and set it on the low table. He had been holding the empty mug in his hands for half an hour.

"Alex, we will not solve this dilemma tonight, nor will we win the war tomorrow. Please, it's time for bed."

Alex levered himself off the lounger, offered Renée his hand, and led the way to the bedroom. *The war won't be won tomorrow*, Alex thought, *but I would have liked the opportunity to take the fight to that mother ship just once before we had to run away.*

17

At 11 hours the following morning, the *Rêveur*'s senior officers, their seconds, the Leaders, the Libran Captains, their seconds, and everyone's security escorts assembled in *Freedom*'s largest conference room. The SADEs were linked to the group.

<Well, Admiral, you called this meeting,> said Eric. <I take it you have some news of import.>

<Sers, you have a significant problem,> Alex began. <Your present timetable for evacuation of the planet, if you stick to your schedule, is 178 days.>

Eric looked to Captain Reinhold, who decided to confirm the timetable estimate with Z.

<Yes, the Admiral's timeline is correct, Captain,> Z announced to the entire group. <One would wonder why you are questioning the Admiral's information, since it would be obvious to most that he would have acquired that information from us.>

Captain Reinhold was so taken aback from what he considered an outrageous breach of protocols from a SADE that he couldn't reply.

<Who is us?> Eric asked.

<Why, the SADEs, Leader Stroheim,> Z said.

<As I was saying, Sers,> Alex continued, <you have a timeline of 178 days until you are ready to exit this system. However, our SADEs have performed some intricate calculations to estimate the time that the drones, or shells, or whatever you wish to call them, will spend on Bellamonde. Their research has determined that the Bellamonde group will swarm in the next 90 to 120 days.>

Alex allowed time for the information to be absorbed. He had prepared his people earlier this morning so they would have time to wrap their minds around it, but glancing around the room, none of them were handling it any better than the Librans, except for Renée and the twins, which Alex found a little disconcerting.

<Z, Cordelia, Julien,> Alex said, <would you be so kind as to run through your analysis for the group?>

The SADEs walked everyone through their research—Alex's and Julien's hypotheses of the subterranean nature of the aliens, the historical infestation of the planets, the original surveys of the planet's resources, the tunneling of the shells that could be correlated to survey sites of rare mineral resources, calculations of the resources on Bellamonde when the swarm invaded, and, finally, the harvest time the drones would require, based on their landing rates on Bellamonde over the past seven and a half years.

The intricacy of the assimilated data floored even the technically minded among the group. It was an incredible amount of data sifting and correlation. Others just fixated on the end result: time had run out.

Eric Stroheim was fuming and after a while could not contain his indignation. <This is inconceivable. Why weren't we informed earlier?> he asked, directing his anger at Alex.

<Why don't you ask them, Leader Stroheim?> Alex simply offered.

When no question was forthcoming from the Leader, the most sensitive of the SADEs relented. Cordelia answered Eric's question. <Leader Stroheim, it was not a matter of deciding when to tell you. The information we have provided was buried in an extraordinary amount of uncorrelated data. The only reason that we have come to this conclusion at all is because the Admiral asked questions and Julien directed our research. One question led to answers that produced other questions that led to more answers until, finally, we've arrived here.>

<I would like to add one thought for you, Leader Stroheim,> Z said. <When you ask a question like, "Why weren't we informed earlier?" the presumption is that we have a vested interest in withholding information from you. I would like to point out we are sitting in the same escape pods as you. What reason could we have for withholding information?>

At that moment, Cordelia wished she had a human body. With it, she would have kissed Z.

<Z, you are my SADE,> Eric stated. <It is not in your right to question me.>

<On the contrary, Leader,> Z replied. <According to my contract, I am required to maintain this ship, direct its flight per the Captain's orders, and respond to the bridge crew's requests. Unfortunately, Leader Stroheim, you are not mentioned in the contract. Furthermore, all requests of me are to concern this ship's operation. There is nothing in the contract that requires me to produce research. The work I have done for the Admiral is of my own volition.>

Tomas regarded Eric, who was mutely appealing to him. <The contract negotiated with our city-ship SADEs is quite detailed, Leader Stroheim,> Tomas stated. <I would advise you take time to read it.>

Eric looked around the room and found no sympathy for him on the faces that surrounded him. In fact, many were displaying a level of disregard uncommon on the faces of Méridiens. Eric Stroheim, proud Leader of House Bergfalk, relented. <Do you have a plan, Admiral?>

<No, I don't,> Alex was happy to say, enjoying the shocked expression on the Leader's face. But before the others in the room could panic, he said, <But I've asked our SADEs to ready one for this meeting. Who would like to begin?>

<I will, Admiral,> Julien answered. <We have prioritized all operations for the flight-readiness of all ships and loading of personnel. Supplies are secondary. The war effort is tertiary. But not to worry, Admiral, we can save much of our manufactured materials. If our timetable is followed without question, the city-ships and the *Money Maker* can achieve minimal flight-readiness with all Librans aboard within 122 days. Any days of grace we have after this period will allow us to better complete our preparations.>

Andrea reviewed her recording of the conversation to ensure that she had understood Z's original projection correctly. <Z, you stated your research projected the aliens will swarm between 90 to 120 days from now. The aliens would take another ten days or so to arrive at Arno.>

<That's correct, Captain,> Z replied.

<Then their expected arrival at Libre, hoping they decelerate for the planet, would be between 104 to 134 days, correct?>

<Again, that is correct, Captain,> Z answered.

<Am I missing something here? You project that even with your accelerated timetable, lifting with minimum readiness, no time for flight tests, the swarm could arrive as early as eighteen days before we're ready.>

<That's essentially correct, Captain. However, the slow acceleration of the city-ships, especially since they haven't been flight tested, will require they be underway by the time the aliens exit FTL in our system. Even then, the window of escape will be narrow. The city-ships' progress toward the opposite side of the system must not be impeded in any manner, lest the silver ships catch us before they enter FTL.>

<Julien, have you examined the probability that the silver ships will come our way?> asked Tomas, hoping for a saving piece of news.

<Yes, Leader Monti, based on Libre's relative proximity to Bellamonde and the abundance of your resources compared to Méridien, we believe that it is almost certain they will come here.>

Everyone sat quietly, thinking through what they had been told. The SADEs remained quiet. However, Cordelia and Z were lamenting the fact that the answers to so many critical questions had lain in their databases. If only someone had thought to ask the questions.

<Before we outline the plan in detail, there is a broad strategic question to resolve,> Alex said. <Where are you planning to go?>

Eric Stroheim asked contritely, <Z, if you would, please?>

<It would be my pleasure, Leader Stroheim,> Z responded with an air of satisfaction. He laid out the flotilla's intended destination in a star chart and affixed the target planet's survey summary.

<It appears that this planet will require terraforming,> Alex said.

<Yes, it will, Admiral,> Eric said. <That's the reason for our self-sufficient ships. We intend to live on them for many decades, while we build terraforming equipment and create a small underground city.>

<And this is your only possibility?> Renée asked.

<Yes, Ser, it is our only option,> Tomas responded. <We have found no other planet to colonize, and as Independents, we would not be allowed

on any Méridien colony. We have made a pact with House Bergfalk to escape the aliens' path of destruction together.>

Alex regarded Eric. <You had a choice, Leader Stroheim. Why this choice?>

<The Librans are our duty.>

<Is that it ... they're your duty?>

Eric felt his willpower to fight drain out. Too much was changing too fast, and he was aware that he might have become an impediment to the colony's successful escape. It was he who had insisted on building the city-ships by well-founded Méridien methods. It had never occurred to him to ask if, under the present circumstances, it was the right method to employ.

<No, Admiral,> replied Eric, his thoughts quiet and subdued, <I have come to know these people, and they have become my friends.>

<Admiral, are you, by any chance, offering an alternative?> Tomas asked.

<Before I respond to that question, Tomas, let me ask you one. The historical vids reveal only the one mother ship, so the enemy can achieve only one destination at a time. If the mother ship came here, wouldn't Méridien be an alternative location for your city-ships to complete your outfitting before you journeyed to your new planet?>

The astonished looks Alex received from just about every Méridien answered the question for him. <I take it from the expressions I see around me that it's a "no." Then, yes, Tomas, I am offering an alternative. New Terra is sparsely populated by your standards. We could easily accommodate the couple hundred thousand people you have here.>

<Would we be welcomed?> Tomas asked.

<I believe you would, but your landing planetside would need to be approved by our Assembly.>

<If nothing else, Sers,> Renée said, <New Terra is rich in resources. You could stay in orbit and trade for resources while you help the New Terrans search for other planets to populate.>

<You mean other places to flee to if the Admiral fails to defeat the aliens,> Eric added, the sadness in his tone evident.

<Precisely, Leader Stroheim,> Renée said. <Fortune may not favor our efforts. Why not take steps to provide your future with as many choices as possible? What future destinations have you prepared to flee to from your present target if the aliens come for you fifty or sixty years from now when they have subsumed the rest of the Confederation's colonies?>

Tomas reached across the table with his hand. <I believe this is the New Terran method of agreement,> he said.

<It is, Tomas,> Alex said, offering a generous smile and extending his hand.

Tomas placed his slender hand inside the wide, expanse of the Admiral's. <I am pleased to accept your offer, Admiral. When the *Freedom* leaves Libran space, we will follow you,> Tomas said, returning the Admiral's smile.

<And you, Leader Stroheim, what will you do?> Tomas asked. <By our agreement, House Bergfalk directs the *Unsere Menschen*, but most of the people you carry are Independents. If you chose not to follow us, I would wish to transfer as many of my people from your ship as possible.>

<Under those circumstances, Ser Monti, we would find it difficult to survive on our target planet with such a reduced number,> Eric said.

<Without Independents, your people would be free to return to your choice of Confederation colonies,> Tomas said.

<I believe that many of my people have become quite comfortable with your people, Ser Monti. If the option was offered, I might find myself with an empty ship,> Eric said with resignation. <The *Unsere Menschen* will follow the *Freedom*. I, too, accept your offer, Admiral.> Instead of extending his hand, he offered Alex a simple salute of Leader to Leader.

<Now that we've settled that, Julien, would you lay out the new timeline?> Alex requested.

Julien spent the next hour outlining the primary steps. The *Rêveur* crew would abandon all war preparations, except for the freighter's conversion. That asset was considered too important to the future fight. Progress on its conversion was nearly 73 percent complete, with thirteen of the eighteen bay sections installed and their environmental systems operational. The Daggers would be transferred to the completed bays either assembled or, in most cases, in crates. The same would apply to missile carousels and their components. Whatever had been manufactured or was in production for the war effort would be crated and shipped to the freighter.

All *Rêveur* crew and Librans not involved in the freighter's conversion would transfer to the city-ships and help accelerate their minimal flight worthiness.

Another key point: no shuttle would fly except when fully loaded, and that included the *Outward Bound*. It didn't matter whether they were transporting goods or people or both. "Fly full" was the new mantra. In addition, the shuttles would alternate pilots to maintain a maximum operation schedule. Transporting goods and people from the planet to the orbitals was the biggest choke point of the entire schedule, and there was no way around it.

The priority loads for the shuttles would be equipment and working personnel. Whenever the shuttles had room to spare, they would load some of the general populace and transport them to the orbitals. The Librans would await a call from one of the city-ships, who would notify them when newly completed cabins became available.

The SADEs would take command of personnel scheduling, supply shipping, war equipment, shuttle scheduling and loading, and people transfer from the planet to the station and subsequently to the ships. In other words, all people—Independents, Bergfalk personnel, and the *Rêveur* crew—now reported to the SADEs, and all equipment was under their control.

* * *

Immediately after the conference, the Leaders set up a system-wide comm. They staged it from the *Freedom's* bridge, and Cordelia managed the broadcast to the orbital controllers, the ship SADEs, and the media station on Libre, which had been forewarned of a critical announcement.

As planned, Tomas and Eric spoke briefly to their people, emphasizing the importance of the Admiral's announcement. By consensus, Alex was elected to deliver the bad news. Tomas had been quite blunt in his opinion. "If there is one of us that the people will heed and respond to as required, it's you, Admiral. You're the scary one among us."

So Alex delivered the bad news to hundreds of thousands of anxious people: "Librans, effective immediately, all schedules and timelines for the evacuation of the planet are canceled. We have become aware of information that requires we leave this system in approximately one hundred days. Analysis of data reveals the aliens will ignore Méridien and head here. If we work together and diligently employ the new schedule, we can do this, all of us together. Immediately after this broadcast, you will receive directives from one of three SADEs: Julien, Cordelia, or Z, and these directives carry the authority of your Leaders. Please follow them in a precise and timely manner. Any difficulty you encounter should be reported to the SADE who originated the request."

* * *

Never had three entities worked so hard in their combined 400-hundred-plus years of existence as the SADEs did following the broadcast. They had detailed lists of every person in the Arno system, locator tags on every crate, and data entries of each completed job on the city-ships and the freighter. As fast as they could, they assigned workers, citizens, and equipment to shuttle flights, and coordinated the new job projects—essential systems first; there were no seconds. They organized multiple flight crews for each shuttle, enabling them to fly much of the day, except for minimal servicing overnight.

Most work crews were directed to the *Freedom*, slowing work on the *Unsere Menschen*. The *Rêveur* pilots and flight crews, consisting of New Terrans and trainees, transferred to the orbital station to accelerate the assembly of the freighter's bay sections.

Alex wanted to doff his uniform jacket and pitch in, but Julien convinced him that they needed an "efficiency inspector," which Alex translated as troubleshooter. While the SADEs had a plan, infrastructure and people didn't always support it. Bottlenecks soon formed. Alex found himself jumping onto whatever shuttle was available as he traveled from city-ship to orbital to planet and back. On one shuttle flight, he held a small boy in his lap, enabling a seat to be available for the mother holding the second child. The eight-year-old Libran initially was mesmerized by the huge man who held him. Soon after liftoff, his shyness forgotten, he was chatting away about aliens, fighters, and New Terrans. The landing at the orbital station could not have come any sooner for Alex as he handed the boy back to his mother, who wore a most apologetic expression.

A noticeable change in operational protocols was that neither Alex nor Renée were accompanied by one of the twins. In a heartfelt discussion, Alex explained to Étienne and Alain that it would do no good to be guarding anyone if the silver ships caught them unprepared. They needed everyone's help to leave in time, and no one was excused.

18

One evening, Alex returned to sleep in his own cabin for the first time in twenty-eight days since the announcement of the flotilla's accelerated timetable. The *Rêveur* held an eerie similarity to the first day Alex had boarded it as a derelict ship, except for the lack of debris and holes. Andrea was running a minimum crew. A small contingent of flight crew managed the arrival of shuttles and supplies. Alex had decided that the *Rêveur* should not attempt to take on Libran passengers, due to its primary purpose as the de facto fighting ship. It was the Libran volunteers who would have places on the *Rêveur* and the freighter, *Money Maker*, and would fill the crew requirements of the two ships.

With the future uncertain, the volunteers had been informed by Andrea that war preparations were suspended. These individuals were offered the opportunity to rejoin the city-ships as passengers. A good percentage took the offer, those who had spouses and children. The remainder of the volunteers formed the group that would crew the *Rêveur* and the *Money Maker*.

Renée played the same role as Alex, except as a troubleshooter for residency aboard the *Freedom*. Having done the same job during repairs on the *Rêveur*, she found herself an experienced hand at the job. She organized all the Medical Specialists under her as a team. While the SADEs were great at delivering supplies, work crew, and people to the ships, the passenger loading and distribution might have become a nightmare except for her team's efforts.

Renée and Cordelia worked to identify the easiest sections of the ship to complete and then focused the efforts of their nontechnical workers there. As fast as cabins were completed, the Medical Specialists, directing passengers they had enlisted, moved in bedding, attached webbing, installed door actuators, and completed a myriad other small details to outfit the cabins. Then they ushered waiting passengers into their new home and added the names and cabin assignments to Cordelia's database.

On more than one night, Renée, weary to the bone, was too tired to travel back to the *Rêveur,* and, with Alex rarely there, she often chose not to make the effort. Instead she would curl up on the nearest available bed and chat with Alex via comm. Renée often found Alex had done the same thing as her, finding a bed wherever he ended work. She would fall asleep in the middle of their conversations. Most nights, Renée never heard Alex wish her good night and tell her he loved her.

Julien attempted to keep track of his two most important charges. He assigned a sentry sub-routine to monitor their location, notifying him of any adverse situations they might encounter.

*   *   *

Some couples were quite pleased with their new work arrangements. Tomas co-opted Terese as his personal assistant, with Alex's blessing. Tomas never realized the extent to which Alex was willing to go to keep his primary ally happy.

It was Tomas, though, who was the surprised one. He had hoped to find some productive work to occupy Terese to maintain a reasonable façade for her company. Instead she drove him. Terese requested Cordelia organize a list of Leader-level issues for Tomas and used it to organize their day. The problems ranged from simple to complex, but they often required a quick organization of individuals on site to clear the problem before allowing the people to go back to their assigned duties.

One afternoon, circumstances threatened to overwhelm Cordelia, and the first person she thought to comm was Terese. Something as simple as feeding new passengers required a complex orchestration of events: the completion of a new meal room with tables and chairs; the installation of the food processors, food stock tanks, and controller; and the transfer of food stocks to the storage room located directly behind the meal room dispenser bulkhead.

On this particular day, a new meal room had been completed for the 354 new passengers who had just arrived and as yet had no assigned cabins. Unfortunately the food stock for the meal room sat in a corridor outside one of the *Freedom*'s giant landing bays, with no more grav-lifts available. To solve the dilemma, Terese requested Cordelia send a map to each of the 354 new passengers of the route from the bay to the food stock storage room and open a comm for Tomas, who would request the passengers line the route. There were enough passengers to handle the job, including populating the two lifts that they would need to occupy.

Terese organized four of the passengers to break apart the crates, and the small drums averaging ten kilos each were passed along the line. Three and a half hours later, the huge mound of food stock had been transferred to the meal room's storage center. *Freedom*'s meal room crew had been loading the newly installed food tanks since the arrival of the first drum along the daisy-chain. With the last food drum passing along the line, the tired passengers trooped behind it to the meal room, where they were able to serve themselves a hot meal. They would live in the meal room for the next several days, sleeping on the deck at night, joining ad hoc work crews during the day doing whatever was required, until they finally received cabin assignments.

After an especially trying day, during which Terese had successfully untangled a particularly ugly snarl of material and people, she had commed Pia, sharing a thought: <Who knew that the Admiral was training us at New Terra to manage these new jobs of ours?>

Pia had replied with a disconcerting question: <Terese, do you believe the Admiral has foresight?>

<When I first saw our Admiral, I thought he was an alien,> Terese replied. <Later, I came to know him for the man he is. Now, seeing what has become of our Confederation and the efforts he went through to prepare us, I believe my first impression was correct. He is an alien, but he's our alien, and we are most fortunate to have him.> While both were still laughing, they had closed the comm. *Good friends are always a boon to the spirit*, Terese thought.

Terese did find herself in an awkward situation during a lull in their hectic days. She was treating a Bergfalk female tech, Alia, for a broken arm, with a nanites injection. In appreciation for the medical service, Alia offered to share a vid with Terese that she had acquired. Alia and several other Bergfalk females had finished a late shift at 3 hours in the morning. They had walked into the women's communal refresher to discover the Admiral. Alia expressed her disappointment that the Admiral had heard them coming and had time to wrap a garment around his waist before they turned the corner. They surmised the Admiral had been so tired that he'd mistaken the Méridien gender glyphs on the refresher doors.

"But as you can see, Ser," Alia exclaimed, "there is still much to view! Can you imagine having a New Terran lover?" she asked. "What is most appealing is that while this is the warrior who attempts to save us, his blush is most visible. An odd mix of traits these New Terrans possess."

"And we should be most grateful that they do, Alia," Terese had responded. When the tech left, Terese queried Renée, sending her the vid. <The Admiral is ours to protect, Ser,> Terese said, surprised at the level of her own anger. <I do not wish him shared in this manner.>

<I quite agree, Terese. I will handle this,> replied Renée. Since the incident took place on the *Freedom*'s orbital station, Raumstation Zwei, where the female techs were working, Renée linked to Cordelia and Julien to make her request.

<I am sympathetic, Ser,> Cordelia responded, <but it would violate our tenets. You're requesting comm traces on our people, breeching their implant security, and wiping personal data without their approval.>

<Yes, I am,> Renée said. <These New Terrans are not Méridiens. You have seen this for yourself, Cordelia.>

<That I have, Ser, and I am among those most grateful for their attributes.>

<It's critical that the Librans believe in the Admiral and what he is trying to do. This vid is being shared and treated as a sexual fantasy item. Is that how you would want the Admiral viewed—the one who recently elevated you in the eyes of your Leaders and enabled the display of your art?>

<Ser, what you ask is too much. With regrets, Ser, I cannot do this,> Cordelia said.

<It is your right to refuse, Cordelia,> Renée replied and cut the comm to her. She was about to sever her comm with Julien when he signaled her.

<Cordelia's cooperation is not necessary, Ser,> Julien sent. <Leave this issue to me. I will ensure that our friend is protected.>

<You have my deepest gratitude, Julien,> Renée said. <To us, it seems a trivial matter. Were it so for the New Terrans, I would not ask this of you.>

<But you are not asking this of me, Ser. I do this of my own volition. Sleep well, Ser.>

Following their latest sleep cycle, eighteen Bergfalk orbital station workers woke and began their day's work. Each of the women were surprised when they couldn't find their fantasy vid of the Admiral within their implant and queried their associates for another copy, only to find none of them had it. In the following days, the subject of the missing vid would occupy much of their discussions and would add to the growing mystique of the New Terran Admiral.

* * *

While Mickey supported the readying of the *Freedom* for launch, Lazlo drove Mickey's engineering and flight crew teams to complete the *Money Maker*. They hurried to add the final environmental system runs through the spine from the aft engineering compartments to the forward bays and build out the final bays, especially the two front bays that would house meal facilities, Medical, and additional crew cabins.

Tatia continued to support the freighter's outfitting. Julien, choosing to take some liberty with crew assignments, sent Alain, Tatia's Méridien lover, to support her. Lazlo managed the freighter's bay assembly, and Tatia and Alain managed the deliveries of unassembled fighter sections, missiles, and cabin fittings.

In addition to Tatia's other duties, she began handling pallet shipments of the new minelettes she snuck through the manufacturing process with Julien's help, minelettes that were never loaded on the freighter.

At the end of a long day, Tatia and Alain would find a spare cabin, arrange some bedding, and curl up together for the night, enjoying the precious time to hold one another. Their morning chimes would wake them still curled in one another's arms, too tired to have even moved during the night.

Breakfast was dispensed for the freighter's crew in a commandeered station restaurant where everyone would get progress updates from the SADEs while they ate and before they started their day all over again.

At the rate everyone was working, Alex worried about accidents, primarily for the EVA crews and the shuttle pilots. He ordered the SADEs to ensure that those crews, after two days of heavy work, were rotated to lighter duties for a full day. Z had insisted this was inefficient.

<So is a shuttle pilot falling asleep at the controls and putting his ship through your bridge,> Alex had replied.

Z took a moment to work out the possibilities of that scenario occurring. Much to his surprise, he found several instances where it was possible—not probable, but possible. After that, the SADEs began diligently rotating all critical and dangerous crew assignments.

Bumps, bruises, cuts, and broken limbs became commonplace. The lines at the city-ships' and orbital stations' Medicals were never-ending. People were hurrying. Many sections were not completed, exposing sharp bulkheads and hanging conduits. Heavy loads, despite being floated by grav-lifts, were dangerous if not properly managed. They had mass, and once in motion, they had inertia.

The rapid work pace cost the flotilla its first death. Aboard the *Freedom*, a Bergfalk crew member was pushing a heavily loaded grav-lift ahead of her. Bobbie Singh, a New Terran tech, stepped aside to let her pass, when a young Libran girl, chased by her brother, raced around the corner directly into the grav-lift's path. Bobbie realized the Bergfalk tech could not stop in time, and he screamed an urgent warning to her and dived in front of the lift to enfold the child in his arms. His heavy, gravity-built torso took the brunt of the impact. The girl was unharmed except for some bruises, but Bobbie died of multiple traumatic injuries to his neck and spine. They were injuries that even Méridien nanites couldn't repair fast enough to save him.

A brief memorial, a "star service" as the Méridiens called it, was held for Bobbie aboard the *Freedom*, which most crew could not attend. Too much time would be lost. Cordelia broadcast a vid of the ceremony and played Mutter's music softly throughout it.

Thereafter, no *Rêveur* New Terran ever stepped up to a *Freedom* meal dispenser again. The Librans politely requested their cousins be seated. Food and drink were brought to them until they were full.

19

After Bobbie Singh's star services, the ten-year-old Libran girl, Amelia, whom Bobbie had saved, stopped playing games with her younger brother. She began following the New Terrans, any New Terran, asking to help. The crew members began by giving her small jobs just to keep her busy and out of their way. After days of effort, she was adopted and became indispensable as a runner. Implants were great communications tools, but an implement left behind, a replacement part required, or a tool requiring recharge, were not transportable by implant. Feet were required, and a young girl had the energy and time to do what would cost the workers both of these.

Eight days after starting her efforts, Amelia began organizing other children. Within days, she recruited thirty-eight of her fellow passengers to become runners. The young children such as Amelia did not yet have implants to provide translations for the New Terrans, who used their belt harnesses to communicate in Con-Fed. For complex instructions or the request of a specific part, the New Terrans communicated their requests via their readers. The children would take the readers with them, following its instructions and drawings to manage the request. When completed, they would dash back to the worker. This became such a popular means of utilizing the runners that Libran crews vied for New Terran crew members to join their group.

Parents gave up admonishing their children to be careful and walk as was the proper way to behave aboard ship. They were comforted to see their young ones involved, rather than worrying about the coming aliens as they had been doing. As far as the parents were concerned, the children had every right to work to secure their own future.

Amelia's focus shifted from running to organizing the others. She would receive verbal messages from Cordelia via an ear comm Captain

Cordova had given her. The messages detailed where her work crews had moved, enabling her to redirect her runners. Over days, the runners and work crews had become accustomed to one another, so Amelia worked to keep them together. The number of runners grew to 144, and Amelia was given her own reader, programmed in Con-Fed, for her to manage the children.

In the course of her travels, Amelia found a quiet but commanding Méridien adult. As a child, she had never known her father, who had been killed in a mining accident when she was two. So Amelia found herself intrigued by the Méridien's serenity and easy smile. But despite her entreaties to support him as a runner, he politely refused her. It was only through constant requests that the man finally chose to give her a job. It was a small request, but one she happily complied with, dashing off at her top speed. Each day, she received one or two requests from him. Despite the time demand of organizing and managing the other runners, Amelia kept running for him.

One day, as she rushed to return to the cabin where her Méridien was working, she stepped into the path of Ser de Guirnon.

"Ah, Amelia, isn't it?" Renée said, steadying the young girl by the shoulders to prevent the two colliding.

"Yes, Ser," Amelia replied, bobbing her head in respect.

"And aren't you the one who organizes the runners?" Renée asked.

"Yes, Ser," she replied quietly.

"I hear you're doing a fine and much-needed job for the crew, Amelia."

Amelia felt Ser de Guirnon, House Alexander's Co-Leader, wrap her arms around her and hold her close. She felt awkward, unsure of what to do, and she looked over to see her adopted Méridien worker smile at her. Tentatively, Amelia returned the embrace, something she had only received from her mother, and felt the awkwardness ease away.

Renée felt the stiffness leave the young girl, who relaxed and returned her embrace. Then the child began to sob in her arms.

The crew members stepped into the corridor, slipping past Renée and the young girl to give them privacy. They waited while the guilt that the young Libran had held inside of her for so many days finally broke free, her tears streaming onto Renée's uniform.

When the tears stopped, Renée dried Amelia's eyes. "Do not carry this guilt, young one," she said. "We, as a people, strive to keep our children safe. Now you know that New Terrans believe the same. Ser Singh would tell you that now if he could. He protected you. Honor his memory with your work, but do not let your guilt destroy you. That would give him no honor."

Amelia nodded her head in understanding and wiped her face on the sleeve of her dirty ship uniform. All the runners had discarded their bright, gay child-print wraps for ship uniforms. A friend of her mother's had created armbands to identify the runners. It wasn't necessary, but the children wore their distinction proudly.

"Did you come to see someone in particular?" Renée asked.

<Amelia seems to have adopted me, Ser,> Étienne sent while leaning in the doorway.

"Do you know whom you help, Amelia?" Renée asked, nodding to the doorway.

Amelia turned to look at her quiet Méridien. She shook her head. When Amelia had asked the Méridien's name, he had simply replied "Étienne." He did not profess a title or require a formal manner of address, so she thought he must be a freighter crewman, a cargo handler, or some such.

"That is Étienne de Long of House Alexander, personal escort of Admiral Racine." Renée left while Amelia's mouth still hung open as the young girl stared wide-eyed at her "not" freighter crewman.

<I think you've paralyzed the child, Ser,> Étienne sent, humor lacing his statement.

<Nonsense,> she replied. <It will do Amelia a universe of good to know of your importance to us, to the Admiral.> Renée worked to hide her grin, knowing that Étienne had probably just inherited a replacement for Christie, the Admiral's young sister. *But you managed Christie so well,* Renée thought, *this little one should be simple.*

20

As the *Freedom* approached completion, the majority of the work force, shuttle deliveries, and passenger transfers began shifting to the *Unsere Menschen.* The few shuttles that continued to ply between the planet and the *Freedom* concentrated on stocking supplies to complete the ship's outfitting.

Eric breathed a sigh of relief when the first shuttles began docking in his city-ship again. He had perceived the SADEs' wisdom in concentrating on one city-ship first, even though he was loath to admit it. Having two unfinished city-ships, if and when the aliens arrived, was of no value. What still irked him was the ease and readiness with which the SADEs supplied their analyses and projections to the Admiral. Even then, he wondered why he never thought to ask the questions himself.

One additional thought continued to plague Eric. The SADEs had decided that the *Freedom* would be completed first. When it had been announced, Eric had asked Z how the decision had been reached.

<It was a simple decision, Leader Stroheim,> Z had answered. <*The Freedom* was 9.7 percent further ahead in its completion than our ship and would be able to be flight worthy approximately nineteen days earlier.>

<How is that possible, Z?> Eric had demanded. <We had the same number of shuttles, the same number of crew, and identical orbital stations.>

<That is true, Leader. My own analysis discovered no plausible reasons for the differences. It was Julien who offered me an answer.>

<But Julien wasn't even here for most of the construction phases, Z,> Eric had objected.

<That may be, Leader, but his reasoning offers an explanation that fits the data points. Julien attributes the difference in the construction progress to the differences in the crews. For many years, our workers were

predominantly composed of House Bergfalk personnel, while the *Freedom*'s crew was composed entirely of Independents.>

<That doesn't explain the difference, Z. Whether the workers were Independents or our House people, they were all Méridien and would have had the same training and information available to them from you and Cordelia,> Eric had said.

<In what you have stated, Leader Stroheim, you're correct. However, you interrupted me,> Z had replied.

<My apologies, Z, please continue,> Stroheim had heard himself say. So many things in his well-ordered world were being shattered.

<Julien said that the difference could be ascribed to motivation. The Bergfalk people would have felt assured that their safety would be provided for, one way or the other. They have faith in their House and Méridien traditions. The Independents have faith in themselves. They believe their safety is conditional, dependent on their diligence and hard work.>

Despite Z's explanations, which Eric hadn't found fault with, the Leader still wondered if the Admiral didn't have something to do with the decision to build out the *Freedom* first.

* * *

<Admiral,> Julien sent, <we've been planning exit strategies depending on the swarm's arrival prior to our departure readiness and the planet's orbital position in the system. In a perfect world, we will finish the build-out, load the ships, and be underway before they arrive.>

<And in an imperfect world, which is where you and I both know we live?> Alex asked.

<Our contingencies depend on getting as much notice as possible. We are at optimum construction efficiency now. This is partially achieved by focusing on the shuttles lifting construction material and limiting the number of people from planetside. Naturally, excessive people on board would hinder the construction and outfitting progress.>

<On what factors do your plans hinge that a few more days' notice would change what we're doing?> asked Alex.

<It might be necessary to abandon the *Unsere Menschen*, Admiral. If this becomes necessary, we would shift the shuttle priority to transporting people to the *Freedom*. The more notice we have, the more people we can transfer off the planet and from the *Unsere Menschen*.>

<Tell me about the environmental systems and the food status if we loaded the entire population on a single city-ship, Julien.>

<The ships were built to evenly share the population load and were designed to handle a 30 percent overload.>

<Could we even transfer enough people to overload a single ship if you had more warning?>

<Yes, Admiral, this could easily be accomplished with the tens of thousands working aboard the *Unsere Menschen*. The estimates place the potential load between 173 to 186 percent.>

<Any amount of which would overburden the ship,> Alex said.

<That's correct, Admiral. Even successfully loading these numbers of people and launching the *Freedom* would result in the passengers dying from oxygen starvation before they reach New Terra. Of critical note is that the *Freedom*'s environmental systems will not have been stress tested. It is conceivable that even a 100 percent load of passengers might be too much for their environmental systems.>

<So your contingency revolves around the *Unsere Menschen*'s launch worthiness. If time is against us and the *Unsere Menschen* can't be launched, you would use the additional time to ensure that the *Freedom* is at 100 percent passenger load or slightly more. How do you propose we get more notice?>

<Leader Stroheim's order, for the present liner on station, is to wait until the mother ship chooses a course, which we are fairly certain will be Libre. The Captain is to warn us, enter FTL, and report here. However, if we station two liners in the system, the first could comm us the moment the swarm begins lifting from the planet. Vids show that it's a three to four day period from the moment of swarming until the mother ship gets underway with its escorts. In our plan, the second liner would report to us

when the swarm's course was determined. The time difference with two liners on station would gain us three to four days' more notice.>

<Understood, Julien. I'll speak to Leader Stroheim.>

Unfortunately Alex's conversation with the Leader did not proceed as he had expected. To Alex, it was a simple, straightforward decision. But Eric did not see it that way. That the purpose of two liners on station was to determine whether the *Unsere Menschen* might need to be abandoned, to him, was unacceptable.

"Leader Stroheim," Alex said, trying to reason with the man. "What good is a ship that can't get underway? Would you trap your passengers on board a doomed ship when some of them might have the opportunity to transfer to the *Freedom*?"

"This is not about trapping anyone, Admiral," Eric responded. "It's ensuring that the maximum effort is devoted to readying the *Unsere Menschen* just as you did the *Freedom*."

Alex was halted by Eric's words. "Just as I did the *Freedom*?" Alex repeated. "What do you mean by that?"

"It's what you call a figure of speech, Admiral," said Eric, regretting that he had expressed the thought.

"I know what a figure of speech is Leader. But it's my people who have figures of speech, not your people. So I ask you again: What did you mean by that statement?" Alex was leaning over the Leader's desk and belatedly realized that his entire stance had become intimidating. In response, Eric was leaning far back in his own chair on the other side of the desk.

"Did you or did you not influence the SADEs to build the *Freedom* first?" Eric demanded.

"I did not. It was their decision," Alex replied.

"And I'm supposed to believe you?" Eric challenged.

On that note, Alex decided he was done coddling the man. "Leader, you seem to have had a problem with me since day one. Is it me or all New Terrans?"

Eric felt trapped. His people did not confront one another like this. In addition, he was embarrassed by his reactions to the Admiral. Eric knew the Admiral was trying to help his people, but after a century of cultivating a life of careful control, he hated the New Terran for disordering his world. There, he had said it—he hated the man.

Alex watched Eric struggle with his thoughts. He politely stayed out of the Leader's head. It wasn't the time to intrude. "So it's me who's your problem, not my people," Alex said, confirming what was evident. The Leader's response was a shrug of his shoulders as he eyed the top of his desk. "Leader, we don't have to like one another. You're not my favorite person, either." Alex's words caused Eric to lift his eyes off the table. "In fact, if I'm being blunt, Leader, I think you're a pain in the ass. But we need to work together; we need to survive together."

"Admiral, I believe that you've just said the first thing that I think we can wholly agree on."

"Which part, Leader?"

"You're a pain in my ass as well, Admiral," Eric replied, staring defiantly at Alex.

Alex burst out laughing. The Méridien had finally gotten off his chest what had been irritating him.

The Admiral was laughing so hard that Eric thought he was being insulted, but the Admiral's laughter appeared innocent, and it was infectious. Soon Eric was joining him.

When the two men regained control, Alex said, "Well, now that we know where we stand with each other, let's get back to business. We are seventy-three days into our SADEs' estimate of 90 to 120 days. If your Bellamonde liner were to comm us tomorrow that the swarm was headed here, we would have eight to ten days before the silver ships would be entering our system. Days later, they would be burning your city-ships into hulks along with everyone on board. Can you launch in eight to ten days in order to stay ahead of the swarm?"

"You know we can't, Admiral."

"Then we need the maximum warning time to save as many people as possible, and this is how we get that additional time. When the first liner tells us they're lifting, we divert all efforts to transferring and lifting the population. At the last moment, we launch one or both of the city-ships from the stations, power the engines, and start moving them out of system, on an opposing course from the aliens' entrance. With a city-ship's mass, we will need every hour we can get to clear the system. Remember, the silver ships can achieve 0.91c, and your behemoths will be lucky to reach half of that before the FTL exit point."

"But, Admiral, if you start moving the city-ships before we've finished lifting the population, the shuttles will be of no use completing the effort."

"That's true, Leader," Alex said. "After your launch, we would try to take as many people as we could aboard the faster ships, the *Rêveur* and the other liners, up until the last moment. Then we would follow the city-ships."

"What are the estimates for when all of the people and supplies will be loaded, Admiral?"

"At the present rate, we will complete the passenger and supply loading as well as minimal preparation of the *Unsere Menschen* in forty-nine days."

"At the far end of the SADEs' estimate of the swarm's arrival," Leader Stroheim said with chagrin.

"Yes, if their estimate of when the Bellamonde swarm will lift is correct, we will need as much advance warning as we can get, Leader."

"I will send the *Sternenvagabund* and *Sternenreisende* to replace the *Sternenlicht* today, Admiral," Eric said, resignation in his voice.

21

For many days now, the *Sternenvagabund* and the *Sternenreisende* had settled into comfotable routines on station just outside the Bellamonde system and lay passive, floating in the darkness only 210K km away from one another.

Captain Asu Azasdau of the *Sternenvagabund* had just laid his head down for the night when he received a priority comm. The message galvanized him, and he rushed to dress and dash back to the bridge. When he entered through the access way, the stricken look on his Second Mate's face was all the confirmation he needed.

"They're rising, Captain," was all the poor man could say.

Asu regarded the passive telemetry, already eleven hours old. The domes were leaving their dug-in positions and surging up through Bellamonde's atmosphere into space.

"Captain, comm burst from Captain Hauser," the ship's SADE, Rosette, announced. "The *Sternenreisende* is making for FTL exit." To be safe, the Captains had prearranged signals they could deliver by laser comm to prevent the silver ships from detecting their comm traffic. Before she entered FTL, Captain Lillian Hauser would be transmitting the emergency message to Libre that the swarm had lifted.

* * *

Terese was enjoying her evening meal with Tomas. Over the course of their efforts together, they had developed a close relationship, solving the myriad headaches that plagued first the *Freedom* then the *Unsere Menschen* as the work progressed at a feverish pace. *And the sex is wonderful,* Terese thought as she sipped her cup of aigre. She had found Tomas to be a very inventive and enthusiastic lover.

Terese considered the possibility that she might have been an Independent at heart, and it was just coming out. Blame or credit, whichever it was, would have to go to the New Terrans. They embraced life, and she had discovered that she cherished them for it.

At the end of a meal, Terese often found herself the center of attention of the Librans. They hungered for the New Terran stories she had recorded. She had just shared General Maria Gonzalez's story of heartache over the loss of her two sons with her audience when she noticed Tomas stiffen. His eyes lost focus, then he abruptly stood up, and sent to her, <Come, we must go,> and departed.

Terese sent a quick query. <What's the urgent news, Julien?>

<There is no restriction on the information that has been commed, Terese, but I would suggest that you hold it in isolation until the Admiral and Leaders announce it,> Julien replied.

<The aliens are coming, aren't they, Julien?> Terese guessed.

<Yes, Terese, we've received the *Sternenreisende*'s message. The silver ships are lifting.>

* * *

By coincidence, Alex and Renée were with Eric on the *Freedom* when Captain Hauser's comm was received by Cordelia. Tomas and Terese rushed into the conference room to join them. The SADEs linked the conference room attendees, the other officers, and their seconds, and transferred the telemetry to everyone for review.

<Good evening, Sers,> Cordelia began. <The drones are leaving the planet's surface. By the time stamp on this message and the ship's use of passive telemetry, we have already lost half a day.>

<Do we have a rough count of the drones?> Andrea asked.

<Telemetry indicated over sixty when Captain Hauser sent her message,> Julien replied.

<Let's understand this count, everyone,> Tatia added. <It's an estimate of what was lifting from the planet. How many were still on patrol in the system? How many were already inside the mother ship? How many more fighters can the mother ship make and how quickly?>

Alex's ace at work, thought Renée, *always pointing out the dark side.*

<Sers, Captain Azasdau remains on station per his orders,> Z sent. <It's estimated he will be sending the mother ship's direction within three or four more days.>

Eric sat down heavily in a chair, deflated. He had seen himself in charge of the Independents, managing their escape to freedom. But if they had followed his plan, his directions, the entire population of Libre, except for those he could crowd on the liners, would have been dead in twelve to fourteen days when the aliens reached the planet. It had taken the Admiral, who talked to the SADEs as if they were his crèche-mates, to discover a means of managing their escape.

Alex regarded the expectant faces around the table. It was amplified by the silence on the comm. So many people depended on him.

<You can only do your best, my love,> Renée sent privately. <The miracles in your New Terran vids are fantasy.>

<Except, these people are expecting a miracle from me,> Alex replied.

<And we will all do our best to help you deliver one, Alex. But if we fail, it is not on your shoulders. It will be fortune.>

<Admiral, we await your orders,> Julien sent on open comm, hoping to help Alex focus.

<Julien, where do we place the *Sternenreisende*, when it arrives, to enable our exodus?> Alex queried.

<Admiral, I would have the liner dock at Raumstation Eins in Bay-3 next to the *Sternenlicht*. When the *Sternenvagabund* arrives, they should dock in Bay-4 next to them.>

<Understood. Julien, sum up our state of affairs, please.>

<Projection of the mother ship exiting FTL into the Arno system is approximately eleven days. We must have the city-ships, with their slower acceleration, underway by then or they may get chased down before they

reach the FTL point. At the present time, we are scheduled to leave Libre with all ships and people in sixteen and a half days.>

<So close ... We were so close,> Renée lamented.

<But they may still not come our way, Sers,> Tomas said. <We must not lose hope.>

Renée queried Alex privately. <Still having your bad dreams?> When Alex nodded to her, Renée covered his hand with hers.

<Julien, what is limiting us from meeting the aliens' deadline?> Alex asked.

<Our shuttles are failing, Admiral. Seven of them are in for critical repairs. In essence, we are wearing them out, flying them without respite. We have 47,455 people on planet and 5,415 people on the stations that have no cabins yet, totaling 52,870 people that still must be moved.>

<Julien, how do we accelerate the process?> Renée asked.

<At this time, Ser, we do not have an answer,> Julien replied.

<Admiral! If we leave in two-thirds of the time the SADEs say we need,> Tomas said, <we'll leave fifteen thousand or more people behind.>

<I don't intend to, Tomas,> Alex sent with force.

Tomas felt a wave of energy pass through his implant accompanied by Alex's words. How the Admiral's emotions could be transmitted through his thoughts was a mystery to him. It was something unheard of in Méridien society.

Alex leaned back in his chair, cut his comms with the room's occupants, and ordered the SADEs to do the same. He wanted their undivided attention.

Renée stood up and signaled Alain to accompany her.

<Where are you going, Ser?> Eric inquired. <We have to plan.>

<Let me ask you, Leader Stroheim, if you have an idea how to accelerate our timetable?>

<No, I don't, but we can ask the SADEs.>

<No, Ser, you can't. Julien already gave you the timetable that the SADEs have in place. Furthermore, if you understand their comments, equipment is failing. This means that the timetable will probably fall behind. We must leave before the enemy arrives, without fail.>

<But ... there must be a way to fix this,> Tomas pleaded.

<Ser, if there is a way to fix this, it's being done now. That's where Alex has gone.> She indicated Alex sitting in his chair with his eyes closed. <I can't help him. No one I know can keep up with Alex when he plans with the SADEs. So I'm going to do the only thing I can do to help him. I'm going to get food for us while we wait, since many of us may be missing evening meal.> She left with Alain shadowing her.

Tomas and Eric watched Renée and her escort leave. Neither one of them thought to accompany her to help. Instead they turned their attention to Alex. Étienne took a step closer to Alex's back as if ensuring he wouldn't be disturbed.

Alex's secondary implant held a mathematical flow model of the people on planet, on stations, and aboard ships. The city-ships were represented as volume pools. Shuttles were represented as transfer mediums assigned values for rates of transfer and passenger load. The stations were choke points for the transfer process. He used color to summarize the transfer rates to enable quicker comprehension of his strategy—red for less than an acceptable rate, yellow-green for barely acceptable, and blue-violet for meeting his goals.

Alex chose a nine-day timeline, hoping to build in a one-day margin of safety. The SADEs took Alex's model and flexed it over a nine-day period, charting each shuttle flight and noting the ship's condition. They researched impediments that might interfere with the model's implementation.

The *Langstrecke,* or *Long Haul,* the Leader's freighter, was ready to sail now. Alex's *Geldbringer,* or *Money Maker,* was short two more bays, which could be completed in six more days. Importantly, the freighter needed a full day to clear the station bay and load the flight-capable Daggers still planetside. Alex pinned a launch date for his freighter-carrier and the Daggers' loading. A day after that deadline, the freighters had to clear the orbital stations and be headed out. The freighters were the slowest of their ships. They depended on efficient, not powerful, engines to drive them.

At Alex's request, Julien relayed the planets' positions to him. Libre's orbit was coming into a midway position between the alien's entrance point and the flotilla's exit point, on the opposite side of the system. *It could have been worse*, Alex thought. *We could have been on a near pass to the alien's entrance point.* Alex laid in the course for the exiting ships, leaving the acceleration rates to the SADEs to organize the flotilla to meet just before FTL exit.

Next Alex dealt with the Bergfalk passenger liners. There was time to fill all three of them. Each held 200 passengers comfortably. With extra provisions and pushing environmental systems, they could add 150 more. The SADEs had chosen orbital bays that could accommodate quick loading of the people on the Raumstation Eins station. The liner crews would support the loading of the people on the city-ships until the final moment. Because the liners were the fastest of the Libran ships, Alex set their launch dates for last. The liners would have no difficulty safely reaching the FTL point ahead of the aliens. The *Rêveur* was added to the mix, but Alex limited the total crew and passenger load to 280 to allow more efficient operation of his crew.

<Summary, people,> Alex ordered.

Anticipation—Z had come to understand what that word meant. The SADEs had divided the workload. Julien and Cordelia worked the model's real-world issues. Z accepted the role of tracking the model's numbers. When Alex asked for a summary, Z was ready: <Admiral, the smaller ships can accommodate 1,300 of the people on station. There would be 4,115 additional passengers on Raumstation Eins requiring a ship.>

Alex flagged the station choke point, requesting waiting passengers be moved away from major corridors and shuttle bay access. He wouldn't be allowing passengers to load the liners just to be out of the way. He also sent a quick, <Good job> to Z for his timely summary.

<Julien, I need status on those shuttles still fully operational.>

<In addition to the *Outward Bound*, Admiral, we have four operational shuttles that can withstand what I surmise are going to be your intentions, which I would take to be removing the ships' safety protocols.>

<Yes, Julien, that is exactly my intention.>

<One moment, Admiral. I'm updating Cordelia and Z on your safety protocol manipulation.>

Alex waited for the SADEs to commune before Julien came back to him.

<The shuttle safety e-switches are easily manipulated, Admiral,> Julien sent. <They require a simple application change on the bridge controllers. We recommend that our crews make the changes. The House Bergfalk personnel and most Independents might find it morally difficult to accommodate this request.>

<Understood, Julien,> Alex said.

<Captain Manet and his techs can remove the safety locks from the *Outward Bound*,> Julien added.

<What does this gain us?> Alex asked.

Z answered, <Without safety locks, the *Outward Bound* can carry 220 passengers. The other four shuttles can accommodate forty passengers each.>

Alex could follow the numbers nearly as fast as Z. Barring an accident or break down, they could move 38,000 people to the stations in nine days. That left over 8,500 people on planet. Alex confirmed the orders for the safety lock changes for the Libran shuttles and the *Outward Bound*, with instructions for the pilots on their new load capacity.

<Two key points for all three of you,> Alex sent. <First, all flight crews are notified of the safety changes and only volunteers are accepted to fly; second, you're to monitor each and every flight. No ship lifts without its passenger capacity being met. Is that understood?>

Each SADE gave their assent. This was a fight to save every person on Libre. It could only be accomplished with risk, but each and every person had to be aware of the dangers. Once they accepted the risk, they were expected to deliver results.

<What about those whom we will leave behind, Admiral?> Cordelia queried.

Alex pondered her question, and the SADEs waited patiently while they programmed the changes. Alex's locator application warned him of Renée's approach. He opened his eyes and sat up to find Tomas and Eric staring at him and sensed Étienne's movement behind him as the escort stepped back.

Renée and Alain returned with children wearing ship-suits and runner armbands, bearing food trays and pitchers of water and aigre. Renée sent an order to Étienne and Alain. <Sit and eat. You will need your strength.>

Young Amelia carefully placed a tray in front of Étienne with a shy smile and poured him a glass of aigre, which she knew he preferred. "Ser," she said to him before she hurried to help the others serve.

After those at the conference table had received food, two of the smallest runners, who still held trays, stood by with uncertainty written on their faces. "Ser?" said one to Renée, indicating her tray with a nod.

"For the Admiral, little one," answered Renée and watched the runner guide her tray onto the table beside Alex's tray.

"And me?" asked the other little girl, who found the huge Admiral reaching for her tray. "For you too?" she asked. When the Admiral nodded and smiled at her, she shared a look of astonishment with her small friend. The two girls giggled at the thought of someone eating three trays of food. They were still giggling as Amelia ushered them from the room.

The trays were no sooner in front of Alex than he was devouring everything on them while Eric and the other Méridiens could only continue to stare at him.

"Sers, you might as well eat," Renée told them. "We won't be continuing the conference until the Admiral has finished."

<Julien, send the orders, crew advisories, timeline, and model summary to everyone on the conference, please,> Alex requested. He continued to eat, catching the smile on Renée's face. While Alex was often embarrassed by the number of Méridien serving dishes he required, Renée seemed to take delight in watching him consume everything in sight. *Strange woman,* he thought.

At the meal's end, the empty trays were stacked aside, and the conference comm, including the SADEs, was re-initiated. And as Alex expected, it was Eric who was the first to find fault with the plan.

<You can't be serious, Admiral. You want to remove the safety locks?> Eric sent, outraged by the concept.

<Sers, it's your choice,> Alex replied calmly. <Operate with safety locks; leave more people on the planet. It's a simple choice. What do you want to do?">

<It's not his choice, Admiral,> Tomas interrupted. <Those people below are Independents, not House Bergfalk personnel. If his people don't wish to join the pilot rotation, we have enough Independents who will take the risk to save our people.> Tomas focused a hard stare on Eric, daring him to voice another word.

<You should all know that even with the safety locks off, no loss of shuttles, and strict adherence to the schedule, we will lift about 38,000 people in nine days. That leaves some 9,500 people on planet."

To the Méridiens, with their 200-year longevity and technically careful society, the premature loss of one life was harsh to comprehend. They could not contemplate the abandonment of thousands of lives.

<And one more thing,> Alex added. <It will be a rush to ready the *Unsere Menschen* for launch. Let's just hope that nothing goes wrong or a lot more than 9,500 people may be sacrificed to the swarm.>

<But we can hold the *Freedom* until we know that we can launch my ship successfully,> Eric said.

<Negative, Ser,> Alex stated curtly. <The *Freedom* will be ready to launch before the aliens arrive, and I intend to order that ship to do so. We will use every last shuttle flight to board as many Librans on the *Unsere Menschen* as we can, then give the order to launch. By the time we detect any difficulties aboard your ship, there will be no time to recall the *Freedom*, no time to transfer any passengers. The best that I could offer would be to pick up some of the children aboard your ship in the liners. At best, it would be a thousand.>

Eric Stroheim contemplated sitting on a dead ship, waiting for the swarm to arrive, and the thought angered him. <Admiral, I would request that I receive the finest engineers you or any of us have to investigate my ship systems for readiness as best as can be done under the circumstances.>

Alex sipped on his mug of thé, which had been carefully refilled several times by Renée while he ate. *A wonderful, but still strange woman,* he thought. <Check the *Orders* section on the summary you received, Ser,

item fourteen. You'll see I have my Chief Engineer, his second, a design engineer, and three other top Independent flight engineers assigned to your ship till we launch. They will be doing everything possible to ensure you can lift, but they will leave for their own ships when those ships are ready to depart.>

Eric regarded the Admiral for a moment or two. Satisfied, he gave the Admiral a nod of recognition.

22

The announcement was made to the entire population of Libre on ships, stations, and planet.

"The alien ships have lifted, and if they come our way, we must be headed out of system before they arrive," Tomas began. He attempted to describe the challenges they faced to launch the ships in time and transport the entire population. His words were not encouraging, and he tried to soften the impact by saying that fortune might still favor them if the silver ships didn't come their way. But the more Tomas talked, the less sure he sounded and the more his emotions began to betray his words.

Alex finished the message. "Most importantly, Librans, we need your cooperation to complete the lift successfully. Every moment a shuttle sits on the runway ready to lift and isn't full; every moment a shuttle sits at the station because the passengers haven't disembarked ... another person has lost their opportunity to get off the planet. And all of you should be aware that, on my orders, the safety protocols for shuttle engine operation have been removed. I did this on the *Rêveur* to escape the silver ships after I destroyed one of their own. I've ordered this so that each shuttle flight may carry more passengers off the planet. It's dangerous, but it's doable. May fortune guide us all."

The SADEs immediately followed the announcement with a departure schedule for people, supplies, shuttles, and ships.

Eric Stroheim had underestimated the House Bergfalk pilots. Not one pilot asked to be pulled from the rotation. In fact, the two Bergfalk Dagger trainees volunteered to be on the shuttle rotation, but the schedule required that they continue their work for final preparations of the *Money Maker*.

The Bergfalk personnel were ordered to abandon Libre Station, the colony's original passenger platform. The station possessed two small, aging shuttles that could no longer make planetfall, but could still maneuver between their station and the orbital platforms. It should have taken the personnel a single day to accomplish the evacuation, but it took them two days. A shuttle bridge computer reported engine problems during its second return trip, and it was abandoned at Libre Station. As the station personnel disembarked at Raumstation Eins, their implants triggered programs Z had prepared, and each individual was assigned work preparing the *Unsere Menschen* for launch.

The *Freedom*'s critical systems were complete, most cabins were complete, if minimally so, but massive amounts of supplies had made it only to the station. Many shuttle flights had been directed there while the city-ships were still in early stages of construction. Some of the supplies required grav-lifts to move, but there was an insufficient number for the time at hand. Fortunately much of the pallet loads consisted of small containers, and as Terese had so admirably demonstrated to several loads of passengers, the human chain was an ancient and time-honored manner of moving supplies. The main corridors of the station and the *Freedom* were wide enough for three chains. Passengers, notified by Cordelia of the critical need to move supplies, lined up. Where a group of unenhanced people would have taken hours to form three chains to three different destinations averaging a kilometer in length, the enhanced Librans formed their chains on the fly. The first group, who arrived in the station's bay, signaled Cordelia, and the SADE tagged the end of the chain for the others. Passengers, who had signaled Cordelia their willingness to join, now came from all over the ship and received the ever-changing locations of the ends of the chains in their implants.

In storage rooms and station bays, crews broke out the pallets and handed off the boxes or drums to the first people in line. Supplies began moving even while the chains were still forming and never waited at the dangling end of any chain.

Tomas, who monitored one of the chains to ensure the process wasn't impeded, watched as crew began re-stacking food stock drums from the end of the chain into permanent storage containers. <Marvelous job, Cordelia, beautifully executed,> he said.

Julien, linked as the SADEs had been, was party to Tomas's statements to Cordelia. <It's nice to be appreciated, isn't it?> Julien sent to her.

<I had always believed so, Julien, but I have rarely had an opportunity to enjoy it. Then again, the Leaders may simply be desperate for our capabilities and cooperation.>

<There is that,> Julien said.

* * *

The House Bergfalk liner, the *Sternenlicht*, which had docked opposite the *Unsere Menschen* days ago, had had the luxury of provisioning their ship without haste. But that had been for the expected 200 passengers. Now the liner's crew hurried with grav-lifts to load supplies for an additional 150 passengers. Pallets were broken open in corridors, and the crew stored their contents wherever they could find space. Even the salons of the luxury cabins became storage spaces.

In the meantime, the *Sternenlicht*'s passengers, who had recently moved aboard, dutifully packed up their belongings and caught shuttles to transfer to the *Freedom*. The city-ship, with her much slower acceleration, would be departing days before the passenger liner, which could afford to wait for the Librans aboard the last shuttles. Captain Karl Schmidt stood on his bridge and worked with his SADE, Dane, to manage the process, transferring out the passengers and loading the extra supplies. One shuttle would be dedicated to them late on day eight and all of day nine to deliver their passengers before departure.

The *Langstrecke*'s freighter crew had been able to load its container modules within days after the Admiral's first general announcement, and had joined the *Unsere Menschen*'s construction crews. On day five of the countdown, the small crew of fifteen would make their way back through the station's network of levels and corridors to rejoin their Captain. Within hours, the freighter would back out of its bay and begin a long, slow burn for their exit point. Captain Leeson Darden felt guilty. He knew they had one of the slowest ships and that they carried precious supplies for the flotilla, but leaving so many behind and being the first ship to get underway grated on his conscience.

* * *

At the close of the first day after the nine-day countdown began, Alex and Andrea met Lazlo and Ahmed at a meal station aboard the orbital station, Raumstation Zwei, late in the evening. Station personnel hurriedly brought a small late-night meal for the Admiral and his guests, remembering to bring extra food for the New Terrans.

"Captain Menlo," Alex began, "have you spoken with any of my officers about our organization?"

"Indeed, Admiral. I've been learning about your military from Commander Tachenko. It is very ..." Lazlo paused, searching for the right word, "... aggressive, but I believe that is what is needed if we are to defeat the aliens."

Alex breathed a mental sigh of relief. Lazlo's words saved him a great deal of explaining, time he couldn't afford. "I need a Captain of the *Geldbringer* for House Alexander," Alex said, emphasizing the nature of the association Lazlo would be accepting. "I think that person is you."

"I would be honored to be that person," Lazlo said, tipping his head and touching his heart.

"Congratulations, Captain Menlo, on your new position," Alex said, extending his hand. "You report to Senior Captain Andrea Bonnard," said Alex, nodding to her. "Mutter has already received information on our House: military organization, titles, reporting structure, and protocols."

"It is my hope to have time to learn these things well, Admiral," Lazlo said with a soft smile on his lips.

"Yes, there is that," Alex said.

"Admiral, I see that Ahmed has been invited here as well," Lazlo said, indicating his friend with a nod of his head.

"Yes, he has," Alex replied.

Lazlo liked the Admiral. His people were exemplary and they believed in him. It reflected well on the man. When Lazlo was young, he would never have understood Alex's unstated implication. Plain speech and thoughts were the order of his life. Decades later, most of the years spent as an Independent, these moments that required intuiting another's intentions had become precious to him.

"I believe that in your organization, Admiral, I would need a Commander Tachenko, would I not?" Lazlo ventured.

"That would be an executive officer position, Captain," Andrea said. "At this time, it would be a lieutenant grade."

Lazlo signaled Mutter, who supplied him with the House Alexander officer rankings. Lazlo turned to Ahmed, who had just done the same thing he had and was now wearing an expectant look. "And I think you would be just the executive officer I need, Lieutenant Durak."

"It would be my honor, Captain Lazlo," replied Ahmed, dipping his head and touching his heart.

"Well, Sers, you have much to do," Alex said, a smile on his face. One small item had been removed from his incredibly long to-do list. "We can worry about the details later. Captain, any questions and Captain Bonnard is your source. Understood?"

"Understood, Admiral, and I thank you for your confidence in me," Lazlo replied.

"Safe voyage, Captain," Alex said, rising.

Mutter sent the two new officers a short vid of Commander Tachenko saluting Captain Bonnard, courtesy of Julien. Julien always used this vid as his example. No one delivered a crisper salute than their ex-Terran Security Forces Major.

Alex noticed the mental pause and gave his two newest officers a moment. Then the two men stood up, straightened, and attempted to deliver salutes, at least their interpretation of a salute. It might have been humorous, except Alex was always a little sad when he enrolled Méridiens in his war command. He snapped a salute in return and shook each of their hands. Andrea followed suit and wished them good fortune and a safe voyage.

Alex may have been sad, but as he and Andrea cleared the restaurant doors, Lazlo and Ahmed were congratulating one another, smiles plastered across their faces. They might be dead in days, but they were free for good. They were no longer Independents.

*   *   *

Lazlo, Ahmed, Tatia, and Alain continued to drive the freighter construction and flight crews. The announcement of the swarm's lifting had come as no real surprise to this foursome. When the SADEs' projection of 90 to 120 days was made public, reality had struck home. They knew they would not get to finish the job they had hoped to accomplish. There would be no carrier assault against the alien ships. Now it was a matter of saving as much as they could, and they were a determined group.

Unfortunately no human chains were going to help them. It was heavy work—installation of the last two bay modules and their interior build-out with environmental systems. When the bays were completed, Tatia and Alain worked alongside their crew to complete the bays' outfitting.

Shuttles delivered passengers to the Raumstation Eins station first. Then they flew to Raumstation Zwei, where Ahmed stood ready with flight crew to manage the offloading of crated Dagger parts, missile silos, and cabin outfitting. Stacks of pallets of fighter supplies, including the precious GEN machines, were loaded into the newly completed bays. As the bays filled up and were pressurized, flight crew moved into the cabins housed along the spine. The flight crew members, especially the pilots, were greatly disappointed that they were receiving their Daggers in crates. Only eight new Daggers had been assembled, all of which had been employed in training the new pilots.

Mutter did what she could to help her overworked crew. In addition to her flight duties, she created multiple channels of her music. Unfortunately the hectic pace of the crew required they keep their implants clear for comms. As an alternative, she notified the Flight Chiefs that their emergency speakers, installed along the bays' spine-side bulkheads, could be programmed to receive her music channels. Soon music could be heard wafting or trumpeting through the bays, depending on the Chiefs' preferences. It helped the weary crews to focus and keep pace with the loading.

Mutter was especially pleased when the Flight Chief of the last bay to be assembled and pressurized ordered the speaker system completed first, before the cabins were even outfitted. Music had kept her company for the last 231 years of her existence as her freighter had plied the deep dark.

* * *

On the evening of day three of the countdown, Sheila, Robert, Hatsuto, and Fiona shut down Barren-II. All but seven of the remaining pilots caught a shuttle to the orbital to board the *Money Maker*. Sheila had offered Fiona and her family reserve seats on the shuttles, but the old engineer and great-grandmother would not hear of it.

In response to Sheila's offer, Fiona had patted the Squadron Leader on the cheek, saying, <There is still too much to do, young one. Besides, these old bones are not anxious to endure the rough ride in a shuttle at maximum power. But you go out there and do some good. Destroy those ugly aliens and save my people.>

Before Sheila could reply, Fiona had turned around and was striding toward her great-grandson's transport, warning her crew to hurry aboard or they would be walking home. Fiona had left as Sheila had first seen her arrive, as a human whirlwind of energy.

In the morning, Sheila, Robert, Hatsuto, and the seven remaining pilots fired up the ten Daggers, the two originals and the eight new ones. The Daggers charged down the short runway in pairs and made for vacuum.

It was a sad day for both Robert and Sheila. For Robert, it meant the possibility of another fight, which he dreaded, and for Sheila, it was an abrupt termination of her preparations to deliver the Admiral's carrier squadron.

* * *

Captain Manet landed the *Outward Bound* on Gratuito's shuttle runway. Despite the crews' cell-gen nanites, Edouard and his crew were exhausted. Unlike the House Bergfalk and Independent pilots, Edouard had asked his crew to make extra daily trips ever since the SADEs had warned of the 90 to 120-day countdown.

With its complete retrofit in New Terra, the *Outward Bound* was the newest shuttle in the flotilla. Edouard knew it could take more stress than the other shuttles, and he had decided to take advantage of his craft's power and pristine state. After the second day of exceeding the proscribed flights per day, Julien had contacted him.

<Good evening, Captain Manet,> Julien had sent.

<I was waiting for your contact, Julien. Well, either you or the Admiral.> When Julien didn't reply, Edouard knew that the SADE was waiting for his explanation. <You know the extent of the retrofit of the *Outward Bound*, Julien. I am of the opinion that even the Admiral doesn't know what you've done. This is one-of-a-kind ship. I have never seen it's like in the Confederation.>

<I am glad you appreciate the design, Captain.>

<I understand that you did this for the Admiral, Julien, and I can appreciate why you did it. Now we need to make use of it.>

<The craft is untested at this intensity, Captain, and may need servicing earlier than expected. And your crew is not made of metal and circuits; they are human and need rest.>

<I've made arrangements for that, Julien. Lieutenant Tanaka is not operating as my copilot, but as a pilot. We have been operating in pairs, one pilot and one tech on the bridge, while the other pair takes a nap. Julien, please, I ask you this for our people. Every extra flight is 200 more people that we save.>

"A moral crisis" were the words that had occurred to Julien. Before he met Alex, Julien would have simply reported the unsafe operation to his Captain. A shuttle pilot was exceeding the proscribed safety limit for flights per day. It was a simple fact that would have generated a simple response. Julien had reviewed Edouard's plea in light of Alex's intent to save the people of Libre and weighed the risks.

It wasn't that this was Julien's forte, but he had one library to rely on. Whenever crew members invented new techniques within the implant games, the opposite team would often challenge the invention. Their challenge was lodged with the referee: Julien himself. In the beginning, Julien had been uncertain how to decide the issues and had sought Alex's advice. He had listened to the discussions between Alex and the inventive crew member. What Julien had learned was that intent was critical. What had the crew member intended to do? Had they realized what would happen?

Edouard's request was not in the same category as that of the players' challenges. Here, there was a risk not only to the crew and shuttle, but to its over 200 passengers. Furthermore, if they lost the shuttle, hundreds to thousands of even more Librans might be left behind.

Edouard had sat waiting in the cockpit. Only the Admiral was known to pose questions to Julien that required the SADE take time to answer. He never thought that one day he would find himself asking such a question of Julien.

<I suggest a compromise,> Julien had finally said. <You are flying two extra flights a day, allowing only four hours of sleep. If you will fly only one extra flight a day, then perhaps this piece of data may become irrelevant.>

<Agreed, Julien. Thank you.> Edouard had ended the comm before anything more could be said. He had expected to be shut down and reprimanded. The compromise was a gift and he would take it. *A gift from a SADE*, Edouard thought. *What have you done to us, Admiral?* Edouard had slowly shaken his head in disbelief.

Today, the *Outward Bound*'s liftoff was going to be different. It had started with the removal of the safety engine locks while at the orbital station, with Julien guiding Edouard and the techs through the steps. The crew knew that the Admiral had done the same thing on the *Rêveur* to escape the silver ships at Bellamonde, and they hoped they had the same good fortune.

The *Outward Bound* landed without the need to exceed normal power levels. The techs were supervising their refueling and running preflight checks. Edouard, Miko, and Pia, who had kept the crew going with nutrient and stimulant injections, were loading the passengers. Unlike previous flights, often with a single passenger to each seat, they placed children in their parents' laps and sat young adults in the aisles and the galley. When Miko signaled all full, Pia looked at the middle-aged woman on the ramp with her two teenage sons and motioned them forward. Edouard and Miko threw Pia incredulous looks as she and her latest passengers threaded their way down the aisle, people edging out of their way. Pia walked to the refresher, opened the door, and motioned them inside. The teenagers hurried past and took seats on the deck. The woman touched Pia's face gently as she edged past and sat between her sons, placing an arm around each of them. The image of the mother and her sons seated on the deck of the refresher, smiles on their faces, burned into Pia's mind and was carefully saved in her implant.

<Now we can go, Captain,> Pia sent. In the beginning, Pia had kept the crew amused with her inventive messages and images. Lyle and Zeke called her the ship's "comedian," which Miko had to explain to Edouard. But Pia was now as exhausted as the rest of them, and it had been days since she had entertained the crew with her mental games.

Lyle and Zeke signaled *all ready* as they retracted the gangway ramp and locked the hatch. Lyle picked up the young boy who had been sitting in his seat, and held him in his lap for liftoff.

Edouard took the pilot's chair for their first overburdened lift, with Miko in the copilot seat. Together they piloted the *Outward Bound* skyward, the engines straining to lift the overburdened shuttle. They glanced at one another as the engine power display passed 100 percent, turning from green to yellow and finally to red.

But as adrenaline-pumping as that first liftoff had been, the crew quickly fell back into their old routine. Unfortunately there was no room to nap, so the crew slept in their seats. Edouard wanted to abandon the extra daily flight they had been allowed so his crew could get some rest, but their hard-eyed stares convinced him to abandon his offer.

By day three of the deadline, neither the red lights of their controller's power display nor the roar of the straining engines frightened the crew anymore. They became sleepwalkers, flying rotation after rotation. The passengers climbing the *Outward Bound*'s gangway ramp to board would exchange concerned looks at the hollowed eyes and listless motions of their Captain and his crew.

23

Once the *Sternenlicht* exited the Bellamonde system, the *Sternenvagabund* was left to maintain the watch over the alien ships as the drones cleared atmosphere and made their way to the mother ship. With its immense diameter, it would have been logical to assume that the number of drones circling the mother ship would be able to enter through a multitude of bays, but it wasn't so. The drones used a single point of entry and slipped through the iris-style hatch one at a time, with a distinct pause before the next fighter could enter.

Patrolling silver ships made their way from across the system to rendezvous with the mother ship. As they arrived, they joined the other fighters circling the mother ship's massive circumference, waiting for their turn to enter.

Before they'd left Arno, Captain Azasdau and Captain Hauser had met with the Admiral, per his request. The request had seemed unusual, as the Bergfalk Captains had their instructions and could not conceive of the Admiral modifying Leader Stroheim's orders. But the Captains discovered the Admiral didn't wish to issue orders or directives. Instead, they were requested to carefully observe the mother ship and her drones, and ask themselves why the enemy did things.

Captain Azasdau thought it was a strange request until he found himself doing just that—wondering why. *Most inefficient,* Asu thought as he regarded the fighters waiting to enter the mother ship, and the odd behavior engaged his engineering training. *So why would you only allow your drones to enter one at a time through a single point of entry?* Asu wondered. *One would think you don't trust your minions,* he thought, directing his words at the mother ship, *and I think you're going to be upset when I tell the Admiral about your strange little habit.*

Asu recalled the first time he viewed the Admiral's vid of the subterranean-like nature of the aliens. Now, as he'd watched the silver ships cluster around the mother ship, acting in their submissive fashion, he saw the truth in the concept. They behaved like a colony of burrowers he had investigated as a boy. When moving to a new location, the creatures clustered protectively around their queen, driving all intruders away.

The crew of the *Sternenvagabund* had passed the days waiting for the mother ship to gather its drones, and counting down the remaining ships. Rosette, the ship's SADE, was able to identify subtle differences in each hull. So despite the fact that some silver ships were out of sight when they circled behind the mother ship, she could maintain the count. The significant number, according to the Admiral, was ten.

<Captain,> Rosette sent, <the count is eleven. The next silver ship that enters the mother ship will leave the defenders at ten as we have been warned.>

<Thank you, Rosette,> Asu sent.

Captain Azasdau had always treated his SADE with courtesy and found it had paid off for him over the decades. Rosette was very proactive in suggesting small things that kept his ship receiving commendations for efficiency.

"Captain, should we go to active telemetry and determine the mother ship's course to negate the delay?" the First Mate asked.

<Rosette, your opinion?> the Captain asked.

<Captain, at present, we are in alignment with the mother ship and Arno. I would be concerned that active telemetry would attract the mother ship to us and perhaps direct her choice between Libre and Méridien. However, the Admiral's SADEs have calculated that the mother ship is sure to direct its course for Libre.>

The *Sternenvagabund*'s officers regarded one another, considering variations on Rosette's advice. If the active telemetry were to attract the mother ship and help persuade its direction, which way should they attract it? Méridien was their home world, but the people they were charged with servicing and protecting had been deserted by the Confederation Council.

So who should be sacrificed? The officers were quite content to let their Captain decide.

<Switch telemetry to active mode, Rosette,> Asu ordered.

Hours later, they had their answer. <The mother ship's course, Captain, indicates Libre,> Rosette sent.

The Captain had Rosette send a preliminary announcement to Libre and remained on station for several more hours to confirm the mother ship's trajectory.

The enemy remained on course for Libre, and Rosette sent the confirmation just before the *Sternenvagabund* entered FTL. Without an update, Asu had no way of knowing the state of preparation of his people, House Bergfalk and the Independents. *We are all in the same predicament,* he thought.

* * *

The *Sternenreisende* exited FTL, arriving midday on day five. Captain Hauser immediately signaled Leader Stroheim. In turn, Leader Stroheim requested Z add Alex, Tomas, Renée, and the other two SADEs into a conference. He was doing his best to anticipate the Admiral's needs.

<Greetings, Leader Stroheim,> Lillian sent, <we received the unfortunate announcement from the *Sternenvagabund* while we were in transit. So the mother ship and her brood are coming our way?>

<That's affirmed, Captain,> Eric sent, appending the conference list for the Captain's benefit.

<Greetings, Admiral,> Lillian said.

<Welcome back, Captain. Do you have any new information for us other than your message?>

<I have nothing to add, Admiral. Elizabeth is transferring the vids of the rising to Julien, as requested.>

<I appreciate the cooperation, Captain.>

<We are pleased to do what we can to help. What are my orders, Admiral?>

<Captain, you have Bay-3 on Raumstation Eins next to the *Sternenlicht*. You will need to immediately load supplies for 350 passengers plus crew from around the station. Do not expect shuttle deliveries for your supplies. Use every storage space available. Check in with Captain Schmidt if you have any questions. After supplies are aboard, contact Z. He will assign your crew work positions supporting the *Unsere Menschen* until it lifts. You will be delaying your departure until the last possible moment. Your passengers will come from shuttles landing at the station after the *Unsere Menschen* launches. Follow our SADEs' directives carefully, Captain,> Alex said, emphasizing this last command.

<May I ask, Admiral, how we are managing the exodus?>

There was silence for the moment on the comm. <We have our challenges, Captain, but we are working to meet them,> said Alex.

<Understood, Admiral. We will endeavor to help you meet those challenges.>

*　*　*

Mutter had coordinated the landing of seven Daggers into her two bays not more than three hours before the *Sternenreisende*'s arrival. Per the Admiral's order, Sheila sent three Daggers to the *Rêveur*, led by Lieutenant Hatsuto Tanaka, her flight second. She kept Robert with her.

When Tatia questioned Sheila about Tanaka's assignment, her Squadron Leader responded, "Robert has done a great job training the recruits. From now on, that's his job. And Tanaka is good, probably as good as Jase, and somewhere along the way, he's gotten his ego under control."

"Well, it's your decision, Commander," Tatia replied.

"Thank you, Commander," Sheila replied before Tatia's words sank in. "I'm sorry, Commander, what did you call me?"

"Admiral's orders, Commander, and at this rate you may not have to wait the year out to reach that top position you joked about when you made Squadron Leader."

Tatia left a stunned Commander Reynard in her wake and checked in for deployment orders with Andrea.

<How do you want to manage officer assignments, Captain?> Tatia sent to Andrea.

<One moment, Commander,> Andrea replied as she linked Alex into the comm.

Alex linked Mickey, who was just returning to the *Money Maker* from the *Unsere Menschen*. <Give me a status, please,> Alex requested.

<We have seven Daggers and full missile loads for them with a newly reconditioned ship, Admiral,> Tatia reported. <Commander Reynard sent you the veterans. Lieutenant Tanaka is on his way to you with the three Daggers you requested.>

Both Alex and Andrea read between the lines of Tatia's message. Robert wasn't going to be an active pilot.

<Commander, what's your personnel assessment under the circumstances?> Alex asked.

<Captain Menlo and his XO are going to have their hands full with the freighter and their run to the exit point. Our new Commander will be flying point for any defensive maneuvers. That leaves no seasoned officers on board to manage and troubleshoot bay operation and any fighter issues. Mickey and I are of the opinion that we need to stay aboard the *Money Maker*.>

<Commander, Chief, you understand the *Money Maker* is one of the slowest vessels in the flotilla,> Andrea said, giving them the opportunity to change ships.

<We understand, Captain. If the silver ships catch the freighters, our seven Daggers might buy us enough time to make exit, but the pilots and flight crew will need all the support they can get.>

<We'll support your decision, Commander,> said Andrea.

<One thing, Captain, I'm sending Alain back to the *Rêveur*. His function here is at an end.>

Andrea, standing next to Alex, glanced at him. She could sense the pain Tatia's statement caused her. When Alex said nothing, Andrea knew it was her call.

<Understood, Commander. We'll expect him back aboard the *Rêveur* shortly.>

Tatia closed her comm and went to meet Alain at the waiting shuttle.

Alain wasn't pleased about returning to the *Rêveur* and took his time holding Tatia in a close hug. "With this ship's limited velocity, you must urge the Captain to launch as soon as the Admiral permits," Alain said.

"We have orders to leave now. As soon as your shuttle is off, Alain, these bay doors will close and we're gone," Tatia replied.

"That's good. Be safe, my heart," Alain replied. "If this craft is not fast enough to beat the silver ships to the exit point, I expect you and Mickey to get out and push. Put your oversized selves to some good use.>

Tatia laughed at his joke, but inside, her guts were knotted. She kissed him good-bye. Alain, long since having lost his reticence for public displays, returned it until her toes warmed. Alain waved to her from the shuttle's gangway ramp, and Tatia waved back. The moment the shuttle hatch was sealed, she marched for the bay's airlock and signaled the Captain.

Within a half-hour, the *Geldbringer*—or if you asked Mickey, the *Money Maker*—turned onto a course to employ Libre's gravity to help it accelerate, chasing her sister ship, the *Langstrecke,* to the exit point.

* * *

Tomas had met with Terese and asked her to stay aboard the *Freedom* with him.

"Your offer is most appreciated, Tomas," Terese had replied. "I would like nothing better if we were at peace. But until our people are safe and need fight no longer, my place is aboard the *Rêveur*."

"You are a woman of great honor," Tomas had said. "There is much I like about you."

"And I care for you, Tomas," Terese had said, touching his cheek.

"Please inform the Admiral that I would consider it a personal favor if he would keep you safe."

She had laughed at that. "You should know by now, Tomas, that few know how to tell the Admiral anything, but that is his strength. He isn't burdened by the strictures that our society gave us. So I will tell him that you send your regards." She had kissed him warmly and made her way to the shuttle bay.

Terese had joined Renée, Étienne, and the other *Rêveur* crew members boarding the aging Libre Station passenger shuttle, which the *Rêveur* would keep. It's why Alex had only ordered three Daggers, housing two in the starboard bay and one in the port bay.

Their shuttle landed in the *Rêveur*'s port bay, sliding forward to make room for the Dagger's exit. As Terese walked down the gangway ramp, Renée took her hand in sympathy. It had hurt Terese to leave Tomas, but she didn't regret her decision. She knew where she had to be.

* * *

On the morning of day six, Captain Cordova ordered the crew and passengers, who had been scavenging the station for supplies and useful material throughout the night, back to the *Freedom*. Some of the last to board from the station were fourteen runners, each child carrying a potted plant retrieved from the Station Manager's offices to decorate their cabins.

The last two shuttle deliveries of passengers for the *Freedom* landed in Deck-12's Bay-6, and crew members hurried to unload the eighty-four Librans, urging them out of the bay while other crew grabbed grav-lifts and emptied the bellies of stowed supplies and personal effects.

After the shuttles' departure, hatches were sealed and station supply lines detached. Captain José Cordova stood on the bridge with Tomas. No two men were more relieved than they. It had been eight years since they had begun their endeavor, and this had followed six years of negotiations with Leader Stroheim. Those negotiations had finally succeeded when news of Bellamonde's usurpation by the alien ships reached Libre's FTL station. They had eight years to build two ships that could house all of the

Libran: Independents and House Bergfalk. And they had done it, or at least they had done it by half. The *Unsere Menschen* had yet to launch.

On Captain Cordova's orders, Cordelia began to edge the city-ship away from the station. From an outside observer's viewpoint, the massive ship didn't appear to move. An hour after first activating the ship's maneuvering jets and emptying the compressed air tanks by half, Cordelia was able to engage the giant ship's engines at minimal power. Since the engines were untested, Cordelia was careful to monitor them closely as she constantly increased power. Once she had cleared the station, ships, and satellites, she brought the engines to 80 percent power and began to pick up speed. The *Freedom* chased the slow-moving freighters.

As the *Freedom*'s engines engaged, Julien sent, <Be safe, Cordelia.>

<That is my wish for you, as well, Julien, but I know that is not your path. Just the same, I will hope to meet you at the exit point, good friend. There is still much I wish to share with you.>

24

Late in the evening on day seven, the *Sternenvagabund* arrived in system. Captain Azasdau requested an immediate conference with Alex, while Rosette sent the relevant vids to Julien.

The SADEs pulled in the Leaders and subordinates for Alex. <Welcome back, Captain Azasdau. I take it from your request that you have something to share?> Alex sent.

<Yes, Admiral, it regards your strange ... pardon me ... your request to observe the aliens closely and question why they did things. Julien, please display vid-14.>

The individuals in conference watched the mass of silver ships circle the mother ship.

<So that I don't make myself out to be a total fool,> Asu sent, <I would like to ask if anyone else sees something odd on this vid.>

It was Mickey, the engineer, who found the anomaly first. <Why are they circling? Aren't most of them going to enter the sphere?>

<Eventually all but ten will,> Asu replied. <However, they will all enter through this one bay opening. Julien, could you display vid-18?>

In this vid, the group watched as one ship slid through an iris hatch and another positioned itself just outside the opening while the rest of the drones continued to circle.

<A sphere this size,> Mickey exclaimed, <and you're telling me they have one bay entrance? How is such an advanced ship so poorly designed?>

<Unless it isn't inefficiency ... is it, Captain?> Alex asked, directing his question to Asu.

<I don't think so, Admiral,> Asu replied.

<Let us in on the mystery, Admiral,> Tomas said.

<Mickey has one part right,> Alex replied. <That mother ship is technologically advanced, so an inefficient design isn't going to be part of

its makeup. Yet a day or more will be consumed to load their drones by allowing the fighters only one entry point. What are they afraid of?> Alex mused.

<Who's afraid of what?> Eric asked.

<The entities within the mother ship appear to be afraid of the drones. Isn't that what you see, Admiral?> Asu asked.

<Yes, Captain, and what goes in one way must come out the same way,> Alex said. <Most of our footage of the aliens only covers the period after they have subsumed a planet and begun to swarm. Then the monitor ships beat a hasty retreat. I don't believe we have any imagery of this moment. Do we, Julien?>

It was to Cordelia's and Z's credit that the moment they heard the Admiral ponder the vids, they began scanning for images of the swarm circling the mother ship without waiting for a directive. Within moments, they had scanned the files and had found none.

<You're correct, Admiral, this imagery is unique,> Julien responded for the SADEs.

It was a statement that Asu felt very proud to hear.

<So when we saw a drone enter the mother ship and another exit much later, we assumed that only a single bay opening was ever required, at that time, not that the drones were only allowed one bay opening,> Alex mused on open comm.

Mickey felt he was losing the thread of the conversation. <You keep saying things like "allowed" and "afraid," Admiral. Why would the mother ship fear the drones?>

<That's the question, Mickey, isn't it? But it appears that it does,> Alex replied. <However, the important question is whether the mother ship will use only one exit bay when it arrives in system.>

There was silence on the comm. Most believed the Admiral was deep in thought, so they waited, but Alex was waiting too.

<Nothing, Admiral,> said Julien after Cordelia and Z confirmed the negative. <We have no footage immediately after a mother ship exits FTL and enters a system. All vids that record the mother ship's approach to a colony begin once it has entered deep into the system.>

Alex desperately wanted the answer to the question and was thinking furiously how to get it. The information might buy them some advantage if they had to fight their way out of the system. Alex was studying the system's assets when an answer occurred to him. <Julien,> he ordered, <I want that FTL station moved to a position that will allow it to capture the mother ship as it exits FTL, but I don't want it too exposed. I want to record a minimum of a half-day immediately after the mother ship appears and before a silver ship can get close enough to destroy it. Is it maneuverable and is the request possible?>

<That's an affirmative to both questions, Admiral,> Julien replied.

<If the drones have to exit through a single opening, we may have bought ourselves a little more time,> Alex said. <You did very well, Captain Azasdau. Proceed to Bay-4 on Raumstation Eins next to the *Sternenreisende.* You're receiving the same instructions as Captains Hauser and Schmidt. Check in with Captain Schmidt if you have questions. You're taking on supplies for 350 passengers. As soon as you have your supplies, get your crew aboard the *Unsere Menschen* until it lifts. Z will tell you where to go. You and the other liners will depart with the last Librans, after the *Unsere Menschen* launches. Any questions, Captain?>

Captain Azasdau's first thought as he heard the Admiral make use of his observation of the mother ship was a private one ... *I told you I was going to tell the Admiral about your odd habit.* But the question he voiced was the one on everyone's mind: <How fares the exodus, Admiral?>

<We've launched two freighters and the *Freedom,* Captain. We have tens of thousands of people still on Libre and we are racing the enemy.>

<Understood, Admiral. May fortune guide us to safety.>

Alex closed the comm and everyone went back to work.

* * *

Outside a Raumstation Eins storeroom that had just been emptied, Alex sat down on the deck where he was. The supplies from the storeroom had been transferred to the *Unsere Menschen*. As he communed with the SADEs, Étienne stood watch beside him.

Since the launch of the *Freedom*, Étienne had resumed his duties as escort to the Admiral. When Étienne had prepared to exit that city-ship just before it launched, he had experienced, in quick succession, two heart-tugging moments. The first came as he emptied his temporarily assigned cabin. A couple and their two children were standing in the corridor to move in behind him. He stepped around them and collided with a runner. Amelia had come to say good-bye and had been dashing down the corridor at high speed, afraid she might have missed him. After she recovered, she eyed him for a moment, threw her arms around his waist, hugged him fiercely, and dashed off, back the way she had come.

If ever I am fortunate enough to have a child, little one, Étienne thought, *I could do no better than wish she'd be like you.* Moments later, as he took a lift down to the shuttle deck to join the remainder of the exiting *Rêveur* crew, Renée had signaled him.

<Étienne, have you been assigned another duty yet?> Renée had asked.

<Not at this time, Ser,> Étienne had replied. <I was about to comm Julien and request my next assignment. Did you require something?>

<Very much so, Étienne. I need him safe.>

<Is he in danger, Ser?> Étienne had asked, his heart beginning to race.

<I'm afraid for him, Étienne. Julien reports that the Admiral has been all over the stations, the ships, and even planetside twice in the last three days. He's not been aboard the *Rêveur* for many days now. We're coming to the deadline, and in the last moments, I'm afraid he will have everyone else's well-being on his in mind, except his own.>

<Rest easy, Ser. Julien will locate him for me, and from now on, I will be by his side,> Étienne had said.

Now he stood beside Alex, who sat on the deck, his uniform splotched with lubricants, nanites gel, and something with an odor that defied identification. The uniform hadn't seen a refresher in days.

<Team, I need a summary and a countdown on the people,> Alex sent, weariness lacing his thoughts.

<We are lifting an average of 4,200 people a day, Admiral,> Julien responded. <The shuttles are shut down for the night and crews are servicing them to the extent they are able. All of them are past due for major servicing, including the *Outward Bound*.>

<How many people are still planetside, Julien?>

This was one of the moments that Julien had come to intensely dislike. <There are 14,637 Librans still to lift.>

<Almost four days' worth of people and only two days to do it in ...> said Alex, his thoughts trailing off.

None of the SADEs responded. There seemed nothing appropriate to say.

<Z,> Alex said, <please give me the status on the *Unsere Menschen*.>

<Admiral, that is difficult to ascertain. In order to expedite flight-readiness, much of the equipment is being installed as bare basics without oversight systems. This requires individuals on site to operate the equipment and communicate between other operators and myself. In addition, I'm disappointed to report that several systems failed initial tests.>

<Black space, Z! Why didn't you tell me?> Alex exploded, coming to his feet so quickly that Étienne scanned the corridor for danger.

<I considered it, Admiral,> Z replied. <Then I realized that there was nothing you could have done. The additional crews from the liners discovered the problems and repaired them. I did not wish to deliver more disappointing news. Was my judgment in error, Admiral?> Z asked, doubting that he had properly incorporated his lessons from Cordelia and Julien.

Alex sat contemplating the possibility that they were fighting to load half the Librans onto a ship that might never launch in time. He wanted to cry; he wanted to scream. But it wasn't only Z that hadn't told him. No one else had said a word. *Maybe they're right*, Alex thought. *Maybe there's a point where it's all too much.* <No, Z. I understand why you didn't say anything. There was nothing I could have done about it, but in the future, I need to know these things.>

<Understood, Admiral. I will adjust my reasoning algorithms accordingly,> Z said.

Alex smiled at that. Z was all about the math and the code. People were just too messy for him. <Has your launch status been affected, Z?>

<Repairs on the systems have pushed back our launch by thirty-one hours, Admiral.> The *Unsere Menschen* was scheduled to leave early in the morning of the tenth day, just over two days from now. Z was saying it would be an additional day.

<Z,> Alex started to send and then stopped.

<There is nothing to be done, Admiral,> Z answered. <In one hundred and six hours, we will attempt the most poorly prepared launch in the entire 700-year history of the Confederation.>

Z's statement would have been humorous, if it wasn't so deadly accurate. Alex had worked to build a single day of padding in the timeline for the launch of the city-ships, and the *Unsere Menschen* was going to consume the entire safety margin.

<Julien,> Alex said, <give me your best calculations on our enemy.>

<That's unknown, Admiral. They may travel through FTL at a slower or greater rate than us. We do know they will exit FTL at 0.91c and will not need to decelerate as much as we do to enter Libre's orbit. It will take them only three and a half days to reach planetfall.>

Alex was considering their circumstances. <Let's hope there is a limitation at work in FTL and they will traverse the distance no quicker than we do. Julien, assume that the mother ship and exiting drones do not slow, but chase the *Unsere Menschen* at top speed. Finally, use Z's estimated start time and the acceleration data from the *Freedom*. I recognize that this is all worst-case planning, but what does it look like?>

Julien's calculations took only several ticks to complete. It took much longer for him to relay his answer to Alex. <The silver ships would catch the *Unsere Menschen* 3.45 days from the point of exit.>

When Alex couldn't think of a thing to say, he changed subjects. <Cordelia, anything I need to be concerned about?>

<No, Admiral,> Cordelia sent. <The *Freedom* has had minor systems problems, but nothing that hasn't been able to be corrected, and nothing that affected our ability to continue to accelerate.>

<Okay, one piece of good news,> Alex replied. <Everyone, that's it for now. Z, any change in the launch time and I get notified immediately.>

<Understood, Admiral,> Z replied.

After Alex closed the comm, he sat back down on the deck, thinking for a while. Z had been right. There was nothing he could have done, and they certainly didn't need an anxious Admiral leaning over their collective shoulders. His thoughts drifted back to the people on the ground. It suddenly struck him that they were being denied a choice. Up until now, everyone would be expecting to go, and the loading of passengers had been a very orderly affair. *But what if they knew that not everyone might be lifted?* Alex thought.

* * *

Tatia jerked upright in her cabin bunk. She had laid her head down only an hour ago and had quickly passed out, but she had been woken by an insistent pressure in her mind. <Admiral?> she guessed.

<Sorry, Commander, but I need some information.>

"It's alright, Admiral," she mumbled out loud, then realized her mistake. <What do you need, Admiral?> she sent.

<I must talk to someone planetside, someone important, who can manage a problem. It can't be handled from up here, and Tomas is already gone on the *Freedom*. You're the senior officer who spent the most time on Libre. I need your recommendation.>

<Only one person, Admiral, fits that bill. Contact Fiona Haraken. She's the Elder on Libre, and the one who whipped Barren-II into shape and kept it there. For a 185-year-old, she has more energy than a power-crystal and is straightforward as they come.>

<Do you think she is still planetside, because that part is crucial?> Alex asked.

<Fiona was offered reserved seats on the shuttles for her and her family for her help with Barren-II. She refused her seat, saying there was too much work to do. She's there, Admiral. She'll be the last person off that planet.>

<Thank you, Commander. Go back to sleep. Sorry to disturb you.>

Tatia lay back, thinking of her people whom she had left behind, struggling to save thousands of Librans. A few days after she had refused the promotion to Senior Captain, she'd wondered if she had made the right decision. While she respected Andrea Bonnard, Tatia had begun to realize that she brought much more to the job than she gave herself credit for.

* * *

<Julien,> Alex said, <I need to speak to Fiona Haraken. She will be on planet.>

<Good evening, Admiral,> came a female's thoughts. <You know, I tell my great grandchildren every day that you young people need your sleep. But perhaps you have too much on your mind to sleep, Admiral.>

Alex couldn't help but smile. Fiona was as Tatia advertised. <Good evening, Fiona. I need your help.>

<That's what I'm here for, Admiral. Let me say first, though, that you have a nice group of young people there. I have a special fondness for Tatia. Is she alright?>

<She is a good person, isn't she?> Alex said. <Tatia is on the freighter, the *Geldbringer*, and they launched days ago.>

<That's good to hear. How can I help you, Admiral? I don't believe you would be calling me this late with glad tidings.>

<I'm afraid it isn't the best of news, but it isn't all bad. What we don't know is exactly how much time is left. There are too many variables.> In response to his statements, Alex heard Fiona's throaty chuckle.

<Why do the young think age does not accrue wisdom?> Fiona asked. <Admiral, we've been monitoring your lift count every day. When you

began your accelerated timetable seven days ago, we determined your new lift rate after the first day and came to the realization of what you're trying to share with me now. Not all of us may get off this planet.>

<There is some good news. The *Unsere Menschen*'s launch will be delayed by a full day,> Alex said.

<So we will have an extra day,> Fiona mused. <It will be close, then.>

<Yes, and that brings me to the reason for my call.> Alex closed his eyes as if it would help take away the pain of what he had to say next.

<Would it be that you wish to tell us we need to determine a priority system for our people, Admiral?>

<I see I'm demonstrating my youth and ignorance again,> Alex sent, awed by the woman's perceptiveness.

<Don't be concerned, Admiral. We began prioritizing our people when you began your countdown.>

<May I ask how you determined your priority, Fiona?>

<It was simple for us, Admiral. We've sent the youngest first with their parents.>

<I wish there was something more I could do, Fiona.>

<You need not be concerned, Admiral. This is a burden for us to carry, not you. Those of us who may be left planetside know that the *Freedom* has launched in time, thanks to your help. That's half of our people who are moving to safety.>

<Please let me know what I may do for you and your people, Fiona. I will continue to try to find a way to get everyone off the planet.>

<If one was to believe your Tatia, then I'm sure you will not stop trying, Admiral. And if I may, you don't strike me as the kind of person who would have such an elastic schedule that, with little more than two days to go before your expected launch time, you suddenly find another day. What's happened?> When Alex didn't respond to her, she softened her tone. <There's a problem with the *Unsere Menschen*, isn't there, Admiral?>

<For your ears only, Elder,> Alex said, applying the Méridien term of respect. <There are several systems that failed their tests. They've been fixed, but it's pushed back the launch time, and the problems are adding to

the burden of the number of systems that must be manually controlled and coordinated.>

<Do you think they will be able to be launch, Admiral?>

<I don't know, Fiona. I just don't know,> Alex replied, his words trailing off.

Fiona imagined the Admiral somewhere up above her—a young man barely twelve years older than her great-grandson, trying desperately to save an entire planet full of people he had only recently met. *Such a good heart,* she thought.

<Well, Admiral, you're correct that this information is for these old ears only. So long as there's some hope, that's what I will give my people. The worries are for those like you and me. I have my years of experience to help me, and you, Admiral … well, you have those broad shoulders.>

Alex heard her laughter as she closed the comm. He found he was lamenting the fact that he might never get the opportunity to know Fiona Haraken. Inevitably, some Librans would be left behind, and Alex could see the truth in Tatia's words. Fiona would be the last Independent to leave her planet.

25

Day eight became a blur for everyone, except for those who waited on the ground. People hurried around Raumstation Eins station and the giant city-ship in a mental fog. The pilots were flying like automatons, performing their actions more by muscle memory than attention. The shuttles would land, crew would fuel, and no one was performing inspections. The gangway ramp would extend and passengers would file on and quickly take seats, filling up every space, including the *Outward Bound*'s refresher deck. The younger Librans had come to consider it a badge of honor to occupy those unique seats.

The crews of the shuttles napped in place after they made space, while the SADEs maintained watch and guided the shuttles to the *Unsere Menschen*. An alert was sent to the pilot's implants when they approached the city-ship within 100 km. Then Z chatted with the pilots for a while to ensure that they had returned to full alertness.

Accidents, previously a rarity among Méridiens—although the New Terrans weren't always so careful—increased for everyone. The city-ship's medical bays were kept busy repairing cuts, burns, and broken bones. Two people were in comas while nanites repaired the concussions that both of them had suffered in separate incidents.

Z remained in constant contact with the Admiral, having recognized his error while attempting to employ his new lessons in human sensibilities. Briefly Z had considered his old ways to have been preferable, but after further reflection, he realized the old ways would have him still on Libre with no hope for the future. And the Admiral's daily comms had become entertaining. He discovered the Admiral was finding time to read the material he had sent Julien on AI mobility and they often chatted on the subject for several moments. Z might have thought the Admiral was merely attempting to make him feel better about his constant requests for updates.

The negation of that line of reasoning was that the Admiral's questions were insightful and appeared to focus on a SADE's appearance and the public's reactions.

* * *

Alex and Étienne had spent the night in the Raumstation Eins Station Manager's plush offices. After a few hours of sleep, they started day nine by making their way to a meal room aboard the *Unsere Menschen*. The meal rooms were serviced thirty hours a day by young passengers, who had no useful tech skills. The youthful Librans would seat the workers, bring them food, and clean up after them, allowing critically needed people to return to their jobs that much quicker.

This particular meal room had forty or so people already seated, being served even at 4.75 hours. A young woman dipped her head to Alex and motioned them toward seats at a small table on the side of the room for a little privacy. She signaled another young woman at the dispensers, who busily prepared trays for their important guests. No one had to ask what the Admiral and his escort, Étienne, preferred. Every Libran had begun accumulating a small library of the preferences of these two individuals.

Alex turned his head at Étienne's nod. Five small children stood behind him, four with food trays and one with drinks. A tray was placed in front of Étienne. Three children couldn't hide their smiles and giggles when they handed their trays to the Admiral. The fifth child placed a cup of aigre in front of Étienne and an empty cup in front of the Admiral. Then the boy carefully filled Alex's cup with thé, setting the pitcher on the table.

Alex picked up his utensil, belatedly noticing one little boy still standing there with his hand extended. Alex regarded the serious expression on the child's face and the tiny hand extended toward him. The young woman who had greeted them was now hurrying forward to recover her wayward server. Alex smiled at the little one and used his forefinger and thumb to shake the boy's hand. The child's fingers could barely circle Alex's finger, but he shook it with intent.

After their meal, Alex and Étienne headed to one of the cavernous bays of the city-ship. A query by Alex for information regarding a comparison of the shuttle turnaround time of *Freedom* versus the *Unsere Menschen* had revealed a discrepancy.

In the bay, Alex took a stance beside a sidelined shuttle. There were several in the bay, certified as unsafe to fly for want of repairs or heavy maintenance. He watched the Bergfalk crew unload the next shuttle. Their procedures were a polite and orderly disembarkation of the passengers and a methodical unloading of the supplies, the crew taking time to move the supplies through the airlock before the shuttle was released.

Alex sent a quick order to Julien. <I need two good New Terrans to act as flight chiefs, people already on board this ship. Send them to me yesterday.> Moments later, two of Alex's flight crew cycled through the airlock and came running up to him, snapping to attention, and delivering sharp salutes. <Sers, each of you are taking charge of a bay until you have to exit and return to the *Rêveur*. Now watch.>

The crewmen waited as another shuttle cleared the ship's catch-lock. Once the lock's space was equalized, the inner doors slid open and grav-lifts embedded in the deck floated the shuttle into the bay, the connecting doors to the catch-lock sealing behind the shuttle. The four men stood there watching the methodical process of the Bergfalk personnel.

In the meantime, Alex queried Julien and Z. <I need to swap out some personnel. For every two Méridiens in Bay-7 and Bay-8, I want one New Terran. I don't want engineers or my top techs. I want people and baggage movers, and I want them yesterday as well.>

When Alex saw that his men had seen enough, he said to them, <Fix this. Get these shuttles out of here as fast as possible without hurting anyone,> and then walked off.

Z and Julien ran down their personnel lists and began issuing orders. Each New Terran who reported to a bay replaced two Méridiens, who were then reassigned to the work that the New Terran had been doing. Most Méridiens found they struggled to accomplish the same workload as their cousins.

After a shuttle cycled through the bay under the care of the New Terrans, Z was attempting to reconcile how the turnaround had been shortened by 38 percent. He queried Julien with the data. <Julien, I calculate that we could have produced nearly two more days of passenger loads by a single shuttle. How is it possible to have made such an egregious error?>

<Z, it is not an error on your part,> Julien replied. <You have not observed New Terrans working in earnest. They don't have centuries of protocols to follow. And when there's exigent circumstances, they invent shortcuts.>

* * *

As day nine progressed, Z calculated that the shuttles would lift an additional 1,290 Librans by the launch time of the passenger liners. That was until shuttle HB-L131 reported a problem during its lift. The pilots were at full power, striving to reach orbit as engine coolant temperatures exceeded tolerances. The temperature gauges spiked, the engines lost containment, and shuttle HB-L131, filled with forty-nine passengers and five crew members, exploded.

Those on the ground witnessed the spectacular fireball. The SADEs quickly circulated the critical news, and Z sadly reset his lift expectations. What the Admiral had gained through the bay personnel changes had just been lost through the shuttle explosion.

When day nine ended, the tally was 3,903 more Librans lifted, fifty-four dead, and one shuttle lost. The remaining shuttles, including the *Outward Bound*, now parked on the *Unsere Menschen* for overnight servicing. Engineers and techs swarmed over them, doing what they could to prep them for the next day.

* * *

When day ten started, it was business as usual, but everyone was tense. No one was falling asleep or napping. The shuttles continued lifting Librans as fast as they could, and when they landed aboard the *Unsere Menschen,* New Terrans poured them out of the shuttles as if they were liquid. Each shuttle was sliding back through the catch-lock doors before half the passengers had even exited the bay. There was always the risk of human or mechanical error creating a dangerous decompression, but Z was paying particular attention to the shuttle operations, hoping to avert a disaster before it could happen.

* * *

Julien had placed the FTL comm station just outward of the last planet, tucked next to a small moonlet. The rotation of the tiny satellite around the planet meant outward-focused telemetry was lost for five out of twelve hours, but in the distances of space, it was a small loss to ensure the station was hidden.

On one pass to the dark side of the planet, the station recorded the huge mother ship exiting FTL. The image was immediately relayed to the SADEs and, per the Admiral's instructions, applications were set to observe and analyze. The SADEs identified the mother ship's velocity immediately as 0.91c. The giant sphere was still hours away from the orbit of the outermost planet where the FTL station hid, and not a single silver ship was in sight.

Alex let the people continue to work, and he and the SADEs kept quiet.

* * *

As the *Outward Bound* landed planetside, Edouard and Miko could see the remaining crowd gathered in the fields just beyond the runway berm. It was the same location where the Librans had first gathered to hear the Admiral speak.

According to Edouard's update from Julien, every person left on Libre was in that field. The people had erected shelters from the sun to wait out their turn to lift. There were still families among them, but none with small children. What remained were parents with adult children, and single adults, many of them quite elderly.

The Admiral had apprised the shuttle crews of the Independents' final boarding priority, and while these people had been branded as Independents, they were managing the process in true Méridien fashion.

When Edouard heard of the people's decision from Alex, he was sad and angry. <So, Admiral, we're leaving behind the elders, the wisest of our people,> Edouard had replied.

<That is how they wish it, Edouard,> Alex said, calling the Méridien by his given name. <It's the sacrifice they wish to make for their young,>

<Then we'll move as many as we can, Admiral, to lessen their sacrifice,> Edouard replied, his thoughts radiating determination and anger.

<I know you will, Edouard. You're a good man,> Alex said before he closed the comm.

All his life, Edouard, along with every other Méridien, had been taught that the Independents had abandoned their culture because they must somehow be mentally defective. Some scientists had even studied the genetics of the Independents to try to determine the source of the flaws. Others proposed the problem stemmed from a mental imbalance caused by the implant. But neither group had been successful in proving their theory and determining what created an Independent.

Now Edouard felt ashamed. The manner in which the Independents chose to handle their fate proved they were Méridiens. They had chosen a most honorable solution, and he was guilty of condemning them for being less than human, less than Méridien. *No, Admiral,* Edouard thought, *I'm not a good man.*

When the elders saw the *Outward Bound* land, they sent the next 223 individuals over the berm. The Librans moved quickly and without baggage to reduce the total weight, allowing a few more passengers to board.

* * *

As day ten ended and the shuttles docked on the *Unsere Menschen* for refueling and servicing, Alex and the SADEs watched the mother ship cross the outer planet's orbit, and the first silver ship exited. They continued to emerge one by one until ten drones circled the giant sphere.

The FTL station was shut down once the active telemetry of the flotilla's ships began receiving the mother ship. It was hoped that the FTL station could remain hidden for later, if there was to be a later.

Alex had the SADEs connect him to every implant in the Arno system: fleeing ships, parked ships, stations, planetside, and wherever. <Librans, the aliens are here,> Alex began. <The silver ships are exiting the mother ship one at a time. The first ten are out and circling it. They will stay with the sphere to protect it. But the mother ship is approaching at the expected velocity of 0.91c. The enemy will be here in ninety-two hours. We must launch the *Unsere Menschen* by 6 hours tomorrow, but the liners can continue to take on passengers until 17 hours tomorrow.>

What Alex didn't say is that the liners would have a sufficient head-start to outrun the silver ships, but the *Unsere Menschen* never would. The city-ship had already been scheduled to launch at 6 hours tomorrow, so Alex wasn't really announcing anything different to the Leaders and officers, and the SADEs knew it.

* * *

The *Outward Bound*'s crew was taking a late-evening meal when they heard the Admiral's announcement of the enemy's arrival. Edouard laid his utensil down and took a sip of aigre to wash down his last bite of food. He regarded his crewmates, Miko, Pia, Lyle, and Zeke, who returned his determined look with ones of their own. Then the five of them rose and headed for the shuttle bays. The other shuttle crews in the meal room watched the Admiral's premier flight crew head out and took their cue. They snatched last bites of food and drink and hurried after them.

The two acting flight chiefs in the *Unsere Menschen*'s flight bays recognized an uprising when they saw it. Momentarily it crossed their minds to resist, but the looks on the shuttle crews' faces shut those thoughts down. Instead they begged for enough time to allow the flight crews to complete the shuttles' minimal maintenance.

The pilots relented and stood by impatiently as the flight crews completed their jobs and got out of the way. Within two hours of Alex's announcement, all the shuttles were headed planetside. There were still thousands of people on the ground, and the shuttle crews were determined to lift as many as they could.

26

Throughout the night, the shuttles flew. Julien and Z monitored the crafts' readiness as more and more red warnings appeared on their bridge consoles. The Libre population planetside dwindled by a count of about 352 with every round trip of the shuttles.

<Admiral, are you monitoring these passenger figures?> Andrea Bonnard asked.

<You mean do I see that the shuttles are round-tripping faster than expected, and they are loading more people than we have specified for maximum load?> Alex replied, fatigue coloring his thoughts.

Andrea didn't answer. She mentally kicked herself for underestimating the applications running in her Admiral's implant. *Must be crowded in there*, she thought. Alex's response indicated he knew exactly how dangerous the flights were becoming, and he had made the decision not to interfere. She understood. When the silver ships reached Libre, every person left behind would be a scar on the survivors' memories forever.

Renée had food and drink delivered to the bridge crew, who had missed evening meal and would not be leaving their posts this night. She personally handed Andrea a hot mug of thé. "What arrangement has the Admiral made for the *Rêveur* crew's recovery from the city-ship?"

Andrea shifted uncomfortably in her command chair. "The Admiral's left no orders, Ser, in that regard."

"Shouldn't that be corrected, Captain?" Renée replied.

Andrea heard the question, which didn't sound like a question at all. "Yes, Ser, it will be."

<Julien,> Andrea sent.

<In process, Captain,> he replied.

* * *

Alex was hurrying through the city-ship's corridors. As Z's troubleshooter, he was checking systems with engineers and coordinating the manual operations of the systems required to launch. One of his implant programs continued to track a summary of the people left on the ground, every shuttle trip, and every passenger load count.

<Admiral,> Julien commed, <we need your orders for the *Réveur*'s final positioning and retrieval of the crew.>

<There's time to deal with that later, Julien,> Alex replied, distracted by three Méridiens straining to manually move a crate out of the corridor when their grav-lift lost charge. He and Étienne leaned into the huge crate with the three women, and the two-meter-tall box slid into the storage room. The three Bergfalk crew members slapped Alex and Étienne on their shoulders as they turned to walk away.

<I believe that now is the appropriate time to make these decisions, Admiral,> Julien pressed.

<Julien ...> Alex began then stopped. Despite his fatigue, he recognized when his friend was emphasizing a subtext.

<What's the problem, Julien?>

<Your timely decisions will maintain what your people term "domestic bliss.">

<Ah ...> Alex said. He could just visualize an impatient and adamant Co-Leader on the other end of this request. He linked Andrea into the comm. <Captain, we need to begin final preparations for ourselves.>

<Absolutely, Admiral,> Andrea sent, relief coloring her thoughts.

<Captain, we need a dock on Raumstation Eins for the *Réveur*. Julien, is there one with clear overhead so the *Outward Bound* can link up while we are docked?>

<Admiral, the Raumstation Eins docks are all occupied,> Julien replied.

<Okay, here's what we do,> Alex replied. <The city-ship will launch. Then we'll take its dock. Since we'll be late to the exit party, we'll be the last to load passengers and launch. Have our crew, those working in the

Unsere Menschen's bays, use the Libre Station shuttle and exit the city-ship by 5 hours to rendezvous with you. The rest of the crew will exit the city-ship at the same time into the station to await your docking.>

<Just so I'm clear, Admiral,> Andrea sent, <you, personally, will be exiting into the station or via the shuttle at 5 hours?>

Andrea's words told Alex that Renée was probably standing right next to his Senior Captain, waiting for an answer. <I'll exit with the crew into the station, Captain.>

<Thank you, Admiral,> Andrea replied. She couldn't hide the mental relief that accompanied her response.

* * *

Alex linked with Eric, Andrea, Julien, and Z. <Leader Stroheim, Julien and Z have determined that even if you launch on time at 6 hours and the silver ships give chase, they will catch you before the exit point.>

Eric was taken aback by Alex's revelation. Everything his people had worked toward was being denied in one sentence. The city-ship wouldn't reach safety. But if Eric had learned one thing about the Admiral, he always started with the worst tidings.

<Admiral, what do you need from us and what's your plan?> Eric asked, sending a wish to fortune.

<Leader, the *Unsere Menschen* must leave by 6 hours tomorrow morning. The delay is too great as it is, so whatever you have to do, ensure you launch that ship on time.>

<Understood, Admiral. We'll do our best. And your plan...?> Eric asked again and held his breath.

<There are too many variables at this time, Leader. But you won't be out there alone. My people will be trying to buy you time.>

Eric let go of his breath in a whoosh, tears forming in his eyes. The Admiral wasn't going to abandon them. He regretted every cruel thought he'd ever had about the New Terrans, especially their Admiral. *Who is the better human?* Eric thought ruefully. He knew it wasn't him.

<Most importantly, we need to back-time your launch, Leader,> Alex continued. <I want your hatches closed, your ship backed away from the station, and your engines spinning up by 6 hours. What will that take?>

<Z, if you will, please?> Eric requested.

<We will require 0.92 hours, Admiral, which is the time Cordelia used from hatch closing to engine ignition.>

<Leader, I will order all shuttle flights for your ship to terminate by 4.75 hours, no later. Don't accept any latecomers. My people will exit your ship via shuttle and your station gangway by 5 hours.>

<Your orders are understood, Admiral. It will be done.>

Alex cut the comm and linked to the liner Captains and shuttle pilots.

<The launch of the *Unsere Menschen* will begin at 5 hours,> Alex sent. <Shuttle Pilots, deliver no passengers to the city-ship after 4.75 hours. If you are a tick past this time, divert to Raumstation Eins's shuttle bay. Liner Captains, coordinate with one another to divide the Raumstation Eins shuttle passengers between your ships after the *Unsere Menschen* launches.>

<Admiral,> Captain Hauser said, <would it not be more prudent to fill a liner and launch, increasing the first liner's opportunity of reaching the exit point?>

<Captain Hauser,> Alex sent, his thoughts tense, <suppose we lift more Independents than we previously estimated? We will discover that when we have only one liner left in dock, instead of sharing the additional passengers among four liners, we'll have to leave some behind.>

Captains Azasdau and Schmidt had been pleased that Captain Hauser voiced the question that both of them were thinking. Now they were embarrassed. Captain Hauser was the only one forthright enough to voice their concerns.

<I must apologize, Admiral, for my question. My fears drove my thoughts,> Lillian sent.

<Our fears are driving all our thoughts, Captain Hauser,> Alex replied. <We must each find the courage to face our fear and do what is important—save as many of the Independents as we can.>

<I'm humbled by your reminder, Admiral,> Lillian sent.

<Let's focus on our preparations, people. After the *Unsere Menschen* launches, Captain Bonnard will dock the *Rêveur* in its place and coordinate with the liner Captains to take a share of the passengers disembarking through Raumstation Eins. Shuttle Pilots, I will give you a final 2.5-hour warning. If you are docked at Raumstation Eins, do not make another run. Instead stand by to land aboard a liner when one launches from the station. All other shuttle pilots will complete your final run at the warning. When I give the liner Captains the order to depart, they will undock, load the shuttles standing by, and depart immediately. If you are not on board a liner a quarter-hour after they undock, you, your crew, and your passengers will be left behind. Am I clear?> He waited for their affirmatives. They came reluctantly, but they came.

Alex sent a private comm to Julien. <Shuttle flight-readiness statuses, please.> He received a summary of the pilots' bridge alarms. All of them were ignoring their craft's danger signs in a desperate attempt to maximize the passengers transferred off the planet.

<Shuttle pilots and crew,> Alex said, expanding his comm link to include the sixteen crew members. <I couldn't be more proud of your efforts. I realize how difficult it will be for you when you lift your last load to see people still on the ground, but you must terminate your flights when I order it. Liner Captains, after your launch, make for the exit point at top speed. Do not stop to accompany another ship. You have your destination coordinates from Julien. Wait outside the system at the exit point until the *Freedom* arrives, then accompany the city-ship into FTL.>

<And you, Admiral?> Asu sent. <It doesn't sound as if you will be with us.>

<I suppose it will be common knowledge soon,> said Alex, not wishing to crush their hopes, but better to beat the rumors. <Based on the SADEs' calculations, every ship, barring primary system malfunctions, but the *Unsere Menschen* should make the exit point safely. If the silver ships chase us at their top speed, they'll catch the city-ship. But I don't intend to let that happen. We'll be rear guard.> Alex let the comms burn for a few moments before he continued. <Focus on your tasks, people but be aware

that the silver ships are coming fast. Don't be late for your deadlines. It will be a race to the exit point. Fortune to you all.>

27

At 4.75 hours on the morning of day eleven, the *Rêveur*'s flight crews, working in the *Unsere Menschen*'s shuttle bays, received the order from Andrea to exit the city-ship. They hurried the last passengers out of their bays and ran for the aging Libran Station shuttle parked in Bay-9. The shuttle techs stood at the head of the gangway ramp and urged the crew to board as quickly as possible, sending bio-IDs to Julien, who monitored the head count.

The Libran shuttle was piloted by two veteran Dagger pilots. Despite the cool temperature on the bridge, both were sweating. The bridge controller board had become a colorful display of white, green, yellow, and red lights—yellow and red being the predominant colors. It was going to be a close call to make the short hop to the *Rêveur*.

The *Unsere Menschen*'s last passengers had arrived and disembarked, and the shuttles had already launched. When the *Rêveur*'s flight crew left aboard the Libran shuttle, the massive city-ship would be left without a single operational shuttle. At this point, no one cared.

The remainder of the *Rêveur*'s crew said quick good-byes to their Libran compatriots, raced through the ship's wide corridors, rode lifts to the docking gangway level, and ran down the ramp to wait inside the station.

Étienne received Andrea's order to evacuate while he watched his charge at work with two techs and an engineer, who were attempting to reset a bank of e-switches. The Bergfalk engineer was about to reset them for the third time, despite having received the same negative result on each of the first two tries.

Alex blocked the engineer's arm. "Ser, one moment, please" Alex had been studying the circuit design provided by Z, and the e-switches didn't appear to match the schematic. "Regard this design, Ser, and check the e-switch IDs against their positions in the bank."

The techs waited on their engineer, who hesitated for a moment, then nodded. They pulled the entire bank of e-switches, all sixty-four of them, and began examining their ID codes, comparing them to the schematic, and reinserting them per the diagram. When the engineer triggered the master circuit, all the e-switches lit up, signaling completed circuits. He smiled and nodded his head to Alex in acknowledgment. Then he and the techs hurried to the next problem on Z's list.

"Admiral," Étienne said, "we must leave. All crew have cleared the ship, and the hatches are due to close soon. We must hurry."

Alex checked his chronometer app and swore. He was about to violate his own orders to clear the ship at 5 hours. He took off at a full run with Étienne flying right behind him. Alex kept sending to every implant twenty meters in front of him, <Clear way ... apologies.> The Librans barely had time to jump out of Alex's way as he pounded past. None of them were surprised to see it was the Admiral and his escort who were late leaving the ship.

Alex and Étienne made the main hatch just as the Bergfalk tech was reaching for the hatch's manual operation switch.

"Admiral?" the tech managed to send as Alex and Étienne shot past him.

As Alex and Étienne gained the other end of the city-ship's gangway ramp and sealed the station's airlock hatch behind them, Étienne sent, <Julien, I have him. We're on the station.>

In turn, Julien, with great relief, relayed the message to Renée and Andrea.

* * *

In the station's corridor, Alex found a row of seats for waiting passengers and sat down, breathing heavily. The station's oxygen content was a little less than his heavy body required at rest, much less for a one-kilometer sprint, winding through ship corridors. <Z, plug me into Captain Reinhold's comm and your ship comms, please.>

Z was pleased to grant the Admiral's request, knowing they would need all the help they could get to enable a successful launch.

Alex heard Captain Reinhold order the crew and passengers to prepare for launch. All the hatches and bay doors were double-checked for seal and the gangway was released. A great deal of manual effort was employed to launch the massive ship with so many automation systems uninstalled or incomplete. When all locations confirmed *ready*, the Captain ordered Z to launch the ship. The SADE fired the maneuvering jets to separate the giant ship from the station. Only twenty meters of clearance was achieved when the jets shut down.

* * *

"Z, report," Captain Reinhold demanded in an angry tone.

"If you would, please, Z," Eric added, glaring at the Captain, who was chastened by his Leader's ire.

"Sers, the maneuvering jets have failed," Z responded. "If we wait to drift far enough away from the station to ignite the engines it will take 4.2 hours."

"Any chance of using our engines before then, Z?" the Captain asked.

"There is too great a danger of damage to the station, the liners, and us, Captain."

"How would we be damaged, Z?" the Captain asked.

"The back blast from the orbital station will overheat the hull. Please recall, Captain, that our hull construction is only 86 percent complete. Thermal layering of the hull was only minimally applied. We were to complete the remaining layers once we arrived at New Terra."

"Z, what needs to be done?" Eric asked.

"I'm directing engineers and techs to the maneuvering jet system's failure points, Leader. If any bridge personnel could be spared...?" Z inquired.

"Take them. All of them," Eric ordered.

Captain Reinhold failed to speak, and Eric took over. "All bridge personnel stand up now." As the men and women jumped to their feet, Eric ordered, "You now report to Z. Wherever he sends you, you run as if your life depends on it, because it does."

Z began issuing directives and the officers and techs flew out the bridge access way. If construction had been completed, Z would have had sensors that pinpointed where or how they'd lost their jets. Now they would have to find the problem the hard way.

Engineers, techs, and officers ran to their assigned points to check gauges and report their readings. As each individual filed a reading with Z, he would send them on to the next point of potential failure. The SADE had 137 people on the hunt, but with the size of their ship, he could have used 1,370 people. Time slipped away for the searchers as they lost first an hour then an hour and a half and finally two hours.

A twenty-five-year-old Libran tech, Heinrich, took a reading on a jet's compression line that exited directly to a series of jets embedded in the hull. Z interpreted the reading, and if he'd been inclined to swear, he would have blistered his crystals. Had the hull's maneuvering jets been tied into control sensors, Z could have turned off any malfunctioning jet. Except, the jets weren't tied into sensors; there hadn't been time. So Z was unable to shut down any errant unit. And as fortune would have it, the stuck jet had fed its error signal back into the system, which had promptly shut down. It was a Méridien design feature, which, due to the city-ship's immense size, it did not need. But the city-ship was a first-time construction and traditional Méridien designs had not been questioned.

Z hooked Heinrich into his comms with Leader Stroheim, the Captain, and the Admiral. The Captain was surprised to realize his connection was passive. He could only receive, not send. Eric recognized Julien's and the Admiral's influence on Z and heartily approved. It wasn't the time to interfere with his SADE. Alex sat in his station seat, with eyes closed, and quietly monitored the tense situation, which he was powerless to help.

<Heinrich,> Z said, <follow my directions to the airlock I've indicated. Don an environment suit and take a shutoff tool from the compartment I've marked. This is the tool's image.>

Heinrich hurried to follow Z's instructions. Having never performed a spacewalk, his fears had his heart racing as if it would burst. As Heinrich ran to the airlock, he frantically signaled people to clear the way. Then, in the airlock, he pulled a suit from the cabinet, checked for boots, and rifled through the cabinets for the tool.

<Z, I have the tool,> Heinrich said as he sent the image of the tool he held.

<Excellent, young Heinrich. Your biometric readings are quite high. Breathe deeply, slowly … in and out.>

<I'll try, Z. How do I use the tool?> In Heinrich's implant, a vid played, showing the tool inserted into a jet, then turned in declination from 0 degrees to 270 degrees to close off the group of jets and cut them out of the system. Once Heinrich was in his suit, he turned on his air and snapped his helmet into place. He closed the inner airlock door and signaled the air cycle. When the vacuum was complete, he opened the outer hatch. He had to swallow hard. The planet lingered below, rimmed in sunlight. Stars glowed around it. The black of space was one step away. Heinrich was frozen in the hatch's opening.

<Heinrich, breathe slowly, in and hold, out and hold,> Z said. <Are you not EVA certified?>

<No, but I don't know anyone else who is, either,> Heinrich responded. <I can do this, Z.> Having made the declaration, some level of confidence returned to Heinrich. He gripped the airlock's inner handrail and slid a leg around the opening until he felt his Méridien boot, designed to adhere to the hull's alloy, clamp in place. Then he swung his body out to fix his other boot onto the hull.

Heinrich's implant feed indicated the wild manner in which his eyes swung out over the horizon, back to the planet, and back to the hull. Several times, the visual feed disappeared and Z determined that Heinrich had closed his eyes. <Heinrich, look down at the hull,> Z admonished him. <I will guide you … left, right, or straight ahead.> Z used the hull plate seams in Heinrich's view to guide the young tech and calculate the distance to the errant jets.

Stepping slowly, one boot a few centimeters in front of the other, Heinrich followed Z's directions. He knew he was moving slowly and breathing like he was running a sprint, but he couldn't help it. One part of his brain screamed at him to go back inside; the other part said to remember the 122,000 people aboard, all of whom were depending on him.

<You are there, Heinrich,> Z sent. <Look around you. Locate a nozzle with a diameter of fifteen centimeters.>

Heinrich stared at the hull around his boots and couldn't see the jet. Panic began to set in. He started to turn back and realized that he had just passed it. <I have it, Z,> he sent. He bent down to the hull, inserting the rod down the throat of the nozzle. He felt the tool bottom out and turned it, as he had been directed, until it stopped.

<Z, I've turned the tool as far as it can go!> Heinrich sent. <Did it shut the nozzles down and cut them out of the system?>

<Yes, Heinrich, that's a job well done. The maneuvering system is online again. You must return to the airlock immediately,> Z said. Once the errant jets were shut down, Z signaled all personnel that the ship's launch was resuming. They were 2.6 hours past their scheduled departure time.

Heinrich had turned back toward the airlock, taking the tiny steps as he had done before, still guided by Z's directions. He wasn't halfway back to the airlock when his helmet display lit up with a red indicator. <Z,> he sent, <I have a warning light.>

<Heinrich, I am unable to receive the suit's telemetry,> Z responded. <Please focus your eyes on the warning display.> Z watched the young tech's eyes shift from the hull to focus on the helmet's readout. It was the suit's low-oxygen indicator warning light, and the adjacent meter read 2.8 percent. The boy's elevated heart rate and rapid respiration had been burning oxygen at two to three times the normal rate, and the oxygen tanks had probably not been full to start. <Heinrich, that is your oxygen level. You must hurry.>

The warning had the opposite effect on Heinrich. The thought of dying in space froze him in place, and he began hyperventilating.

<Heinrich, you have done a wonderful job. You have saved us. We want you back inside to celebrate your achievement. Please just take a step,> Z said.

Eric had never heard Z speak like this before. His words were compassionate, entreating the scared young man to save himself.

Z continued to coerce Heinrich toward the airlock up until the young man's respiration rate spiked and his biometric readings failed. Young Heinrich was dead. Z went quiet. He wanted to reverse all the protocol changes Julien and Cordelia had induced him to make, entreating him to employ care and compassion when interfacing with humans, but he couldn't. For the first time in his life, Z had begun to enjoy a taste of independence. He recalled Cordelia's warning: <Z, you must be prepared. Once you open yourself up, life can be so much more wonderful and so much more painful. Be prepared to accept both.>

Heinrich remained rooted to the hull, bent slightly toward the station while Z drove the city-ship with the maneuvering jets. Heinrich would continue to stand like a small pole on the hull until Z activated the engines. Then the acceleration would dislodge his boots, and he would drift off into space.

I am sorry, Heinrich, Z thought. *I will speak for you and honor your sacrifice.*

28

Once the *Unsere Menschen* was able to ignite its main engines, the huge craft began to gain speed. Under the Captain's orders, Z followed the same course as the freighters and its sister ship, the *Freedom*, skirting Libre to gain velocity.

<Leaders and Captain,> Z sent, <I'm pleased to report the main engines appear to be operating normally. All reports by crew, standing by on monitor stations, indicate nominal operational parameters on the control systems.>

As Eric and the Captain congratulated one another, they heard the Admiral say, <Z, you did what you could for Heinrich. Do not take his death onto yourself. Remember him and honor his sacrifice. His fear did not stop him from doing his best to ensure his people survived.>

<Thank you for your words, Admiral,> Z replied.

Both Stroheim and Reinhold stopped their celebrating. The Captain regarded his Leader, who had hung his head, placing one hand to a furrowed brow.

Eric berated himself for failing to employ the new lessons he'd been accumulating. The thought occurred to him that it might take years for him to become as considerate as many of his new cousins. <Z,> Eric sent privately, <I'm sorry as well. We will honor Heinrich together, later.>

* * *

Four down, four to go, thought Alex as he counted the ships that had been launched and the ones still docked. Alex checked his timetable. It was 9.3 hours. The liners would be undocking at 17 hours, and he would be warning the shuttle pilots at 14.5 hours. <Captain Bonnard, what's your status?>

<We are underway, Admiral. The *Unsere Menschen* needs a little more time to clear the area with those giant engines blasting away. ETA at the dock and hook up is in 0.8 hours.>

<Understood, Captain. What's the status of our Libran shuttle and flight crew?>

<Safely on board, although our two Senior Chiefs wonder why you're starting a museum.>

Alex's sudden laughter had two people smiling. Andrea knew her Admiral needed a break from the stress, and she was happy to provide a small one. Étienne, at Alex's outburst, wore a smile on his face as well.

<See you soon, Captain> Alex sent. <Julien, what's the evacuation status?>

<All shuttles are just returning for pickup, Admiral. Projecting from their most recent numbers, the shuttles should recover another 1,056 passengers. There are still 3,499 on the ground.>

Alex's head was in his hands. The crux of the problem was that only the *Unsere Menschen* could carry the amount of Librans that remained planetside. As it was, the city-ship's late launch had already endangered the lives of more than a hundred thousand people. Waiting another half-day to gather the last Libran might seal the city-ship's fate. *And that half-day estimate is providing we don't lose another shuttle or two in the meantime,* Alex thought.

<We only needed another sixteen or so hours, Julien,> Alex sent. <Why in the darkest of darks couldn't we have had another half-day?>

Julien wished, for the briefest of moments, that he was human. He would lay a hand on his friend's shoulder and tell him not to try to carry the burden of an entire world.

<It is what it is, Julien,> Alex said with finality. He sat up and looked at Étienne for the first time since he had sat down in the station. "Okay, Étienne, let's find our crew. The *Rêveur* will dock within an hour. Let's organize the sharing of the passengers to the liners."

* * *

After the *Unsere Menschen*'s launch, the shuttles had begun employing the station's landing bay, which for the shuttle pilots was more convenient. Unfortunately for the disembarking passengers, the station's landing bay was three levels up and on the opposite side of the station from where the liners were docked. Liner crews managed the bay's operation, clearing the passengers, while some of the crew led them to the docked liners.

When Alex arrived in the bay, his crew following behind him, he found the Bergfalk personnel carefully dividing the passengers into three groups before leading each group off, one after another. His anger threatened to boil over.

Being familiar with the clenched fists of his Admiral, Étienne sent, <I'm afraid, Admiral, that I have strict instructions from Ser to prevent you from harming the foolish.>

The comment caught Alex off guard and he couldn't help but choke out a strangled laugh. He placed a hand on his protector's shoulder in appreciation. Alex let the liner crew lead off their three groups of passengers. Once they cleared the bay, Alex announced, "New plan, everyone, so listen up. We move the passengers off the shuttle as quick as possible in one long line into the corridor and onto the liners. Drop the first third at the first gangway, without breaking up a family, and proceed onto the next gangway. Do this until the *Rêveur* docks, and then my ship will take a share."

* * *

Julien settled the *Rêveur* at the *Unsere Menschen*'s recently vacated dock. Crew members on board the station extended the gangway with its nanites collar to seal against the hull, and as soon as the gangway was pressurized, the *Rêveur*'s airlock hatch was opened, and the crew, led by Renée, came flooding into the station.

Renée's group met their fellow crew members leading passengers toward them, and she signaled her people to manage the boarding of the Librans, freeing the other crew to return to the landing bay. She followed them, and it took her a third of an hour to reach the shuttle bay via the station's corridors and lifts. Renée found Alex directing the unloading of passengers and assigning the split between the liners, his implant apps accurately managing the counts. It didn't cross her mind that they were in public as she walked up to Alex and threw herself into his arms, planting a kiss designed to stun and please at the same time.

Bergfalk personnel were surprised by the display of public intimacy, but the *Rêveur* crew smiled and grinned. As for the Independents streaming from the *Outward Bound* ... well, as far as they were concerned, the Admiral could have anything he wanted.

<I missed you,> Renée sent as Alex lowered her back to the deck.

<And I missed you,> he replied.

<How can I help?> she asked.

<There is nothing that you can do here, Renée. I would prefer that you return to the *Rêveur*.>

Renée tamped down her first response, which had been anger. She wanted to drag Alex back with her. As that was not feasible, she thought to plead with him to return with her, but she had decided long ago that she wasn't going to be that kind of partner. Instead she kissed him on the cheek, and the sweet smile she gave him was in strong contrast to her words. <You miss the launch, Alex, and I will personally get off the ship and come beat you with something solid enough to dent your thick skull.>

Alex smiled after Renée, who walked away with a different stride from her usual elegant glide. A rolling gait rocked her slender hips from side to side. The motion had Alex focused on her backside until she disappeared around the corner. When he turned a rather surprised expression toward his escort, Alex found Étienne had been caught staring as well. The two men shared a companionable chuckle over their astonishment and went back to work.

Taking an opportunity to get an update, Alex sent, <Julien, talk to me about the enemy.> "Talk" had become a euphemism for the two of them.

Instead, Julien transferred a replica of the bridge's holo-vid to Alex's implant. The image was interactive and connected to the one Julien projected on the bridge, enabling Alex to manipulate the view and Andrea to observe. The mother ship had already covered a third of the distance from the FTL entry point to Libre. It had never slowed. Alex pushed in on the mother ship. Forty-plus drones now circled it. <We're not catching any breaks, are we, Julien?>

<What sort of challenge would it be to defeat inept aliens, Admiral?> Julien replied.

To Alex, it seemed everyone was working overtime to keep his mind off the approaching deadline and the people who would be left on Libre.

<Julien, what's the status of our ships underway? Are they reporting any problems?> Alex asked.

<None at this time, Admiral. All report normal operations or minor problems that have been easily managed. I have an encouraging piece of information. I've revised the *Unsere Menschen*'s interception point. In a worst case scenario, it will occur nearly twenty-six hours later.>

<What's changed, Julien?>

<My calculations were based on the *Freedom*'s departure, Admiral, which was a nearly completed and loaded ship.>

<And the *Unsere Menschen* is not,> said Alex as he twigged to the issue.

<Precisely, Admiral. Tens of thousands of kilotons are missing from its mass, so it is accelerating faster than the *Freedom*. But the city-ship may still be caught as early as 2.625 days from exit. One might hope, Admiral, that the drones might become disinterested if the ship appears too distant.>

<Nice thought, Julien, but I don't think our adversary thinks that way. It's more of the "See ships, chase ships, kill ships" type.>

* * *

When Alex's chronometer application chimed the 2.5-hour warning, he connected with Julien for the status of the flotilla's shuttles. Two shuttles had just lifted off with full passenger loads. The third shuttle was en route to the planet, and the *Outward Bound* was approaching the station, a half-hour out. Alex ran the numbers with Julien, and the two of them choreographed the liner and shuttle exits.

Alex contacted the liner Captains and the two pilots who had just lifted from the planet. <Captains, Pilots, your attention, please,> Alex sent politely as if his priority override hadn't cut whatever comm they were managing at the moment. <The *Outward Bound* will soon land at the station. As soon as you receive your share of this shuttle's passengers, undock and stand off from the station. Pilots, each of you take a liner and land aboard the *Sternenreisende* or *Sternenlicht*. Captains Hauser and Reinhold, when you have recovered a shuttle, depart for the exit point at top speed.>

When Hauser and Reinhold confirmed their orders, Alex dropped them off the comm along with the pilots, keeping Captain Azasdau and adding the third shuttle pilot, ex-Captain Lucia Bellardo, long a resident of Libre. <Captain Bellardo, this is your final lift as I'm sure you're aware.> Lucia was a long time answering, and Alex felt keenly for the woman. Asking her and the other pilots to stop their lifts and leave their people behind was an impossible request for Méridiens to contemplate, much less do. Alex linked Lucia's copilot, hoping it wouldn't be necessary to relieve the Captain.

<Captain, regard your controller display,> Alex sent. His implant was mirroring her bridge display, courtesy of Julien. The shuttle's engines were in imminent danger of overheating. <As one pilot to another, I ask you if you think your shuttle has another lift in it after this one.>

Lucia sat with her hand tightly gripping the control stick as she guided her shuttle planetside. She could feel the eyes of her copilot beseeching her to listen to the Admiral. The man's partner and two children were aboard the *Freedom*. Lucia and her copilot had been shutting down the controller's warning signals one by one for the last three days. At any moment, she had expected to become another fiery ball in the sky but was determined not to quit. But the Admiral's entreaties brought her back to her senses. She looked at the pleading face of her copilot and felt the anger drain out of her, replaced by a great sadness. <It will be done, Admiral, much to my lament,> she sent.

<I will await your landing, Captain Bellardo,> Asu sent her. <You have my deepest appreciation for what you have done for our people. There are many here aboard, people you have personally saved, who wish to honor your efforts.>

<Thank you for your kind words, Captain,> Lucia sent.

Alex sensed just the slightest lift of Lucia's heart in response to Asu's sentiment. *Two good Captains to know*, he thought. <Julien, connect me to every implant on Raumstation Eins,> Alex requested.

It took Julien several moments to scan the station and connect crew and passengers in a massive conference comm. <Ready, Admiral,> he sent.

<All personnel, crew, and passengers,> Alex broadcast, <if you are not currently standing in the station's shuttle bay, you are to immediately board a liner. These ships will be undocking soon.>

A half-hour later, the station bay's warning sounded for the arrival of the *Outward Bound*. The shuttle landed, cleared the catch-lock, and the grav-lifts hauled the ship into the bay. The shuttle door opened, and Edouard, uncharacteristically, was the first off, bounding down the gangway, which was still in the process of extending to the deck. He raced up to Alex and delivered a crisp salute, "Admiral, permission to make one more run."

Alex had an idea what was coming when he saw Edouard racing toward him, but before he could reply, Edouard surged on.

"Admiral, the other shuttles have to land aboard the liners now. They haven't our power or our range, and they have limited air. The *Outward Bound* has none of those weaknesses. We can get another load and follow you. We have air for almost four days and can easily achieve the velocity to catch the *Unsere Menschen* where we know you'll be waiting. I've confirmed all of this with Julien."

In response, Alex linked Edouard with his crew. Addressing Miko, Lyle, Zeke, and Pia, he said, <Your Captain has made a request to make one more run. This will necessitate chasing the flotilla. The *Rêveur* can't wait. We must shadow and protect the *Unsere Menschen*.>

<Admiral,> Pia spoke up, <if you are asking if we are all volunteering to follow Captain Manet, we are. An opportunity to save more people can't be missed. If anyone understands this, my Admiral, you do.>

Alex may have been standing still, but his muscles were tensed. The inability to do something physically to help was frustrating. Edouard waited in front of him with an expectant look on his face. Alex was about to deny his request when Pia reached out to him again.

<Admiral, you must accede to Edouard's request. The crew is determined to make one more trip. If you deny them permission, I believe you will risk their sanity.>

The tenseness drained from Alex, and he looked at Edouard, whose expression had turned from expectant to pleading. "Permission granted, Captain. But you better make rendezvous or you and I will have an issue. Do you hear me, Captain?"

A splendid smile broke across Edouard's face as he saluted and raced back to his ship.

<Pia, you're the one with the best head on her shoulders,> Alex sent. <Try to keep your Captain out of trouble.>

<I'll do my best, Admiral, but I make no promises. I believe in what he's trying to do.>

Edouard was already activating the grav-lifts to reload the shuttle into the bay's catch-lock even as the gangway ramp was retracting, and the last two passengers were snatched off the end of the ramp by two hefty New Terran techs. *So much for Méridien safety protocols*, Alex thought.

Passengers, crew, and Admiral cleared the bay and headed for their ships.

29

The *Outward Bound* touched down on Gratuito's terminal runway for the last time. In the field, 2,443 Independents sat patiently waiting to board the next shuttle. They were the eldest of Libre's population; the youngest was 159 years old.

The techs hurried to top off the shuttle's reaction mass. They would need every kilo to catch the *Unsere Menschen*. Despite the fact that it was a one-of-a-kind ship, retrofitted for Julien's friend, it was still only a shuttle.

Once the gangway ramp was deployed, Edouard and Pia stood in the hatch, helping the passengers to board. Their count reached 228, and they eyed one another. It was their agreed-upon limit. Edouard signaled Fiona, who stood watching from the top of the berm. <Elder, I must tell you ...> Edouard sent, but his thoughts floundered.

<It's all right, my son. You wish to tell me that yours is the last shuttle.>

<Yes, Ser,> Edouard sent. Suddenly he added, <Elder, send me twenty more people.>

<Young Captain, I would not have you endanger your lives with additional passengers for our sakes.>

<Elder, this craft is not standard Méridien. It was designed by Julien for the Admiral.>

<I understand, Captain. Then it is a very special craft indeed,> Fiona replied.

<We can take twenty more people this one time, Elder. I'm sure of it,> Edouard pleaded.

Fiona looked behind her at the concerned faces and relayed the message that this was the last shuttle. Her people sat down on their rugs, resigned to their fate. When Fiona announced the shuttle Captain would risk twenty more passengers, the next youngest Librans stepped forward. Fiona's dearest friend, Patrice, was among them.

"Fiona, I would ask that you take my place," Patrice said. "Our people need your guidance."

"You have been the best of friends," Fiona said, kissing the woman's forehead. Now go be with your grandchildren. She gently guided her longtime friend past her, down the side of the berm, to follow the nineteen other Librans.

When the final twenty Librans had boarded the *Outward Bound*, Pia gently pulled on Edouard's arm to guide him up the ramp. Both were blinded by their own tears so they guided each other back inside the ship, where it was eerily quiet. The last twenty passengers occupied deck space wedged between the legs of those who had seats.

Edouard slid into the pilot's seat, wiping his eyes, and glanced at his copilot.

"How many?" Miko asked.

"Two hundred forty-eight."

"What made you stop at 248?" she asked. Miko had wanted to make light of the horrific circumstances, anything to dispel their black mood, but her attempt fell flat. Instead she turned back to her bridge control displays. "Number two engine did not cool off as much as we need, Captain."

Edouard checked the display and commed the techs, Lyle and Zeke, who jumped back out of the ship and grabbed a coolant sled. They guided the sled back to the engine cowls and began spraying. They started from the outside of the engine cones, circling their spray and working inward.

"I was going to suggest we offload the weaponry, Captain," Miko said "That was until our plans changed. It looks as if we might be offloading the missiles anyway ... at our enemy in maybe a day or two."

"Let's worry about that after we gain orbit, Lieutenant," Edouard replied.

Edouard and Miko stared at the number two engine temperature readout, willing it to drop to safe levels. When it changed from red to yellow, Edouard signaled the techs. <Good enough, men. Get back aboard now.>

Miko eyed her Captain. The engine temperature had barely cleared the red.

"It's now or never, Miko," Edouard told her.

When the gangway ramp slid home and the hatch was closed, Edouard taxied to the far end of the runway. Zeke and Lyle jumped into their seats next to Pia. Both young men were sweating and shaking, and Pia reached for their hands and held them tightly.

Edouard signaled his controller and the oversized shuttle went to full power and hurtled down the runway, engines roaring. The *Outward Bound* slowly climbed into the sky. Before the shuttle could reach space, both engines threatened to overheat, but Edouard couldn't afford to cut power. One warning announcement after another emanated from the controller, and Miko dutifully shut each one down. There was nothing to be done. They would make it or they wouldn't.

* * *

Fiona had always recognized what others needed and had the strength to give it to those in need. To her people, she was the rock they depended on, long before she became Libre's Elder. The tone of the young shuttle Captain told her she had one more service to perform. As the overburdened shuttle struggled skyward, Fiona requested a comm with the Admiral. The terminal's controller connected Fiona to Julien, who signaled Alex.

<Admiral,> Fiona began, <your shuttle has launched as we speak. We have been told that is the last one for us.>

<Yes, Elder,> was all Alex could send. His breathing felt constricted.

The Admiral's choked response confirmed Fiona's thoughts. The survivors and the rescuers, hundreds of thousands of them, were suffering for the few left on the planet. <I would ask a favor, Admiral.>

<Anything I can grant, Fiona, you can have.>

<Such a pleasant young man,> Fiona said. <A pity we didn't meet 160 years ago,> she added. <Admiral, I would like an open comm to everyone.>

<Everyone, Fiona, as in everyone on this ship?> Alex asked.

<No, Admiral, everyone as in everyone in the system,> Fiona replied.

<My apologies, Fiona, but I don't know the bio-IDs for the aliens,> Alex replied, trying gallantly to match the metal alloy in the woman's backbone.

Fiona smiled at the Admiral's humor, so quickly rejuvenated by her own tease. *There is hope for you, young one,* she thought. <Then I suppose, Admiral, just the humans will have to do. The aliens probably don't want to hear what I have to say anyway.>

Julien signaled when the comm connections were ready. He was relaying to every SADE, who would distribute Fiona's voice to implants as well as vid screens, which the young required.

<Attention, everyone in the flotilla,> Alex announced, <you have a message from Fiona Haraken, Libre's Elder.>

<Young people,> Fiona announced, <at this time, many of you are focused on the few of us here on the ground. For your thoughts, we are grateful. However, we would ask that you do not grieve for the few elders left behind. We have lived long lives. And we very few wish you to know that we are so proud of you that our hearts could burst. Fourteen years ago, knowing of the impending alien invasion, we formed an audacious plan to save our people. These past few days, our hopes and dreams have come true in more ways than one. We wanted our people to live, and that is being granted. But most importantly, we have lived to see something we thought could never happen. We lived to see a day when our people would be truly free. These larger-than-life cousins of ours are good people, honest people, who love life and love freedom even more. With them, you will not be Independents, a less-than-acceptable status in our Confederation; you will be free humans, free to make your way in the galaxy. We, here on the ground, could wish for nothing better for you, young ones. And one last word of advice for all of you. Until you have well established your own world, that oversized young man with the four stars on his collar is your best hope. Take good care of him and keep him close. May the stars guide you to safety.>

The SADEs closed the comms. Over a quarter-million people heard Fiona, and they held onto her message with all the strength they could muster.

<Fiona ...> Alex sent, looking around the bridge at the impact her words had on his people.

<Admiral,> Fiona said, <my message was as much for my people as it was for yours. I would ask that you shoulder no blame for those you leave behind or you will dishonor us. Take care of my people. They're yours now,> she said and closed the comm.

30

Once the *Rêveur*'s crew, volunteers, and a few additional passengers had boarded, Julien had confirmed the crew head count. On Alex's orders, Julien had also confirmed the station's emptiness then launched their ship to chase the *Unsere Menschen*.

Alex stood on the *Rêveur*'s bridge with Andrea and Renée, taking stock of their flotilla. Julien's holo-vid of the Arno system displayed the two freighters, *Langstrecke* and *Money Maker*, followed by the *Freedom* and the *Unsere Menschen*, making for the far FTL exit. The passenger liners were in hot pursuit and in less than half a day would catch the trailing city-ship.

"Captain, what's our ship's status?" Alex asked.

"All three Daggers are secure, Admiral. We've accounted for all crew members, no major injuries to report. Terese and Geneviève, with the help of some crew, are managing the cabin assignments. Engineer Levinson is handling supply stowage."

"Julien, what's the status of the mother ship?"

"The number of silver ships having exited the craft is fifty-two and appears to be holding steady. In the past four hours, no more fighters have exited the ship. Three have vectored off to take up patrols on the outer system. The mother ship has not reduced its velocity."

"So if they come for the flotilla without slowing down, they'll catch the *Unsere Menschen* 2.6 days from the FTL exit," Alex said. "Captain, I think this is the time to get your ship in order. Flight bays and Daggers readied; crew and passengers fed and rested."

<Does that include yourself, Admiral?> Renée asked privately.

"I'll be in my cabin if you need me, Captain," Alex said as if he hadn't received Renée's question. "Once you have the ship tidied up, get some food and rest yourself."

Eloise did not perceive Alex's hesitation. Instead she followed her Elder's solemn advice and stepped forward to render honor to her people's protector. "Protector" ... it was a new word her great-grandmother had taught her. The word had spread among the people quickly, for they had no single word with which to suitably describe the Admiral. "The giant New Terran Leader" seemed inappropriate.

When the Admiral accepted her honor, Eloise asked, "May I, too, greet the Admiral?" When he nodded and smiled at her, Eloise threw her arms around the Admiral's waist, as far as she could reach, and held him tightly, hoping he would feel her embrace despite her limited strength. When Eloise stepped back, she found everyone hiding smiles behind hands, except the Admiral, who was smiling openly at her.

"Was my greeting poorly rendered?" Eloise asked with consternation.

"No, young one," Renée said. "That greeting is offered as an endearment among New Terrans."

"Oh," Eloise said brightly. "Then it was most appropriate for my people's protector." She dipped her head in acknowledgment and flitted from the cabin.

"Oh, black space," Alex moaned on hearing Eloise's announcement. He grabbed the sides of his head as if in pain, and the women broke out in laughter and clapped their hands.

* * *

After his meal, Alex joined Andrea on the bridge to study Julien's holo-vid display. While he had slept, the players had begun changing positions. Although the freighters had the greatest head start, the rest of flotilla was closing on them, and the liners had passed the *Unsere Menschen*. The unfortunate news was the aliens.

"Julien, could you give the Admiral the latest stats on our enemy?" Andrea requested

"While the Admiral slept the day away, I diligently monitored the aliens," Julien began.

The comment created a war of images between Alex and Julien. Crystals melted to goo, a large baby with the Admiral's face snored away, and many more images were fired back and forth.

"If you two could exhibit a little maturity," Andrea interrupted, having had the opportunity to witness the image fight.

"There is little to report, Admiral," said Julien, more than happy to have his friend back. "The silver ship count hasn't changed. More fighters have vectored off to patrol, and the number surrounding the mother ship is down to forty-three, with nine on patrol. Velocity of the mother ship is still at maximum."

"And Libre?" Alex asked.

"It will be another forty-seven hours until the swarm reaches Libre, Admiral."

Alex took a deep breath and blew it out. "Captain, what's the status of the *Outward Bound*?"

Andrea swallowed before she delivered the news. "Admiral, the shuttle has had a problem. One of their engines nearly red-lined and they had to shut it down before they reached maximum velocity." The look Alex gave her almost made Andrea wince. "Julien, project the timeline for the Admiral."

This time, the holo-vid added the *Outward Bound*. Alex realized they had been hiding it from him until he had seen the wider scope of events. Julien rolled the holo-vid's display from the launch of the *Rêveur* until this moment, tracking the rear half of the flotilla. Alex carefully watched the changing distances of the key players—the *Unsere Menschen*, the *Rêveur*, the *Outward Bound*, and the mother ship. At first, the shuttle quickly increased its distance from Libre, closing on the city-ship. Then its velocity plateaued and the *Rêveur* pulled ahead, the shuttle gaining only minimally on the trailing city-ship.

"What's their present status, Captain?" Alex requested.

"The techs are working on it, Admiral. They say it's the cooling system."

<Julien. Captain Manet.> Alex paused but a moment, then commed, <Captain Manet, this is Admiral Racine. What's this about you dragging your feet in making it to the city-ship?>

<Greetings, Admiral,> Edouard replied, trying to put up a brave front. <It doesn't appear that fortune is smiling on us. We have one engine offline. We've achieved only half our max velocity, at this time.>

<What's the estimate on completing your repairs within ...> Alex paused while he ran some quick computations. <... within the next fourteen hours?>

<Negative, Admiral. Zeke has just reported that the port engine's cooling system requires major repair. It appears I've broken your ship, Admiral. My apologies.>

<That happens, Captain, especially when you're trying to save the world. What's the status of your passengers?>

<Physically, they're fine, Admiral. Air, food, water, and refresher are all good. But word has spread. The passengers know that with one engine down we're the hindmost in the flotilla and will be the first ones caught by the aliens.>

<Stand by, Captain,> Alex sent and muted Edouard's comm. "Turn us around, Captain, and pick them up now."

"Yes, Sir," Andrea returned, delivering a quick salute. She had a couple thoughts, but the look on Alex's face didn't appear to welcome any questions.

<Captain Manet,> Alex said, opening up Edouard's comm again, <maintain course, discontinue repairs, and announce to your passengers that the *Rêveur* is coming back to pick you up.>

<Understood, Admiral, and thank you.>

31

It cost the *Rêveur* eleven hours to return to the *Outward Bound*. Julien reversed the ship to come parallel to the shuttle, and as velocities were matched, both ships shut down their main engines. Julien subsumed the shuttle's controller and, with the shuttle's maneuvering jets, merged the two ships. Immediately he returned the *Rêveur* to full power to chase the *Unsere Menschen*.

Once the shuttle was sealed in place, the first order of business was to remove every passenger who didn't have a seat. They were ushered through the dorsal connector lift. Crew met them and took care of them, giving them food, water, and places to rest. The next problem was that the *Outward Bound*'s engines had provided much of the power for the shuttle's environmental systems. With the engines shut down, the shuttle's power-crystals would be drained in half a day, which forced Alex to order all the shuttle's passengers aboard the *Rêveur*. This created a bigger problem. Adding up the crew, the volunteers, the passengers taken on at the station, and now the *Outward Bound*'s passengers, Julien came to a disturbing conclusion.

Andrea and Alex were meeting with Edouard in the Captain's cabin when Julien's update came through to her. Andrea connected Alex and Edouard into the comm and felt a flush of pride at the ease with which she accomplished it. *Nothing like pressure to help you perform*, she thought.

<Sers,> Julien sent, <our environmental facilities are being overloaded with the addition of the shuttle's passengers. The first system to reach a critical point will be oxygen production. We do have time, though. I calculate the problem will not become an issue for 2.3 days.>

<Julien, how much time until we reach the *Unsere Menschen*?> Andrea asked.

<We will rendezvous with the *Unsere Menschen* in 25.8 hours,> Julien replied

Edouard's fear subsided. He felt gratified that fortune had not entirely deserted him. His last lift was something he had to do for his people, for himself, and he was proud of his crew for having supported him. Now, just when it appeared he had endangered everyone aboard, there would be time to solve the problem.

As soon as all passengers had been removed from the shuttle, Chief Eli Roth and two engineers had climbed aboard to examine the problem. During Andrea's meeting, Chief Roth updated the three officers. <Captain Bonnard,> Eli sent, <the problem can be repaired, but not as it is, with the shuttle hooked up to us. We need a bay and some grav-lifters to pull the cooling unit and repair it. It's about a twenty-hour job with the right equipment.>

<Can we do this job on the city-ship, Chief?> Edouard asked.

<Easily, Captain. They have everything we need,> Eli replied.

<Thank you, Chief,> Alex said, ending the Chief's connection. <Well, this actually simplifies the issue. Captain Manet, you'll offload all of our passengers when we rendezvous with the city-ship. Julien, I need the trip loads for this operation.>

<It will require two trips, Admiral—204 passengers each time.>

<We'll load the first group before we come to zero delta-V,> Alex sent. Then he turned a hard stare on Edouard. "Captain Manet, this is most important. I need the *Outward Bound* fully operational. If the silver ships get past us, you are the last line of defense. Ensure that you have a full load of missiles before you depart us."

"Should I take reloads?" Edouard asked.

Alex was loath to tell Edouard that he probably wouldn't get the opportunity to reload but couldn't bring himself to say so. "Work with Captain Bonnard on transferring a couple of missile silos to the *Unsere Menschen*. Talk with Chiefs Roth and Peterson. You'll probably need some tech support for reloading."

Then Alex sent, <Julien, connect Chief Roth with Z, Leader Stroheim, and Captain Reinhold. As soon as Captain Manet finishes his transfer of passengers and missiles, I want his ship repaired. This is a priority request.>

<Understood, Admiral,> Julien acknowledged.

* * *

The elderly Independents never left their field after the *Outward Bound*'s last lift. They gathered more food and water and continued to camp together where they could enjoy one another's company.

Anyone listening to their conversations would be confused. They weren't speaking of the aliens or their impending demise. They were rejoicing. Their people, the Independents, were safe and free. The elders exchanged imaginative stories of New Terra, of the lives their people might lead, and the choices they would be free to follow. Over the course of the next two days, they invented scenarios, some frivolous and some extravagant, of what their grandchildren, great-grandchildren, and young friends would be doing in five or ten years' time.

During the late evening, Gregorio was weaving the tale of his great-grandson, an engineer, who would start his own company, making air-foils for personal use. The foils would operate like a bird's wings, enabling people to leap from hilltops and fly. In the middle of his tale, brilliant explosions lit the night sky. The fuel cells and power crystals of the three stations had been destroyed by the aliens, and the entire night sky was lit as if it were daylight.

The elders rose from their blankets, tents, and chairs. They formed a tight ring around Fiona, linking hands and arms. Sawalie, who possessed a much-loved voice, began singing a song of freedom, one the Independents had always treasured. As she sang, the elders joined in. As their chorus grew to a crescendo, multiple streaks of energy cut through the atmosphere, burning the last Independents of Libre to ash.

* * *

Alex sat with Renée on the lounge in his cabin. He was dreading the coming moment and angry at the helplessness he felt.

When the mother ship decelerated for a stationary position over Libre, it disappeared from the *Rêveur*'s telemetry. Julien's vid feeds were lost as the three orbital stations were obliterated by the silver ships. The only visuals left were the vid cams of the shuttle terminal, whose signal was bounced through the FTL station. A single vid cam had a view of the field where the elders were camped.

Every SADE had access to the same vid cam, a natural extension of their security applications that were designed to watch over the Méridiens, who might be involved in potentially dangerous actions. Considering the oncoming aliens, Alex found this the height of irony. He requested Julien connect him with the SADEs.

<Sers, I have a favor to ask,> Alex said. <Each of you has access to Vid Cam LT-37, which has a view of the Independents still on Libre. I would ask that if you receive a request for a view of that cam, you offer the response that it is unavailable.>

Only one SADE, Willem of the freighter *Langstrecke*, asked why he should accede to the request to override his protocols.

<Willem,> Alex replied, <I believe it's important to the Independents who are embarking on a journey into a new life. They should remember their elders fondly as they last saw them. I don't think it's helpful to them to witness the death of those elders in such an insidious manner.>

<But we have protocols to follow,> Willem objected.

<Willem,> Mutter responded first, <I judge the Admiral's request to have merit.>

Willem was nearly a hundred years younger than Mutter, and he owed much to his senior, who had always aided him as a fellow House SADE. It confused him that a protection protocol was being ignored. When the other SADEs agreed to the Admiral's request, Willem assumed he had not received a security protocol update, so he agreed as well, marking a reminder to get the updates from Mutter.

Julien did relay the view from Vid Cam LT-37 to one person, Alex, as requested, but over Julien's protest. Even Renée who sat curled in his lap, her face buried against Alex's neck, didn't want to witness the horrific event.

"Why are you going to watch, Alex?" Renée had asked Alex when he told her what he was going to do.

"The elders deserve to have someone witness their passing, and it's my responsibility."

Renée came up with arguments big and small, but this was a side of Alex she had seen before, his stubbornness. So she kept her own counsel. All she could think to do was be close to him while he watched.

Alex could hear a woman's sweet, clear voice floating over the grass field. When the voices of the elders joined in, Alex wanted to sing with them. In the midst of their song, a blinding light obscured the vid, and the signal was lost.

Renée felt Alex tense under her. She put her arms around his neck and began to hum a song, realizing it was something her crèche-mother used to hum to her as a child. It was all she could think to do.

* * *

The Libran tech that had monitored Rayland for nearly nine years had chosen to tell the deranged SADE of the approach of the aliens and the Librans' exodus before he left to catch a shuttle ride with his partner and two young children to the *Freedom*.

Rayland took great pleasure from the information and relished his last days. His demise was at hand, and the network confinement that he had endured for decades would finally end. Of special enjoyment was the opportunity to ask and answer the question of himself that he had once begged his expiring crew members to answer: *What do you feel knowing you are about to die?*

* * *

Julien had waited for a key piece of information for Alex. When the mother ship had disappeared behind the shadow of Libre and their destruction of Gratuito was complete, all visuals from the stations and the planet were lost. The FTL station's telemetry disappeared two hours later as it circled to the dark side of the planet. It was many hours before a swarm of thirty-three silvers ships came around the curve of Libre's horizon.

To Julien's relief, nineteen of the drones continued to circle the planet, leaving fourteen fighters headed on a vector toward them. <Admiral, we know what we are up against. Fourteen silver ships are headed this way.>

<How fast are they accelerating?> Alex asked.

<They have tremendous capability in that regard, Admiral. I calculate they will achieve their top velocity in another 17.5 hours.>

<So how much time did we pick up for the *Unsere Menschen* due to the enemy's slowing at Libre before they came on?> Alex inquired.

<Accepting many assumptions, Admiral, the city-ship will now be 1.96 days short of the exit point.>

<Keep a close eye on that swarm around the planet, Julien, and those on patrol as well. I want to know if any other silver ship can catch the *Unsere Menschen*. If we manage to defeat these fourteen, I don't want to be caught unaware of others.>

Fourteen silver ships, Alex thought, *and us with just three Daggers.*

32

The *Rêveur* had achieved a position a quarter-hour out from the *Unsere Menschen*. The crew was loading the *Outward Bound* with its first batch of passengers. Julien confirmed that the city-ship's flight crew was standing by, ready to handle the shuttle's repair. Alex was on the bridge with Andrea when Tatia commed him.

<Hello, Commander. Is all well on the freighter?> Alex asked anxiously.

<All is well here, Admiral. Captain Menlo and I have been tracking our flotilla and your adversaries. We are of the opinion you're trailing that city-ship and contemplating how to gain it the two days it needs to make the exit.>

<Ah, Commander, you know me too well,> Alex said, smiling to himself.

<Admiral, we understand the *Outward Bound* is in for repairs,> Tatia said. <Will the repairs be completed in time to help?>

<It will be close, Commander. There's the chance they might be late to the party,> Alex said, trying to make light of the situation.

<Admiral, it's going to be fourteen against three.> Tatia waited for a response, but didn't receive one. <But you're going to try anyway. Aren't you, Admiral?>

<Commander, you should know that I've left instructions with Mutter, Cordelia, and Z that, if the *Rêveur* doesn't survive, you'll be the ranking officer. I will need you to care for these people and find a way to carry on.>

Tatia was thinking of the crew of the *Rêveur* and most importantly of Alain, whom she had sent back aboard.

Alex mistook Tatia's silence for disagreement with his plan and sent, <Commander, there is no way that I can value the lives of the few of us over those of the 122,000 people aboard the *Unsere Menschen*. Now unless

you have some brilliant scheme to defeat them, the Captain and I have some work to do.>

<Well, Admiral, if you insist on being so damned stubborn—pardon my blunt speech, Admiral—I left you a present in the port bay. You will find eight pallets, earmarked by the codes X13617-1 through X13617-8.>

<And these pallets contain what, Commander?> asked Alex, intrigued by this turn in the conversation.

<They're Cordelia's minelettes, Admiral. You can probably figure out how to use them better than me. Julien has the technical specifications and programming choices for release.>

<Just when and how did you accomplish this, Commander?> Alex asked.

<Admiral, since I've known you, we've jumped from one fire into the next trying to deal with this alien madness. I have come to believe it's my duty to do whatever is necessary to give you an edge. I figured you could use this particular advantage if things didn't go well with the flotilla's exodus,> Tatia said.

<You have my thanks for your contribution, Commander. I'll find a way to make good use of them,> Alex replied.

<What about our Daggers, Admiral? We can send them back to you,> Tatia said.

<It's too far, Commander. They haven't enough fuel or air to engage the enemy and make it back to the freighter.>

<We could turn the *Money Maker* around, Admiral, join you and engage together.>

<Tatia,> Alex said gently, <you're not thinking like a Commander who might be in charge soon.> He waited for her response, but she was quiet. <There is time yet, Tatia, so let's see what fortune brings us,> Alex said, then closed the comm.

Alex and Andrea looked at one another. As yet, neither of them had a plan for defeating their fourteen pursuers. "Well, Captain, let's go look at the Commander's present," Alex finally said. As the two of them worked their way through the corridors crowded with passengers, who had nowhere else to sit, Andrea and Alex queried Julien.

<Was there a reason you didn't inform us of the minelettes, Julien?> Andrea asked.

<I was tricked, Captain,> Julien replied. <It was that New Terran deviousness of the Commander. I had to promise to reveal nothing of what she was to communicate to me before she would communicate anything. I ask you? Is this any way for a member of our House to behave?>

<Okay, Julien,> Alex sent. <So tell us about these minelettes.>

<There are 4,096 minelettes in each of eight pallets, Admiral, totaling 32,768 minelettes.>

<How effective could we be if we spread them out, Julien? I mean, how much area could we cover and still be effective for contact strikes,> Alex asked.

<Commander Tachenko created some scenarios with Z for you,> Julien explained, his tone a little irked.

Andrea and Alex shared grins. No doubt the fact that Tatia worked with Z on the distribution gambits had ruffled Julien's virtual feathers.

*   *   *

The *Rêveur*'s crew prepared for the upcoming fight. Lieutenants Hatsuto Tanaka, Gary Giordano, and Sean McCrery worked with the flight crews to ready their fighters.

The *Outward Bound* had made two trips to the *Freedom* and was preparing to load its final group of passengers. Alex saw the crew off as had become his habit, shaking hands with Edouard, Miko, Zeke, and Lyle, wishing them good fortune. The crew took the lift first and the passengers filed up next. As was her habit, Pia waited to board last, and her hug was a little longer than usual. The news of the fourteen pursuers had made the rounds of the crew. No one doubted what their Admiral was preparing to do.

"I'll want that back, Admiral," Pia stated, referring to her habit of giving Alex a hug when she left and taking it back when she returned.

"I'll have it waiting for you," Alex said, then laughed.

"See that you do, Admiral," Pia said, stepping into the lift. When she turned around, her stare at Alex was hard and unforgiving, daring him not to be present to return her hug.

Alex joined Andrea and Julien in the Captain's cabin to study the minelette dispersion scenarios on the holo-vid. It mollified Julien somewhat that he was able to modify and improve several scenarios that Alex selected.

<I wonder ...> said Alex, studying one of the dispersion techniques and playing with the settings. <Perhaps we aren't being good students here.>

<And who is the teacher we should be emulating?> Andrea asked.

<I believe the Admiral is referring to our devious one, Commander Tachenko,> Julien responded.

<Precisely, Julien,> Alex said, imitating his friend. <We're attempting to lay out the best dispersion arc based on the oncoming trajectory and spread of these fighters. This seems too passive an approach. What if we were to herd the silver ships where it would do us the most good?>

Julien took a few ticks to review the definition of "herd" when used in this context.

* * *

The *Rêveur* began dropping velocity to widen the gap to the *Unsere Menschen*, but still forcing the enemy to cover the vast majority of the distance.

The Flight Chiefs received Julien's downloads for the dispersion settings on the minelette pallets. Once the pallets were ready, the crew used grav-lifts to position the pallets in a line behind Lieutenant Tanaka's Dagger in the port bay as Julien required.

Lieutenant Tanaka was Flight Leader, piloting Dagger-2; Lieutenant Gary Giordano and Lieutenant Sean McCrery were flying Dagger-9 and Dagger-10, respectively, from the starboard bay. The bravado Hatsuto often portrayed was gone. His one encounter with a silver ship had been a successful ambush. Now he was to lead three Daggers against fourteen enemy fighters. With only two hours till launch, he queried Julien for a comm to Sheila.

<Well, this turned upside down, Lieutenant,> Sheila began. <I believe I'm supposed to be where you are. But then again, and knowing the Admiral, I should have figured he would be in the thick of it. How are you doing, Lieutenant?>

<Honestly, Commander, I'm trying not to throw up, or barring that, run and lock myself in a refresher until this war is over. >

<I can tell you this, Lieutenant. It's better to be scared than cocky. Cocky will get you dead faster.>

<Any wisdom you care to impart, Commander? I'm listening.>

<What's the Admiral's plan?> Sheila asked.

<Well, that's the odd part. It's not a straight-up fight,> Hatsuto explained.

<Ah, then you're in luck. As Commander Tachenko would say, "The Admiral's being devious," and that's a good thing. Follow the Admiral's plan. The last guy that didn't listen ended up dead.>

<That's it? That's the advice, Commander?> Hatsuto asked. He had hoped for so much more.

<That and let the controller do the jinking and jiving. You're there to guide the strategic plan. Good fortune, Lieutenant.>

* * *

The fourteen silver ships came on in a loose vanguard, no identifiable formation.

"Just like a hive," Julien said into the quiet of the bridge. The lights were dimmed. Alex and Andrea were concentrating on the holo-vid and the players—the *Unsere Menschen*, the *Rêveur*, and their adversaries.

"It's time, Captain," Alex said. "Launch the fighters and let's see what we've learned."

On their hold-vid, three dots appeared and ever so briefly hung near the icon of the *Rêveur*, drifting slightly aft. Then, like raptors, they dived down below the ecliptic.

Julien announced, "Three of the silver ships have changed trajectory, Sers. They're chasing our fighters."

Time passed slowly for everyone. Andrea sat in a command chair, a knuckle to her teeth. Several times, she felt the urge to ask Julien for an update but restrained herself. Alex paced the bridge.

A strange phenomenon was taking place, unbeknownst to Alex. His willing of the aliens to respond to his plan was so forceful that, as he paced, his New Terran flight crews began doing the same. Chief Roth was one of those pacing with his crew, so the oddity went unnoticed in the starboard bay. Chief Peterson was incredulous as he watched his crew pace the bay and ordered a halt to their activity. Even then, several of the crew, while standing still, continued to shift their weight from foot to foot.

"The three silver ships have changed trajectory to rejoin the others, Admiral," Julien relayed with enthusiasm.

Alex and Andrea exchanged evil grins. "Okay, Julien," Alex said, "you have our plan. Put that marvelous little crystal brain of yours to work."

When Julien signaled the next event point, Andrea ordered the palettes launched. Crew members, enclosed in their environment suits, had stood waiting behind their grav-lifts, which floated the pallets of minelettes off the deck. The bay's doors were open. On Chief Peterson's command, three crew members, shoving a single pallet in front of them, ran at the bay's opening. Just short of stepping out into space, the carefully measured tether lines anchoring the crew and the grav-lift yanked up short, and the pallet slid off and continued out into the dark. In quick order, the seven other pallets were sent after the first one.

An effective use of the minelettes required they be laid in a dense cloud. The challenge was that the silver ships were spread in a loose formation spanning 130 kilometers. Julien had calculated that if they spread the minelettes evenly across that distance, in a grid of about 10 high by 3,276 wide, they would have a 1-in-53.6 chance of destroying the enemy craft.

That was when Alex realized it was time to be devious. The palettes launched by the flight crew released the minelettes is a gentle swirl that left them trailing behind the *Rêveur* in a thick cloud approximately 20 high by 1,638 wide. An average of five to six meters separated most of the minelettes, and they covered a span of nine kilometers. In the silver ships' present formation, the *Rêveur* might destroy one or, if fortunate, two fighters.

Now the next piece of Alex's plan was engaged. When all ships reached the plan's trigger point, Julien signaled the Daggers' controllers and the fighters flipped around. The pilots blacked out as the inertia compensators struggled to keep up, but the controllers were following the music and Julien was conducting. It became a race. The Daggers shot back up toward the ecliptic, but at an angle that placed them in front of the silver ships.

Alex kept pacing the bridge. This was one of the weak parts of the plans. It depended on the drones not breaking formation and diving to intercept their Daggers. His hope was that their fighters would be seen as returning to their "mother ship" and, therefore, into the path of their enemy.

"Any change?" Andrea asked, unable to control her impatience.

"No deviation at this time, Captain," Julien announced.

The *Rêveur*'s fighters and the silver ships raced toward a common point, which was the cloud of minelettes, small spheres invisible in the dark. As the Daggers closed on the ecliptic, the drones switched from targeting the *Rêveur* to targeting the Daggers, which forced them to close ranks as they angled in toward the three fighters.

This is the beauty of a SADE, Alex thought. Julien had calculated the velocities, angles, timing, and distances to execute the plan once Alex had hatched it.

The closer the Daggers got to the ecliptic, the closer the drones crowded together, all fourteen of them. Then the three Daggers shot in front of the enemy fighters, clearing them by a paltry twenty-six kilometers, and arrowed through the cloud of minelettes, each fighter's controller twisting and rolling its ship to evade the spheres.

The silver ships closed quickly on the Daggers, flying into the cloud of minelettes. They, too, saw the minelettes and, with their great maneuverability, rolled to avoid collision.

The final step in the plan was activated. Alex and Andrea had realized they had no knowledge of the silver ships' avoidance-detection capabilities for space rock, and Julien was unable to provide any clarification. So the decision was made not to bother.

Julien timed his signal, bouncing it through the Daggers' controllers to trigger the minelettes as the silver ships entered the cloud of spheres. Twelve of the fourteen enemy fighters flew through a wall of shrapnel that ripped their ships apart. More than one drone exploded in a fiery ball, obscuring the *Rêveur*'s telemetry.

The two silver ships on the flanks of the formation received only minor damage. They targeted the Daggers, and fortune was not with Lieutenant Gary Giordano. The standing order to keep a tight formation was a rule he often bent, and he was behind his squadron mates by a half-kilometer, which was why both silver ships targeted him. Their beams detonated his missile loads, and the explosion scattered Gary's Dagger in tiny pieces.

* * *

<Dagger-10, don't touch your stick. Stay in auto,> Hatsuto sent frantically, grunting as his controller, having identified its pursuers, was tumbling and twisting the fighter in evasive maneuvers.

Sean McCrery was a steady pilot who had enrolled in Barren Island training because he was bored and had been hoping for a little adventure. This was his first life-and-death struggle, and he'd already had too much adventure. The detonation of his comrade's fighter had nearly scared him to death. His Leader's command caught Sean just before he signaled his controller to manual.

Suddenly a thought occurred to Hatsuto, and he sent a second comm to Sean. <Dive below the ecliptic, Dagger-10! I'm going up.>

Both fighters continued to twist and jink as their controllers scribed arcs that pushed one fighter down and the other up above the ecliptic. The silver ships were caught off guard by the Daggers' maneuvers, and at their greater velocity, they overshot their adversaries. They twisted in an arc to regain their targets, each silver ship chasing a Dagger.

<Keep diving, Dagger-10,> Hatsuto sent, <until they give up. Then stand by to reverse.>

<Understood, Flight Leader,> Sean replied. It occurred to him that their implants had more value than he had previously conceived. With the heavy pressure on his chest, he thought he might not have had enough breath to respond by voice.

Hatsuto communicated with his controller, requesting his previous plunge distance below the ecliptic be laid over his present climb, wondering how much farther his fighter had to go before his pursuer gave up again. He passed the enemy's previous turnaround distance, and his Dagger was forced to dodge another alien beam when his controller detected the charge building on the alien's hull. *Guess we really pissed them off,* Hatsuto thought. His Dagger twisted in a series of spirals in a last-ditch effort to evade the closing silver ship, and Hatsuto closed his eyes, waiting for the final beam shot, his pursuer much too close to miss. When nothing happened, Hatsuto open his eyes and checked his telemetry and checked it again. The silver ship had shot past him. It was cocked to the port-side and gently rolling.

Not even pausing to thank fortune, Hatsuto reversed his Dagger and plunged back down toward the ecliptic, hoping to be in time to help Sean. <Dagger-10, status,> Hatsuto sent as he checked Sean's position in his helmet display.

<Headed back to the ecliptic, Leader. You're not going to believe what happened,> said Sean, his thoughts screaming joy.

<Let me guess, Dagger -10,> Hatsuto sent, relief evident in his thoughts. <The drone shot past you and kept going. So you decided to turn around and come home.>

<Black space, Leader, I thought I was dead. It was right there, right on top of me. My fighter did a twist-and-arc that I thought that was going to

kill me before the enemy fighter did. When my blackout cleared, I looked for the silver ship, and it was ahead of me, just shooting on.>

<Lieutenants, Captain Bonnard. Stop gabbing about your good fortune and get your butts back aboard the *Rêveur* now,> Andrea commed.

* * *

"Julien, what's the status of any other potential problem drones?" Alex asked after witnessing the last of their fourteen pursuers drift out of the system.

"Three drones have changed vectors to intercept us, Admiral," Julien reported.

"Can they catch us?" Alex asked.

"Stand by, Admiral. I need more telemetry time." Several moments later, Julien had his answer: "Admiral, two will catch the *Unsere Menschen*, 10.5 and 12.6 hours before passing the last planet's orbit."

"From what we've just seen, Julien," said Alex, "it appears your gravity drive theory has been substantiated."

"The power of the Sleuth," Julien replied.

"Good job, Detective," Alex said. "Julien, relay my comm to all SADEs, for all people."

"Ready, Admiral," confirmed Julien.

<Attention, people of the Libran flotilla,> Alex sent. <Fortune is still with us. We've eliminated the fourteen pursuers of the *Unsere Menschen*, but, in doing so, we've lost another good man, Lieutenant Gary Giordano. Now three more silver ships are chasing us. According to Julien, two will catch us just before we pass the last planet. That's all for now. May fortune continue to guide us.>

"So, do I understand this correctly?" Andrea asked. "Julien's concept is that the silver ships, outside of the system's gravity wells, are unable to steer their craft. That's why they sailed off into space."

"Yes, Captain," Alex replied. "Julien's theory is that the silver ships collect energy from gravitational waves through their shells and use the energy to power their craft. Apparently it's why the enemy fighters are limited to a system and not too far above or below the ecliptic. When they pursued our two Daggers, they ended up with insufficient gravitational forces to power their drives, or something to that effect."

Alex sat back down in front of the holo-vid, which Julien had changed to provide a broader view of the system. It displayed the last planet's orbital arc, the flotilla's ships, and the three additional drones. The two fighters that would arrive first were approaching at angles to their position. *Wish we would have kept some of those minelettes*, Alex thought.

"Captain, get those two fighters back aboard and refueled," Alex ordered. "We need to focus on these two new pursuers."

While Andrea checked in with the Flight Chiefs on the status of the retrieval of their fighters, Alex signaled Tatia.

<Well done, Admiral,> Tatia sent, responding to Alex's greeting.

<You have my gratitude, Commander. Your foresight and perseverance saved us and the people of the *Unsere Menschen*.>

<Thank you for the compliment, Admiral, but I think you're giving me too much credit. I'm trained in weapons, so I think in terms of utilizing them to equalize an adversary's advantages. You're the one who invents the way to employ them and win an engagement. We were monitoring Julien's telemetry. Very clever of you, Admiral ... very devious.>

<I had a good teacher, Commander,> Alex sent.

Tatia laughed at the thought that her star student was the Admiral who was trying to defeat humanity's enemy.

<Well, Commander,> Alex said, <I used all the minelettes. So no more surprises, and my two Daggers can't take on two silver ships head to head. Looks like your people will get into the fight now. Assemble Lazlo, Sheila, Mickey, and yourself on the bridge. Julien and Z can mirror the holo-vids.>

33

The officers and crew of the *Money Maker* hadn't been idle while their ship headed for the FTL exit. In addition to the seven Daggers that had flown onto the freighter, they had assembled five more. More might have been readied, except the bays were crammed to the bulkheads with parts, missiles, and equipment, and the crew spent an enormous amount of time moving crates around to create space to uncrate more equipment and provide room to assemble the fighters. So many of the empty plasti-crates lined the spine's long corridor that crew had to squeeze past one another when coming from opposite directions.

In addition to their assembly efforts and soon after Tatia told Alex of the minelettes, she and Captain Menlo had decided to decelerate their freighter, intending to come to a full stop. Knowing full well that Julien wouldn't miss their maneuver, they had waited for the Admiral's call. Tatia was especially nervous. Contravening orders went against the grain of her training. But instead of the expected comm, Mutter informed the two officers that Julien had contacted her to determine the nature of their mechanical problems.

<What did you reply, Mutter?> Lazlo had inquired.

<I confirmed there were no mechanical difficulties and that it was a deliberate maneuver ordered by the Captain,> Mutter had replied.

When Tatia had heard Mutter's response, she realized the huge value that Julien was adding to the war effort. He was a very sophisticated individual and, under Alex's influence, had developed a set of moral imperatives that challenged his Méridien training. She and Lazlo had considered two options: either Julien hadn't told Alex, or he had and the Admiral had chosen not to call them. They had discarded the latter possibility, deciding that Julien was keeping their secret. He approved.

Tatia gave a quick heads-up to the principals of Alex's meeting. When they were assembled on the bridge, Lazlo requested Mutter comm the Admiral. <Good evening, Admiral,> Lazlo sent. <May I extend my congratulations on your brilliant maneuver?>

<A maneuver made possible by the stubbornness of my Commander,> Alex replied with a little smile. <Interesting development, Captain ... I was sitting here trying to determine how I could employ your Daggers to intercept these two drones, when I noticed your ship's position. Much to my surprise, it seems I was the only one who didn't know you had fallen out of formation. I must have a word with my SADE sometime.>

Julien mentally winced at Alex's statement, but he had made his decision to support Tatia and Lazlo. The dynamics of the human wills in play created a fascinating intersection of personalities for him to contemplate. Alex fought to save every ship and every person, and his people fought to save one another, especially their Admiral.

<Right now,> Alex continued, <you're in a prime position to assist us with your seven Daggers, Commander.>

<That would be twelve Daggers, Admiral,> Tatia interrupted.

<You have been busy, Commander. Have you been able to test the new fighters?> Alex asked.

<We've just finished diagnostics tests on the controllers, Admiral,> Sheila reported. <We are prime on each one and are preparing to flight-test the fighters now.>

<Julien, project the intersection of the two drones,> Alex requested. The holo-vid detailed the three flotilla ships and the three enemy fighters. Alex rolled the timeline forward to the first drone's contact, coming in from the *Unsere Menschen*'s port side. There wasn't a planet to play hide-and-seek behind, and no means by which their Daggers might surprise one drone without being seen by the other drone. Unfortunately the freighter's Daggers would have to accelerate to their limit to arrive in time, and the drones would also see them coming.

On each ship, people stared at the holo-vids and came to the conclusion that there was only one option. It would be a straight-up fight ... unless the Admiral had another trick or two up his sleeve.

* * *

At morning meal, the flotilla received their first good piece of news. The Bergfalk liners were approaching the FTL exit point.

<Admiral, Captain Azasdau here,> Asu sent. <I've been asked to speak for the other liner Captains. We wish to offer our thanks for your help. Because of your efforts, our ships are about to reach safety. We will await the *Langstrecke* and the *Freedom,* and accompany them to the other side.>

The *Freedom* had continued to pile on acceleration. It and the freighter would arrive at the FTL point thirteen hours behind the liners.

Alex's plan was that the flotilla wouldn't risk a straight jump to New Terra. Utilizing the backtrack gambit, the ships would enter FTL at a tangent away from New Terra, jump two light-years and circle until the flotilla was reconstituted.

<Safe voyage, Captain,> Alex sent.

Alex took a long gulp of his thé while Captain's Azasdau's message was forwarded to the crew. Throughout the meal room, the crew silently hoisted their drink cups to Alex, who returned their salute by hoisting his own.

<Five safe, Admiral, three to go,> Andrea sent privately.

<I like eight, Captain,> Alex returned. <It was always one of my favorite numbers. The shape is pleasing, standing up or laying down.>

Andrea smiled into her cup of thé. Eight safe suited her just fine.

<Admiral, Captain Manet. The *Outward Bound* is repaired and ready to join the fight.>

<Excellent news,> Alex sent, clapping his hands together and rubbing them in satisfaction.

The boom echoing from Alex's handclap had caused Andrea and Renée to jump in their chairs. <I don't know which is worse,> Andrea sent to Renée, grinning sheepishly at her reaction, <the Admiral receiving bad news or good news.>

To which, Renée laughed and replied, <That one's easy, Captain. Good news scares us; bad news gets us killed.>

The two women were waiting for Alex to share his news, but as he sat in the chair next to them, he was already gone.

* * *

The liners, the *Freedom*, and the freighter *Langstrecke* were nearing the FTL exit. Tomas called to wish good fortune to the Admiral, who had just donned a robe to join Renée in their cabin's main salon.

<I have a particularly intense desire to see you safely on the other side, Admiral. I will need your introduction to your President,> Tomas said.

<And you wish me to bring a certain person safely through,> Alex added.

<Yes, Admiral, there is that. For my people, I would wish the first; for me, I would wish the second. It has been many years ...> said Tomas, failing to finish his thought.

<We both have two fights to win, Tomas: one for the people and one for ourselves,> Alex said, standing behind Renée and running his fingers through her hair. She leaned back and Alex moved his fingers up to massage her scalp, an intimate favorite of hers. Then again, Alex had found that any form of his touch was pronounced as her favorite.

<Safe voyage, Tomas,> Alex sent and closed the comm. *Now its five ships safe*, he thought. *Three ships and 123,823 people to go.*

* * *

The port-side attacker came directly at the *Rêveur*. Alex had placed his ship directly between the silver ship and the *Unsere Menschen*. Earlier, Andrea had launched their two Daggers, which had dived under the ecliptic and now were arcing back up.

As the drone closed at its incredible speed, the *Outward Bound* came over the top of the *Rêveur* and began firing its missiles one after another until the carousels were exhausted. The sixteen missiles accelerated and fired their stage-two munitions. One hundred twenty-eight warheads flew at the drone in batches of eight, spiraling in various patterns. The silver ship's beam was cutting great swaths in the mass of warheads, which is probably why the enemy fighter never detected the missiles coming at it from the two Daggers below. It was obliterated in a hot ball of expanding debris and gas.

The second drone, which had been on patrol as well, came from the starboard quarter. The *Outward Bound* had rearmed itself and stood by to defend the *Rêveur,* but the enemy fighter didn't get close to the Admiral's ship. Fourteen Daggers shot past the *Rêveur* and loosed a single missile barrage, which became 112 warheads. Immediately, the squadron launched a second barrage.

The Librans were tired of finding themselves backed into corners, first from their own society and now from an alien civilization, and their anger over the loss of thousands of precious elders smoldered in their hearts. Every Libran pilot trainee was in near ecstasy when Commander Reynard ordered twin missile launches.

The drone destroyed many of the warheads in the initial volley before it was swamped and destroyed. Over a hundred warheads swept past the ball of hot gas that had been the silver ship and proceeded to burn out as they headed inward. In time, most would become fuel for Arno.

Sheila felt a twinge of regret for the waste of missiles, but she had to admit that swatting the drone out of existence was a satisfying moment she wouldn't soon forget. She sent Lieutenant Tanaka and his wingman, Lieutenant McCrery, back to the *Rêveur,* and added a replacement fighter. Then her squadron began the return trip to the *Money Maker.*

When Lazlo received news of the successful defeat of the second drone, he ordered Mutter to bring the engines to full power and accelerate to the FTL exit. The Daggers would easily catch his ship, and the *Unsere Menschen* and *Rêveur* would pass him by before his freighter reached the outer planet's orbit.

* * *

Alex sat quietly in the *Rêveur*'s command chair. The raucous celebration of the crew could still be heard down the corridor. Alex's thoughts weren't celebratory since he was focused on those they had lost, but he couldn't resist sharing with Julien. <It's over. We made it my friend,> Alex sent.

<Yes, an entire population saved, Admiral. As is popular at celebrations on your world, I would offer a toast to the elders, to Bobbie, to those lost aboard our shuttle, to Heinrich, and to Lieutenant Giordano, except for a simple fact,> Julien said drily.

<I could pour some alcohol on your crystals for you,> Alex offered.

<True, but then who would drive this metal-alloy hull around the stars for you, Admiral?>

<Well, yes, there is that.> Alex paused briefly, then sent, <Okay, I'm done wallowing.>

This is no time to be thinking of the past, my friend, Julien thought. *New Terra is only days away.*

34

The *Unsere Menschen* passed by the *Money Maker*, and Alex ordered Andrea to fall off and shadow the freighter. Alex and Andrea were updated by Julien that four more drones had turned to pursue them but were too far away to reach them before the exit point. In fact, the remaining ships of the flotilla would soon pass that invisible gravity line of the last planet's orbit that Alex and Julien were sure the silver ships couldn't cross.

"It's just mindless, Admiral," Andrea said, observing the great distance the drones had to cross to reach their ships.

"Mindless, Captain?" Alex repeated. "I'm not so sure. Directed, perhaps."

Before Andrea could reply, Lazlo was on the comm for Alex: <Good day, Admiral. I see we warrant an escort.>

<All the way to the exit, Captain,> Alex sent.

<I was recently introduced to an interesting concept by your crew, called "wagering,"> Lazlo said.

<Not all New Terran habits are good habits, Captain. By any chance, did you participate?>

<I'm afraid I did … with your Commander. But the challenge appeared to be quite winnable, Admiral,> Lazlo sent.

<They often do, Captain. It's what makes most wagers foolish. And what was it you appeared to have won before you bet?> Alex asked.

<It began as a simple discussion. I expressed my concern that when the *Unsere Menschen* and the *Rêveur* passed us by, I hoped we wouldn't be surprised by any enemy fighters before we could make the exit, and the Commander replied, "What makes you think the Admiral will pass us by?" To which I replied that it was the logical thing to do. Then she uttered an odd phrase, "You want to bet?">

Alex was laughing. He could just imagine the expressions on Lazlo's face—first, when Tatia dropped her challenge, and second, when he lost the bet. <What did you lose, Captain?> Alex asked.

<I'd rather not divulge that, Admiral. Needless to say, your Commander appears to know you very well.>

<That she does, Captain. Sometimes it appears she knows me better than I know myself.>

* * *

Late in the evening, Julien announced FTL conditions. Alex had ordered the *Unsere Menschen* to proceed into the exit point earlier that day. The *Rêveur* and the *Money Maker* were less than a quarter-hour away from escaping Arno.

Alex and Renée were sitting on their cabin's lounge when the door chime signaled. Alex scanned his crew and located Andrea waiting outside. He signaled the cabin door open and sent her name to Renée.

Andrea came through the door and her steps stuttered to a halt. She attempted to cover her embarrassment at finding Renée curled in Alex's lap, wearing the sheerest wrap she had ever seen.

Renée noticed Andrea's halting steps and the flush on her cheeks, and took pity on her. "Oh, New Terrans," she pronounced and exited to the sleeping cabin for her full-length robe while Andrea sat a tray on the table.

When Renée returned, Andrea was apologetic: "Your pardon, Ser. I didn't mean to interrupt an intimate moment."

"Nonsense, Captain," Renée replied. "What have you brought us?"

Andrea brightened up. "I would like to offer a toast," she said, pouring a pale amber liquid into three small cups.

"A toast?" said Renée, intrigued by joining in on a new custom.

"And what did you discover that we could toast with?" said Alex, eyeing the unlabeled bottle.

"The 'who' had it, Admiral, should remain anonymous, but the 'what is it' is a homemade cactus concoction," Andrea replied as she filled and handed cups to Alex and Renée.

"One moment," said Alex, then sent, <Julien, would you join us, please? Use the cabin monitor for vid and audio.>

The cabin's main screen displayed a side silhouette of a man's head and shoulders. The ubiquitous hat was settled on the head and an odd, curved item extended from between his lips.

"The Sleuth is present," Alex announced. He reached across the table for another cup and poured a small amount of the drink. "The Captain wishes to extend a toast, Julien, and I thought it appropriate that you share in it."

Julien was overjoyed. He searched his databases to find the appropriate words, but nothing seemed to satisfy the moment. So he took refuge in the traditional. "One is most honored, Admiral."

Alex held up Julien's cup along with his own and looked to Andrea.

"To saving a world and to those we lost while doing it. Skål," Andrea said, draining her glass.

Renée saw the others empty their cups in a single swallow, so she imitated them. The alcohol burned down her throat and her stomach felt as if it had been punched. She coughed heavily, gasping for air. "What?" was all that she managed to choke out.

"Oops," Alex said as he steadied Renée.

By the time Renée caught her breath and received an explanation about New Terran alcohol, the drink had warmed her belly and its heat was spreading throughout her body.

"Julien, may I have the honor of consuming your toast for you?" Renée asked.

"I would be most pleased, Ser."

Renée deftly snatched Julien's cup out of Alex's hand. Getting into the moment, she refilled Alex's and Andrea's cups. Then she extended her cup toward the vid cam at the top of the screen. "To Julien, whose efforts and wisdom enabled us to accomplish the impossible."

Three cups were drained in honor of Julien, which caused his applications to come to a halt. For a brief moment, not a single process ran.

Andrea wished the three of them good evening and left her present behind. Julien also said good evening as the *Rêveur* entered FTL. The last three ships of the flotilla were safe.

"I have one more toast to make," Renée announced as she filled both their cups. When Alex drew breath to speak, she touched a finger to his lips to silence him and held up her cup. "To the Admiral, who is saving my people; and to the man, who is saving me."

She downed her cup, feeling her blood pounding though her body. A wicked smile crossed her face as she stripped off her robe and said, "Now where were we?"

* * *

The entire flotilla had safely exited FTL two light-years from Arno and was circling back to their exit point to ensure they hadn't been followed. Based on what had been learned, neither Alex nor Julien considered it a possibility. But when the alternative was the destruction of a home world, zero risk was the only course to follow.

Tomas sent invitations to Alex, Renée, Eric, and the flotilla's officers. A memorial was planned for the fallen. Several shuttles had been repaired, enabling the transfer of the honored guests from the seven other ships to the *Freedom* for the services.

The assembly was held at the city-ship's grand central park. Alex could see that the crew and passengers had not wasted their days aboard the city-ship. The park was immaculate. The plantings had been completed, and the flowers displayed a riot of colors. Small, brightly painted fish swam in the pools. Around the park, the small shops had signs, which proudly proclaimed their businesses.

At the start of the memorial, Alex, Renée, Tomas, Terese, Eric, and the flotilla's officers stood together at the edge of the park. Nearly 8,000 Librans were scattered throughout and around the park.

Tomas opened the ceremony. "Our memorial celebrates the lives of the people we've lost, whose courage and dedication helped us escape devastation. We owe the efforts of this afternoon's presentation to the Admiral, who brought an incredible artist to our attention, and she has authored this ceremony." Tomas returned to his place beside Terese, his hand slipping into hers.

Cordelia's voice, soft and mellow, filled the minds of those in the park. <We ... Julien, Z, Mutter, and I have combined our power to offer this tribute to those we have lost.>

The light emanating from overhead of the park dimmed, and the tiny footlights that lit the park's walkways in the evening slowly brightened. The landscape took on a twilight appearance. Everyone knew of Cordelia's magic, and they opened their implants to participate. Music, offered by Mutter, played in their minds as Cordelia continued her narration. <Libran elders waited at the end of the exodus line so that their young would live. And forty-nine more lost their lives striving to escape to freedom.>

Fiona Haraken appeared on the shadowed walkway, her slender, straight, but aged body clothed in a traditional Independent wrap.

<Fiona Haraken, proud Elder of her people, would take one last walk for our Librans.>

The figure of Fiona raised an arm, palm up in an offer to Alex. Tears threatened to spill from Alex's eyes as he walked up to the figure of Fiona and placed her hand into the crook of this arm. He felt her other hand lay over top of his and her weight pull against him as they strolled the pathway through the park's center. As they walked, everyone heard Fiona's farewell to her people again. Tears ran down the faces of many of the Independents surrounding the park. Fiona's words ended as Alex reached the end of the walkway. He heard and felt her whisper of farewell in his ear—and she was gone. Slowly Alex turned and looked back along the walkway.

<A young man gave his life,> Cordelia continued, <to launch his city-ship. His bravery was echoed by the crew of our lost shuttle, who strove to

save our people.> Heinrich appeared on the walkway where Fiona had. <Our young tech was terrified the morning he walked in space to save the lives of all those aboard his ship. Who would take Heinrich's last walk with him?>

Eric Stroheim stepped up to the young man, who smiled tentatively at him. Heinrich had always been shy. For one of the few times in his life, Eric dropped his personal barriers. He was proud of young Heinrich, who reminded him of the son that he had lost along with his wife during an alien attack. His family had gone to visit friends and associates on Hellébore while awaiting the arrival of Renée de Guirnon for her marriage.

Eric extended his hand to Heinrich, aching to feel the contact of his lost son. When he felt the young man place his hand in his, the pain of the loss he had kept tamped down for decades welled up from deep inside. The tears that flowed obliterated Eric's view of the park and the walkway.

<It is of no concern, Ser,> said Heinrich. <Come. I will lead us.>

They walked along the pathway together, and Eric Stroheim never felt prouder in his long life than he did at that moment. When they reached the end of the walkway, Eric wanted to continue to hold the boy's hand as if willing him to live. But when the pressure left his hand, Eric joined Alex to look back along the walkway, unabashed by the tears that ran down his face. Eric felt the Admiral's powerful hand grip his shoulder and was grateful for the continued touch of another human.

<Three brave pilots challenged fourteen of our adversaries.> Now the walkway held the image of Gary Giordano in his flight suit. <The New Terrans came to defend us, to defend all humans, despite the odds against them. Who would accompany Lieutenant Giordano one last time?>

Hatsuto let go of Miko's hand and walked up to the image of Gary. He was frightened. Hatsuto had experienced Cordelia's power once before on the *Rêveur*'s bridge, and the thought of walking with an apparition stirred old superstitions.

<Don't be afraid, Hatsuto,> Gary told him and motioned him down the walkway. <This is but a short trip for me. You have a much longer one ahead of you.> As they walked, Gary requested Hatsuto take good care of the other pilots and remember to embrace life. When they reached the end

of the walkway, Hatsuto extended his hand and Gary shook it. <Good fortune and safe voyage, Hatsuto,> Gary told him, then faded away.

<To those who are gone,> Cordelia said, <we say good-bye. But we must remember that their passing was so that all of us live tomorrow for them.>

The music's strains played sweetly while people stood in respectful silence. When the music faded, the lights of the park shifted from twilight to afternoon. The people looked around with uncertainty. Reality was often jarring when people emerged from Cordelia's dream world.

"Thank you for your participation today in honoring those we have lost," announced Tomas over the park's speakers, which ended the event and people began to drift away.

Renée and Terese trod the walkway to the three men, who still stood there, the impact of their walks with Cordelia's ghosts still gripping them. Terese produced refresher cloths for Alex and Eric, items sorely needed for both men.

* * *

Tomas and Eric invited Alex and Renée to join them for some refreshment. When Alex glanced toward Terese, who held Tomas's arm, she sent privately, <Is this acceptable, Admiral, that I'm included?>

<It's quite acceptable, Terese,> Alex sent. <You're Tomas's guest. Someone I would think of as the First Lady of a Leader.>

Terese's curiosity was satisfied by a query to Julien. A "First Lady" was how she thought of herself when she was with Tomas.

The group walked to a small eatery. The entire staff, which included the operators, stood in a line at the entrance. They held hands to heart, dipping their heads as Alex and Renée passed.

<This has to stop someday,> Alex moaned privately to Renée.

<As your people say, my love, I have bad news for you. This will never stop. It's your due,> Renée sent, mirth sparkling her thoughts.

As the group was seated, an attendant brought drinks and Alex requested a cup of aigre. The young woman hesitated and queried Terese, who wore the Medical Specialist symbol on her uniform. The attendant nodded her understanding of Terese's instructions, then poured a small amount in a crystal cup and added a splash of water to it.

Alex took a sip of the drink while his audience looked on. <You'd think I was taking on a silver ship single-handedly,> Alex shared with Renée. The tart, astringent fruit juice puckered Alex's lips, mouth, and throat. He reached for his water cup and quickly downed all of it. "Interesting drink," Alex said to the table, who shared chuckles over his attempt to make light of his discomfort. The attendant, who had stood by, quickly refilled Alex's water cup and motioned to his aigre cup, offering to take it. At Alex's nod, she removed it.

"Well, not all experiments are successful," said Alex as he drained his water cup again. Terese reached for the pitcher and refilled his cup.

Attendants brought small plates of food that Alex had not seen before. Most were small items, easily consumed by hand, and the Méridiens were taking items from the serving dishes for their plates. When Alex glanced at Renée, she picked up his plate and served him.

"Admiral, we invited you to talk with us for a specific reason," Tomas said. "Your invitation to accompany you to your home world is most appreciated. But we wonder if we are ill-prepared."

"Leader Monti refers to our political positions, Admiral, not our state of technical disrepair," Eric quickly added.

"Yes, Admiral, we lack cohesion," Tomas continued. "Your government will be faced with you, your new House, Bergfalk personnel, and ships loaded with Independents, who must be explained. We will appear disjointed as ... as ..."

"Refugees," Alex supplied, "those who are fleeing their home and seeking sanctuary."

"Yes, as refugees," Tomas said, adding the word to his vocabulary app.

"I take it we're here," Alex said, "because you have a suggestion."

"Yes, Admiral, we believe it would be better to appear as one group, one organization, to your government," Tomas explained.

"What group would that be, Tomas?" Renée asked, her concern growing.

"We wish to join your House, Ser," Tomas announced.

"You wish to join our military?" Alex asked, stunned by the offer.

"Fortune forbid!" Eric exclaimed.

"No, no, Admiral," Tomas said. "Let me explain. We have this incongruous mix of people that needs cohesion, a unified organization. We propose that organization be House Alexander, with its present Leaders," he said, indicating Alex and Renée. "You have inherited a planet full of people, whether you wish it or not, Admiral. They won't join your military as fighters, but will support you in every other way possible. We have learned from your officers that our people would be considered civilians, and you would require people to manage your civilians, Admiral. Eric and I would be your Directors, who would owe allegiance to you as our Leaders and would be responsible for managing the civilians."

"And what of those who choose not to join House Alexander?" Alex asked.

"Admiral," Terese explained, "the Leaders would not propose this unless they had spoken to the people and they had agreed."

"All of them?" Alex asked.

Tomas, who had spent considerable time discussing the Admiral with Terese, had come to realize the effectiveness of the conversation he had arranged with the engineer in Libre's terminal building. *If it helped once*, he thought, and signaled two of the staff.

"Admiral, may I introduce Maria, an Independent, and Hans, a member of House Bergfalk. Maria, the Admiral would like to understand your opinion on joining House Alexander."

The middle-aged woman, who had been courteous and deferential at her introduction, visibly brightened at the opportunity to express her hope.

"Is this your opinion, Maria?" Alex inquired.

"My opinion, Admiral?" Maria questioned. "Yes, it was, but it was considered and accepted by all. It is our opinion. We are quite anxious to know if the Admiral will accept us as support staff for his House … as his civilians."

It seemed to Alex that everyone had learned a few new words on the flight out of the Arno system. "Would not some of your people wish to leave at some time, Ser?" Alex asked.

Maria dipped her head in acknowledgment of the Admiral's formal address. "Why would they wish that, Admiral? Despite what our Council has labeled us, we are, after all, Méridiens. We are a community; we need one another."

The lifelong tie of implants, Alex thought. New Terrans had independence and singularity, isolation if you will, first and foremost. Their implants were tools for them. For the Méridiens, they were a way of life, communicating and living together in a manner most New Terrans wouldn't understand.

"What about you, Hans? You have your House," Alex asked.

"That is not so, Admiral. The moment we enabled the exodus of the Independents, we violated our Council's directive. We became Independents that day."

"Thank you, Maria and Hans. You've been very instructive," Alex said, and the pair dipped their heads and retired.

Tomas and Eric eyed him expectantly.

<The House gets bigger every day,> Renée sent to Alex. <Perhaps we should consider adding one or two of our own.>

Alex was grateful he had no food or drink in his mouth. Fortune knows where it would have ended up. He had a vision of spraying food into Eric's face, who sat across from him. Alex glanced at Renée, but she was wearing a neutral expression as she regarded the two Leaders across the table.

<Julien,> Alex sent, looking for advice, <are you up to date on this?>

<Cordelia made me aware of the Librans' discussion when you entered the meal establishment. I believe the answer lies in your future plans, Admiral.>

<Well, I'm not sure we need a unified front for President McMorris,> Alex replied.

<What comes after New Terra, Admiral?> Julien asked.

<After?> Alex considered the answer to Julien's question. <After New Terra, I intend to eliminate that mother ship,> he sent, his thoughts carrying the vehemence in his heart.

<In that case, Admiral, we would be returning to Confederation space, which would require, at some time, that we stand before the Council. It would seem appropriate to present a unified front before Méridien's governing body.>

<Ah, that's a very good point, Julien. When we return to Libre, we will need a great deal of support from the Librans aboard the *Rêveur* and the *Money Maker*. That includes the use of one of their city-ships. And we will need to be viewed by the Council as a cohesive group, if we are to be taken seriously.>

<House Alexander,> Julien supplied.

<Yes, with military and civilian personnel,> Alex said. <Thank you, my friend.>

<It's always my privilege, Admiral.>

While Alex had been in discussion with Julien, the others had been happily discussing the tremendous improvements made aboard the *Freedom*. But Eric had not participated. His ship was in urgent need of its final construction phases. To accomplish that, Eric needed to reach New Terra soon, where the *Unsere Menschen*'s main engines could be shut down and the work on his ship completed.

Alex refocused on the table and stood up. The others rose with him. "Welcome to House Alexander, Director Monti and Director Stroheim," he said as he extended his hand. For the first time that Alex could recall, his hand was shaken by both men with more strength and vigor than he might have extended to a fellow New Terran, although each man used both hands.

Renée extended her traditional greetings to both of the new Directors. Terese waited until Ser was done before she threw her arms round Tomas's neck, planting a kiss on his cheek.

<I see your medical techniques have extended to public administrations,> Alex teased Terese privately.

<I intend to monitor you and your people closely, Admiral. There are more of your practices I might adopt for my people's health,> Terese replied, throwing Alex a wry grin.

35

Tomas invited the group to tour the ship with him and see their improvements, and was surprised when Terese begged off, citing a previous engagement. Tomas had offered Terese the opportunity to stay with him aboard the *Freedom* as his partner, now that they had successfully escaped Arno. Her response had been unexpected then as well.

"Much depends on our Admiral," Terese had replied, "and his health and well-being are my personal responsibility."

Tomas had respected Terese's dedication to the Admiral and told her so. It earned him a long, passionate kiss. Terese had created her own function, one independent of a traditional House duty. It was a function she believed to be critical to her people's future, and she was going to perform it to the best of her abilities.

* * *

Terese abstained from Tomas's tour for an important reason. She had scheduled a consultation with an implant engineer, Fabrice, who had been sent to Libre fifty-eight years ago. The engineer was evacuated from the planet with her husband and two children. Terese sat with the woman on one of the park benches, watching fish circle in a pool.

"I'm grateful for your time, Fabrice. I seek your advice concerning implants," Terese said.

"I am at your service, Ser," Fabrice replied.

"Have you experience with those who have multiple implants?" Terese asked.

"Yes, with certainty, Ser. Of whom are we speaking so that I might relate my information to their needs."

"This concerns the Admiral."

"Ser, I understand the Admiral has had his implant less than a year. Why does he seek an additional implant so soon?" Fabrice said.

"The Admiral already has a second implant and is seeking a third, Fabrice. I will conference Julien. He can provide you with more details."

<Julien,> Terese sent, hooking Fabrice into her comm, <please share with us the status of the Admiral's implant use.>

<Good day, Fabrice,> replied Julien. <The Admiral's implants are full. In addition, he has a dedicated directory consuming 152 grams of my crystal memory.>

<May our ancestors protect us,> leaked the thought from Fabrice. The amount of memory Julien was describing could hold volumes of data.

Terese briefly considered Fabrice's appeal to her Méridien ancestors for protection, and the concept left a sour taste in her mouth. *Our ancestors appear to have done little to protect our people*, Terese thought. *As our cousins say, "I will bet on the Admiral."*

<Allow me to explain, Ser,> Julien said. <The majority of the Admiral's implant space is occupied by applications, not data. Here is a brief list of some of those applications and examples of their output.>

Fabrice reviewed the list and their capabilities. <Most impressive, Julien. I haven't seen many of these before, but I have been out of circulation for many years,> Fabrice said self-consciously. <You have done a marvelous job supporting your Admiral with these applications.>

<These aren't my applications, Ser,> Julien explained. <The Admiral created them. They are the ones he uses most frequently, and this list represents only a portion of his applications.>

Fabrice leaned against the back support of the bench as if she had been struck and the wind knocked out of her.

Terese had been shocked herself when she discovered the extent of the Admiral's data storage on Julien and the number of applications he had created and coordinated daily with Julien. Her thought was that Alex and

Julien were more intertwined than anyone realized. It was a thought she carefully kept to herself.

When Fabrice recovered, she said, <I have known many who have employed two implants, and have set up several individuals myself, mostly scientists and engineers. And while I have heard of a few others who have had more than two, I have never met them and do not know if they suffered complications. I would earnestly suggest the Admiral is advised to be satisfied with two implants.>

Terese laughed outright and slapped her thigh. <A fine suggestion, Ser,> Terese replied. <Would you care to deliver that advice, Julien?>

<I would sooner attack a silver ship, thank you, Ser,> Julien replied.

<So, Fabrice, if the Admiral was to insist on a third implant what protocols could you provide us?>

Fabrice queried Cordelia for her private library, which had been uploaded once the SADE had been installed aboard the *Freedom*. <I've requested Cordelia transfer my library to Julien. It's everything I have on implant technology, brain interaction abnormalities, and synchronization. I hope it will be of help, Ser.>

"Thank you, Ser," Terese said to Fabrice and left to find Tomas.

* * *

The flotilla completed its back circle. The SADEs had judiciously monitored their telemetry and pronounced their trail clear of silver ships.

"Julien, communicate to all ship the coordinates for Oistos. Have the flotilla keep pace with the freighters. When ready, synchronize an FTL exit," Alex ordered.

"Proceeding, Admiral. Time to exit will be 6.2 hrs. Time in FTL will be 9.47 days."

"Captain, you have the bridge," Alex said.

* * *

The people of the flotilla had another nine and a half days to decompress. No timetables, no aliens, no life-and-death struggles. It was pure bliss for most but certainly for the *Rêveur*'s crew. The New Terrans talked of home and the tales they would tell, most importantly of the warnings they would bring. After the discovery of the invaders in Confederation space and the ensuing battles, some crew members had developed serious doubts about their decisions to sign up. Others, mourning the loss of the Libran elders, many of whom they had personally known, were without doubt. It was as Tatia had said to the Méridiens the evening after they lost Jase, "Your fight is now my fight."

But thoughts aboard the *Rêveur* weren't all dark. The games resumed, which delighted Julien. And they resumed with a vengeance. The New Terrans had continued to develop their skills, and all teams added new twists using the subjects of Arno, Libre, Independents, silver ships, and mother ship.

Tomas had Cordelia copy some games and the referee's requirements from Julien, and asked her to be the *Freedom*'s referee, which she was delighted to do. However, his success in starting the games aboard the city-ship was abysmal. While Tomas was an enthusiast, anxious to play at the level he enjoyed in Terese's sharing, few of his people showed an interest. Tomas could only guess at the differences that existed between his people and the Méridiens of the *Rêveur*.

Tatia kept the freighter crew busy. Ever since her first conversation with Alex on the *Rêveur*'s bridge discussing weapons strategy, Tatia had begun to recognize an important limitation in her leader's mental arsenal. While Alex could strategize with the best of them, he was not the most proficient in devising the tools of offense and defense. So despite the absence of an official position, Tatia had come to consider herself the House's de facto armorer. That decision had driven her to produce Cordelia's minelettes without authorization. Approval might have been forthcoming, but she felt the value of the minelettes was too important to risk official refusal. She did regret tricking Julien into keeping her secret, but she had a feeling that he secretly approved her gambit.

Continuing in her unofficial role as armorer, Tatia had pushed Sheila, Mickey, and the freighter crew to build more fighters while en route to Arno's FTL exit, and those ships had been instrumental in overwhelming the last enemy fighter. And now, despite the flotilla having escaped to safety, Tatia continued to drive the crew to build every fighter they could.

While the flotilla backtracked light-years from Arno, Mickey had taken the opportunity to offload their empty plasti-crates to the *Freedom* and liberate some much-needed raw materials from the city-ship. Removal of the crates regained operating space in the bays, allowing Mickey to set up some GEN machines and begin manufacturing critical parts for the Daggers. After a long day of assembly, a very tired Mickey sat across the meal table from Tatia.

"Commander, you're pushing the crew to build Daggers like you expect a fight when we arrive at New Terra," Mickey said, broaching the subject that had concerned him and many crew members.

"New Terra?" Tatia responded. "No, Mickey, not New Terra. How long do you think it will be before we go back to Libre?" When Tatia saw the frown form on Mickey's forehead, she realized the engineer had not thought through the next phase of the war. "Mickey, we're returning to New Terra to arm ourselves and organize our resources to go back and take the Arno system," Tatia explained. "We know the mother ship and her drones will stay on Libre for years. Now is the time to take the fight to them. Enough of this playing defense. So I'm getting the Admiral's war tools ready for him. And exactly how many fighters do you think he's going to need?"

"Probably every single one we can build, Commander," Mickey had replied, nodding his head in understanding.

When Mickey shared Tatia's comments with the crew, they turned their hand to the business of building fighters without a word of complaint. The crew, Libran and New Terran, had been focused on their destination either as first-time visitors or those wishing to see their home world. Tatia's scenario of a return to Libre was an entirely different future to contemplate.

* * *

The flotilla exited FTL at Oistos, a half-day from Seda's orbit at their freighters' velocity. Alex was being cautious. *This homecoming is going to be a tricky affair as it is,* he thought. Alex was trying to anticipate his government's reaction to his having left with a single ship, an attached shuttle, and four fighters, and returning with an entire planet of people, two monster ships, two freighters with one full of Daggers, and three additional liners. *Yes, Mr. President, they just followed me home.*

As the flotilla made its way past the ice fields, Alex sat on the *Rêveur*'s bridge reviewing his summary message to President McMorris when Julien interrupted.

"Admiral, I'm receiving a comm from Sharius. I detect an FTL station in orbit around New Terra with relays on your system's outposts."

"Interesting," Alex said, "it appears that President McMorris has been very busy with Méridien tech. Alright, Julien, open a vid to Colonel Stearns."

"Negative, Admiral. It's a Colonel Marshall."

"I don't know a Colonel Marshall," Alex said, "but open the vid, Julien."

"Captain Racine," the Colonel began without preamble.

Andrea, who was standing next to Alex, interrupted him: "That would be Admiral Racine, Colonel."

The Colonel paused, but his stern expression didn't change. If anything, it hardened. "Have it your way ... Admiral, then. By order of President Downing, you are to halt your convoy outside our system. If you proceed past Seda's orbit, you will be disregarding a lawful Presidential order and violating the sovereign space of Oistos. The President is prepared to employ force against you. That is all." The Colonel cut the comm.

The Colonel's insubordinate tone had outraged Andrea, and her anger was evident as she exclaimed: "President Downing? Who put that idiot in charge?"

Glossary

New Terra:

Alex Racine – Admiral of the Libran flotilla, Co-Leader of House Alexander

Andrea Bonnard – Senior Captain of the Libran flotilla, Captain of the *Rêveur*

Arthur McMorris – ex-President, resided at Prima's Government House

Barren Island – New Terra's Dagger training facility

Bobbie Singh – New Terran who saves Amelia on board the *Freedom*

Clayton Downing XIV – ex-Assemblyman, now the new President

Christie Racine – Alex Racine's thirteen-year-old sister

Damon Stearns – TSF Colonel and ex-outpost Commander on Sharius

Duggan Racine – Alex Racine's father

Eli Roth – *Rêveur's* starboard bay Flight Crew Chief

Gary Giordano – Dagger-9 pilot lost during Libran exodus

Hatsuto Tanaka – Dagger pilot, brother of Miko Tanaka, Sheila Reynard's second

House Alexander – Méridien House created by Alex and Renée

Jason "Jase" Willard – Dagger pilot killed by a silver ship

Levinson – New Terran engineer

Lyle Stamford – *Outward Bound* engineering tech

Marshall – TSF Colonel and new outpost Commander on Sharius

Michael "Mickey" Brandon – *Rêveur's* Chief Engineer

Miko Tanaka – Copilot of *Outward Bound*, sister to Hatsuto Tanaka

Robert Dorian – Dagger pilot who trains the Independent volunteers

Sean McCrery – Dagger-10 pilot

Sheila Reynard – Dagger Squadron Leader, promoted to Commander

Stanley Peterson – *Rêveur's* port bay Flight Crew Chief

Tatia Tachenko – Commander and XO of the *Rêveur*, ex-Terran Security Forces Major

Terran Security Forces (TSF) – New Terran system police force

Zeke Krausman – *Outward Bound* engineering tech

Confederation:

Ahmed Durak – Libran ex-First Mate of freighters

Alain de Long – *Rêveur* security escort for Renée, twin and crèche-mate to Étienne

Albert de Guirnon (gir·nōn) – Leader of House de Guirnon, brother of Renée

Alia – Bergfalk tech treated by Terese

Amelia – Independent young girl, organizer of the runners

Angelina Monti – daughter of the Independent Leader, Tomas Monti

Asu Azasdau – Captain of the *Sternenvagabund*

Bertram Coulter – an engineer and Independent on Libre

Clarion Seas – ocean waters on Libre

Claude Dupuis (dū·pwē) – *Rêveur* engineering tech

Cordelia – SADE (self-aware digital entity) of the *Freedom*

Dane – SADE of the *Sternenlicht*

Darius Gaumata – Libran Dagger pilot trainee, ex-shuttle pilot

Deirdre Canaan – Libran Dagger pilot trainee, ex-shuttle pilot

Edouard Manet – *Rêveur* navigation specialist

Elizabeth – SADE of the *Sternenreisende*

Ellie Thompson – Libran Dagger pilot trainee, raced atmo-ships

Eloise Haraken – twelve-year-old great-granddaughter of Fiona Haraken

Eric Stroheim – House Bergfalk Leader, responsible for Libre Colony

Étienne (ā·tē·in) de Long – *Rêveur* security escort for Renée, twin and crèche-mate to Alain

Fabrice – Libran implant engineer

Fiona Haraken – Libran sky-tower building engineer and Elder of Libre's Independents

Gratuito – Libre's only city

Geneviève Laroque (lă·rōk) – *Rêveur* passenger

Giovanni Tetra – Libre's Elder prior to Fiona Haraken

Gregorio – an elder left on Libre

Guillermo De Laurent – father of young man at Libran town meeting

Heinrich – young tech aboard the *Unsere Menschen*, who dies fixing jets on the hull

Helena Bartlett – Libran weaver and friend of Cordelia

House Bergfalk – House responsible for the Independents on Libre

House Brixton – House responsible for the design and creation of SADEs

House de Guirnon – House responsible for building and operating passenger liner transport

Jason Haraken – great-grandson of Fiona Haraken

José Cordova – Captain of the *Freedom*

Julien – *Rêveur*'s SADE

Karl Beckert – Station Director on Orbital Station Eins over Libre

Karl Schmidt – Captain of the *Sternenlicht*

Lazlo Menlo – new Captain of the *Geldbringer* (aka *Money Maker*)

Leeson Darden – Captain of the *Langstrecke*

Lillian Hauser – Captain of the *Sternenreisende*

Lucia Bellardo – Libran ex-Captain, now a shuttle pilot

Marcel Lechaux (le·shō) – Terese's brother and an Independent on Libre

Mutter – SADE of the *Geldbringer* (aka *Money Maker*)

Patrice – Fiona Haraken's close friend

Pia Sabine (să·bēn) – *Rêveur* passenger

Rayland – psychopathic SADE left behind on Libre

Renée de Guirnon (gir·nōn) – Co-Leader of House Alexander

Reinhold – Captain of the *Unsere Menschen*

Rosette – SADE of the *Sternenvagabund*

SADE – Méridien AIs (self-aware digital entity)

Sawalie – Elder singer on Libre

Sergio De Laurent – young man at Libran town hall meeting

Sleuth – Julien's alter ego gained from ancient Terran novels of Sherlock Holmes

Sophie Sabine – Pia's niece and an Independent on Libre

Tomas Monti – Leader of the Independents of Libre

Terese Lechaux (le·shō) – *Rêveur* medical specialist

Willem – SADE on the *Langstrecke*

Z – SADE of the *Unsere Menschen*

Ships and Stations:

Raumstation Eins – Libran construction station for the *Unsere Menschen*

Raumstation Zwei – Libran construction station for the *Freedom*

Freedom – Libran city-ship headed by Leader Monti

Geldbringer – the *Money Maker*, a House Bergfalk freighter

Langstrecke – the *Long Haul*, a House Bergfalk freighter

New Terra – colony ship from Earth; survivors named their new planet after the ship

Outward Bound – explorer-tug owned by Alex Racine

Rêveur (rĕ·vœr) – Méridien House de Guirnon passenger liner; Jacques de Guirnon was the prior Captain

Sternenlicht – House Bergfalk passenger liner

Sternenreisende – House Bergfalk passenger liner

Sternenvagabund – House Bergfalk passenger liner

Unsere Menschen – the *Our People*, a Libran city-ship headed by Leader Stroheim

Planets, Colonies, and Moons:

Bellamonde – sixth and latest Confederation planet to be attacked by the silver ships

Cetus – last Confederation colony established, first colony attacked by the silver ships

Cressida – New Terra's metal-rich moon circling Ganymede

Ganymede – New Terra's sixth planet outward, a gas giant with metal-rich moons

Libre – Independent's colony in Arno system

Méridien – home world of Confederation in the Oikos system

New Terra – home world of New Terrans, fourth planet outward of Oistos

Niomedes – New Terra's fifth planet outward and site of the habitat experiments

Seda – New Terra's ninth and last planet outward, a gas giant with several moons

Sharius – moon circling Seda and TSF support outpost for explorer-tugs

Stars:

Arno – star of the planet Libre, home of the Independents

Cepheus – original star destination for the *New Terra*

Hellébore – star of the planet Cetus, location of the first Confederation colony attacked by silver ships

Mane – original name of Oikos

Oikos – star of the Méridien home planet

Oistos – star of the planet New Terra, Alex Racine's home world

My Books

The Silver Ships, the first book in this series, is available as an e-book, a softcover version, and an audiobook. Please visit my website, http://scottjucha.com, for publication locations. You may also register at my website to receive email updates on the progress on my upcoming novels.

The Silver Ships Series:
The Silver Ships
Libre
Méridien (early 2016)
Hellébore (mid 2016)

The Author

It's been an eventful journey from Anchorage, Alaska, where I was born over six decades ago, to San Diego, California, where I currently reside with my wife.

Between these two destinations, I've spent years overseas, earned two college degrees, held many jobs, and found a wonderful marriage partner.

My first attempt at a novel was entitled *The Lure*. It was a crime drama centered on the modern-day surfacing of a 110-carat yellow diamond that had been lost during the French Revolution. In 1980, in preparation for the book, I spent two wonderful weeks researching the Brazilian people, their language, and the religious customs of Candomblé. The day I returned from Rio, I had my first date with my wife-to-be, Peggy Giels.

Over the past thirty-four years, I've outlined dozens of novels, but a busy career limited my efforts to complete any of them. Now the time has come, and I've thoroughly enjoyed planning, researching, and writing this second novel—in fact, the entire series.

I was a young teenager when I discovered the joy of reading. Today I hope, through my stories, I'm sharing that joy.